The Madrigal

CHRISTOPHER LEE

The Madrigal

SINCLAIR-STEVENSON

First published in Great Britain 1993
by Sinclair-Stevenson
7/8 Kendrick Mews, London SW7 3HG
an imprint of Reed Consumer Books Ltd
Michelin House, 81 Fulham Road, London SW3 6RB
and Auckland, Melbourne, Singapore and Toronto

Copyright © 1993 by Christopher Lee

A CIP catalogue record for this book
is available at the British Library

ISBN 1 85619 119 2

Phototypeset by Intype, London

Printed in Great Britain by Clays Ltd, St. Ives Plc

1

Whitehall was at a standstill. In Parliament Square, the late summer drizzle seeped through the paper-seller's stand. A union of trench-coated tourists, plaid linings flapping, disgorged itself from a hissing coach and threaded through the chaos of diesel cabs. The tour guide raised her scarlet umbrella and triumphantly led the way to the refuge of the wide pavement in front of the Treasury building.

A tall, hurrying figure, hands clenched deep in his raincoat pockets, collided with the tail end of the tour and cursed their politeness.

He was late. He was always late. He had been born late. His mother said by three weeks. His father, a benign country doctor, said it was normal for the first to be late. The next, he promised, would be on time. Perhaps early. The child's mother, a solicitor whose sense of lineage had been dulled by the experience of pregnancy during an exceedingly warm summer, rejected gynaecological complacency. She refused to give her husband the opportunity to satisfy his hypothesis. David was to be the Sanctuarys' only child.

He had been late for the train on his first day at boarding school and for a term he lived with the stigma of everyone believing he was a cry-baby.

'An only child. Ah yes,' Sanctuary's housemaster had intoned during one winter's tea. No one had asked for more. The explanation was sufficient.

At Cambridge, Sanctuary had been late for his interview. He had been to a Schools rugby football trial and missed the King's Cross train. The college was not unimpressed. He was offered a place. That was twenty years ago. Since then he had missed planes, but always arrived. At the time it seemed important. It rarely was.

He blundered around the corner into the fool's shelter of King Charles Street. Beyond the arch, the drizzle had become rain. Head down, he avoided a black-slickered figure gleefully scratching make and number in the uncompromising ledger of illegal parking. Sanctuary turned right, waved vaguely at the cubby-holed security guard and crossed the cobbled quadrangle and mounted the steps into the warmth of the Foreign and Commonwealth Office.

The blue-overalled attendant smiled and said it was raining again. Sanctuary fumbled for his pass, grunted his good morning, turned left and headed for the broad staircase and the first floor. Instead of left towards the dark-oaked sanctum, he turned right and then through a series of small corridors. When he had gone beyond the walls and frames where once great glossed linens of India were lowered from squeaking pulleys, he let himself in through the cream-gloss door and into the end room. He left the door open. It was after nine-thirty.

The room was larger than might have been imagined from its entrance. Three tall windows overlooked Downing Street – as, sometimes, did its occupants. A second door was covered in dark green baize. There were three desks, all wooden, all facing into the room. A small fan heater stood unplugged, insignificant in a grand grey and black marble fireplace. Whitehall wallahs no longer struggled with scuttles, nor was toast made against the glowing basket of fire. The monument to an age when maps were predominantly pink was now sealed by perforated hardboard. Postcards and invitations reminded a casual browser that there was life beyond the Department and that perhaps, after all, its influence was ever somewhere bathed in sunlight.

The woman on the telephone smiled a welcome and gave a half-wave with her yellow fountain pen. He grimaced as he wrestled with his dripping coat. He didn't much like it over here. Preferred Carlton Terrace.

'So glad you could join us.'

Priestly was thin. He didn't look up. Instead, he made short,

2

ticking notes on the brief in front of him. His slim gold pencil had been sent by an aunt, from Asprey's.

'Sorry. It's raining. Couldn't get a cab.' He turned as his sodden macintosh slithered from the wooden corner-stand to the green carpet.

Priestly passed a hand across a smooth head of black hair and looked up. He smiled. It was a slightly crooked smile. It ran parallel to the blue stripe in his tie. Not for the first time Sanctuary eyed the romantic portrait hanging behind Priestly's desk. Lawrence of Lucknow. A well-fed Priestly, he thought. The Lucknow smile. It could have been Priestly's. He wondered if Priestly practised in front of the imperfect oil every morning before the others arrived.

Priestly was good at smiling. He had worked hard at it since his prep school. The aunt who travelled from Yorkshire to shop at Asprey's thought it genuine. There was a family portrait somewhere, perhaps in the great house, of an eighteenth-century Priestly who was equally engaging. Priestly was her favourite nephew. She always sent him two greetings cards for his birthday and the two main Christian festivals. There would always be someone sending Priestly something extra. Everyone knew Priestly would get a good posting. Eventually a Section. Maybe more.

'Five minutes. All right?' He was saying. Not asking.

'Sure. No problem,' Sanctuary replied. They both knew he was lying.

Dorothea said a quiet goodbye into the telephone and looked across from her word-processing screen. She smiled.

'Here.' She offered him a red folder. 'Just as you asked. I've marked the pages. The If Asked ones should be pretty simple. Mostly monitoring stuff. The detail will be coming from the JIC minutes.'

She handed him the Joint Intelligence Committee folder, tatty and scuffed from many thumbs and coffee cups.

'Page seven. It's all there.' Her wink was discreet.

'Eh. Yes. Thanks.' He hadn't asked.

'Any time.' She smiled again. 'Any time.' She meant it. She rather thought she might be in love with him, a thought her

3

husband would have found irritating but nothing more than that.

Priestly made a final schoolmaster's squiggle on his file, closed the folder, tapped it with his pencil and leant back.

'One really must resist the urge to pamper our David.' Priestly piped the final vowel a half-octave higher as a nanny might call to her disobedient charge. There was no love in Priestly's tones. Priestly would never love.

Dorothea was back at her screen.

'What's that supposed to mean?' Her voice was easy. She had no reason to upset Priestly.

'David must learn to do his own homework. You cannot be forever running after him.'

Sanctuary dripped onto his desk, rubbing his wet sandy hair with a large green spotted handkerchief and urgently flipping over the pages in front of him.

'Come off it, Chas.' Sanctuary was deliberately provocative. Priestly glared. His skin, so exquisitely barbered, was taut with annoyance. Priestly hated being called Chas. He would have liked to be known by his second name, Rupert, but it was too late. He was certainly not a Chas. He was Charles. One day his knighthood would prove it.

Sanctuary stopped rubbing his head and tossed the damp handkerchief in the tray marked Specialist Cables. He creased back a page and ran his finger beneath a paragraph.

'What's this about Poss GRU out?'

Dorothea had read the Intelligence Summary file, had meant to make a note for him so he wouldn't have to ask.

'The backnote on the Intsum. It's there. One's out at the moment, off base.'

'Who? Anyone we know?'

Priestly was rubbing at his nails with an impeccable handkerchief.

'That hideous man Ignatiev. Or so they tell us.'

Sanctuary looked up. He had known Ignatiev, had followed his career from Moscow to London to Cairo and back to London. A man for whom cruelty was a pastime. Ignatiev's file said 'Sadistic Tendencies'. Sanctuary had written the file.

4

'And he's down as Poss? There's nothing Possible about Ignatiev. He's Positive. He's been in their Military Intelligence for years.'

'Who knows nowadays? It's not just the mighty who have fallen. I will have you remember . . .'

Priestly did not finish whatever it was he was about to have them remember.

Another blue-overalled figure, a Tudor crown brooch on her lapel, appeared at the door with a slim wire-basket trolley.

'It isn't 'alf raining,' she said. 'Chucking it down it is. Well, chucking it down I tell you.'

She seemed delighted. Her blood-red lipsticked smile had been introduced early that morning while she half-watched the weather-centre lady forecasting gloom. It made her feel good to be in the know. She dumped a pile of buff Registry files in one tray and took a similar pile from another. No one spoke. Priestly smiled. Shaking her peroxided hair, she trundled away along the aisle of diplomatic special offers and foreign policy loss leaders.

The door to the inner room opened. Nothing happened. The two men stood, waited and then, as the door swung wide, Priestly, by seniority and even birthright, led the way. Sanctuary picked up a coffee mug from Dorothea's desk and took a quick sip. He looked back and mouthed thanks before closing the thick door behind him. He still had the mug.

The telephone rang and Dorothea, smiling, lifted the receiver.

'Hello.' She didn't identify the Department. 'Sorry, he's in a meeting right now. Can I get him to call you?'

In a firm, open fist, she wrote a name and then a long telephone number and read it back, then bent her head as if the line were poor.

'Say it again.' She added a sentence to the telephone number. There was a pause. The mantel clock, booty from some shut-down Government House, whirred biliously as it roused itself to the quarter-chime.

'I'm not certain,' she apologised. 'Not before noon. He's only just gone into his meeting and it could be some time.'

The red light disappeared on the green plastic board. The message was simple, a name and a number. She frowned. The call had come in through the greenline and not the FCO switchboard or Whitehall circuit. She turned to the screen, tapped three commands and then typed the word, Fisher, followed by the number.

It took thirty seconds to re-run the scan and search. One channel was bare. The other listed four Fishers. Two were Department. Two dormant. Neither matched the number. She tapped a cross-check command. No Contact. Not Registered.

2

Surrounded by the flat marsh, the grey water sprawled anonymously. The breeze flicked and slashed at the shallows. The reeds stirred, still firm with late summer growth.

The man in dull green overalls lay unseen, as he had since eleven o'clock.

Without shifting, he flexed his stiffening limbs. It was a slow, rehearsed movement. First the shoulders, the joints hardly moving, down through the biceps, the forearms firming along their slopes, then the hands, fingers outstretched to the very tips, slowly relaxing like some retreating wave from a sandy beach, until the shoulders softened but never sagged. An exercise learned in another land. At another time. His bottom lip jutted, he blew away moisture from his nostrils and settled once more, the rain-hood carefully rolled back and button-clipped so that nothing should dull sight or hearing. His body, like his mind, carried no extras.

He tracked a dipping sandpiper, anticipating each tick of the short wings above the mud-edged inlet opposite. Then it was gone. He could hear the distant puttering of a small diesel but little moved to interrupt the dull greens and browns and slate of the creek: a yellow buoy, a rusting can. The sandpiper returned. Still searching. But the man took no notice. The puttering was sharper, the beat easier to count. A small sloop, its forestay bare and its white mainsail furled along the horizontal boom, drifted across his vision. He watched a deckhand hanging blue fenders over the side before making his way aft to where the helmsman leant at the tiller. If they said anything, the man did not hear. The boat gradually disappeared, hidden by the thick reeds, though he heard the increased revolutions as the skipper turned her across the channel and headed for the basin entrance and the lock-master's paternal wave. The man returned to his waiting.

At first he was not sure.

On the far bank a dark figure smudged the uncertain path that ran from the burned and blackened rope-store. The man slowly wiped droplets of water from his eyebrows. Without haste, without even looking, he folded back the waterproof covering at his side.

The meandering figure was clearer.

He ran his hand the length of the long barrel, the black metal and then the bandaged stock, as a widow might caress a sleeping cat. Then he gently pulled the weapon into his shoulder, raised the cold metal breech to his cheek and with thumb and forefinger turned the bezelled ring at his eye until the distant figure cleared. A fraction more and the image sharpened.

The figure was limping.

He smiled.

Hidden from the open waters, the *Madrigal* barely moved on the slack tide. Her white springs, stern and head ropes lay easily from the slime-planked landing stage. Her slim blue hull was dulled by the overcast weather and her scrubbed cream upper decks misted with rain. She was neat. Well cared for. Her warps and lines were looped and tied and coiled to be set free, untangled at a moment's tug. The foredeck was long and uncluttered; the newly painted anchor lay fore and aft, incongruously scarlet and unmoving in the grip of two well greased shackles. The slightly raised coach-house, running abaft the tall mast to the cockpit, seemed a solid and sure shelter. The ends of two lines, one running from the forestay and another from the covered boom, were neatly coiled like large folk-woven teapot mats. The *Madrigal* was tied down and secure. Ready for sea.

He limped, still half-bent though there was little wind and the drizzle was friendly enough. At the bank's edge he paused, looking down at the slippery jetty. The effort of the path behind him, he stooped and rubbed his aching knee. It was not a new pain and he massaged from habit rather than hope. Straightening, he seemed a powerful figure. He swung a bulky orange

8

bag to his other shoulder and looked across the flats to the raised headland. His eyes quartered the wooded rise that protected the sheltering waters. He grunted. Satisfied. There would be wind enough. He could slip on the turning tide and drift down to the headland in an hour. He glanced back to the hull as the creak of tightening moorings told him the slack water was giving way to the ebb. It was time.

From the opposite bank, the man watched through the tiny cross-haired glass. The light was cleaner now. The wind had freshened, maybe half a knot. He felt the reeds shift with the tide's turn. He took a long breath, frowning at the pulse which beat at his temple. The hush was broken by the descant triplet of the returning sandpiper. The man held his breath as if he had been discovered. The temple vein continued to throb.

The blue figure turned to one side. With his weight on his sure leg he carefully negotiated the three muddied wooden steps cut into the bank. On the landing stage he steadied himself, legs firmly apart, testing the rotted surface. With a coalman's heave, he tossed the bag into the cockpit. The *Madrigal* rocked slightly, the white tube fenders squeaked against the boat's side as he gripped the port shrouds, took the weight once more, paused and bent his knee as he prepared to swing himself aboard.

The man gently squeezed the trigger.

3

Sanctuary let himself into his small hallway, hung up his macintosh and glanced through the mail on the side-table. His bank statement suggested there was little point opening the three brown envelopes and he tossed the whole lot onto the couch. Then he poured himself a small whisky. The telephone answer machine was silent and he was about to make his duty call to his father when he remembered the message Dorothea had handed him. It was still in his shirt pocket. He let the number ring for thirty seconds. There was no reply.

4

It was dark now. The child was scruffy and miserable. Should not have been there. He'd get into trouble. It was late. Gone tea-time. Muddy, wet, jeans cold on his legs. He wanted to pull up his socks to keep his legs warm but he was too frightened to move. Instead, he tried to fidget one up at a time by rubbing the back of his ankle up the other leg. The woman looked at him.

'You want the toilet?'

He didn't say anything. He sat still and shivered.

'You cold?'

He shook his head. The dark-blue quilted anorak with its mock fur-edged hood and orange lining was torn down the left sleeve. He wondered how it had happened.

'Sure?'

He shook his head again, still shivering. He sat further into the soft back seat of the police car, its doors gaping open, and said nothing to the unmotherly woman constable. She was asking him again. He blocked her out just as he did with Miss. She was always asking him things just because she knew he didn't know them. Especially sums.

He twisted at the dirty purple rag in his lap and kept his chin down in his chest. She had fat ankles. He wondered if she'd hurt herself. She started asking him the same question *they* kept asking him. Her voice was kind. He didn't answer. He ran his hand along the torn sleeve. What was his mother going to say? They were sending for her. They'd done that when he'd broken the window at school. She would be here shortly, they said. He was glad his dad was away. That would have been trouble. She touched his arm and he shrugged it away. He didn't want her to do that. She had no right to. He switched

11

off again and stared at nothing. Why did they have to have two fire extinguishers in the front? And all those papers and that list of things? Policemen always had lists of things. He looked at the back of the driver's head. He didn't say anything to anyone. Just tapped his pencil on the steering wheel. He had a boil just under his cap. The boy wondered if it hurt much. He'd never had a boil. Kev had. On his face. Lots of times. He wondered where the other one had gone. The sergeant. He couldn't see him.

They'd got big lights going. It was a bit like floodlit football at The Dell. He'd been there with his dad a couple of times. Across the way, near the yachts, the ambulance was white and shiny. The back doors were shut now. One of the policemen had one of them yellow anoraks. Like *they* did. Had them on the roads and all. He was talking to the ambulance men. The driver was leaning against the bonnet. He was smoking. They always did. Then told you not to. But they always did. The other one was writing something in the gravel with his foot. He did that sometimes on the beach at low tide. The panda car was there. Still got its engine on. Could run out of petrol, he thought. His dad had a car. Sometimes his dad turned off the engine when they were going down-hill, like he'd done when they went to Cornwall or somewhere. He couldn't remember. His dad said it saved petrol. He wondered where his mum was. But he didn't ask her. In the marina lights he could see all the masts and wires of the sailing boats. They were making that tapping noise in the wind. He liked that. Sounded good.

The police radio started to chatter. He couldn't understand what they were saying. He saw one of the men in the other car with the mouthpiece to his face and the radio went dead.

'What they say?'

'Oh, nothing.'

She was a prat. They always said that. He stopped listening as she started talking to him. Wanted to know if he'd seen anything. She kept wanting to know. There was music some-where. Probably the yacht club. It was just over there. The windows were steamed up but he could see them inside. Old music. Gross. His mum had worked in there when they had parties. He'd heard her tell his dad that some of them got sick a lot. His dad said it was typical. Wasn't that smart anyway. Brown wood and patio doors. They had patio doors at home. His dad had done them himself. He was clever, his dad was. Those crates of empties and orange gas bottles outside. Really scruffy. He didn't reckon the club. Not like the places he'd heard about on the island. His dad had told him. His dad knew. He'd worked on the boats. Still, his mum said it was nice to work there. They always gave her a lift home at night. She didn't like him coming down here. Thought he was going to drown, she'd said. Couldn't swim, could he? Got hit because he couldn't swim. That was at school. Didn't want to swim anyway.

The man was coming back. The one that had talked to him first time. He could see him. The lights were really bright. He could see him along the path that came up from the creek. He didn't look so big as before. The other one, the fat one with the chewing gum and the black beard, was behind him. That one had got a book and kept writing things down. He didn't like him. He was gross as well.

She was going on again about seeing anyone. He didn't say anything. He watched the man and the one with the book reach the end of the path. He wondered if they knew about the slimey bit by the rope-store. He'd seen rope in there. His mate Kev said there were lots of rats. They'd never seen any though. But there were anyway. Everyone knew that. The fat one started to slip. That was good. He didn't fall in. Pity. He was gross. The other man ducked under the yellow tape they'd put across the end of the path. The driver with the boil saw them coming and got out and went to meet them. He couldn't hear what they were saying but they looked over. The man shook his head a couple of times and stared at the ground in front of him. He was wearing an old raincoat like that cop on the video. The one with the funny eye. And he had his hands behind his back. Just like him. He reckoned he was gross too. But he was better than the fat one. Not much. But he was. He said something else to the driver and the fat one, then looked at him. They were coming. The other one walked with his hands behind

13

him and stared at the ground as if he were looking for something. The boy started shivering again. From the far side of the timbered club the lights of an approaching car danced up, down and across the lumpy track where it said BEWARE CHILDREN! and swung in behind the ambulance. He was here. He stood for a moment, one hand on the open door, and looked at him. He smiled.

'Anything?'

'No, sir. Nothing.' She really did have a kind voice. He wished he'd said something. He didn't want her to get into no trouble. The man smiled again. He had bushy eyebrows and glasses. He didn't know police were allowed glasses.

'Listen, Bennie, you're sure you didn't see anyone?'

The fat one had come up from behind. He could hear him chewing. He made sharp snapping sounds. He reckoned he must have two sticks of gum. You couldn't make noises like that with one. He had his book out. The boy stared at him and said nothing. The man looked over his shoulder.

'See who that is, will you?'

The fat one nodded. He looked at the boy, then turned. He walked with both arms stiff and slightly out, as if he were carrying shopping bags. The man waited until he was out of earshot, then crouched by the back seat. He smelt like his dad did when they'd had a curry. The boy didn't go on that much.

'When you found him, didn't you look up or anything?' His eyes looked bigger than before. He was still smiling.

Bennie didn't like his eyes. Spooky. He looked away.

'You must have seen something. Worried, were you? Bit scared?'

He said nothing. Just twisted and twisted the purple rag around his fingers. It hurt.

'Were you?'

From where the new car had stopped, a woman's voice, reedy, uncertain, frightened.

'Bennie?'

He started to get out of the car.

'Bennie? Bennie?'

The woman constable put a hand on his sleeve where it was

14

torn. He stopped. Half out of the car. The man sighed and shook his head. She took her hand away and he ran. She was standing with the fat one. He could feel the other man looking at him. He didn't care. She held him tightly, one thin arm about his shoulders, the other hand pressing his head to where it just reached below her breast. He was shaking.

'He'll be all right, missus.' The fat one's voice was high. Like a girl's. He hadn't heard him say anything before. It frightened him.

'There, there. Come on, Bennie. Let's go home.'

'When you're ready, missus. It's all laid on. We'll come round later.' It was almost a squeak.

'There, there.' She was stroking his head now. He was shaking still. But there were no tears. Not here.

'They're giving us a lift. In the police car. You'll like that.'

He pressed his face into her old green coat. It was rough but he could smell her. That's all that mattered. Through one eye, he peered across the threadbare of her sleeve to see if the fat one had gone. He was walking back to the police car. Arms straight. Still carrying bags. There was nobody else near them. He was safe. The music from the club was louder. It was gross. He saw the man by the crates watching him. The one in the green overalls. He didn't care. He was going home. He hoped his dad wasn't in.

5

The second telephone call had been mysterious but not melo-dramatically so. Dorothea had described the caller as crisply polite.

'Ask Mr Sanctuary to read page four, bottom-right-hand corner of this morning's *Daily Telegraph* and then 'phone me at his convenience.' He had said his name was Roberts and had left an evening telephone number.

Dorothea had drawn a blank on Roberts's name and tele-phone number. There was nothing in the computer. It was the newspaper paragraph that set off the alarm bells in Sanctuary's head.

Murder Hunt
A man who died from gunshot wounds in Chichester
harbour yesterday afternoon has been named as Stuart
Fisher, a former Royal Naval Officer. Sussex police say
that in spite of an intensive search no weapon has been
found.

Sanctuary went through his private list of numbers and names. Nothing under Roberts. Stuart Fisher was quite different. Num-bers and memories galore. But not for some time. Especially the memories.

When Sanctuary returned his call that evening, Roberts had said very little. Almost evasive. He said that Fisher had said that if anything should happen to him he was to get in touch with Sanctuary at the Foreign Office. There was an envelope, Roberts had said, and no, he would not post it. Fisher had said he must hand it to Sanctuary and no one else.

16

'Oh. Just one other thing. He said I was to say "Sad Sam Theory". Just that. "Sad Sam Theory." '

That had made up Sanctuary's mind.

Dorothea had said nothing when Sanctuary announced that he would not be in the next morning. Fridays could be as dull as ditch-water and an excuse labelled 'family reasons' was hardly unknown in the Department. Fisher had never been 'on the books'. For the moment, Sanctuary saw no need to let the rest of the Department hear the alarms. If it came to nothing, so much the better.

Priestly had looked put out and his well-bred spitefulness had been predictable and ignored.

'Yet another grandmama?'

Sanctuary had not bothered to explain.

Priestly used one of his smiles and continued in case explanation might foil his enjoyment.

'How sad. Please accept one's condolences. The arithmetic of the Sanctuary bereavement cycle is as puzzling as it is distressing. One shall watch *The Times* with interest.'

The drive down from London had been dreadful. The chill rain of the past days had turned to an annoying drizzle seemingly with nowhere else to go. The treacherous dual carriageway had become an adventure playground for salesmen, contemptuously spraying the windscreens of the more timid. But, once the other side of the Downs, Sanctuary had outpaced the rain. The road was easier. The sun was bright. He rolled down the window and rested an arm on the sill as he watched for the promised signpost pointing him away from the trunk road to what Dorothea, who seemed to know everything that he didn't and needed to, had called The Witterings. They had laughed over imagined scatty spinsters fussily getting ready for church and rabbiting on to a sighing but polite nephew paying a duty visit. He liked her. He wondered how married she might be.

Now, seventy miles away from Priestly's internecine career politics, Sanctuary humped the Alfa over striped sleeping policemen. He slowed to allow three mallards to waddle to the safety of the bank before turning easily into waste ground

17

between the shipyard and the yacht club. He didn't bother to lock the car. He never did.

Sanctuary tugged on his dark blue jacket, stood listening to the frapping and slapping of shrouds, and breathed deeply. Line upon line of hulls and masts were neatly pontooned into the harbour like some water-logged arboretum. Here and there figures were tidying and stowing. There seemed little urgency. Across the way in the yard, a nose-masked workman was sanding the deep fin beneath a high, dry and pit-propped cutter. He could smell paint spraying onto a preening hull from the open cavern of the boatshed and from somewhere unseen came the sharp-pitched chorus of chipping hammer on iron; between clangs, a fair-haired man rasped a counterpoint of sandpaper on a wooden dinghy hull. The raucous splutter of a blowing exhaust made him step back. A small once-red truck pulled up alongside. The exaggerated suspension was slow to settle and complained noisily yet the back was empty save for two green diesel cans hemp-roped in the offside rear corner. The front tyre nearer to him was worn and the rusting wing mirror had a wing but no mirror. He looked around as the driver got down and slammed the creaking door. She tossed her sunglasses through the cab's open window and smiled. Friendly. Not familiar. Blonde hair casually tied and old sun-bleached T-shirt. He looked quickly beyond her lithe figure. He felt overdressed.

He heard himself saying 'Good afternoon'. It came from the back of his throat. Too casual. No authority. Not his voice at all.

'Hi.' She smiled. Didn't stop.

He didn't follow her. Instead he watched a top-heavy cruiser glide along the centre channel between the pontoons, her gleaming superstructure and ostentatiously raked chromium stanchions space-aged and incongruous. The tall-masted and well-bred sloops and ketches, firmly and traditionally moored, ignored her wash and grumbling diesels.

Sanctuary looked back beyond the red truck. The girl had gone.

The yacht club was a ramshackle single-storey building, the sort of place forever needing a coat of paint and a carpenter.

18

Backs of stickers and small posters blocked part of the windows. A tan and black mongrel lounged against the sun-warmed wall and eyed him without malice. Where the paint wasn't peeling there wasn't any. It wasn't what he'd expected. A tubby white-haired man in faded denims held the door and smiled hello without removing a smouldering meerschaum.

'I was looking for the Secretary. A Mr Roberts.' Sanctuary made it sound like a trespasser's excuse.

'Ginger? Sure.' The man's teeth were old. He pointed with his yellowing pipe. 'He's in there. Try the bar. Club tie. Orange juicer. Can't miss him.'

Inside, the notice said: Members & Guests Only. Visitors Report to the Secretary's Office. There were no directions. He tried the bar. It was a big, oblong room, scattered with brown tables and chairs. Through the plate-glass windows he could see a lawn with white benches and canopies and a white flag-pole in the middle. Beyond, the upper reaches of the ragged harbour were clear and still.

Roberts was short. Very upright. The navy-blue club tie was tightly and neatly knotted with the preciseness of a 1950s banker. He was sitting on a high stool, a frosted orange juice at his elbow. He was talking to the girl. At the other end, a beefy red-faced man, two packs of cigarettes and a half-finished pint of beer in front of him, was talking to the barman. His eyes flicked at Sanctuary. The barman, a sparse figure, caught his glance. So did Roberts.

'Mr Roberts?'

'That's right. Mr Sanctuary?' It was not really a question, more the voice he kept for brewery reps. David Sanctuary recognised the clipped, assured, navalised tones he'd heard on the telephone.

'Sorry I'm late.'

The girl smiled at Roberts. It was a well-brought-up expression. There was little warmth. No intimacy.

'I'll see you later.' She turned and walked across the room and out to the terrace. Roberts didn't reply. Instead he nodded his dismissal, even though she hadn't waited.

'What'll you have?'

19

The barman was hovering, wiping the spotlessly clean mahogany surface with a red-checked cloth. Roberts was grinning from one side of his mouth. Sanctuary had been watching the retreating girl. So had the red-faced man. She must have been about twenty-five, twenty-six. The shorts were decent. Just. To an older man they wouldn't have been.

'G and T? Beer?'

He shook his head and then changed his mind.

They took their drinks into Roberts's pokey office overlooking the harbour. Sanctuary leant back in the tubular chair. He could see everything without moving his head. Roberts didn't close the door. An ancient computer screen showed a membership list. The rest of the room was stacked but not cluttered with files, a few books and a wallpapering of lists and pamphlets, pictures of warships and yellow while-you-were-out notes stuck wherever there was space. In the outer room he could hear a woman's harsh voice demanding the free-flow times through the lock. She sounded like someone who has missed a bus and wants to know what the inspector's going to do about it.

He looked back at Roberts. It was an intelligent face. Winter-pale under closely waved, marmalade short-back-and-sides, the shaving line high above the ears. He was Ginger all right. The eyes pale blue. Water-coloured. Expressionless. He looked in his early forties.

'Is this official? I mean Foreign Office official?'

Sanctuary shook his head.

'No, not at all. What made you think that?'

'I didn't say I did. I was asking.' The tone wasn't unfriendly.

'No reason it should be, is there?'

'You tell me,' said Roberts. He didn't blink very often.

'There's not much to tell. I didn't even know he was dead until you 'phoned.'

He had no intention of telling Roberts that Stuart Fisher had tried to get in touch. Not yet anyway. Perhaps guilt. Perhaps there was no need. Perhaps instinct. The woman outside was complaining about queuing at the lock. Roberts got up and closed the door.

20

'We're okay, you know. I'm cleared,' he said.

He settled with a wriggle in his chair. The mock leather sighed its readiness to be privy to some conspiracy.

'I'm not sure I'm with you.' Sanctuary's tone was polite.

The crooked smile seemed part of the confidence.

'I was in Whitehall Wireless.'

'I see.' He didn't.

'Comcen.'

'Oh, I see.' This time he did. 'Communications Centre's something I've never had much to do with.'

Roberts gave a slow nod.

'Need-to-know basis only.'

'Of course. Hence you are cleared?'

Sanctuary paused, not quite knowing what was expected of him.

Roberts nodded again.

'Still? Isn't there something about being renewed or updated?' Sanctuary didn't want to offend the other man.

Roberts watched. There was no blink of embarrassment.

'I keep in touch.'

He paused as if waiting for a response. There was none.

'So if there's anything you need to say on the old net then fire away. Get my drift?'

Sanctuary leant his large frame back in the precarious balance of the tube and canvas chair.

'I'm not really sure why I am here to be frank.'

'Early days yet. I expect you've had the police report.'

'No. Why should I?'

'Understood.'

The Secretary pulled open the bottom desk drawer with the toe of his shoe and propped his foot. Sanctuary wondered if he read Dashiell Hammett.

'In actual fact I knew all along that this couldn't be straightforward.' The crooked grin winked confidentially. 'Obvious, you know.'

'I'm afraid, Mr Roberts, you have the advantage.'

'Not had time to read in? Understood.'

21

Sanctuary could hear the woman outside. Now the reputation of the harbour master was feeling the edge of her tongue.

'Truthfully, there's nothing to read. Stuart Fisher was a friend, really an acquaintance. He had nothing to do with the Foreign Office if that's what you're suggesting.'

Roberts's stare was blander than ever.

'Roger. But you two were pretty close, I expect?' His voice suggested that he knew there was a deeper reason.

'Not really. I met him about eight years ago. Exchanged Christmas cards, we saw each other occasionally but usually by chance. That's about it.'

He paused. An innocent would have nothing to hold back. It was sufficient for now. Roberts said nothing. Out on the water, the cruiser gave a double blast on her klaxon.

Roberts cocked his head in the direction of a photograph. The ship was easily recognisable.

'We were in the *Britannia* together.' He smiled his one-sided grin. 'Well, not exactly together. I was on the lower deck. Stuart was an officer.'

'You were . . . ?' He made it appear that he hadn't quite caught what the other man had said. He didn't know what else to say.

'I was a Chief RS then. Coms. Mind you, that was a few years back. Then we met up again in the biggy. By that time I'd been commissioned. SD.'

Sanctuary was lost in the jargon. He didn't worry. It would all come out if Roberts wanted it to. Roberts shifted his chair. There was a photograph of a warship behind his head. He nodded backwards.

'Then we went south in her.'

'You mean '82? Falklands?'

Roberts nodded.

'You know what happened to her. In actual fact, that's where he did his leg. Still, could have been worse. Was for a lot of them. After that he did the Russian course.'

'You're a Russian speaker?'

'Me? You're joking. *Da* and *Niet* and that's it. Not me. I had enough. Knew I wasn't going anywhere. Then this number

22

came up and I put my papers in. I met him here. That was just before he went off to Sovland.'

The wardroom accent had slipped, elbowed aside by jargon.

'I met him not long after that,' said Sanctuary.

His mind went back to the brittle dinner party and the lamb chops imported from Copenhagen.

'Moscow,' he explained.

'You were in the Andrew?'

Sanctuary frowned his incomprehension.

Roberts smiled. Glad to help out.

'Obviously not. Andrew. The Navy.'

'Oh no. Not me. Not bright enough.'

Roberts liked that. Sanctuary fed him more.

'I was in the Embassy. I moved into the same apartment block. It was the ghetto for junior Dips. You mentioned it. Sad Sam.'

Roberts laughed.

'I thought it was some code.'

'It was. For lousy living. *Sadovo Samotechnaya*. Everyone called it Sad Sam. Still, the central heating worked.'

'Embassies must be a bit like a ship. Everyone mucks in, I suppose.'

'Not that one. Your lot, the military, made the ambassador nervous. In those days they worked in a separate block over the way from the main building. Kept themselves to themselves. Locked doors, did their own sweeping. He made sure they did. In a place like Moscow ambassadors get twitchy. All the defence attachés are doing the business – they could get bounced at any time.'

Roberts looked down at his desk. Using the side of his hand as if gathering tobacco dust, he slid a green plastic paper-knife until it was in parallel with his yellow note-pad. Without looking up he said, 'Stuart mentioned he got mixed up with the Poles.'

'Really? How do you mean, "mixed up"?'

'Said he was there. Thought you would have known.'

'He doubled as naval attaché to Poland. Went down there on the train,' said Sanctuary.

Roberts sipped his orange juice.

23

'Beautiful Russian spies creeping into your bunk at night, eh? Very sweet-smelling. Tasty. Did his lady go with him?'

'Jane? Sometimes. Wives were encouraged. It avoided unwelcome situations.'

'She was strange, wasn't she?'

'I honestly don't know. As you know, they, well . . .'

'She chucked him. A Yank, wasn't it?'

'I'd left by then. He told me a bit about it when he got back.'

'Happens. Like I said, bit like a ship. She was a model, wasn't she?'

Sanctuary nodded.

The grin was back.

'Said to have been a bit Page Three.'

'Certainly attractive. Yes.'

But Roberts wanted more.

'And?'

'Boredom perhaps? Moscow's all right at first, but then you find yourself in the circuit. Insular.'

It wasn't the word he wanted, but Roberts knew what he meant.

'Lunching with the same old crowd. Probably sitting next to the person you were down to dine with that evening. Incestuous.'

It still wasn't the right word. Roberts was racing ahead.

'He said she was living in Washington.'

'I didn't know that. I wonder if she's been told.'

'No need. Not if they were divorced.'

'I'm not entirely sure they were.'

'That right?'

Roberts rattled the ice in his glass, drained the pale orange water, then studied the dregs.

'They say she, eh, was very sociable.'

'Who are they?'

'You know, on the old net.'

'No, I'm afraid I don't.'

'I heard her idea of a good time didn't come up to diplomatic expectations so to speak.'

'She found Moscow difficult, yes.'

24

'Poor sod.'

'She wasn't the first wife to suffer.'

'No, I meant him. Stuart. What happened?'

'Nothing much. The system copes with these things. As soon as it started to go wrong they shipped him home.'

'Before the old KGB got on to him? That's what he said. Did they get him?'

'Not that I know. What did he say?'

Roberts looked out of the window as if trying to remember a difficult text. The cruiser had reached the end of the approach channel and was heading for the line of mooring buoys.

'He didn't. But I often wondered.'

Roberts sounded mysterious. Knowing.

Sanctuary shook his head.

'What made you wonder?'

Roberts tilted his head and his next words were muffled by ice cubes.

'He goes out there as a two-and-a-half. Comes back to Greenwich and does the Staff Course. Gets his brass hat while he's there and then leaves.'

He put down the glass and wiped his mouth with a white handkerchief.

'Didn't make sense. Even if he wasn't getting a ship, that stripe meant he was on the way up. Most don't make commander.'

'Well, there's your answer. They wouldn't have promoted him if he'd been nobbled.'

'Assuming they knew.'

'You really think so?'

'Possible. In actual fact they don't always. Not until it's too late. We both know that.'

Sanctuary stretched and stood. He felt cooped up in the tiny office full of files, trophies and innuendo.

'You mentioned an envelope.'

Roberts nodded.

'I need ID.'

Sanctuary took a small plastic-coated identification card from his wallet and dropped it onto the desk. Roberts assumed the self-importance of a Third World immigration officer as he examined the photograph and then the freckled features of its bearer.

'D'you mind telling me what Department you're in?'

'Does it matter?'

'Best to be sure.'

'You've no way of checking and this won't tell you.'

Sanctuary picked up the card. He was getting tired of the game.

'True.'

Roberts had conceded the game, but not the set.

'I'll let you have it Monday. Ten-thirty here.'

Roberts smiled again.

'Stuart didn't want it falling into the wrong hands. It's in my bank. They're closed for the weekend.'

Sanctuary's shoulders heaved with the same strength that had pricked the nerves of many a Rugby threequarter. Roberts, invulnerable, simply smiled. Sanctuary was putting on his jacket.

'Have you mentioned this to the police?'

Roberts shook his head and carried on smiling.

'Why not?'

'Why should I? He wanted you to have it. Not them.'

'But this is a murder inquiry.'

'I don't think so.'

Sanctuary was puzzled.

'I'm not with you.'

'I think you are.'

'You mean suicide?'

'No gun.'

'Then it must be murder. What else could it be?'

'Come now, Mr Sanctuary, you people know the answer to that, otherwise you wouldn't be here, would you?'

6

Detective Chief Inspector James Hodge Boswell Leonard
wiped his gold-wired glasses on his tie, re-crossed his ankles on
the edge of his desk and squinted at his brown toe-caps. Twenty
years before, as an impecunious undergraduate, Leonard had
bought a pair of well-worn boots in the charity shop. He'd worn
boots ever since, even with a black tie at police dinner dances.
His colleagues thought him something of an eccentric. For a
start, he had never looked like a policeman. The granny spectacles hadn't helped. He was thin and stooped, with the deft
hands of a model-maker, little used to feeling the collars of
minor villains. The uniform razor-cut hair particularly designed
for policemen and Association Football managers had passed
him by. His brown, tousled and fringed locks owed more to
Rome than to Simone's Unisex Salon.

Leonard was a loner. As a child he had treasured rare
moments of privacy in the orphanage. Nights were his own and
it was only years later that he longed to share dreams. But he
did not. He was not particularly academic but he had got a
good law degree, perhaps because he never paddled in the
upmarket redbrick social whirlpool. Couldn't afford it. After
two years in unfashionable chambers he had left the bar with
his own form of disillusionment and perceptions of injustice.
He went to Florence, by himself, fell in love and when that
love died returned to his private dreams.

At his preliminary interview, a very correct Inspector asked
how he had got his string of Christian names. Leonard thought
it none of the man's business. But did not say so. Instead he
asked the Inspector what made him think the names were
Christian and they moved onto the safer routine of why he
wanted to join the police. Leonard gave the answers the board

wanted to hear and six months later they handed him a pair of their regulation black boots and a peak cap which slipped to his ears, just as the rough, yet perfectly judged issue uniform always seemed two sizes too large. At the station they had, at first, called him The Professor, but he was never popular enough for a nickname to stick. No one, except for the very proper Inspector, thought he would last the course.

The half-glass door opened and the Fat One came in. He was eating a half-pounder. The smell of onions was disgusting. He dropped a green folder in front of Leonard.

'That's the outline. The rest's coming from something called DNSy. Could take a week or two.'

He plonked on a wooden chair, his grubby white mail-order shirt taut across his overhanging gut.

'DNS – what?' Leonard sniffed at the onions. 'D'you have to?'

Perkins took another bite and dropped the half-eaten burger into the waste-paper basket.

'Sorry. Bit peckish.'

He wiped his thin lips with his sleeve. There was still onion on his beard. He might notice before he went to bed that night. Leonard doubted it. When Perkins spoke again, the onion flicked in time.

'Director of Naval Security. Seems whoever-he-is-when-he's-at-home locks files away and it takes a month of Sundays to get them back.'

Leonard put on his glasses and blinked at the folder. Across the top, in red felt tip, was the murdered man's name. S.M.D. Fisher (Commander Royal Navy Retired). He tapped it with a middle finger.

'What's this say?'

'Not much. Stuart with a U Michael David Fisher. Born 1949. Parents deceased. Only child. Married. Wife's name Jane. Separated three years ago. No kids. Left the Navy early last year. Lived by himself. Local. That's about it. Had a few friends. Nothing special.'

Leonard opened the folder and peered at the passport photograph. The face was expressionless. Dead ones usually are, he thought.

'What's that mean?'

'What's what mean, guv?'

The Fat One didn't want to shift from his chair.

'Few friends, nothing special.'

'Well, nobody we know. No villains or anything.'

Leonard buried his thoughts in his conversation with the yacht club secretary. He didn't want to think about his sergeant. How could he have got this far? He looked at him for a long, quiet minute. Perkins squirmed. Leonard blinked. Influential friends, there could be no other explanation.

'Who'd he work for?'

'He didn't, guv. Well, as far as we know. Seems spent most of his time doing up his cottage and messing about with his boat. Been abroad.'

'Most of them do. Where? Cherbourg?'

'And other places. Spent some time in the Med. According to the boatyard.'

'Where's his wife?'

'Nobody knows.'

'Someone must.'

'Spose so.'

He took out a once-white handkerchief and blew his nose. He stared indifferently into the damp rag.

'Summer cold,' he explained. 'Spoke to his solicitors this morning. Tupmans. They wouldn't say much – you know bleedin' Tupmans – 'cept that he didn't have no maintenance. It was all done on separation. She may have done a runner. Hasn't been heard of since. She may be in America.'

'Why?'

'Spose she likes it.'

The high-pitched laugh came out as a giggle.

'No. Why d'you think that?'

The Fat One looked down at his trousers, then at the reeking waste-bin.

'Something Tupmans said. Want me to give them a bell?'

Leonard shook his head. Somewhere he could hear a telephone ringing. He looked at his pocket watch. Snapped it shut. Three thirty. The doctor had promised his report by lunchtime. Knowing the doctor, Leonard expected it by six accompanied with all the standard complaints that this one wasn't easy.

'Customs got anything?'

The Fat One nodded.

'A bit, but nothing helpful.'

He smiled a small flicker of triumph, even initiative.

'Had a word with the Harbour Office as well. Nothing there. All registered and paid, he was.'

Leonard peered at him, searching for a glimmer that this intelligence suggested he had been wrong about his sergeant. He didn't really think so. The fat stomach rumbled and the intricate engineering of gas inlets and outlets effortlessly directed the vapours towards the only convenient exhaust valve. The smell was disagreeable.

'Haven't got much, have we, guv?'

The statement didn't hide his embarrassment.

Leonard got up and opened the window.

'What about the lad? We sure he didn't see anything?'

'Says he didn't. He's a good nipper. Good family.'

'Frightened?'

'Rosie, uh, WPC Rose, says that his mum says he's had a couple of bad dreams.'

Leonard poked at what had once been a thriving tradescantia. He pulled at the scrawny stems and left them on the window shelf.

'He might remember something. Tell Rose to stick with it. Be nice to Mrs Lomax. Go gently.'

'Don't want to frighten him, guv. He's a good sprog.'

'And we don't want his dreams. We want his ears. It could be too late.'

The Fat One scratched his swollen belly. The shirt was surprisingly uncreased.

'If there's anything there it'll come back, don't you think?'

Leonard shook his head.

'His eyes will see his dreams. Tell her to see if he remembers

30

what he heard. Kids don't dream sounds. What he heard is still in his head somewhere.'

Perkins had learned something. It didn't dawn on him to question Leonard. Leonard was different. He watched him rubbing the dead leaves and stem in his fingers. Staring out of the window. Perkins wondered why Leonard had let the plant die. That wasn't like him. Maybe he only liked flowers. Himself, he liked bushes and chrysanths. Not white ones. White ones were funerals.

'Worth having a word with young Bennie yourself, is it?'

Leonard didn't reply. The lad needed the confidence of just one of them. Eventually he'd tell if he had anything to say. Too many of them would confuse. Frighten. The WPC would do. Maybe he'd tell his mother. More likely there'd be no telling. Just a remark. Leonard hoped Mrs Lomax would know if she heard anything. Perhaps she wouldn't. Perhaps she wouldn't tell them even if she did know. Wouldn't want to get involved. Protect her son. A kid shouldn't find a bloodied body. He remembered when he was eight. Watching a fisherman in a punt far out on the still, warm lake. Bank weed, dark green, and long-tailed, transparently winged flies. No one knew he was there. The fisherman had placed his rod neatly in the craft's flat bottom and then carefully rolled over the side into the water. There had been nothing but a gentle splash. No protest. No cry. He had watched. Nothing. An empty still punt. An old hat floating on a glass summer lake. A dragonfly. For a day. He had returned in time for tea. Said nothing. Had cried that night. Had wondered each day. Then he cried because of fright, guilt, helplessness. Later, dry tears because he glimpsed the beauty though he could never understand the tragedy.

He turned from the window. Perkins was waiting. Faithful Perkins. If only he had a biscuit to toss. He opened his silver half-hunter. A quarter to. Snapped it shut, picked up the file and, without saying anything, headed for the corridor.

Upstairs, the Chief Superintendent was in a bad mood. His secretary was juggling two telephones and flipping through the pages of the official diary and comparing it to the private dates.

She often wondered who was running the division, the Assistant Chief Constable or her boss.

'He's waiting,' she said without looking up.

Leonard tapped on the inner door and went in.

The Old Man was signing letters. It took time. His was an exact signature. Very readable. Precise. No flourishes. No ambiguities. This was his last job before retiring. He didn't want to go. But go he would and he wanted a clean desk when he did. He waved Leonard to the side seat. Anyone sitting there couldn't put an elbow on the desk without knocking over the four photograph frames of Herself, the two children and the blue-background grandchildren. The pen-scratching stopped. He screwed the top on the ink bottle and put it in the middle drawer. The Old Man didn't like clutter.

'What have you got to tell me?'

Leonard polished his clean glasses.

'Nothing beyond the file other than conjecture which I won't.'

'Try me. It's been two days. I've had the Press Desk on.'

He smoothed his blue-and-white-striped tie down his stiff shirt front. Leonard noticed the bony wrists, the copper bracelet. There had been a science master with bony wrists, but no bracelet. He would have regarded that as hope over experience.

'I'll have the medical report by this afternoon.'

'That'll not tell you much you don't know. You know what I always say, Dead is dead. Up-to-no-good dead is murder. This is murder. You don't need that old fool to tell you that.'

Leonard was blinking. He didn't say anything.

'Talk me through. I'm seeing the ACC this evening. He'll expect me to know.'

Leonard understood. A display of knowledge, however incomplete, was far better than a display of ignorance. There was always the hope that the retirement OBE might, just might, be a possibility. The division hadn't had anything for some time.

The other man gave a grunt and maybe a nod. Leonard wasn't quite sure about the nod.

'Right.'

Leonard ran his hand over the closed file as if seeking spiri-

32

tual warmth from the sparse sheets. The slow blinking kept pace with his delivery. The old man liked it this way.

'Single round through heart. Entry and exit wounds suggest high velocity. 303, 762. Unconfirmed. Range 100 metres. Also unconfirmed.'

'How d'you know?'

'We think we've found the site. Across the water. On the other bank.'

'Where else?'

The sarcasm was faint but felt.

'Could have used a boat.'

'Oh no. Not at that range. Too unstable for accuracy.'

Leonard hadn't thought of that.

'Usual signs. Flat grass. Boot marks. It was wet. Too grassy for good prints.'

'The boat? His?'

'Mm. Mm. Forty foot. Inboard. Sailing vessel.'

He leant across with the file, careful to avoid the pictures.

'Apart from detail, the backgrounder from the yacht club secretary's the only thing to work on.'

'And?' The Old Man was scanning the typed sheet.

'I'll see him again as soon as we've finished.'

The Old Man swivelled his high-backed chair in his best boardroom manner and gazed at the Constable reproduction before speaking. He would look the part in the security firm next year.

'This one's not straight up and down, is it?'

'Thus far no. It . . .'

'. . . Doesn't conform. Doesn't conform.'

He was tapping his nose with a paper-knife. Leonard wondered which letters were left to him to open.

'If I may, sir?'

'Mm. Mm.'

He was still examining the print. Looking for a flaw.

'The thing that bothers me is the distance. A long-range like this wasn't a pot shot. If it had been the usual in-the-family mess then it would probably have been close-range.'

'And probably not as he was about to climb aboard. Probably not even there.'

'Right, sir. Let's tick them off. Wife? As far as we know, she's not even in the country and hasn't been for years. As far as we know.'

'Drugs? A forty-footer could be used to bring them in.'

'No signs. We've been over it. Sniffed it. She's clean. Customs say there's nothing known. Mind you, if he was good at it, then Customs wouldn't know, would they?'

'But the dogs would.'

'Probably, though it's pretty simple to clean up the smell, especially if the boat hadn't been doing the rounds for a couple of weeks. Even one.'

'Anything on the hull?'

Leonard shook his head. The *Madrigal* had been craned out. She was clean.

'Well if it's not that, and not his wife, what about girlfriend?'

'With a 762 at 100 metres? Some girlfriend! Mind you, that does leave jealous boyfriend.'

'Go on.'

'There's not much to go on with, that's why I want to have another word around the club.'

The Old Man was now ceiling-gazing. He really would look good in the boardroom.

'It's the set-up, isn't it, James?'

The Old Man always called him by his full name. He was never Jimmy. But then the Old Man was always very correct. Always had been. Long before that first interview.

'Most people, James, don't have access to this sort of weapon. Mm?'

Leonard blinked. Waited. There was more.

'Most people don't have the balls to set up something like this. Most people don't have the skill to bring it off. Mm? One round, you say? That's either very lucky or very, very skilful. Mm? Most people would not have dug in, waiting for him to turn up. That's not lucky. That's knowing.'

'A pro.'

The chair creaked as the Old Man swung back. It was not very good theatre, but it would do for the boardroom.

'That's correct, James. A pro. That's not very good, is it? Amateurs cry about it. Mm? That's why they're easy to nick. Mm? But pros. Oh no. They don't even smile. This one's different, very different.'

Leonard knew that.

'I'm going to need help. Foot soldiers.'

'Of course, of course. I'll see what I can do. But . . .' the sigh was as predictable as it was exaggerated, 'you don't need me to tell you that we're stretched.'

Leonard got up. The Old Man was smiling. For a long time in this job he'd considered himself too important to smile. Very correct. Serious image. He might not have got as far as he should, but he had done rather well for himself.

'You're lucky on this one. You've got a good sergeant.'

Leonard waited. There had to be more.

'Aye, very good indeed. A bit limited in some respects, but good local knowledge. A good all-rounder. Knows the right people.'

Leonard nodded his goodbye. So, he'd been right.

7

It was Les the barman who convinced Sanctuary that something was wrong. Or, rather, something Les gave him.

A murder, he thought, however horrid was a police matter. Nothing to do with him. Even a friend's murder. Friends, he thought, don't get murdered. Acquaintances don't. He had never known anyone who had been murdered. Never known anyone who had known anyone who had. He had heard about it in the Department. Mostly the old days. The Eastern bloc had thrived on it. Some of them did still. But none of this had ever touched Sanctuary. There were those who said he was too easy-going for the Department. Lacked an edge, they said. He wasn't sorry he didn't know about murder. Ordinarily, he thought, he could have walked away from this. Left it to the local Mr Plod.

The difference was that Stuart had been known to the Department. As his minder, his Friend, Sanctuary had to see it through as discreetly as possible. At the first whiff of official investigation all sorts of fans would be turned on. The Special Branch would be in demanding a briefing and that meant the Security Service would hear about it. Before anyone could sneeze, the whole area would be crawling with plods, clumsies and shadows as Dorothea called the police, MI5 and the Foreign Intelligence Service. Sanctuary wondered if he should bale out and let someone else stir the buzzing nest.

Roberts had said his goodbyes and had left the club for 'a bit of business in the smoke'. They had arranged to meet the following Monday. Roberts said he would have the package by then and No, he wouldn't reconsider the idea of posting it.

Sanctuary wandered onto the club terrace. He wanted to

36

think through what little he knew. At some stage he had to decide what to recommend and whether or not to return to London. The terrace was flagstoned and rose-walled. A good place to sulk. It was empty. The girl had gone, perhaps through the small gate and across the old canal lock and into the copse on the other side of the dank waterway. The black and brown mongrel appeared and slumped and then settled into the baking warmth of the stone wall. It panted once or twice in Sanctuary's direction.

Sanctuary pulled at his tie and undid his collar as the sun baked his shoulders. There seemed more water in the approach channel than when he'd arrived and he watched a broad-beamed, long, white ketch glide from the open basin to make her way towards the first curve of the shore. Two young men, very blond, their backs and feet bare, were in the bows. One of them, his arm raised, steadied himself with the forestay, yet there was no swell. A third, by his beard older, steered easily from a wheel in the centre cockpit, occasionally spying the mainmast top though no sail was set. Instead, it lay bunched along the spars like bleached and crumpled Monday washing. There was hardly enough wind from the boat's passage to spread the ensign from its stern pole, but Sanctuary could see the Frenchman's tricolour. A woman, long dark hair loose, from a distance voluptuous in her scarlet bikini, emerged from below deck and handed the helmsman a can. He wondered who they were. Where they were bound. How they could afford the time. How they could afford the sparkling-hulled vessel with its two silver masts stretching to goodness knows where. He wondered about the woman as she too stretched and made his every nerve stare. He wondered about the Lotus Eaters and the desire to never return home and understood why but not how.

He shivered. Suddenly cold. He looked about. Quickly. A child scurrying by a locked November church. The path across the canal lock was empty, the copse shadows innocent, the club house corner sharp, indifferent, the rose bushes trustworthy, offering no hide. Yet he felt watched. And then it was gone.

The sun's warmth told him not to be silly. He picked up his jacket and went in. There was nothing here for him.

The barman was alone with his polished glasses. He smiled. Sanctuary gave a half-wave, a salute, and would have walked straight through, but the man, on one foot then the other, seemed to be waiting. Had something to say.

'It is Mr Sanctuary, isn't it?'

He nodded.

'That's right.'

'Les. That's me. Les.' He seemed ashamed. 'Thought so,' he went on. 'Heard the Sec, you know.'

When he smiled, he looked down, modestly.

Sanctuary said he was sorry to have kept him waiting and hoped that it was all right to have sat outside. The barman's head bobbed and he smiled like a kindly marionette.

'No problem. Plenty to do.'

He rubbed gently at the glass in his hand.

'Mr Fisher gave me a letter for you.'

He reached into his back pocket and pulled out an old wallet, decorated with camels and pyramids and double-jointed Pharoahs. It was much-repaired. The envelope was blue, scuffed and bent at the top and corners where it had been too big for the bum-boatman's money holder.

Sanctuary looked at the front. Someone had printed in ball-point capitals his name and an address.

DAVID SANCTUARY Esq.,
c/o FOREIGN OFFICE,
WHITEHALL, LONDON, SW1.

'When did you get this?'

Now the barman was embarrassed. The head and shoulders weaved.

'That morning. The one when he was killed. You know?'

Sanctuary put his jacket on the bar and half-leaned, half-sat, on one of the high stools. He held the small envelope in both hands like a prayer book.

'You didn't post it?'

38

'I meant to. Then, with everything happening. I didn't. Just didn't. You know? Didn't know if I should or not. You know?'

'Tell me what happened?'

The barman looked confused.

'Tell me when you saw him and when he gave this to you.'

Les was rolling a cigarette. His hands weren't shaking, but he was having trouble with it. He licked the paper, slid it between his fingers and nipped out the ends of golden shag. The Zippo set fire to the cigarette rather than lit it. The barman took a deep pull. He wheezed. It sounded painful. Sanctuary waited.

'Well,' the barman looked from side to side like a backstreet tout, 'he came in like he usually does. About mid-morning. We're not really open, but he comes in gen'ral.'

He took another drag on the cigarette. It had gone out. The click of the Zippo was nervously loud in the long bar.

'What did he do?'

Sanctuary was trying to help him.

'Looked at the barometer out there.'

He nodded towards the hallway.

'Not many does. He does.'

'Go on.'

Sanctuary wanted the man to get on. He didn't know why, but he felt they might be interrupted and he'd never know the story. He wasn't even sure there was one. The letter remained unopened. The explanation was probably there. Perhaps there was nothing to explain.

'Well . . .'

'Go on,' he said again as the barman started to speak then didn't.

'First thing he says is have I got any change. He wanted twenty 50ps. For the telephone. Off he goes with that lot and five minutes later he's back for some more. Then he wants 20s.'

'Who was he 'phoning. D'you know?'

The head was bobbing and weaving like a tethered shadow boxer.

'No. Can't hear from here. Anyway I wouldn't, would I?

39

You know? But it must have been long-distance. Trunk call, you know?'

'Why?'

'Well, you can't use up ten quid's worth in four minutes on local calls, can you?'

'And that was it? He didn't say anything?'

'Well, he started to, then she comes in and they goes over there.'

He pointed to the corner table. The cigarette was out again.

'Who do you mean? She.'

'Forget her name. Local. Eh, Isobel. That's it. Pots. That's her. Makes pots, they say. She's not a yachtie or nothing. He had some charts, you see, in one of them black folders. You know?'

Sanctuary didn't but it didn't matter so he nodded.

'What happened?'

This time the Zippo nearly burned the barman's nose.

'He gave them to her. The lot. And off she goes.'

'That was it?'

'Yes. Almost. She says she'll do them straight away. That's what she says.'

Sanctuary looked at the envelope.

'And what about this?'

'Well, soon as she's gone, he asks me for some paper and goes back over there, same table. I gave him the envelope.'

'Why did he give it to you to post? Why not do it himself?'

Les was busy lighting up, holding the half-smoked cigarette at the bottom of the lighter's flame. He sounded like a bad ventriloquist.

'I offered. I was going into town for the Sec.'

The twin smoke-streams twitched his nostrils and he rubbed at them urgently with the back of his hand.

'Said I'd bung it into the main post office. First class, he said.'

'Thanks.'

Sanctuary left his jacket on the bar and walked over to the terrace doors. The mongrel raised his head, peered at him,

40

then dropped back into a panting slumber. The letter was short, neat, the uniform writing slightly backward-sloping.

11.00 Wednesday

Long time no speak. Tried to call you all morning. Couple of things you should know. If I'm right, Sad Sam Theory was right on. Now it's all breaking up as we once knew it would, someone's put a big one into the bazaar. Sorry to be so dramatic but if I remember correctly you can read between these lines, especially if you're still in the same business. If I guessed right you'll know what to do. I've been tied in with people I thought were on our side. Now not so sure. I've run out of people I can trust. This sounds daft, but I think (I really *know*, but *think* will do for now) that someone on our/your side knows and is keeping mum. Don't ask why. I don't know. I've put most of what I know in a letter with my solicitor, Tupman. He's in the local book. Hope it doesn't come to that. If it does, get the letter. Also, package with YC Secretary. He knows nothing. Give me a ring asap.
Stuart Fisher.

PS I haven't flipped my lid. Got a couple of names. One from Sad S. Remember I? Don't know about the other one. S

Sanctuary reread the letter. He remembered their Sad Sam Theory. It was really Fisher's. He believed that, when the Cold War was over, there would be too many interests and ideologies surviving in back rooms of high places for the Intelligence battle to melt away. The new Cold War would be fought in an ever-deeper undergrowth of subterfuge and mystery. And he believed that the back rooms would build snags and snares to keep their masters full of suspicions about what they both thought would be the inevitable thaw in East-West relations. That was Part One.

Part Two was frightening to them both during that long night in Sad Sam. Too much to drink and too much time to think in fantasies. Jane had laughed at them. Neither cared if she never smiled again. Fisher believed that when the crash came the Kremlin would lose control of the regions, the Republics. Everyone and everything would be for sale. There would be a long queue for sales goods. Even the most hideous of things. That was Fisher's hypothesis. It did not take much to prove it – especially if you happened to be in the trade. They had taken it to the next stage and both knew that an increasingly influential element in the Intelligence community saw their ways and lives threatened by a new détente. That night they'd been drinking too much, spilling too much but not enough to take themselves too seriously. A couple of old reactionaries before their time was Sanctuary's thought. Yet they both knew enough about the collective paranoia of Downing Street and Pennsylvania Avenue to realise that the doctrine of the CIA and the Foreign Intelligence Service would find house room in the sanctums of Whitehall and Foggy Bottom. They believed, but could never know, that twilighters would spread rumours of plot and counter-plot to stop Cabinets going soft.

They had never much developed the theory. In Sad Sam you never knew which radiator was listening. They had been neighbours. The cotton-wool poplars, the tenement yard. The European cars jealously guarded by the locally employed drivers possessive of their Western horsepower as Newmarket boys of well-marked thoroughbreds. The draughty arch and the brown wooden-slatted three-pack of militiamen. Black-and-white-ringed and ever-swinging pashalsta sticks. Smiling 'please' in threes, never in ones. Watching each other. Ever-watchful. Ever recording the comings and goings of the foreign residents. Quietly checking. Quietly guarding. No one entered, no one left, without them knowing. All this had changed, which was why Sad Sam Theory had surfaced.

He looked across the calm water. The French ketch had gone. He thought of the girl with the beer cans and remembered the evening when Fisher had been away on one of his summer trips down to Warsaw. On the top floor it was airless. Jane had knocked at his door just after midnight. Bored. Just back from a dinner party. She dressed expensively and, in that heat, flimsily.

She'd seen his light on. That's what she had said. The door was solid. The carpet thick to its bottom edge. He hadn't argued.

He looked at the letter. The handwriting was a mystery. There was no reason he should remember Fisher's fist, if he'd ever seen it. A package. A letter. A premonition. No. A calculated prediction. Fisher was not someone who thought much about premonition.

They had met once more at Lord's. They sat on high stools in the Long Room. A damp, slow, cheerless charade at the season's start played out in silence beyond the warmth and comfort of the glassed pavilion's nave. They talked about Ignatiev. *Sotto voce.* No irritable head would turn. Coded asides. No suspecting ear would tune in. Ignatiev had gone back. They had talked again and wondered. Ignatiev was coming out. Fatter this time. London. Fisher reckoned he was handling. British? Fisher didn't know. Ignatiev had gone back. Gone elsewhere. Now they said he was out once more. And Fisher was dead.

He heard the click and snap of the barman's Zippo. Caught the first sweet scent of golden and shredded Virginia. Les was smiling. Waiting. Polishing still.

'Everything okay?'

Sanctuary went in. Picked up his jacket.

'Sure.'

The barman watched him tuck the blue envelope in his breast pocket.

'Not bad news I hope, Mr Sanctuary.'

Sanctuary stared at him for a few seconds. The invisible strings jerked the barman this way and that. There was no attempt at humour, even less at irony. Sanctuary shook his head, sandy hair disturbed and flopping. Smiled as best he could.

'No. Not at all. Personal.'

'Bad business.'

'Yes. Tell me. Where's somewhere reasonable to put up for a few days?'

8

Sanctuary had cleared with the Department. There was no great problem. Fisher had been a contact. They had worked together albeit nothing had come of their liaison. Yet he had been known to them. A Casual. Sanctuary had been his Friend. Fisher was dead. Had attempted to get in touch on the day he was killed and there was acceptable evidence that he had something which he believed the Department should know. As his Friend, Sanctuary should take a look. Seemed reasonable as long as it came to nothing. Better to be sure.

Dorothea had met him in the office. Deserted on a cheerful Sunday lunchtime except for the casually jacketed and smocked duty staff. Red-striped shirts, suede brogues, razor-pressed levis, not a paint dab to be seen, mixed and matched early Liberty prints. They smoked more on Sundays. Dorothea had photocopied the letter, put the original on file. The accessed constabulary code took time. When it came there was little to go on.

The medical report summary skipped what Dorothea called the lingua pathologica. Fisher had been killed by a single shot in the region of the heart. The small entry and large exit wounds at that range suggested a high-velocity round, maybe with a softened head. The chest was a mess. The victim had otherwise been in reasonable condition for his age. The left leg had been damaged some time earlier and plated and pinned. There was extreme wastage of the left quads which was to be expected from such leg damage. The pathologist had no medical evidence to suggest how the leg came to be in such a scrapyard state. Roberts had said it was '82. He hadn't said how. The police report mentioned that background on the deceased was being sent from DNSy.

44

It was then that Dorothea told him there was nothing in the
Green Bank about Fisher. Odd? Sanctuary put it down to cock-
up rather than conspiracy. The system was a year old. Fisher
wouldn't rate an entry until the Also Knowns came through
the weeders' files. She reminded him to get a receipt for his
hotel, to remember the daily allowance, check his mileage and
to avoid the chambermaids. He was embarrassed. She laughed.
But not noisily. She wished she hadn't been so obvious.

They walked through St James's Park. He paid for deck
chairs by the lake. Age, he thought. Ten years ago they'd
have sat on the grass. She bought ice creams that dripped and
chocolate flakes that crumbled over her soft pink skirt.

'You know you're trespassing? Charles says it's strictly SB,
nothing to do with us.'

'How does he know I'm there?'

'Deputy Dog told him.' She licked at the fast-melting cream
mush. 'Don't look so disgusted. Of course he told him. After
all, Dear Charles will have to look after your desk if this takes
some time.'

'By the way, where's Ignatiev's file?'

'Why?'

'Charles will need to keep it updated.'

'In Black Section.'

'Restricted?'

He nodded. She smiled.

'That'll give him more to do.'

'That's why he's warning me off?'

'No. He's right.'

'When isn't he?'

'Someone gets killed. He's not ours. Let the local police
handle it. It's a murder job. Isn't it? Maybe Charles is right?'

He liked lakes and ponds. They reminded him of jars of
tadpoles. Warm days. Lying face down staring into the brown
waters. Tickling minnows. Wanting a proper rod with a line
and a hook. Making a net from a garden cane and old muslin.
Too embarrassed to touch his mother's cast-off laddered stockings.

Dorothea was speaking. Bare-legged. Tanned. Full calves.

45

Toes stubby and brown in old leather sandals. He wondered about the thin gold ankle chain. He'd never before noticed it.

'You'd do best to contact the police. Be open. You're a chum of his. Saw it in the paper. Nothing more than that. If they suspect you're sniffing about they'll get ratty and start hitting the 'phones. Just don't mention the Department.'

'You sound like an Inter City briefing.'

His voice was sharp. He could still see the faces of candidates before they ran on evasion exercises in Germany. Bright. Self-assured. Bit of a game. Ignoring the obvious. Each getting caught. Ignoring the obvious.

'Charles would be in there like a flash. He's just dying to write his I-told-you-so memo to Deputy Dog.'

'Priestly's a shit.'

'Even more reason to watch your back.'

Behind them, through the trees, the white-helmeted Royal Marines oompahed in six-eight with no straining at the brass-buttoned blue tunics. Through half-closed eyes he watched picnics and strollers and wondered at the innocence of the afternoon and why Fisher lay shrouded and naked and puttied in a cold drawer, one big toe buff-tagged in recognition that once he too had picnicked, marched in step and dripped ice cream.

'I thought you did that for me.'

His voice was far away. Frogspawn swept into a jar. A strand of green weed wisping about the spotted jelly forms. Smells. Earth. Dock leaves rubbed on nettle stings. First scents of wild garlic on the bank by the summer house. Discarded stockings. Torn at the thigh band. He shuddered.

'You cold?'

He shook his head.

Dorothea put a hand on his arm.

'I do. You know that.'

He looked at her hand then into her face but not her eyes.

'Do what?'

He'd forgotten.

'Watch your back.'

'You think I need it watched?'

46

She nodded.

'It should be simple. Murder is always simple.'

'Family or robbery.'

He knew the routine of why-people-murder figures.

'Often. But Davy, don't forget, everything you've told me about this is different. Assuming he was right.'

'But I don't know what he was right about.'

'What did he mean by a big one?'

'Don't know.'

He did.

The band had stopped. An Indian family ambled in front of them. The father flabby, white-shirted. Carrying an executive briefcase. The children well-behaved. Grandmother scraggy with hurting feet and grey-tinted glasses. The wife cool, elegant in turquoise and lemon.

'Sure?'

'No. But he might have been guessing.'

She'd turned against the deck chair's curve. The unbuttoned T-shirt gaped. She was very brown. He wondered how. Where. She smelled warm. He looked away.

'You say he wasn't a nutter. A good Casual. You knew him.'

He wondered if he did. He wondered if Fisher had known. Dorothea had paused. Sensing his mind's wander. He looked back. This time at her eyes.

'Not that well.'

'Well enough for him to 'phone.'

'And then he's murdered.'

'Or?'

The Indian family had moved on, eyes averted from the lakeside. Very British. A young woman held a toddler. Both hands beneath its thighs. Cradled as it peed into the water.

'Or nothing. He was shot through the heart from long distance.'

'Very professional.'

Her voice was easy. Not challenging.

'It didn't say that.'

'It was.'

'Very murdered. So there's no "or".'

47

He was challenging. She took it.

'Murder's when someone gets it in the family, or out of jealousy or villainy.'

He stared at the young woman. The child, bare except for a white sunhat, was cackling. The mother was washing her ankles in the water.

When he spoke it was as if he were coming to a reluctant conclusion. He wasn't. He'd been there for some time.

'Assassination?'

'Is something quite different.'

'Different rules.'

'Not different, Davy. None at all. Take care, won't you?'

9

The package, when he got it, didn't tell Sanctuary much.

He'd arrived back the night before, booked into the hotel and started his case note. There was very little to record. He had wondered about going to the yacht club. Roberts had said to drop in any time and left instructions that he should be signed in as Secretary's Guest. But he didn't go. No point. Not yet. Didn't want to be too obvious. That's what they always taught. Be as inconspicuous as possible. Being six four, with sandy this-way-and-that hair and a nose that had played one game too many against the front row, made that difficult. He wrote two pages. It was mainly names and first facts. Nothing much but it could mean something later. No conjecture. Not if Fisher were half-right. He marked the top copy HOLD FOR RETURN which meant that Dorothea would glance through it and action anything she thought necessary. He could trust her. He slipped on his jacket and strolled out into the town and posted his own copy into the Royal Bank of Scotland letter-box. It would be in their Drummond's Branch by the following evening. He would pick it up when he needed to. It was better to be safe.

The next morning, Roberts, as promised, met him in the yacht club office. Fisher's package was on his desk. He made a point of saying that he had not gone to the bank at opening time.

'Didn't want to make a big deal of it.'

Sanctuary nodded. Didn't say anything. Roberts was right. To admit so would suggest there was more to his interest than he had let on. He didn't want to encourage Roberts. He was not on the team. There was no team.

The Jiffy bag was small, letter-size, bound with red insulating tape, clearly marked with his name in that same neat row of block capitals which he had to assume was Fisher's. Sanctuary had asked Dorothea to get a hand-writing sample but that was going to take time unless he could get into Fisher's home.

Roberts folded his arms and the shoulder-tabs on his crisply laundered shirt arched in authority.

'I was wondering if I should mention this, eh, this little lot to the police. If you get my drift.'

He pushed the upholstered envelope across the desk, now surprisingly clear of clutter and correspondence. He had taken the telephone off the hook.

Sanctuary leant against the filing cabinet and looked down at Roberts. It was a long way down. Roberts didn't seem to mind. The packet remained on the desk.

'Mind you, depends what's in it.'

The odd grin was there again. But Roberts wasn't smiling.

'You must do what you think correct.'

He had no intention of opening the envelope in front of the Secretary.

'Look, Mr Sanctuary, I don't want to stick my nose in. But I tell you something: it's a very good nose. If you'll excuse the pun so to speak, it knows its way around.'

'I take your point. But I'm telling you, what I said on Friday was true. There's nothing official in this. I'm naturally curious about a not very close friend's death. Understood?'

The office door had swung open. Maybe the breeze. Maybe the cockeyed angle of the whole building. It seemed a good signal for Sanctuary to leave. He picked up the package.

'Before you go, Mr Sanctuary, before you go.'

Sanctuary paused, the envelope insignificant in his large hand. His hesitation was answer enough for Roberts who had swung his foot onto the open bottom drawer. Sanctuary looked at him, half-smiled. Friendly without offering a promise of friendship.

'Yes?'

He dredged the forbidding tone from clear memory of a housemaster who knew instinctively that some privilege was to be requested. Roberts was no boy oppressed by the authority

50

of office. Blank eyes. Open for ever. Pressed into his scrubbed and shorn countenance by an apprentice waxworker. The perfect NCO. Sure of his empire. Safe in his patronage. Out of his class in the high-flying wardroom but rarely out of his depth.

'I hear what you say, Mr Sanctuary. What you do is not my part of ship. But I was a good Jimmy. I've got good ears and eyes. If you need a hand, you may save a lot of time.'

The smile was a leer. Just. He wasn't done.

'Another thing, you could save yourself a lot of unwelcome questions from other parties by coming to me first. Understood?'

He was probably right. Sanctuary knew that. Roberts knew that. Sanctuary knew that, unless they were silly, then the local police would know that.

'Thanks for the offer.'

This time, Sanctuary put a little extra into the smile. They shook hands. He tried another smile. Roberts didn't blink.

Outside, the sun had dried the puddles of overnight rain. Ducks waddled, paused, then waddled on. In the basin, a workboat slipped an unmanned sloop onto its berth and waited while a youth in shorts made the yacht fast. The harbour seemed in no hurry. Les the barman was talking to the drayman, brawny and leather-gloved. He waved, crashed an unsuspecting gear and rumbled towards the service road alongside the canal.

'Off to see the old boat then?'

The unlit cigarette was stuck to his bottom lip.

'What old boat?'

'Mr Fisher's. *Madrigal*. You know? They brought her in last night. She's over on S.'

He pointed to the other side of the basin.

'You can just walk over the lock.'

'I thought she was in the creek. Wherever that is.'

'So she was. So she was.'

Les was all-knowing. He looked down. Smiling and modest in his moment of importance.

'They had her out of the water a couple of times. Then put her back. All taped off, she was. Couldn't get near her. You

know? Yellow ribbons and things. But that was then, wasn't
it?'

'Why bring her in here?'

Les was shaking his head from side to side. But he did know.

'Keep a better eye, I suppose. The ways I hear it, last night,
you know? They were saying . . .'

He stopped.

'Saying what?'

Now the head moved faster.

'Nothing. Bye.'

David watched him go. A spare figure. Stooped but not old.
The head in rhythm with his fox's trot. He didn't look back.
Didn't look up. Didn't pause as he skirted the Secretary stand-
ing in the clubhouse doorway.

He watched for a moment after the door clacked closed
behind them both. Across the path, propped hulls, scraped
and part-scraped, fouled and anti-fouled, named and unnamed,
waited the attentions of owners, surveyors, chippers and scrap-
ers and painters. Wasting ashore instead of being afloat. A
middle-aged woman, stocky in royal blue and red-spotted ker-
chief, balanced atop an aluminium ladder. A plastic bottle in
one hand, a rag in the other, she was polishing the bow of an
elaborately superstructured motorsailor. He wondered if it
were called *Dunrovin* and had net curtains, and then felt guilty
at his instinct to sneer. The man who had been rubbing at a
dinghy was still rubbing. His back to Sanctuary, the shoulders
easy, the arm rhythmically sure. No hurry. No tide to catch.

Sanctuary looked back to the clubhouse. Nothing. Nobody.
Yet, he felt . . . he didn't know what he felt.

He walked towards the lock, passing the woman polishing.
She looked up. Surprised. Then friendly. Smiled hello. Gold
and white framed in blood-red. He nodded and walked on.
Wished he'd said good morning. Loudly. Cheerfully. But he
hadn't. He felt annoyed with himself.

To his left, the harbour stretched as far as he could see,
bound by tree-lined shore. The distortion of distance gave the
impression of hulls and bare poles haphazardly moored. He
supposed there was some order. To his right, pontoons lay

52

like double-edge combs, each tooth holding a boat either side. Whites and blues, greens and reds, hulls and multihulls, spars and masts, cabins and gin decks.

At the lock he rested against the rail as a young, bare-chested man called in a motor cruiser. The boat seemed to be going quickly. Reverse thrust. It veered. Banged hard against the wall. A high-pitched Midlands voice from the cabin yelled an obscenity at the woman on the foredeck who was grappling with a holding rope from the lock top which she couldn't see, trying to keep her balance, and to fend off from the green-slimed stone sides. The gates closed. Trapped. Water going out. Boat going down. The woman more confused. Bent forward, deep-sided unromantic drawers outlined beneath stretched lilac tracksuit. For a moment, she looked back in mutinous hatred.

Sanctuary watched on until the front gates opened, the offending ropes were released, and the turboed cruiser came gargling and spluttering into the channel. The young man smiled at him. There was no malice. He'd seen worse. And somehow they all made it back. He settled into his chair and worked on his tan.

Sanctuary followed the low concrete wall until it gave way to bushes and thin woods. He dropped down to the shingle and sat facing the harbour. He could see the cruiser. Even the helmsman. There was no sign of the woman. She was probably clapped in irons by now.

The foreshore was smeared with sea weeds, scattered with stones and wafted smells which were full of childhood. Shrimping summers among rock pools. He could see his father who had never been young. He remembered the kindness, the patience. He trusted him. He remembered the blue pail. The sand in the bottom. The water and the starfish. Maybe it was dead. Maybe it wasn't. It curled when the water moved. In the morning it was gone. The pail upside down and dried by the bath's edge. His mother telling him not to be silly. It was dead. It stank. Hotel bathrooms, especially her hotel bathroom, were not for dead and stinking starfish. She told him never to forget that. He hadn't. He wouldn't.

53

The package ripped as he unwound the red tape. He pulled out a cork ball with a short line attached and a stainless-steel ring. A mortice key, barely strong enough to secure a wardrobe. The blue tag said, *Madrigal*. He recognised the writing.

She was easy to find. He thought there might have been a helmeted constable. There wasn't. The yellow tape had gone. She lay bow to the pontoon, the second boat in the double-banked line of craft. Even to his untrained eye she was beautiful. Long, sleek, bigger than he had imagined, perhaps low in the water, perhaps slim, but unquestionably beautiful. He had sailed with an uncle for four or five seasons. Once in the Solent they'd seen something similar.

The *Madrigal* looked good. Her mooring ropes still clean fore and aft. The springs crossed, holding her steady. The white decks uncluttered. The hull, dark-blue, glistening, reflecting the doubtful waters of the basin. Sanctuary stopped a few yards from her long bow. She seemed serene. Untouched by tragedy. A white notice, tied by baler twine, was cockeyed on the stainless-steel pulpit. It said to KEEP OFF and was signed Police.

Sanctuary fingered the cork ball and key in his denim pocket. Notices didn't mean not to look. He walked aft noting the taut rigging, the keenly furled foresail, the mainsail rolled and tucked beneath its blue boom cover. In the cockpit, ropes remained neatly coiled on the after benches. The police had looped a strong security wire across the padlocked hatch door.

The notice had been ignored. The wire cut in two places. The padlock, closed tight and useless, lying in the cockpit well. The oiled teak doors jemmied from the top.

Sanctuary looked about him. Nothing. Nobody. He swung himself aboard and into the cockpit. He used the key to ease open the port-hand door and then his elbow to lay them both flat. Prints hardly mattered. It was best to be sure. Whoever had been below before him had successfully finished an advanced vandalism course. This was no burglar in search of unmarked boat jumble booty. Bilge hatches neatly laid aside. The batteries out and emptied. Berth cushions razor-ripped. The oil lamp reservoir unscrewed. The fire extinguishers blown. Barometer and clock lay in one corner. A knife had sliced the top from a

54

soft-soap dispenser. Instant coffee was spilled in a pyramid of slashed packet soups. The VHF radio was unscrewed from its bracket. Only the navigation repeaters were intact, one of them incongruously showing some faraway latitude and longitude.

He pushed the starboard bunk cushion back in place and sat down against the chart table. Some mess. He could hear Dorothea's husky warning. Very professional. Very different. Not murder. Vandalism? Couldn't be. Search? Damned right, he thought. But for what? He hadn't a clue. He had decided that it was time to go when he sensed, rather than heard, a light step along the main pontoon. He crouched further into the berth and held his breath better to pick up the sound. Definitely footsteps. They stopped. He guessed at about the bow. By the police notice. He felt the pontoon sway as the steps, cautious, came alongside. A chromium-plated winch handle was in the bulkhead socket by his shoulder. Very carefully Sanctuary slipped it free and took a firm grip. For the life of him he couldn't think that he would have the right angle, nor the purchase to use it. Too cramped. Trapped. Slowly, very slowly, he pulled one long leg under him, ready to spring. There was nowhere to hide. He could hear breathing. Controlled. Professional. There was a lurch and a dip.

Had he been watched? That cold sensation earlier. Seen? He lowered his hand, ready to underarm the shiny missile at the first chance just as he heard the intruder put one foot on the side deck and jump aboard. The handle was useless. What if there was a gun? He tried to turn his head to see from the small side windows. Couldn't. Had to watch the hatch doors. Only way in. Only way out. The footsteps had stopped. Silence. Then a scuffing as whoever it was crossed the deck and started to edge down the port side and to the open cockpit.

10

Priestly had lunched well. The food at the East Indies was perhaps less than distinguished, but Priestly thought it agreeable and he so enjoyed a seat at the window. He liked to be seen by those he valued as they passed through St James's Square. He always prayed in Wren's church in Jermyn Street. Just to be sure.

Lunch done, he had left, discreetly after his guest, and had then crossed Pall Mall and dropped in to see another Friend, this one in Carlton Terrace. They had talked quietly and with some circumspection. Then Priestly had taken his hat, his stick and his gloves and had walked, rather jauntily in the sunshine, down the steps and across the Park. He had paused just off the path, listened for some minutes to the band, and then humming contentedly continued his way across the road to the side entrance of the Foreign Office.

Dorothea was listening on the telephone when Priestly walked in. She half-smiled. But looked worried. The window was open but it was hot and Dorothea's rather thin frock, he thought, looked very cooling. She was almost, well, quite Rubensesque. He was sure it was the right phrase. He supposed her bosoms rather large but that she might make someone a splendid sister and, later in life, a sleepy grandchild would find her comfortable and warming at Christmas. Dorothea put down the receiver.

Priestly smiled. But in good humour.

'Have we heard from our David?'

She shook her head.

'No. He said he was going to 'phone in.'

'I'm told he may be fishing on dangerous ground.'

She ignored the bait.

'The Deputy wants to see you.'

Priestly lost a little of his smile and humour.

'I hope you told him mine was not an idle lunch.'

'I didn't. I didn't know.'

She had. She wasn't telling Priestly that. The bait was visible still.

'What d'you mean dangerous?'

'Red Flag stuff, my dear Dorothea. Red Flag. Strictly No Bathing.'

The Government House timepiece whirred fussily and began its delicate quadrille. Priestly buttoned his jacket and headed for the internal door.

'But I did warn him, didn't I?'

He paused before going in. Turned. The smile had gone. Now there was a beam. Priestly's aunt would have been positively overwhelmed.

11

The face that appeared at the cabin door looked as startled as he felt. There was a scream of mixed rage and terror and a flurry and scramble to escape. Sanctuary jumped up and crunched his head against the overhead light. Crouching and still grasping the winch handle, he pushed himself through the doorway and leapt onto the pontoon. With the violence of his jump he nearly lost his balance. The T-shirted figure, less sure-footed and scrabbling to escape, fell.

Sanctuary stepped close. Not too close. His right hand raised in conquest. From where the girl lay, Sanctuary's large shaggy-haired frame, bleeding from the temple and threatening with a chromium steel bar, must have looked awesome.

'Keep away. Keep away.'

It was pathetic.

Sanctuary looked at her. The same tatty, scrubbed shorts. The same thin T-shirt. Nothing else. No gun. No knife. No grenade. No thuggee's wire. He grinned. Stretched out a hand.

'You can't run far in flip-flops.'

She didn't move. She was panting. Puffed. Frightened. He looked at the winch handle, still half-raised, turned and tossed it into the cockpit.

'I'm sorry. I thought you were . . .'

He shrugged. He didn't want to say what he thought.

The girl wasn't impressed. Unsure. She didn't move. He wondered what he would do if she tried to make a run for it. Stop her. She wasn't a killer. Where did it say that? Part of team? He wanted to know what she was doing on the boat. He waved at the *Madrigal*.

'She belongs, or rather belonged, to a friend of mine. Stuart Fisher.'

58

There was no movement.

'But you probably knew that anyway.'

Slight nod.

'I simply wanted to take a look. Someone's already done that in a big way. I was wondering what to do when I heard something. You. I'm sorry.'

A cruiser's klaxon blasted outside the basin entrance. The girl jumped. He put out his hand. She ignored it and got up, still keeping her distance. Way up on the bank, a green-overalled figure had emerged from a concrete wash-house. He was watching them. Sanctuary felt embarrassed.

'I'm David Sanctuary. The Secretary in the club will vouch for me.'

'I know who you are.'

'I saw you in the car park.'

He pointed again at the *Madrigal.*

'Look for yourself.'

'Why?'

'So you can see I'm telling the truth.'

Her eyes were frightened. He stood out of the way.

'Don't worry. I'll stay here.'

'Why haven't you called the police?'

Sanctuary was surprised. She was more Scottish than he'd imagined from the monosyllables. Too blonde. The eyes too round. Yet the burr was there. From where, he didn't know. The Islands? He blinked as blood dripped to his eyelid.

'I would have. But you turned up. By the way, you don't have exclusive rights to being frightened. Sneaking up like that was pretty nerve-racking.'

He smiled. Dabbing with his forearm at the cut temple. He was supposed to look boyish and harmless. From where the girl was, he looked grotesque.

'I wasn't frightened.'

Defiance. Definitely the Islands.

'Not really.'

She was wary. But she had accepted his story. Or appeared to. She stepped around him and easily aboard the *Madrigal.* She said something. He didn't catch it and started to follow her below. Then didn't. She knew the *Madrigal*. Said it had always been neat. Immaculate. But, as far as she could see, nothing was missing. The expensive binoculars lay in pieces, their lenses unscrewed. The old vernier sextant was in a corner, its wooden box so ruthlessly searched that the tiny filter tray had been levered from its compartment.

'God. Look at this.'

He took it as a vote of confidence and ducked below. Isobel's confidence came with their shared disgust of what had happened. It dawned on her that this tall and obviously very strong man didn't frighten her. She had been frightened by what had happened. Still was. But not of him.

This time the footsteps had no ring of furtiveness. They were sharp. With purpose. Confident of their right or reason to be there. Sanctuary put a finger to his lips. The girl didn't need telling. Now she was doubly frightened. She felt caught. Snared as much as anything else by the sense of energy in the man's frame as he moved surprisingly quickly in such a confined space. Sanctuary wasn't about to be trapped again. He started for the cabin door just as the footsteps turned onto the pontoon and the boat lurched with their weight and rhythm. He reached the cockpit and looked up. There were two men. One was big. Unsmiling. Blue pinstripe cut and stitched for a Romanian wrestler. The other was thin. Round spectacles. Bushy eyebrowed. Herringboned. He wore green bicycle clips.

12

It took a bit of explaining.

The blue flashing lights had followed. A slack-busted redhead in a long green singlet had appeared from the cabin of a nearby cruiser. A male voice from below was demanding to know what the hell was going on. So was Leonard, though no one had disturbed his more basic needs. The Fat One leant forward, but not too near. A blue-backed identity card.

'Police. Who you?'

Leonard blinked furiously. Waited. The Fat One nodded his support.

Sanctuary relaxed his grip.

'Thank Christ for that.'

He grinned. Nearly. The girl came to the companionway.

Leonard stopped blinking. Somehow he didn't believe he'd nabbed a killer. Certainly not two. Perkins was confused.

Sanctuary explained. It was the concise form. Grade IV Sitrep. He'd done it dozens of times. Hard outline. No adjectives. Pause between sentences. No more than three paragraphs. Explanation would come later. It was now important to cool down the local plods. Situation Reports were buckets of water. You used them to put out bonfires or to wake up sentries.

'David Sanctuary. The chap who owned this was a friend. I'm down from London and thought I'd take a look at her. She's been broken into. I was having a look when Miss, eh . . .'

'Isobel Rolfe.'

The voice didn't have to say if it were still frightened.

'When Miss Rolfe arrived. She, she, eh, was a friend of Stuart's. Stuart Fisher. We were checking the damage.'

Sanctuary switched off. Transmission ends.

A gangling uniformed figure, middle-aged and moustached, dot-and-carried one down the slope in their direction. Leonard still had not spoken. His weariness and frustration escaped in a hiss as the marina guard approached, looking this way and that in nervous self-importance.

'Security. What's up then? What's up?'

The Fat One didn't have to go through his card routine. They knew each other. Leonard said nothing. Perkins said something about routine. Sanctuary ran a knuckled grip through his hair. The girl had stubbed her flip-flopped toe and was rubbing it to hide bewilderment still tinged with fear. The security man puffed and gasped into his two-way which squelched and spat static and unintelligible squawks from an adenoidal control somewhere across the basin.

'Gotta report in,' he said. He was blue-denimed and silver-badged. Very important. 'Gonna have to have to see someone. George oughta be here. He's on the roster.'

Leonard waved a hand and the man headed for the ramp, keys, torch and pouch swinging from his black leather belt, muttering that George had no sense of 'dooty'.

'Never on dooty when he's supposed to be.'

A marina van was exceeding the speed limit in the direction of the constabulary pit stop. It was becoming very crowded. Very public.

Leonard stared across at the cruiser. The redhead stared back.

'Not a good place, guv.'

Sanctuary was surprised at the shrill pitch of the Fat One's voice. He remembered a long summer. A forgotten palace in Nawanagar. The eunuchs' soft hands.

Leonard was walking back to the Vauxhall.

'You'd better come.'

Perkins wasn't certain if he was supposed to be arresting anyone. They stepped ashore and he backed off to the end of the berth. Two constables were waiting. Just in case. There was no need. They weren't under arrest. But Perkins was right. Not a good place.

It took time. The windows in Leonard's office were open, the blinds down. They rattled drily in the breeze. But it was cool. At first they had been separated. Then she came back with the Fat One. They talked for two hours until it was time to close the windows. It wasn't cold but the girl was. A WPC found a winter sweater in her locker. Leonard scribbled on a pad, tore off the note and gave it to Perkins. Perkins handed it to the WPC. She left. The WPC was big. The sweater fell below the girl's shorts. Leonard kept looking at the white scar above her left knee. Wanted to ask how it had got there. He hadn't seen it until she put on the sweater. He thought she was quite nice. Maybe. He smiled, which said that that was almost that. Just a couple of small points.

The girl's stomach gurgled. Perkins didn't write it down. But he looked on in sympathy, then at nothing. But he could smell. He could smell the spare ribs his mum had promised that night. She always cooked when she came round. Liked to be busy, she said. Probably, she'd bring him a bread pudding. His favourite.

The WPC returned. She stood in the doorway like a man. The doorway was hers. The uniform did something for her. Sanctuary thought he wouldn't recognise her off duty. Nurses were the same. Her shoes looked very serious. They must walk a lot, he thought. Her ankles were heavy. Perhaps swollen. Perhaps walking did that. The other room was free. Perkins and the WPC left with the girl. She paused for a moment by the doorway. A passing WPC stared openly at her legs. She smiled at Sanctuary. Not very confident.

'I'll wait for you,' he said.

She nodded. Interrogation formed instant friendships.

'Now, Mr Sanctuary, tell me more.'

'About what?'

'You say you'd had a call from Fisher, but you hadn't seen him for some time.'

Sanctuary wanted to ask what was happening to the girl. He knew why they'd been separated. The police had done the course. Divide and conquer. Same questions. Different rooms. Doubts. Uncertainties. Resort to cover story. Then compare answers. He remembered the tricks. Easier in a foreign language. Resort to the I-don't-understand ploy. When they brought in the language expert, act normally. Time gained means confidence. The girl wouldn't know. Would she? Forget the girl.

'That's right.'

'Then why should he call you?'

'That's what I wondered.'

Sanctuary could not place the neutral accent. He was wary. Leonard wasn't a plod. He was all wrong. He could smell Dorothea's scent. He looked at the plant on the window ledge. It was parched. Forgotten. Best take the initiative.

'We were neighbours once.'

Leonard looked up from his pad, the doodled teddy bear not yet finished.

'Here?'

Sanctuary shook his head.

'Moscow. He was a junior naval attaché. I was in the Embassy. Cultural attaché.'

'Culture.'

Leonard made it sound very un-English.

'Isn't that a euphemism?'

'For?'

Sanctuary knew what was coming.

'Espionage.'

The policeman was peering at Sanctuary's mouth ready to lip-read the lie.

'Sometimes. Wish it had been. Moscow's brilliant for your career. Not much else.'

Leonard went back to his teddy bear.

'And for unusual friendships?'

'We kept in touch. Not sure why really, but we did. Anyway, when I heard that he'd been . . .' he paused.

'Killed?'

'Murdered.'

'Is that what it was?'

Leonard's dark pencil strokes were slow, contemplative.

'You're the policeman. You tell me.'

64

Leonard looked up. The blink took its time. A tired punkah wallah late in his day. He ignored the question.

'What did he say when he called?'

'To me, nothing. I wasn't there. It was a message. Get in touch.'

'That it?'

'More or less.'

'I would like a recording of the message. Can that be arranged?'

'There isn't one. It's not that sort of Department.'

There was. It was.

'Who took the message?'

'One of my colleagues.'

'And if I wanted to talk to him? Is it that sort of Department? I could?'

'She.'

Leonard was annoyed with himself. Sanctuary wasn't playing a game. He looked at Sanctuary's mouth. Leonard believed he could tell more from mouths and hands than from eyes and voices. Sanctuary was amiable. Strong. The nails were clean, clipped but not filed. If there was vanity it lay deep in this man. He took an unnecessary breath. The question would have been clever. Sanctuary cut him off.

'What you should know is that while there is no official interest in Fisher's death it's quite natural that the Department would understand my interest in the event.'

Leonard was surprised. He didn't look it. If Sanctuary were to be hinting at some unofficial inquiry then there was something much bigger going on than he imagined.

'Mr Sanctuary, let us for a moment step back one pace. You are here because you, and Miss Rolfe, were found, to say the least, in suspicious circumstances in suspicious surroundings. In short, you were not supposed to be there. You were, however. We were alerted to your being there because of a disturbance which, it seems, focused on both of you. We had sealed the cabin of this vessel. When we arrived, the seal had been broken and the inside of the cabin ripped to pieces. It had been turned over.'

He paused. His perfect impression of one of the most boring styles of the Old Man had been effective. Sanctuary looked puzzled. But his hurt innocence was wasted on the policeman. Leonard had removed his spectacles and was furiously rubbing them with the end of his tie, exaggeratedly peering for smudges. Sanctuary's big hands were back in his denim pockets, scratching impatiently at his thighs.

'Bolt cutters.'

Leonard peered. Blink. Blink. Blink. Pause. Blink. Blink. Blink.

'What?'

An irritable archdeacon chastising a rector.

Sanctuary's eyes were wide. A cartoon of innocence with a plastered temple for good measure. His hands spread, offering himself for some imaginary frisk.

'We would have needed strong shears. Probably bolt cutters. Where were they? On board? Then how did we get to them?'

Leonard blinked.

'You could have dumped them.'

Sanctuary smiled. It said Nice Try.

'Overboard? I bet there's no more than eight to ten feet of water there. If we did, they shouldn't be hard to find.'

'That doesn't prove anything.'

Leonard was losing. Didn't mind. This time. Sanctuary was something else. Sanctuary was not frightened. Sanctuary was not worried. Sanctuary was not a local villain. No bombast. No four-bedroomed two-car fraudster full of bluster before tears. Leonard was happy to let him go on. He was learning more about this large, open-faced man.

'And in broad daylight? Come off it, Chief Inspector. We both know that Miss Rolfe and I are not villains.'

Leonard's spectacles were off once more. He rubbed at them and then laid them on the desk, the gold wire arms opened, the lenses sightless. Waiting for an image.

'Do we?'

'Of course we do.'

'Of course we don't, Mr Sanctuary. I agree the chances of

you both being involved appear slim. But that doesn't rule out the thought that one of you is, to use your phrase, a villain.'

Sanctuary shook his head. He had thought Leonard intelligent. He even looked intelligent. Whatever that meant.

'She hardly looks the type who would blow a man's head off at fifty paces. Come on, man.'

'Legs and soft eyes impress you, do they, Mr Sanctuary?'

'What do you think?'

'I think that on your basis for value judgements then neither your legs nor your eyes absolve you from suspicion.'

Sanctuary smiled. Relaxed. A little.

'Of what?'

Leonard wanted to put his feet on the desk. He didn't. He wasn't yet in command. He envied Sanctuary his big, bare feet in old canvas deck shoes. He understood physical confidence because he had never had any. He admired Sanctuary's broken nose. It wasn't from a school of hard knocks. It had to be hard play. It would have been good to have had the choice.

Tap-tap. The door opened. A middle-aged woman in a blue smock dragged in a black plastic bin-liner. She apologised and emptied Leonard's waste-paper basket, apologised again and closed the door. Leonard said nothing. He was giving his teddy bear a bow tie. He spoke without looking up.

'I imagine you can tell me where you were when Fisher was killed.'

'London. In the office.'

'You know then what time it happened?'

'No, I don't know. I do know that I was in the office all week other than Friday. The Department will confirm that.'

'Why not Friday?'

Sanctuary had broken the rules. Never display knowledge. Answer the question and nothing else. The policeman was doodling. Waiting.

'A day off.'

He had broken another rule. Leonard could easily find out from Roberts that he had been to see him. He might find out about the package. He was about to catch up. To explain. Damage limitation. There was a knock. It was the Fat One.

He was in his shirt sleeves. Scratching his beard. Grey patches spread from each armpit. The stench of spin-dry shirt drifted on the draught from the open door. He shook his head. They had done for the time being.

Perkins had organised a panda car to take them back to the yacht club.

The girl's truck was parked on the edge of the boat yard. Sanctuary suggested a drink in the club. He wanted to find out what the police had asked her. What she had said. She wasn't keen but said yes. They saw Roberts. He had his back to them. He was standing by one of the houseboats talking to the tubby man with the meerschaum who nodded in their direction. Or was it the girl's? Roberts turned. Even from a distance, the crooked grin, a smirk where Priestly's was a groomed smile, was all there. The eyes were not. He met them by the door.

'So. I hear you've been doing business with the local fuzz.'

The other man had gone.

Sanctuary was humourless.

'News travels.'

'Too right. It's my part of ship to make sure it travels to me.'

The girl walked on, ignoring Roberts.

'Madam seems a bit flushed. Not used to having the bracelets clapped round her dainty wrists.'

Sanctuary heard the viciousness in Roberts's tone and wondered why. Roberts liked people to think him important. To take him seriously. Spitefulness a big-product of scorn? Sanctuary looked at Roberts. The face grinned to order. Had the policeman talked to him? The washed eyes said nothing. Sanctuary decided that, for the moment, he needed Roberts. For the moment. He smiled, confidentially.

'They're all the same these women, aren't they? Take themselves too seriously.'

Roberts's grin was real. This Sanctuary was one of the lads after all.

'Right little prick-teaser that one. Do her good to get turned over by the law.'

They started for the door.

68

'What happened then? Heard you got bundled into the old hurry-up wagon. What was that all about then?'

Sanctuary told him. Why not? He was going to have ten versions to choose from. Sanctuary didn't mind being the horse's mouth if it meant keeping Roberts on the phantom team.

Inside, the girl was sitting at a table talking to Meerschaum. She gave a half-wave. Roberts went off to hold court at the other end of the bar. The red-faced man with the barrister's stripe and leather-thonged deckers was still auditing the room. He gave Roberts a friendly punch on the biceps and signalled to the barman. Another double bank of cigarettes and half-empty beer mug were in front of him. It was his place at his bar. Les kept polishing and tried not to look over. His head bobbed and he muttered something to the dark-haired girl pouring a gin and tonic. She glanced at Sanctuary who had dropped onto the bench between the girl and the pipe-smoker. Most people were trying not to look across. Most people were.

The man's name was Pete.

His grip was calloused. A black-rubbered digital watch on his right wrist suggested left-handedness. He said hello with his right. It didn't matter. He was Isobel's friend. She introduced them. Explained they'd known each other for years. Since she was a teenager looking for a sailing berth.

'I'm the only one round this place who's not trying to get her into his bunk.'

'Thanks very much.'

She wasn't indignant.

'True. There isn't one of these bullies who wouldn't want to wake up at O Six Dubs with this one alongside.'

He pointed at her with the stem of his pipe. There was a small dribble on the end with the finest of spider's spittle trailing from his lip. He wiped his mouth with the back of his hand and laughed. It made a rasping sound. Dry. Sore-throated. Open-mouthed.

Sanctuary was embarrassed. The girl looked at him as if to see his reaction. She and the man were easy friends. He said he had known Fisher. To take a drink with.

69

'Likeable hand. Good for a run ashore. Bad business this.'

Sanctuary, suspicious, wondered if the nautical jargon was for his benefit. Pete could have been sixty and a lot more. Solid. Stocky. The vee of his unbuttoned shirt framing a cravat of spring-wound ancient hairs. Small white veins in a burnt face which should have been brown. The sandy, sparse hair was showered and salt-fed dry. Faded red trousers. The scrubbed, sun-bleached and wind-dried shirt said designer sailor. But he was too easily confident to be anything but the real thing.

Sanctuary listened and watched the girl relax. She was sure with Pete. Her shoulders were still straight, but easy. Her eyes younger. Fisher and this man had talked boats. Repairs. Maintenance. Sail-stretching. Anti-fouling. Roller-reefing. Nothing about where he sailed to? Sanctuary remembered something the barman had said. The girl had taken Fisher's charts. He didn't mention it. Listened.

'Not really. Some don't. Some do. It's not special. He didn't have anything to prove. Falklands, you know? The stink boaters around here, well, they're full of it. The sort of stuff they come out with, well, you're not allowed to pump into the harbour. Most of the sailors' tales you hear, well,' he paused, laughed again, 'from them, well, most of them, haven't got beyond the head and that was on the free flow.'

'Western end of the harbour.'

Isobel had caught his question. He wouldn't have asked anyway. Pete had said his fill. He eyed Sanctuary, as if from a distance.

'What about you? Must have known him well to come all this way and then get duffed up by the rozzers. Eh?'

For the tenth time it seemed that day, David explained that Fisher had not been a close friend. Pete wanted to know what had happened. He was openly curious. Sanctuary didn't mind. The sailor might give something in return. But not in the bar, where like a well-behaved audience there was hardly a murmur from those leaning by the pumps or squatting at the nearest tables. Pete looked about him. His eyes rolled, but not in disgust.

'Drink up. Let's have one on board.'

He stood, not waiting for an answer. He picked up the empty glasses and stacked them at the end of the bar.

'Night, children.'

The one in the red stripes scowled good night. Pete was whisking away the stars. As the three left, the bar went into a huddle of speculation.

Pete was ahead, He moved quickly. On the balls of his sandalled feet. Almost a trot. His hard, round belly leading the way. His aertex shirt a canopy over the swelling. He had a car, a well-preserved beer barrel Rover, leather and wood and springs that creaked as they rolled over the sleeping policemen and left behind the houseboats, the dozing ducks, the smart tiled cruiser bar, and drove without speaking around the yacht basin until they reached a point almost opposite to where they had been in the yacht club. It wasn't that far from the *Madrigal*. Sanctuary saw the uniformed man at the top of the gangway to the pontoon. He might have said something about bolting horses but didn't. Pete waited until they were out, locked the passenger doors from the inside, then the driver's, then checked the boot lock. Then, from the outside, tried the passenger doors. He grinned at Sanctuary. Shrugged his shoulders.

'You never know nowadays, do you, matey?'

They came to what looked to Sanctuary to be a big ketch. Bigger than *Madrigal*, he thought, broad and tall. A storm lamp burned from the mizzen. Yellow behind the smoke-stained globe. He could see a glow from the main cabin and was relieved when Pete called out. Sanctuary had had enough drama for one day.

'Get the booze out, you little runt. We've got visitors.'

He paused on the deck to hand them both over the side. There had been no reply. Then a tinkle of glass and bottle below made what Pete clearly decided was a welcoming sound.

'Thought the little shit had turned in.'

The face that stared up from the cabin was large. A caricature. The chiselled chin of a matinée idol. The eyes elliptical. The soft brown of an abandoned brindle. The big forehead was lined as if in constant surprise and the actor's curls silky-soft. Washed by fine rain. The head ignored Pete and stared at

Sanctuary. At his eyes. He felt uncomfortable. He wanted to say hello and couldn't for the life of him understand why nothing came out. Then he felt it too late.

'Hello, Rusty. How are you?'

The girl's voice was soft. Islands. yes.

The head jerked to her. A flickering silent movie villain. Hero? Sanctuary saw him smile. Large, exaggerated, white teeth. The eyes even warmer. Then he turned, scurried as only the smallest can on a boat, to where bottles and glasses were wedged in a for'd rack. He took down another glass, put it on the main cabin table with the others and then sat cross-legged in the corner. The boat was considerably bigger below than the *Madrigal*. There was even headroom for Sanctuary. Cotton-cushioned side benches. On the starboard side, a chart table with dials and switches and a small radar screen above. Opposite, a stainless steel sink and cooker. Small round lights in the deckhead and an unlit and gimballed oil lamp on the thwartships bulkhead. She felt like a small ship.

Pete was messing for a tobacco tin in the navigator's locker, muttering something about knowing where it was and accusing Rusty of hiding it. Isobel introduced Sanctuary. Her voice was formal. The camaraderie of the cells had fallen by the quayside.

'Welcome. Why don't you sit down?'

The voice was unreal. Bass baritone. Vowels slowly rounded. The head darted, guiding Sanctuary to the cotton cushions. A knowing unsmilingness. The head steady, then electric. Staccato movements. Somewhere a hidden electric motor. Muscles and sinews in relays and parallels. Sideways. Stop. Sideways. Stop. The head never up and down. Instead the body leaning to offer a better view. The head of a giant. Too heavy for the stubby, miniature body. Sanctuary wanted to look away. Could not. He said something about there being a lot of room below. Isobel agreed. Pete, cussing a jumbled locker, gasped triumphantly and levered with a coin at the airtight tin.

He filled and lit, then settled on the companionway steps and puffed. The smoke drifted into the warm night where moths buzzed about the hanging lantern. Sanctuary and Isobel told a story of finding the pillaged *Madrigal*. Instinctively, without hesitation, they kept to themselves the fears and drama of their meeting. Told of their interrogations, and Sanctuary for the first time heard what had happened when Isobel was led away.

The Fat One had hardly looked at her. She had been frightened as he made laborious notes in his book. She had been so aware that everything was being written down. What would they do with it? She had wondered if she were telling the same story as Sanctuary.

The Fat One had wanted to know how well she knew Fisher. When she had seen him last. What they had said. What he had told her. What she had told him. Kept coming back to how well they had known each other. At one point she had asked him what he meant by knowing. She shuddered, remembering his expression. It was the only answer he had given. Then he wanted to know about Sanctuary. When had they met? Before the boat? Must have done. Tried to confuse her. The WPC had said nothing. Just stood by the door. Not even looking at her. Something from a poster. Inanimate. She had not said that. But that's what she meant.

Now, as she spoke, Isobel kept looking across at Sanctuary. Uncertain. Wondering if she were saying the right things. Rusty watched. The great weight propped steady. Pete poured more whisky for himself.

'What do you think?'

She seemed to trust this harsh-tongued sailor. He rubbed a hand over his belly and cocked a bare foot across his knee.

'I think someone's in the shit, missy. Deep in it. That right?'

His look and challenge to Sanctuary said it had to be. He made no effort to hide his thought that Sanctuary was anything but an innocent friend of a murdered man. Sanctuary leant further back in the cushion until his hands clasped behind his head came in contact with the bulkhead.

'I assume we can rule out vandalism?'

Pete nodded.

'Damned right we can. Nothing missing, was there?'

'And vandals don't ignore police notices and carry their own bolt cutters.'

73

'They do but let's not piss about. Whoever went below was looking for something.'

Isobel rubbed at her head. She felt tired, dirty. Wanted a shower. Then bed.

'What are we doing? We sound like conspirators. This hasn't anything to do with us. Even if it has, I don't want it to.'

Pete sipped. Looked at Sanctuary.

'Well, master. Nothing to do with us? Is the missy right?'

Sanctuary wanted to go. He did not understand this group. He could feel the brown eyes from the corner cushion. He wanted to look. Not allowed. Rule. Ignore the silent observer. Pay respect. Pay the price. Rule.

'Yes and no.'

A puff of sweet-smelling smoke.

'Yes and no? Ah! So you really do turn-to for the Foreign Office. Well, let's forget the no. Tell us about, well, the yes. Yes?'

Pete belonged to nobody. Hard. The pipe perfectly paced. No irritating scratching of match after match. Ready to wait out Sanctuary's patience.

'The yes means I want to know why he was killed. I've told you I knew him. In many ways it was more than that. We were friends. He'd had a rough time. His wife pushed off. He was pretty cut-up about it. I often wonder if that's why he left the Navy. It just seems to me that it was a lousy end to a really nice chap. To the police it's nothing more than a murder case. To me, well, I suppose I'd like to find out for myself. Especially as someone seems to feel that killing him isn't the end of the matter.'

Pete sucked at his pipe and looked over his shoulder and to the open deck.

'What you say, pig?'

The clumped fist didn't shift. When he spoke the eyes never left Sanctuary's face.

'A man is not murdered when he dies like this.'

Isobel stretched, her eyes closed, her brown stomach showing beneath the loose waistband. Sanctuary remembered the park and the running ice cream. He looked up to see those steady

74

brown eyes watching. He wondered what more they had seen. Isobel's voice was weary. She had no mind for riddles.

'What's that mean? No one is trying to claim Stuart wasn't murdered. Surely?'

Rusty smiled. A white stockade of teeth.

Pete tapped the meerschaum against the heel of his cupped palm.

'What the little runt means, missy, is that, well, motives are, shall we say, different when murder is more accurately called assassination. Isn't that right, master?'

'There's a difference?'

Pete gave his hushed laugh. There was no humour.

'Look, Mr Sanctuary, the way I see it is this: someone we knew and liked has been killed. The police are investigating. They're looking for a murderer. We all know, or at least you and I think, that Stuart was not the sort of hand who goes around getting himself murdered. Right so far?'

Sanctuary said nothing. It was answer enough for Pete. His attention was steadily on Sanctuary's face. Watching for a twitch of expression on which he could pounce.

'I think he was up to something. You, master, at a guess, either know or think so too. I want to know what.'

'Why?'

'Well, master, apart from anything else, I think it beats sitting on my arse waiting for a tide and another rabbit run to Cherbourg. If there's a bit of action about, I wouldn't mind some. That right, pig?'

The great head nodded.

'But not tonight.'

The eyes flicked to Isobel. The face had relaxed. Almost asleep.

'Time to turn in, children.'

Sanctuary offered to walk the girl to the truck and to follow her home. She said no. He told her he was in the hotel in case she wanted anything. She said no.

Pete laughed.

'Best kip here tonight, missy. You can sleep for'd.'

Rusty nodded. The toothy smile was a leer but not to the girl. To Sanctuary. He'd been dismissed.

Some of the moon was left. It was enough to see where he was going along the sparsely lit harbour wall and the walkway across the lock. But not much. It was black, gloomy. Great square shapes changing form in the reflected light as he approached. He needed to let the Department know about his playgroup session with the local plods. There was a telephone box near his car. The duty officer would tinkle the alarm at the Deputy's nine-thirty prayers. There would be time enough to spread aniseed.

Cold.

The same cold in the warm garden. He shuddered. Looked about him. Nothing. Shadows. Water. Still in the deep lock. A voice. A long way off on the all-but-silent harbour. Hailing. But not him. He stopped. The sound was nothing. It was not there. But he could hear it. He wasn't alone. Yet nobody was there. He started again. Stopped and looked back. Down. The lines of boats quite clear in the pontoon lights. He could see the yellow deck lantern on the ketch's aftermast. Nothing else. No one. No brown eyes. Yet he could still feel their stare. Not hostile. Just something he did not understand.

Then warm.

He passed the girl's truck. Windows wound down for the afternoon breeze. When he reached the yacht club, his old Alfa Romeo stood out where earlier it had been surrounded. He tugged at the door. It was locked. They all were. He never locked. The keys were in the ignition.

He found the telephone box. Made one call then turned back towards the car and pulled out the wire hanger from the aerial socket. It took fifteen seconds and the driver's door grated at his tug. For a while he sat in the dark. Waiting. Watching. Waiting. He banged his hand against the wheel. Of course. That's what was he was meant to do. Wait while someone finished the night's business undisturbed. Sanctuary switched on.

The night porter said, No Messages. No Visitors. He wouldn't know.

76

Someone had been through his room. Nothing he could spot. He just knew. The professional touch. He too was a professional. That was why he knew. There was nothing to see. Nothing to take. That in itself would tell a professional something. His case book was safe. The two blank pages after the notes were always destroyed. It was surprising what impressions could be seen using funny lights. He checked the door again. The lock. The window. He was wasting his time.

He had been in bed for about five minutes when the telephone rang. It was Pete. He was checking on him. The girl had gone up to the wash house. Somebody had been waiting nearby. She had seen the shadows before the person. Normally she wouldn't have associated them with human form. Now she was screwed up. She had screamed. Pete had been on deck. Waiting for her. There had been someone there. A man – or someone who ran like a man – had escaped down to the wood by the foreshore.

'I'll come down.'

He was already out of bed.

'No you won't, sunshine. I was just checking. You couldn't have got back that quickly. The missy's all right. The pig's given her one of his exotic potions or some such shit. She'll be okay.'

He didn't say goodbye. No pips. Silence. The payphone was ungenerous. He listened. The line was clear. The night porter was probably doing whatever it is night porters do when they're not listening in to night calls. Taking stock at one in the morning is not a good idea. It was hot but he locked the door and the window. No great protection, he thought, but more warning. He turned on his back. He tried to catnap but was soon sound asleep.

13

The Duty Officer recorded Sanctuary's call at 00.43. Seven hours later, Dorothea picked it up from the Overnight Log. She was first in. She was glad. Priestly had been taking pot shots. She was not sure that the Deputy took any notice. He was hardly a fool. He knew what Priestly was up to. Damn the opposition. Caress its lost chances. Priestly would never have gone. Priestly never left the Department if he could help it. The Department was the Centre. The Centre was Power. Power was promotion. Priestly knew what he wanted. Dorothea made three telephone calls. Took one. By the time Priestly arrived, Dorothea had made sure that no one would be surprised when the police report surfaced. When they went into Prayers, the Deputy knew all about it and gave the nod. One of her calls had been to the Deputy at home. He liked to be kept informed even when he did not need to know. That was the instinct, the nature, of the Department.

Priestly wondered aloud. Dorothea listened to the sharpening of his stiletto. The Deputy disagreed. There was no need to agendarise Fisher. CSIS did not like to know unless he had to. He knew that the Deputy did and would. Another week. It was a compromise. It was always a compromise. Anyway, the Deputy was going on leave at the end of the month. He liked to leave a clear desk. Priestly said he would keep an eye on matters. The Deputy said he was sure he would. No. Not a fool. But he did not matter. By Christmas he would have gone. Retirement. Nothing more than something in the New Year Honours List.

Afterwards Priestly telephoned his friend in Carlton Terrace. They arranged to lunch. His club. Priestly did not give up. CSIS would know by the end of the afternoon.

Dorothea left the room, walked along the corridor to the gallery and the stairs. There was an empty office. She knew. The telephone was not on the Department circuit. She wanted to speak to Sanctuary. Somewhere in her head alarm bells were ringing. Instinct. It was not in the Field Manual. The man coming towards her smiled. He thought her rather attractive. Preoccupied. He liked serious people. Wholesome. He had not seen her before. He wondered where she worked. What she did. Why he had not seen her before. He said good morning. So did Dorothea. She smiled. She thought it odd that he should look so out of place in a corridor. His place was behind grand desks, in conference rooms, at the Dispatch Box. Not by himself in a corridor seeing people he had never seen before. Foreign Office corridors were best kept empty.

The office was empty. She left the door open and dialled the hotel. She left her home number when they said Mr Sanctuary was not in the hotel. She would be alone. Mr Dorothea was prosecuting in the provinces. On the way back to the Department, the alarms continued. Priestly would lunch spitefully. She would have to be nice to him for the rest of the morning. Perhaps longer. Smile at his wimpery. There was no one else along the corridor. The great oak door in the gallery corner was closed. People who should have been were in their rightful places. Except Davy, she thought. She wondered why he had not answered. She wished that his Case Note had arrived that morning as it should have done.

14

They found the body at five o'clock in the morning.

Leonard didn't hear about it until later. He was at home mending the chain on his bicycle. He wanted time. He wanted space. By the time Sanctuary had gone the previous evening he really didn't know any more about him than was in the thin folder. He knew Sanctuary was an oddball. But which one? The girl was straightforward. Good-looking. Nothing heavy. Caught up. But Sanctuary was something else. He wondered if there was a connection with Roberts. He didn't think so for long. Sanctuary was too smart. Roberts was smart but he was small beer.

Roberts was either living in another world or knew something. He didn't have an idea what it was the Secretary could know. He wasn't even sure if the Secretary knew. Leonard recognised the type. In the know. Official. An inner mafia of Service and ex-Service people who assumed the guise and air of the insider, when there was no inside. No secrets. No mysteries.

The cogs looked right. The old bicycle was upside down, a pad of long-ripped viyella protecting the sprung leather saddle. He turned the pedal. The smooth chain whirred over the crank and hub. He flipped the thumb lever and the easy click and pace of the changing gear was satisfying. Everything dropped or rose into place. Well oiled. Well balanced. The ratios correct and mathematically sensible. Mechanical Advantages proved.

Sanctuary and Roberts, though, they weren't so easily oiled.

The side-gate squeaked. A high-pitched squeak. It was better than any expensive burglar alarm. It was the Fat One – or at least his face from the nose up peering through the slit between the top of the door and the frame. The door chain kept the rest of him at bay.

80

'That you, guv?'

He left the back wheel spinning and opened the gate. Perkins smelled of fried breakfast. Leonard didn't say anything. Perkins followed him towards the kitchen.

'We got ourselves another one.'

He eyed the tea cosy. He was rubbing his mouth with another dirty handkerchief.

Leonard had his feet on the kitchen table. It was polished antique pine. It matched the brown of his boots. He poured the tea. Listened while the Fat One told him about the body. It had been found in the trees by the foreshore by a constable two and a half hours earlier. Just light. Low tide. Someone had raised the alarm. A big man, they said. There was no positive ID.

Leonard scratched. He shouldn't have been out of touch.

'Old Man was asking for you.'

Leonard looked up. Blinked. He had switched off his bleep and the telephone.

'How'd it happen?'

'Haven't seen it. Looking for you, I was. Doc says busted neck. Deliberate, he says. Bit of cold bruising.'

'Shit.'

'Roberts any flavour then, guv?'

He was trying to help.

'Might be. Run him past the Wizard, will you?'

'Got previous then?'

Leonard didn't know and sighed as much. The light-box on the wall blinked. He flipped a switch. The telephone on the dresser shrilled. It was tall, thin, black Bakelite, 1920s. Leonard held the mouthpiece just below his lip like a sports commentator.

'Leonard.'

He listened for some moments. Said 'Mm, mm' a few times. He didn't say goodbye.

'Everything all right, guv?'

The high-pitched voice was really concerned. Perkins was confused. Nobody was telling him anything. Leonard never did much. But the nick was the same. Something was up but nobody was saying. He'd got up. The kitchen chairs were uncomfortable. Most were. His crotch was sore. He scratched, then looked embarrassed. He took out his spiral notebook. He had nothing to write but Leonard might say something. Leonard didn't raise his voice. Perkins liked him. He wondered if Leonard liked anybody.

'That was him, the Old Man.'

He was back at the table. The tea was cold. Perkins had finished his.

'I'm seeing him at nine. He wants a result.'

'Yes, guv.'

'Yes what?'

He watched the confusion in Perkins's eyes.

'I meant, okay.'

'Think we're missing something?'

'Villains usually have the same MO. This one weren't a shooter, was it?'

'A connection doesn't necessarily mean one man two jobs.'

'You mean a team? What here?'

'I mean maybe there's a connection. Nothing more.'

Perkins was clearly disturbed. He looked at the teapot and Leonard nodded. It wasn't hot but Perkins had something to do. Leonard bothered him. Everyone knew he wasn't normal. Not married. No girlfriend. Not the other way. Kept himself to himself. Didn't do any police dos unless he had to. Didn't seem to know anybody. You had to know people in this job. That's how you did it. Leonard was all theory. But he had good form. Plenty of places and a couple of tasty winners. Only he didn't run with the rest, then come through. He was always on the outside somewhere. Waiting. Making his own running. Perkins sipped noisily at his tea.

Leonard got up. Stretched. Perkins gulped down the luke-warm tea as if he'd heard the four-minute warning.

'I got my wheels. You want to take a look at it, guv?'

Leonard nodded. Turned over the Murder Report and glanced at Location.

'Body gone?'

'Doc's got it.'

82

Leonard glanced through the kitchen window to the clear sky and picked up two green bicycle clips from the dresser.

'See you there.'

15

When he arrived by the sea wall, Perkins's green Vauxhall
was parked. Empty. The window was open. He could smell
chocolate. Brightly coloured wrappers and screwed sweet
papers were scattered across seats and floor. Another car, its
blue light still, was in front, a blazered detective constable
putting black plastic bin-liners into the boot.

Leonard leant his bicycle against the driver's door. Three or
four children stood across the way. They stopped talking when
they saw him. One, in Reeboks, multi-coloured tracksuit and
Ray Bans nudged another, making him lose his grip on a
screaming green skateboard. A woman, clutching a Yorkshire
terrier, eyed him suspiciously.

'Local paper?'

The cigarette wagged.

Leonard nodded. The woman went off to speak to the boys.
The constable guarding the path to the beach grinned and
flicked him a salute as he went by.

16

The Old Man was in his braces. His white teacup had a gold rim. Leonard had been given the green canteen china. There was a chip in the saucer. At least he had a saucer. The Old Man sipped tea. Never drank it. He liked to tell people about tea. He said it was in the blending and the water. His secretary used tea bags. Never told him. He would have been hurt. She even put a silver-plated tea-strainer with a windmill handle on the round tray at his elbow. Two years of it.

'A lovely cup that. It's the blending, you know. Makes all the difference. And the water of course.'

Leonard nodded. Didn't mind the routine.

'Of course.'

He wondered why the Old Man had never asked about the tea leaves. Never looked in the pot. Everyone knew except the Old Man. Perhaps he did.

'This is not good, is it? I mean, two down in two weeks. What's the tie-up?'

Leonard didn't know. Said so.

'Security guards get knocked over in blags. This wasn't. Down at that place they're nothing more than boat prefects, making sure the odd outboard doesn't go for a walk. Right?'

Leonard nodded.

'Then why? What's the score?'

'Could be coincidence.'

The Old Man sneered. They both knew that was unlikely. Leonard put his hands behind his head and leaned back.

'The guard was supposed to have been guarding the pontoon. Everyone thought he'd gone missing. Girlfriend. Laziness. Something like that. These security firms have a big turnover. They're used to no-shows.'

85

'Why was he on the pontoon?'

Leonard unclasped his hands and straightened in his seat.

'As you said yourself, sir, we're pretty thin on the ground. We didn't mind when they offered to do a daylight shift. Anyway, they feel they've got some obligation to the boat-owners in the basin.'

'Damned right they have with the prices they charge.'

'Getting murdered is a bit unnecessary when it comes to obligation, isn't it?'

'So was that, James. So was that.'

'Sorry.'

The Old Man waved a hand.

'Anything? Anyone in mind for this one?'

Leonard shook his head. He wished that he had. There was nothing at all. No sign of a scuffle, which was odd. The guard was big and a fitness fanatic. Squash three times a week.

'Which suggests he knew whoever it was?'

'Maybe, sir, maybe. It certainly suggests that it was a surprise. A snapped neck is.'

'It would be. Not that he'd have known much about it.'

'Someone did.'

The Old Man was scanning the buff file open in front of him on the blotter.

'This Sanctuary chappie. He's kosher?'

Leonard said he did not know. Told the Old Man about his call to the Foreign Office. He had spoken to a woman in the same office. Something to do with overseas relations. What else in the Foreign Office? Anyway, she had said that, because Sanctuary had known Fisher, he'd requested a couple of days' leave.

'So it's not official?'

'Difficult to tell. If it is, they're not saying. I've spoken to the Branch. They'll give me a steer. She says that murder's not their line of business, so in that sense it's private. However . . .'

'If anything came up?'

'Something like that. But not exactly.'

Leonard felt cheated. Sanctuary was not just a friend of

86

Fisher's. A casual friend did not show this sort of interest. Leonard sensed the system at work.

'I should forget him. It's hardly worth it.'

Now Leonard looked surprised. He moved in his chair, recrossing his ankles.

'Forget what?'

'Back burner. Sanctuary's clearly no problem.'

'Really?'

'You said he's kosher.'

'With respect, sir, I didn't. You asked if he were.'

The Old Man shrugged, finished his tea. He placed the cup and saucer on the tray neatly alongside the damp strainer. Nodded his approval. The Unbeatable Taste. A million perforations could not be wrong.

'Someone broke into the boat.'

'Vandalism. Happens all the time.'

'And nothing stolen?'

'Disturbed probably. Or lost their nerve.'

'Why?'

'Probably kids, that's why.'

The Old Man was casual. The irritation was not very far below the skin.

'Okay, James?'

'No. Who's turning which screw?'

That first time. That interview. They had not clashed. They would not. The Old Man, then a Very Correct Inspector had said yes when others had shaken their heads. He had read and reread Leonard's background sheet. He had thought about it over lunch before the interview. Uncompromising. That had been his Reason for Recommendation. He had never written that before. Nor since. It had never been written for any other candidate. The Very Correct Inspector was exactly that. Uncompromising. He had wanted Leonard. He looked at Leonard now. Uncompromising. He looked away. He was tired. There came a point when compromise had its advantages. Higher interests. That's what he had been told that morning. Higher interests. Whose? He hadn't asked. That was another compromise. Vows. To whom? A ritual of silence when it

87

mattered. An apron tightly and squarely tied. No undoing the knot after so many years. He looked back.

Leonard's gold round-rimmed spectacles seemed pressed closer than ever to his serious eyes as if he were trying to see through opaque reason. Knowing that something was on the other side. Knowing it was not far. The blink was slow. Equally spaced. Uncompromising. Always uncompromising.

The Old Man sighed.

'Look, James . . .'

'Who?'

The Old Man swivelled his chair. Leonard's voice followed him.

'Who?'

He didn't turn.

'I am told there are higher interests.'

'Whose?'

This time he did move. Both hands flat on the desk. In charge. Very correct. The sigh was deeper. Not given in. But still the Very Correct Inspector. Not yet the Old Man. Staring hard at the clean blotting paper. Not at Leonard. Not yet.

'Okay. For the moment, James, just for the moment, easy does it. Forget the lay off. But easy does it. Okay?'

He looked up. Leonard was heading for the door.

17

Sanctuary found the River Pottery along a side-lane leading to
the upper reaches of the natural harbour. Fields, hedges and
trees. Oak front doors already ajar for the morning sun. The
clean air was late summer-scented. The grass banks lazy and
inviting. He saw the truck and then the tiny flint house. Two
storeys. Thin. Slate-roofed. Clean white window frames. At
the roadside terracotta pots beneath a wooden shingle said it
all. The converted sharp-stoned barn was open. A black and
white sign said so. The girl was inside. A man's collarless
shirt all but hiding her threadbare denim shorts. Brown leather
sandals. A zinc dustbin lid in her hand.

She jumped when she saw him. It struck him that she must
have heard his car even though he had parked in the lane. After
yesterday, he thought, it was a wonder she hadn't dropped the
lid.

'Dustbin day?'

He tried to sound casual. Cheerful.

'Clay.'

She clanged the lid. Smiled.

'No one's invented a better bin for it. Coffee?'

Not really, but he nodded.

'Please.'

She was rinsing her hands beneath a hard-running tap ignoring the splashes from the sink. He looked about him. The kiln
was on one wall and the wheel by the window. The rest of the
barn was shelving. Mainly plates and jugs. Oatmeals and slates,
terracottas and greens. Leaves and stems on the plates. He
turned to look at the back wall. Those same brown eyes. The
slightly bowed, oh so heavy head. Propped on the ever-
clenched fist. Cross-legged, unspeaking, on a corner chest.

89

'I didn't see you.'

It sounded obvious.

'There was no need.'

The girl laughed. She liked Sanctuary. She made quick judgements. She was often wrong. Sometimes she liked people because they liked her. She knew which ones liked what about her. Roberts wanted her. He was a toucher. She had made it clear: No Touching By Order. She didn't get on with many people even when she liked them, especially women. She liked Pete. He was rough. Very intelligent. She adored Rusty. She felt guilty when she thought about it. She adored him in the same way that she would a Labrador dog. He was faithful. Undemanding. There to please. Responded to affection. Sensitive to a raised voice. He had come back with her to make sure she was safe. She had started to say, 'What could you do?' Seen his eyes. Had not.

'What could you imagine would happen to me?'

It was not her syntax. They both knew.

She had once loved deeply. They had forgiven each other in advance for the pain they knew would come one day. They thought themselves sophisticated. Clever. Free. They had thought of pain as something experienced with disappointment. She was much younger five years ago. He was now dead. Neither had thought it would come that way. Cheating was a misdemeanour. That sort of pain. Not a tragedy. That pain was different. She had learned not to ponder and calculate human values for long. They might change. They might too easily slip away and then too late. So she now said yes and no to herself. Lived with the judgement of yes. Struck from her life the judgement of no. Now she liked this man. She did not yet trust him. But that did not matter. That might come if it had to. He looked like a good big brother should look. Tall. Strong. Broadshouldered. Battered and straggly-haired. Everyone's hero, she thought. She laughed again. This time to herself. Private joke.

Rusty was smiling. He could be quite sinister when he did that. Like now. Deliberately in the corner. Deliberately in the half-shadow. Deliberately mysterious. He took advantage. Then why not? Advantages for him were hard to come by.

Equality was a benefaction. Pete did not treat him as an equal. To Pete that would have been condescending. The two were friends. She had never known how they had come together. It was too late to ask.

The coffee was from a pot on a gas ring. The mugs, squat, earthy, unglazed.

'Yours?'

She gave Rusty his first.

'Rejects. The first things I did when I got this place. They're about the only things I haven't managed to break.'

'When did you come here? Straight from art college?'

He was truly interested. Isobel looked at Rusty and they both smiled.

'Art college? You're joking. Until three years ago the only thing I was throwing was plastic food and duty frees.'

First package holidays. Great on the way out. Dreadful drunks on the way back. Then it was short haul. Then one day Cairo.

'That was where I met Stuart. We were on a stopover and he was in the Hilton.'

Sanctuary felt brown eyes on him. How would he react?

'What was he doing in Cairo?'

'Working.'

Her voice had enough surprise in it for him to offer an explanation.

'I thought he was in the Navy then?'

'I suppose he was. Oh, I don't know. Attached to something, wasn't he?'

Sanctuary had to be careful. He was. He had not known about Stuart Fisher's attachment, if that was what it had been. He would ask Dorothea. She might be able to run it through the All Agency File. Now he went through the routine of not having known him that well and of having more or less lost touch after Moscow. It was true. He needed to know more. Cairo. Wanted to ask about Ignatiev.

The voice was deeper than last night. The vowels rounder. The consonants still incisive. A brown voice gravelled by smoke and blended spirit.

91

'At some stage, Mr David, it might be useful for all concerned if the fences collapsed and those who now sit astride
decide in which garden they wish to land.'

The eyes were wise. The head slightly forward so the brown
ellipses peered from beneath the lined dome.

Sanctuary was breaking rules. He kept to his own. Ignored
the suggestion in the ponderous, almost thespian statement.

'Stuart left me the key to the *Madrigal*. I don't know why.
Someone has turned it over. I don't know why. Someone frightened you last night. I don't know why. He was murdered. I
don't know why.'

'Many questions, Mr David, but perhaps one answer for
them all?'

The girl looked tense. In the best movies, he thought, she
would now light a cigarette. Hand shaking. The lighter catching
on the fourth attempt. A deep lungful of smoke, a silhouetted
stream from a head-back pose by the window. Instead she
plonked down her mug and splashed the still-hot coffee on her
hand.

'Oh, shit!'

She looked up. Her timing was perfect. Two of them grinned.

'Sorry.'

'About what?'

He was being brotherly. She ignored his question. He played
the innocent.

'Tell me more about last night. Did you see who it was?'

She shook her head.

'A fool, Mr David. A loiterer. Maybe a person of no consequence. A thief, a vagabond waiting to steal. Nothing more.'

'But of enough consequence for you to be here.'

The great head rocked in disagreement.

'The company of a jester, Mr David. I'm lending my soul for
the morning. And you? You will stay?'

'I care enough to find out.'

Rusty went back into a shell. Staring. Unworded questions.
Unnerving. Deliberately? It didn't matter. Sanctuary had now
established his authority. He left him marooned on his fool's
cushion.

The girl had gone outside. She was sitting on a weathered bench, long legs stretched, head tilted back in adoration of a sun god that would be gone in a few weeks, maybe days. She didn't open her eyes when he sat down. At the other end of the bench, a ginger cat lay humped.

'When was Cairo?'

He needed to know. It would save Dorothea time.

'Just before I left. It was my last summer. I was getting money together for this and night school. The house came first. I opened up here twelve months ago.'

'Hidden talents.'

'Temperament. My father was a potter. I knew what to do and occasionally did it. I don't do anything I can't. Plates, bowls and jugs are pretty basic.'

'Why here?'

'Reasons.'

She opened her eyes. Looked at him. Shut them again.

'And?'

'The reason is no more. But I stayed. It's warm. Anyway, I make a living. Just. A lot of people here think it's smart to have a tame potter.'

'Tell me more about Stuart.'

'About a year ago. He came in. He'd bought a cottage and was doing it up. Wanted to buy some dinner plates. I made him some.'

'Coincidence.'

'Not really. He had a good memory. When we met in Cairo I'd told him I intended to set up around here. He promised to look me up. It's the sort of thing people promise by hotel swimming pools.'

'Especially in Cairo.'

This time she turned her head.

'What's that supposed to mean?'

'Exactly that. If I got chatting to a pretty girl by a pool in Cairo, I'd promise to look her up.'

The cat, disturbed by unnecessary vibrations, stretched to its paws and stalked in the direction of the pottery.

'And he did.'

Her eyes were again closed.

'That's right.'

'Simple as that.'

'That's right.'

'Nothing more.'

'That's right.'

'You saw a lot of him?'

'Why?'

'He's been murdered.'

'You're not a policeman. Just a friend. Remember?'

'Did he ever tell you anything that might get him murdered?'

'No. Why should he?'

'No, or you don't think so?'

'Suit yourself.'

'Where was he sailing to that day?'

There was no answer.

'Where?'

He sensed no defiance. What then? Dawning? He tried again.

'Where?'

'Portland, I think.'

'Not Poole?'

'Why?'

'Doesn't spring to mind as a place people often go for pleasure.'

The girl tucked her legs onto the bench. Her arms wrapped around her knees.

'He didn't do much for pleasure. I don't think.'

Sanctuary was surprised. Not for the first time he realised he really did not know a great deal about Fisher. In Moscow they drank and ate at the set-piece dinner tables. Their evenings of hypotheses and ramblings had been about other matters, not their own. Fisher had once asked Sanctuary if he had ever married. Sanctuary's simple no had been enough and somehow the rest of his private life had been blocked off. Fisher had mentioned once or twice that Jane found the diplomatic round difficult. Sanctuary remembered the summer night and had said nothing. It was always easier to talk theory and shop. He had never really known him. Later in the London pubs, there had been something ineffectual about their clandestine meetings, which weren't at all clandestine because neither was hiding. They would have liked to have been, but it was only the few weeks when they thought Ignatiev might jump, come over, that those lunchtimes had been anything but charades played out among the twilight rules of never saying anything outright. The result was that they talked in an improvised code which meant that afterwards neither really knew what had been said. That way was best. The Department liked to live in the twilight where everything that was not in shadows was grey and where minds need not be changed because they had never been made up. No. He did not know much about Fisher. He wondered how much Isobel knew and how she had got to know.'

'What were the charts you corrected for him?'

She was surprised. Had she forgotten? No.

'How did you know about them?'

He came out of the shadow.

'The barman mentioned them. He said you'd collected them and promised to correct them by noon. Or something.'

'I did.'

'Why?'

'He asked me to.'

'But why you?'

'I do it for a lot of them. People buy charts and they're already out of date. Sandbanks are always shifting, buoys get replaced or drag. There's always something to correct. I get the Notice to Mariners and do it. They leave their . . .'

He interrupted her.

'Who are "they"?'

'About twenty of them. Mainly the weekend sailors. They leave them on Sunday nights and pick them up next time they're down. Usually yachts. The powerboaters don't bother so much. I don't charge much, but it's worth it to me.'

'I would have thought it was the sort of thing Stuart would have done for himself.'

'He did. It was the first time. I volunteered.'

'And they were all Portland?'

'And Plymouth.'

95

'Plymouth? So why d'you think he was heading for Portland?'

'Because he said he'd see me by the weekend. Assuming he was going to stay there, Plymouth and back would have taken longer.'

'So you don't really know.'

'I didn't pretend I did.'

Her voice had a defensive edge.

'He didn't actually say where he was going?'

'He never actually said anything about anything. He wasn't the type. I'd have thought you'd have known that.'

'Did he say why he was going?'

Isobel shook her head.

'And you didn't ask?'

'If he'd wanted me to know he would have said.'

'Weren't you curious?'

'Yes.'

'Would he need updated charts for Portland?'

'Of course.'

'Why?'

'It's not the sort of place you just breeze into.'

'Why not?'

'It's Navy.'

'When you gave him the charts back, what did he say?'

'I didn't.'

'Didn't what? Give him them back?'

'No. When I'd done them, I couldn't find him. I went to the boat and he wasn't there.'

'Where was he?'

'Don't know. I never saw him again.'

Sanctuary had turned. No longer lounging in the sun. No longer casual in conversation.

'So where are they now? The charts, I mean.'

She nodded towards the pottery.

'Still on the drawing board.'

He wanted to look immediately, but he didn't know what he expected to find. If there were clues, they would be unsuspecting. No marks of Stuart Fisher's. The girl sensed his change of mood.

96

'You're more than a friend, aren't you? So what are you?'

She looked at him. A sideways look. The head now resting on her kneecaps. Almost childlike. Snugly watching a story-teller. There was no belligerence in her voice.

'I've told you.'

His voice was firm. She was tired but not sleep-doped. It was the best time to be firm.

'Pete was right. We can sit here waiting for the police to do something or we can do something ourselves. I'm for doing something.'

Her head was back. Not sun-seeking. Deciding.

'That doesn't answer my question.'

'It's the best you're going to get at the moment. I want to find out why he was killed. If we do that we find out who.'

'Then what?'

'Depends what we find.'

'We?'

'Okay. Me. I need your help. You can answer questions. You know far more than you think you know. I want those answers but as yet I'm not sure I know all the questions. Without being corny, you've got to trust me.'

The look was harder, the pause longer, the voice more suspicious.

'Why should I? If I know anything why don't I simply tell the police?'

'Tell them what?'

'Perhaps I don't have anything to say.'

'To a killer it's all the same.'

'What's that mean?'

She had been swaying. A comforting rhythm. Now she was still. Waiting for his answer. It came from behind them. A brown, solemn judgement.

'If our murderer lingers it may be to destroy evidence. If he thinks you know something, then he may regard you as, I'm afraid, evidence. Yes, Mr David?'

Sanctuary nodded. The girl looked from one to the other. She got up. Stretched. Rubbed her bare brown arms. They were covered in goose pimples. The sun was warm. She looked about as if expecting to see the poison of danger.

'If you're right, then I'm not the only one.'

'I can look after myself.'

He wished he hadn't sounded so corny.

'Mm. As far as I can make out, you get paid for being big and brave. I didn't mean you.'

'Who then?'

Rusty got there first.

'Perhaps, Mr David, and perhaps is nothing more than perhaps, then perhaps we have to think about who else knows and who might have seen.'

'Could be a whole list of people, starting . . .'

He paused. Rusty finished the sentence.

'The child?'

18

Mrs Lomax was a woman forever drying her hands. She washed. She cleaned. She cooked. Her life was threadbare.

Lomax was the first of his family to stand still. Once a traveller, always a traveller. That's what they said. Everyone said it. One day, Lomax had said no. No more sites. No more being moved on. No more vans. No more being looked at. No more seeing mothers tug children out the way when he stopped to buy. No more being pulled when a car radio went missing. No more car breaking and dogs without collars. He had stopped travelling. They had met. They had married. There had been no romance. No courtship. She loved him. Lomax was a good man. He could whistle like nobody else. Lomax was a hard worker. He had to be. He had no education. No papers. No exams. He was nowhere near as bright as he thought he was. Mostly he had a job. Mostly it was not the same one as last month. Cleaning. Broom pushing. Store rooms. Painter. Mainly painter. Lomax had a beer when they went on holiday. A caravan week in Cornwall. The Lomaxes lived on the edge.

When Mrs Lomax opened the door to the man she was drying her hands on a tea towel. She was frightened. It did not show.

'Yes?'

Her voice was sharp. Forbidding. In the kitchen, Bennie listened. He was frightened. This was not the woman with fat ankles. She was nice. Really nice. His mum said so. His mum said there was nothing to say, but the policewoman came back. This wasn't her. He knew that as soon as his mum spoke. Her voice said she did not know the person at their door. Bennie knew that. There had been lots of people at their door. Then he heard the man's voice.

'Mrs Lomax?'

'Yes.'

She wished Lomax were there. He was up Midhurst or some-where. Painting. Council job. Wouldn't be back until late.

'I wonder if I might have a word.'

She looked out to the road. This was not a policeman. His car was red. Old. The man smiled. She knew when smiles were put on. The insurance man did that. Especially when they hadn't got the money that week. The headmaster had one of them smiles when they called her down the school about Bennie. When they had asked about his saying nothing. He was a dreamer that one. She had told them. They smiled. Didn't understand. This one was put on. He was after something.

'What about?'

He looked wrong. She didn't know what. But he looked wrong. There was another car. Across the street. She knew most of the cars around there. Didn't know that one. A man was reading something, then looking over. Funny place to read. Especially with the windows up. Must be hot. She put her hand to her forehead. Shaded her eyes though the sun was high. He was saying something. She didn't hear properly. Her from number 47 went by. Had a good look. Stuck up. Nosey. The man looked at the gate. It was open still.

'D'you think I could come in. It's about your son.'

She wasn't daft. She was scared too. She shook her thin head. He could see the fear. Could smell the soap. Could see the worn hands. He felt sorry.

'You police?'

He started to explain. She butted in, not hearing anything he said.

'They know. There's nothing to say.'

She closed the door. He could hear her calling to Bennie to close the back door and get upstairs. A thin voice. On another edge.

19

Tupman was easier to find – eventually. The building was tucked into a courtyard near the cathedral. The brass plate was polished, the lettering Victorian. Tupman & Frobisher Solicitors. Sanctuary wondered about Frobisher and then which Tupman sat in cracked and creaking leather two slim storeys above the crooked pavement. The receptionist insisted it was impossible to see Mr Tupman Senior without an appointment and Mr Robert, presumably Tupman Junior, thought Sanctuary, was abroad. She made it sound as if Kitchener had called for him. An appointment could be found within ten days. Sanctuary had to insist before she sent a note through to say that he was here at Fisher's behest. A note came back. Would eleven o'clock be suitable? It was now ten-thirty. It would be.

When Sanctuary returned, the receptionist was hostile, her feeling of being overruled had not softened during the thirty minutes he had wandered through the cloisters and along the plaques to long-ago bishops, deans and justices of peace. He was five minutes early. She reminded him that his time was not yet and, when a plaid-skirted woman in her late twenties, bobbed and ash blonde and sweet-smelling, appeared with a bright smile to usher him upstairs, the receptionist irritably crossed her ankles and muttered into her twinset and pearls. The secretary said her name was Nell and she hoped he had not been waiting long.

Tupman compensated for her easy friendliness. He did not look up immediately the door was closed behind Sanctuary. When he did it was with all the friendliness of a Victorian tutor. Sanctuary felt ill at ease. He was meant to. Tupman was in his middle fifties. Portly, stiff-collared, dark petulant eyes deep in a podgy face and nearly bald head. His handshake was limp and

101

he looked down and to one side as they exchanged greetings as if he would have wished to avoid the perfunctory custom. He sat back in his leather and buttoned throne, highly polished with an elaborate scroll at his head.

'How may I help you, ah . . .' he leant forward and examined the piece of paper on his desk '. . . ah Mr Sanctuary?'

'Stuart Fisher. I understand you were his solicitor.'

'Do you indeed? How very interesting.'

'Why?'

'Very few, even friends, are aware of legal arrangements enjoyed by others.'

Sanctuary was irritated. Why was everyone a games player? He took another breath and tied a reef in his temper.

'I had a letter from Fisher. He said that I should get in touch with you if anything happened to him. I assume that's not a problem?'

'The circumstances of Commander Fisher's unfortunate, eh, death, present many problems including the execution of his will of course.'

Sanctuary found it odd hearing his friend called Commander. It pointed to the other world in which Fisher had lived and about which Sanctuary knew little.

'I'm not interested in his will. I wasn't family nor was I that close.'

Tupman raised an eyebrow, sniffed and opened a buff file that rested in front of him like the charge and evidence at a court martial. Though he must have known the file's contents he announced his finding with deep suspicion.

'In that case you will be surprised that my client gave mention of you – although not in his will, I hasten to add.'

He looked up. Sanctuary had said nothing. The big hands were back in his pockets, fingers scrubbing at the tops of his thighs. He wondered how Fisher ever came to appoint this man as his lawyer. Tupman was cold, almost sneering, a small-town bully. Fisher was easy-going, sometimes anxious, straight-talking. Often he talked too much. Perhaps that was why. It would be like Fisher to think a step ahead and find a lawyer with whom he would never become friends, somebody with

102

whom he would never talk too much. First kill all the lawyers. And now he was dead. Sanctuary dropped his gaze from Tupman's framed certificates of law to their practitioner's eyes.

'What's that mean? In simple terms.'

'It means, in the most simple terms, that Commander Fisher has left you something. Not, I hasten to add, in his will. Beyond it and before it. Though I must advise,' Tupman turned a page in the file, 'that a letter to the matter was received by me and pre-dates his will. There is no legal problem although I imagine that the police may have some charge on the bequest, we shall call it that – for the moment anyway. And I have to warn you that the beneficiaries of my client's estate may contest the gift. All this you should know.'

Sanctuary said nothing. Tupman was going through his routine. He would let him. Then he would know. Tupman looked up from the file like a pathologist demonstrating the malfunctioning of a gut to a student. The sneer was the nearest Tupman ever got to a smile.

'It seems that the Commander thought fit that you should, eh, become the owner of his boat, the, eh, the *Madrigal*.'

'But not in his will. I don't understand.'

'Sometimes, indeed it is not uncommon for people to make special provision of a gift to be made in the event of his or her death. That provision is often made outside the terms of a will although it would normally be considered as part of the execution of the estate.'

'But this isn't.'

'But this indeed is not. It appears from Commander Fisher's clear instructions that you, should you have accepted the offer, were to become the new owner of the vessel on the very day that I received his written instructions which were signed and witnessed in this very room. No, this was not a bequest. It was an instruction that did not anticipate his death, nor one which I should advise is invalidated by his death although there might be some who would contest that judgement.'

'They would be successful?'

'I think not. It was not so much a gift as a transaction. You

103

had I believe agreed to accept the vessel, the *Madrigal*, in lieu of a debt owed you by the Commander.'

'I see.'

'Not, eh, everything, Mr Sanctuary. Not everything. You will see there were and are conditions.'

The lawyer was turning pages though he probably knew full well what he was to say. Sanctuary stared at the top of Tupman's head. It was smooth and mottled though very pink and very bald except for small, surprisingly black tufts above the ears. He looked up.

'Yes, conditions. For example. You will not be able to sell the vessel for twelve months. Nor will you be able to lend or charter it however attractive a fee may be offered. Nor must you, eh, lay up is the expression used by my client, the vessel during that twelve-month period. It, or as Commander Fisher chose to call the vessel she, must remain in the water other than for essential hull repairs and must be cared for and maintained by you and by no other person. It seems that all the equipment on board was included in the transaction and the whole is full and final settlement of the debt outstanding in your favour. As you had, before Commander Fisher's death, agreed to take the vessel in lieu of payment, the matter remains straightforward unless you now raise objection.'

'Me.'

'Yes, eh, you, Mr Sanctuary. The legal arrangements concerning this, eh, transaction, are not as straightforward as you might imagine.'

'I would not have thought anything else.'

The sarcasm was not very good and anyway wasted on Tupman who carried on as if he had not heard Sanctuary's intervention.

'The capital value of the vessel might be considered as part of Commander Fisher's estate although that is not excessively large. His letter however appears to anticipate that difficulty, hence the agreement by you to accept the vessel as full and final payment. However, you may have to show proof of that debt and you may also be required to wait until the boat is valued to see if it matches that debt, although I must say, once

104

again without prejudice, that as the matter was settled and Commander Fisher's signature and presumably your agreement predated his, eh, unfortunate passing, then serious difficulties will not arise although cumbersome ones may. Mm?'

Tupman, with all the care of a stamp collector, handed Sanctuary a single-page document and, while he scanned the transfer of ownership, Tupman pressed a buzzer on his desk and unscrewed a fat, black and gold fountain pen. By the time that Sanctuary had read the document, the cheerful Nell was standing at his side ready to witness signatures. Did he want to sign? Why did Fisher want him to have the boat? What debt? Fisher had never owed him money. At first he thought the whole idea preposterous. Perhaps so, but he knew instinctively that, however he might try to dismiss the idea as melodrama, the *Madrigal* held the key to Stuart Fisher's death and that he, Sanctuary, was now committed to finding that key. In two minutes, it seemed, the *Madrigal* was his.

Tupman had not moved. He would say goodbye if urged. Nell, who appeared to be Mrs Dent, held the door open. But Sanctuary was not finished. He had not come for any inheritance but for a letter. He could remember Fisher's instructions, word for word. 'I've run out of people I can trust. I've put most of what I know in a letter with my solicitors, Tupman in Chichester. Hope it doesn't come to that. If it does, get the letter.' And now he wanted the letter. A quite different will and testament and one which Fisher would never have let Tupman read.

'I came here because Fisher told me that you had a letter from him addressed to me. I'd like it.'

Tupman looked right through him. Said nothing. Mrs Dent quietly closed the door on her way out.

'That was it, Mr Sanctuary, the contents of which entitled you to a very generous gift. Now if you'll excuse me?'

He was reaching for a pink-ribboned document.

'I think not.'

Sanctuary was standing. A long way up to the sitting solicitor. Tupman hardly noticed. This was, after all, the tutor's study.

105

'Then, my dear Mr Sanctuary, I think you should. There is no other letter. Goodbye.'

Sanctuary's voice was hard. Challenging.

'Look, I happen to know that Stuart Fisher wrote to me shortly before he was murdered. Murdered, Mr Tupman.'

No reaction.

'He left that letter, unopened with you, to be given to me in the event of his death. I want it. Where is it?'

Tupman was reading a document. He did not look up when he spoke.

'Mr Sanctuary, you may happen to think a letter was written to you, you may even know that Commander Fisher wrote to you, though I suspect that your evidence is somewhat circumstantial. But I must tell you, yet again, there is no letter here. Nor has there been. You are misinformed. You are also exceedingly ill-mannered. Should there be need to contact you, then we shall.'

He did raise his head. The eyes contained too much cruelty in them for a small-town bully.

'Now, you will kindly leave.'

20

Leonard was also easy to find. Sanctuary had not been looking for him.

When he got back to his car the Fat One was leaning against it eating a bun. Strings of iced coconut stuck out from the corner of his mouth as he chomped. They walked over to the police station, Perkins screwing up the stained bag and dropping it into the entrance litter-bin. He was always very tidy. His jacket made a good hand-towel.

Leonard beckoned him in. Leonard was not of his century. He beckoned instinctively. A silent courtier. Contemptuous of the system.

Leonard was not a good policeman. A good policeman, or so his contemporaries pointed out, was one of the team. That way, the right crimes were solved in the right order.

Convictions came when they mattered. Some of his colleagues, for he had no friends in the Job as they called it, regarded their task as one of containment. Some let crimes go undetected. Gangs did their own policing. They did not like freelancers. There were those who didn't mind that. Keep the land fit for cowards – not for heroes. Leonard was intolerant. He fought the system as well as the criminal. The Old Man had said Leonard would have been happier in a French provincial town. He was wrong but Leonard knew what he meant. Sanctuary had saved him a journey.

'Is this official?'

Sanctuary winced even as he asked, but he was on the offensive.

'Murder's always official. Isn't it?'

'You tell me. You're the policeman.'

Leonard nodded as if that had once or twice crossed his mind also. He blinked rapidly. Then screwed up his eyes behind the thin-rimmed spectacles.

'I'm glad you see it that way. So you won't mind explaining why you've been pestering a witness? Or was that official?'

'Tell me more.'

Perkins had left them. Now he returned with three beakers of coffee. It was from the machine. Even Perkins's voice was apologetic. Leonard ignored his apology.

'What were you doing at Mrs Lomax's house this morning?'

He waved away the coffee. Perkins looked hurt.

'I wanted to hear what he had seen.'

There was a long silence.

'That's not unreasonable. Fisher was my friend.'

'More so by the day.'

Sanctuary let it pass. It was better to do so.

'His mother seemed nervous.'

It must have been Mrs Lomax who'd told the police. Must have been.

'A murder inquiry's not exactly her bag.'

'I didn't intend to frighten her.'

The hand came down with a crash. Perkins had left one of the beakers on the desk's edge. It spilled. Leonard was half across the doodled blotter. He was not shouting his anger. No need.

'What the hell is your game, Mr Sanctuary? Apart from frightening the hell out of a very nice lady, this is a police inquiry. You are to stay out of it. Okay? And so is your friend.'

'Miss Rolfe is hardly a friend.'

'Don't unbright me, Mr Sanctuary. This isn't the MI6 mastermind course or whatever wall you've come off. Now, come on. Who was he? Or isn't it that sort of Department? He doesn't exist.'

Sanctuary sipped at the coffee. He didn't want it, no one would. But he sipped all the same. It gave him time and the edge on Leonard. Maybe the policeman wasn't so smart after all.

'What friend?'

If he had wanted to set Leonard into a rage he couldn't have

108

made a better fist of it with a week's notice. Down came the hand. Up sprang the plastic ruler. Perkins understood this tactic, but he was nervous. This wasn't Leonard's style.

'Don't give me this crap. You and another man went to Mrs Lomax's house, right?'

'Wrong. I went to Mrs Lomax's house. By myself.'

'Then you met someone there.'

'Wrong again.'

'Look, Sanctuary, let's get a few things straight. I know who you are and who you work for. And I'm telling you, I'm not having Spook and Company poking its nose in police work without an official entry door. Right? If you people have interest I want it declared through the Branch. Okay?'

'I hear you. But I tell you, there was no one with me. There was no one I know in the area.'

'Then who was the other man in the other car? The one with the you-can't-see-me newspaper? Come on, Sanctuary. Mrs Lomax may not be one of your Sloanes but she's not daft. And nor am I. So let's have answers. And now.'

Sanctuary looked at Leonard. This was not what he'd imagined from the local plods and he was fed up with being treated like a fool. First Roberts, then Pete, Tupman and now Leonard. He looked over at Perkins and then at Leonard. The policeman flicked his head in the direction of the door and Perkins struggled to his feet and waddled out.

Sanctuary switched on his confidential tone. It usually worked when he needed it. Now he wasn't so sure. Dorothea had been right, as usual. He should have gone straight in and played the rules.

'I've already told you my Department's interested.'

He raised the flat of his hand as Leonard started to gasp his disgust at going over old, and what he thought was phoney, ground.

'So it is. At this stage it is unofficial. Fisher was known to us, but not in any formal way. That means that I'm looking around, but not in any formal manner. If it came to that then things would be different. For a start I'd go back to London and other people, probably another Department would take an interest. And, for what it's worth, what I've told you so far is between you and me. The Department does not exist and even if it did it would deny any interest. Sorry, but that's the strength of it.'

He leaned back and waited. Leonard had been watching his hands. They were in his pockets. Scratching. The policeman swung in his chair. It was not constabulary theatre. It was a change of thinking angle. Perkins was right about him. Leonard was different.

'I said I know who you are.'

'I heard you.'

'It took only one telephone call. Why didn't you tell me in the first place?'

'You might not have made the call.'

'Mr Sanctuary, the idea of someone being at the scene of a murder in the most suspicious circumstances and then claiming to be a member of some clandestine government Department is the sort of fool's question thrown on the most basic senior-officer qualifying course. The rules are simple, Mr Sanctuary. They say this man is lying. The task is to find out why. Nutter? Villain? Cover story?'

'What did you mean then? Scene of what murder?'

'We have a second body, Mr Sanctuary. The missing security man, George, has turned up – with quite a bit of his head facing the wrong angle.'

'Shit.'

'He probably thought so. But I'll pass on your sentiments to his widow.'

'That's not funny.'

'None of this is funny, Mr Sanctuary, which is why I can do without tripping over your cloak and dagger.'

'But you're not suggesting for one minute that I, or Isobel Rolfe, had anything to do with this?'

'Why not? The man was murdered on the foreshore in front of the woods. That's about three hundred yards from where we discovered you and the delightful Miss Rolfe in a ransacked boat – which was, in fact, the scene of a previous murder. Why shouldn't I make the connection?'

110

'Because it would not be true.'

'It's never true, Mr Sanctuary. Nothing is ever true. I have your version. I have Miss Rolfe's version. I have my own version. When they are pasted together and we think we have done with the whole affair, then the file is closed. But it is never, Mr Sanctuary, thrown away. Because . . .'

'Because a series of facts and fictions produced a result that satisfied the process of your law but not that of someone else's curiosity at some later stage?'

Leonard had, that morning, spoken to a friend he had made on a staff course two years before. The return telephone call said that Sanctuary was listed Attached Foreign Office. MI5? The friend said not. MI6? The friend would not say. Anything else? The friend thought it unlikely. There wasn't anything else.

'If you had thrown some ID on the table in the first place, we wouldn't have had this problem.'

'I owe you.'

'What I said stands. This is policework. I won't have unofficial snoopers on the patch. That's not petulance. That's being in charge of an investigation. So stand back or else.'

'Or else what?'

Leonard was leaning forward again. The eyes through the gold-rimmed spectacles were blinking furiously, pulsing warnings straight at Sanctuary's battered face.

'Or else I shall start to make public noises of mysterious circumstances and government interest. Not official interest, you understand, but government interest. That's political interest.'

'Don't be daft. There isn't any political interest.'

'I know there isn't. But the innuendo will be enough to get your backside hauled to London and then kicked into the darkest corner behind whichever set of lace curtains it is you hide.'

Sanctuary believed him. He was probably right too. He could almost hear Priestly's razor stropping, as the Departmental strings were cut, denying all knowledge of the less than favourite son's existence.

'Okay. Okay. Truce?'

'You're in no position to parley.'

It was Sanctuary's turn to sigh.

'Fisher was not what you would call an agent. He really was a naval attaché. However, on more than one occasion he passed on information, just as you would probably do if something came your way.'

'Would I?'

Leonard was busy with his pencil once more.

'Probably. You may not tell the same people but you'd know where to go to make sure it reached the right desk.'

Leonard was nodding. Maybe not in agreement. Sanctuary pressed on.

'He had an idea that he had come across something that was not simply a security problem. It seemed, from my reading anyway, to be a security problem within a security problem.'

Leonard looked up. It was question enough. Sanctuary didn't know the answer.

'Haven't a clue. The worrying part is that there is nothing to go on. Names, recent history, associations, reports, all the normal routine matters are missing from this one. Including our computer file on him. Everything's so clean it's almost as if someone's wiped it clean.'

'Well?'

'That's it. I haven't anything else. I'm not saying I'd tell you, but I haven't. That's why I'm working on instinct rather than the routine of the department.'

'Whichever one it is.'

'Whichever one it is.'

'That doesn't answer everything.'

'What's left?'

Leonard shook his head.

'Who's working with you? Who was it?'

'Where?'

'Mr Sanctuary, please. Who was the other man outside the Lomax house?'

'I don't know. I didn't see anyone.'

Leonard looked, then looked away, then back again. It was too stupid a reply for it not to have some truth.

'She did.'

112

'Perhaps. If she's as nervous as you think, then perhaps she sees all sorts of strangers.'

'I believe her. She 'phoned from the corner box as soon as you'd gone. He was still there. We sent a car.'

'So?'

Leonard sighed. He had read his riot act. It was time to behave. Whatever their methods, they did after all have a common interest.

'And the bloody fools belled it. According to Mrs Lomax he was away as soon as he heard them. Probably half a mile off and he was straight out onto the dual carriageway.'

Leonard snapped his fingers.

'Gone.'

Sanctuary told him about the previous evening. A shadow. A figure. Probably a man. Possibly no connection. But who could tell? Leonard wanted to know why the police had not been called immediately. Sanctuary shrugged. And then it struck him.

'Where was your man last night? The one guarding the *Madrigal*.'

'Doing exactly that.'

He had been there when they arrived at Pete's boat. He had not been there when Sanctuary left. Nor when Isobel went ashore. Leonard picked up the telephone. Asked a question. Listened. Asked another. Did not listen. Replaced the receiver. He offered no explanation.

'Why did you not tell me earlier?'

He shrugged again.

'It's been a busy morning. You rather grabbed the offensive.'

For the first time, Leonard seemed to relax. Sanctuary doubled his guard.

'By the way, I appear to be the owner of the *Madrigal*. Any problems?'

Sanctuary told the policeman the story of the meeting with Tupman but left out the letter which Fisher had sent to Tupmans for safe-keeping. Sanctuary did not believe the *Madrigal* letter was the only one. Fisher had been explicit. He had run out of people he could trust. Sanctuary decided that Tupman was one of them. He knew how Fisher had felt. He wondered about Leonard.

'So why did he leave you the boat?'

It wasn't a casual question.

'Haven't a clue. But we'd be kidding each other if we didn't wonder how much it had to do with him getting killed.'

Leonard was doodling yachts. Dark sails stretched to windward. Short, choppy seas with angry slashes of wave-tops battering and breaking over the bows.

'We've combed it. Everyone has. No drugs. Nothing. Nothing you wouldn't expect to find on a boat.'

'Nothing on the hull?'

'We craned her out. Clean.'

He was drawing a hand clawing for life as it all but disappeared beneath the waves.

'You must have been good friends.'

'I've told you. Not really.'

'Then that means he hadn't any others.'

'Possibly.'

'Doesn't that strike you as odd? No one else has come forward and offered information about him. We had to go to the Navy. Got some background, but not much. And when a sailor leaves his most prized possession . . .'

'Was it?'

'Must have been. His cottage is clean, neat and that's about it. The bank hasn't anything surprising to say. No hidden security boxes. No hoards of jewellery. Nothing obvious but the boat and he leaves that to an acquaintance for a special reason without, it appears, telling him what that special reason is. Now that's a prized possession, wouldn't you just say so?'

'Put like that.'

'Well, how would you put it, Mr Sanctuary? You're the one with the training for solving dark secrets. I'm just a policeman.'

Leonard's seascape was getting darker. The more his pencil worked its thick lines across the soft blotting paper, the more the seas rose and the winds blew.

'I wonder what his wife will think.'

114

'I shouldn't think she'd know. As far as I can make out Jane went back to the States and no one knows where she is.'

'Jane? You knew her.'

He was looking. Looking hard. It was a long time ago. Six years? A long time?

'Vaguely.'

'Does that mean not very well or not important?'

'It means I knew Stuart, not Jane. Embassies tend to be like that.'

'Right.'

He appeared to understand.

'Especially when one of you is a euphemism.'

He didn't look for an answer. But, if Leonard were chalking, it was another point to him. Sanctuary brushed aside the jibe.

'Anyway, I hardly think she comes into this one. Do you?'

Leonard shrugged. This was theatre.

'Why not?'

'She's miles away for a start. She left after Moscow and that was that.'

'That was what?'

'The last anyone saw or heard of her. Anyone back here that is. I should imagine it's not very likely that she knows anything about this.'

Leonard had finished. The wind, now in full fury, was blown by a puffed-cheek woman, eyes fiercely uncompromising, jet-black hair streaming in the gale's force she blew. The policeman tossed the pencil on the paper. There could have been a smile in his eyes. Sanctuary was not to know. Not yet awhile. More theatre.

'Not true, Mr Sanctuary. Not true at all.'

21

Sanctuary spent the afternoon at the yacht basin. He talked to Roberts again. The whole club was talking about the second murder. Roberts was between a hard spot and a stone. He revelled in the intrigue and gossip. The local television stations had interviewed him twice and the television in the bar was on in case he should be starring in the next hour's news flash. But he was also a good Secretary. He had anticipated the down side of the basin's spotlit stage. Yachtsmen and their spending friends would be keeping away. Fear is bad for business. Roberts wanted his figures balancing for the next annual general meeting. He liked his job. Sanctuary cheered him up with new information to boost his imagined reputation as the yacht basin's Inside Man of the Month.

He had not heard about the change of ownership. Roberts would relish the moment when he broke that news. It would boost his standing at the bar. He would be the fount before which red stripe and his cronies would have to genuflect. Roberts imagined himself in deeper than ever confidence with Sanctuary. He saw the *Madrigal* as what he called 'a nice little windfall'. He was also smart enough to think that Sanctuary must have been closer to Fisher than he made out. Fisher simply wasn't the type to give his boat to someone he hardly knew. Roberts had made his own telephone calls. He didn't have the access that Leonard had. The 'old net', as he called it, was not very fine. Anything of any importance either slipped through or never swam in the channel Roberts and his friends had fished. He knew that. They knew that. But they speculated with their eyes and knowing nods. Sanctuary was obviously on the big inside. For the moment Roberts would ask no more in case the door he thought ajar was slammed in his face.

116

Sanctuary was tempted to ask Roberts if he had heard from Jane. He could think of no sound reason why he should have done but there was always the chance that she too might have had a telephone call from the Club Secretary. It was just possible that Fisher had left a second set of instructions with Roberts. Fisher would have had some contact address for his wife who, after all, was not legally the former Mrs Fisher – not until someone killed him. Temptation was set aside. If Roberts knew anything he would tell, eventually.

Leonard had surprised him. Jane Fisher had surprised Leonard. According to the policeman, she had telephoned out of the blue asking about her husband's death. Yes, they had never been divorced. She had picked up a pile of newspapers from a friend at the British Embassy in Washington where she lived. Or so she said. She had, thought Sanctuary, possibly read the same paragraph as he had. Leonard had told her very little. He knew very little. She had seemed curious rather than concerned. Said she would keep in touch and had rung off before he could get a Washington number for her.

Sanctuary thought it would not be difficult to find the friend in the Embassy. Then he wondered how well she knew this friend and saw that it might be difficult to find him. Instinctively, Sanctuary felt the friend would be male. The Jane Fisher he had known in Moscow had few female friends.

Roberts was prying once more.

''Spect the fuzz was a little suspicious so to speak? The boat and all that?'

Sanctuary was once again happy to let Roberts into what were not secrets.

'Curious. They couldn't figure why he's done it. Frankly nor can I.'

'Understood.'

He didn't but his own knowing look and sense of at last being into something big convinced him he did. His diagonal grin switched into automatic. Now it was his turn.

'Pete Hogarth was looking for you.'

'Who?'

'You know. Pete.'

The surname had thrown him. He made a note to feed it into Dorothea's green screen. It was supposed to know all. It didn't, of course – only what someone else had fed it.

'What did he want?'

Roberts shrugged. Pete treated him with contempt as he did anyone who didn't drink, especially people he called 'orange juicers'. Pete was of that school. Roberts wasn't bothered. He looked after himself. Gym three times a week. Three miles first thing in the morning. He'd see them all dead. A six-ton ketch didn't buy you time.

Sanctuary left the club office and headed towards the jetties. The policeman was back on duty. He said there had been an all-hands call at about midnight. A car on the by-pass had exploded, big fire ball and everything, he said. All standbys and special guards had been called into the centre. That time of night there wasn't much back-up. No, it hadn't come to anything. Bloke from the squad said it was nothing. Big bang but no one hurt. In fact, no one at all. Curious. Didn't seem much point to it, he thought. Maybe some joker from the barracks a couple of miles away. He wasn't on anyway, but his mate reckoned he hadn't got back to the boat until six. It was light then. The constable was pretty relaxed and was happy to talk but, no, he couldn't let Sanctuary on board. His instructions were 'to guard it not act as a bleedin' doorman for guided tours'. Sanctuary explained he was the new owner of the *Madrigal*. The policeman said 'nice boat'. He knew his instructions. Look. No touching. It was simpler that way. They stood and talked some more and Sanctuary ran his eyes the length of the dark blue hull and the height of the sturdy mast to the tiny spikes and spindles of electronic sensors. Nothing special that he could see or that others would have missed. But he felt the urgent need to get on board. He didn't doubt Leonard. They had found nothing suspicious. No clues to anything unusual. But the idea of Fisher giving him the boat was too absurd unless there was something that would lead him to the reason for the man's death. Sanctuary and Leonard were apparently working towards the same end, which was why the Detective Chief Inspector had more or less agreed to turn a blind eye, for the

118

moment. That moment would be brief. That was clear. But appearances were deceptive. Leonard was looking for a double murderer and the evidence to convict. Sanctuary regarded justice as a secondary consideration. He wanted to know what Fisher had found out that was so important that he had to be assassinated. Fisher was dead. Hard luck. The reason for killing him was not dead. Fisher had talked about the big one. That was kiloton talk. If Fisher had been right, that was reason enough.

By evening Sanctuary wanted to step up the pressure on Leonard. He left a message at the police station to call him as soon as possible and then went over to the club house. He was hungry.

Les the barman was nervous. He was always nervous. He gave the impression that he didn't want to be seen talking to Sanctuary. The Secretary came into the bar for a few moments but by the time he had figured that Sanctuary had nothing new to tell him it was time for him to be gone. He gave Les a hard look and said something about being at home if there was any trouble.

The barman relaxed once he heard the back door click to.

'She gives him a bit of stick if he's not home for his tea on time.'

He grinned that someone somewhere had Roberts under the thumb.

'Mrs Roberts?'

Sanctuary hadn't thought of Roberts having a domestic life. He seemed too self-contained.

'That's right.'

The bobbing and weaving had started. Les had something to say.

'She's a strange lady that one. Used to be a nurse, they say. Keeps an eye on him, specially in the season. Too much totty round here for her liking.'

Sanctuary wasn't interested in Roberts's private life though it would explain some of his animosity towards Isobel. Les was busy setting himself on fire. The skinny roll-up cigarette caught

119

and curled a sliver of paper ash and Les coughed his appreciation.

'Mind you, there's not much of that hanky-panky stuff going on round this place. Not really. I mean, a lot of people thought your mate was having some from that blonde party. I don't think so. I see quite a lot, specially when they've had a few. You see a lot of what they're really like from this side of the bar, specially about eleven o'clock.'

For the barman this was a speech. He had plenty to say now Roberts had gone. Sanctuary nodded towards the cider tap and Les fetched a fresh glass.

'I suppose you heard that *Madrigal*'s mine now?'

Les nodded.

'Not surprising though, is it?'

He smiled and carefully placed the brimful of cider in front of Sanctuary.

'How so?'

'Well, it was more or less like he said.'

'You knew? He told you?'

The ducking and weaving had started. Les had been caught out and he was trying to get back in.

'Not in so many words. He just said that you were interested in her. That's why you was meeting up, I suppose. Wasn't it?'

'When was that?'

Sanctuary tried to sound casually interested. But he knew that, if he asked Les anything at all, he had to be specific in his questioning. The barman couldn't cope with teasing and roundabout questions.

'Well, like he said to me.'

He dragged on the fading cigarette and then scrambled on the back shelf for his lighter. The double click produced more flame and Les coughed contentedly. He seemed to have forgotten the conversation.

'Said what?'

'Oh that, yes. Well, he said that he expected to meet a friend of his, that was the next morning.'

'The one he was killed?'

120

Les looked at him as if Sanctuary were simple. It was obvious to Les. It should have been obvious to anyone else.

'That's right.'

'Did he?'

'Did he what?'

'Meet his friend?'

'Well, I don't know, do I? You should know that. It was you he was meeting.'

'You're sure?'

Les puffed and picked up the towel. He'd said as much as he wanted. Almost. The barmaid was taking care of red stripe and his friends at the other end. Les leaned over, the cigarette's smoke scorching his half-closed eye.

'Had to be. Unless,' he was looking up and down the bar's alley once more, 'unless it was the bloke he was with the night before.'

'Who was that?'

'Don't know. It was getting real dark. Must have been eleven-thirty. Down by the boatyard it was. This bloke sees me on me bike and moves back behind that old workboat they'd been burning off. So I didn't really see him, did I?'

The barmaid was being teased. She blushed easily. When you had big breasts you either blushed or you didn't. She did. It wasn't an ideal sensitivity in a barmaid. Les went off to rescue her as the hall telephone shrilled.

It was Leonard. He was answering Sanctuary's pressure. Okay. There was no further reason to prevent him going aboard. There would be a further search in the morning and then he could take over on the condition that he didn't sail the boat out of the harbour. It was still evidence. Sanctuary thanked him. Asked him how things were going. No change. He sounded like a ward sister.

When Sanctuary got back to his hotel there was a message at the reception desk to call Dorothea on her two-star number. That meant home. It was urgent. It meant also that she did not want to use the Department board, which was odd. So, urgent and something wrong. He had left 'phone cards in his room. It

121

would be better to get them and then find a public call box. He never used hotel switchboards for Department business.

As he opened the door he stopped. Instinct? He knew someone had been in. His hand was still on the key, holding the door steady, when he heard a calm voice from inside.

'Mr Sanctuary? Do come in.'

He had to let the door swing wide before he saw the man sitting in the room's only armchair to one side of the sashed window. He was as tall as Sanctuary but elegantly and darkly tailored. The high forehead beneath greying, brushed-back curls had mandarin stamped right across it. Sanctuary swept the rest of the room, or as much as he could see. More or less as he had left it. Except for the bathroom. The door was closed, but not quite. He had left it open. Wide. He always did. Just in case. The maid? Perhaps. He didn't know. He said nothing. Along the corridor a door opened. Sanctuary stepped back and to one side, slightly out of sight of the stranger. But only slightly. A man and a woman came out. Closed their door. Tested that it was locked. They didn't want burglars. As they passed they smiled and the man, looking like a retired colonel, said good evening. Sanctuary nodded. The woman glanced into the room, more to see if it was nicer than theirs than because of any sense that something was wrong, and then they were at the top of the stairway and going down. The colonel looked back as they rounded the bend. Curious, but minding his own business. They would mention it over sherry.

'Do please come in, Mr Sanctuary, after all it is your room.'

The voice was cultured, not cultivated. The authority of ancestral order and assurance. Sanctuary entered and leant against the inside wall. The door was open. He could hear his mind demanding, Who the hell are you? What the hell d'you think you're doing in my room? Instead he said nothing. He pulled the door to, almost, and waited. The man did not get up. Not bad manners. Unprovocative. He was smiling. Not grinning. Not mocking. Smiling. Almost friendly. Sanctuary's father had a similar smile which he kept for his surgery. It was meant to be reassuring. Relaxing. It normally worked unless people were really ill. Sanctuary did not relax for one second.

122

The man stirred, very slowly. His elbows rested on the chair's arms, his finger tips touched. If English proconsuls had ever wanted to build pyramids, this was how they would have described them. Sanctuary noticed the slim gold wrist-watch. It was shortly after nine. The smile was there still. It was like Priestley's except this was the real thing.

'I do apologise for startling you, Mr Sanctuary.'

He indicated the writing-table chair.

'Won't you sit down?'

Its back was to the bathroom door. Sanctuary didn't move. He said nothing.

'This is all very difficult. I assure you, I mean you no harm.'

Silence. Sanctuary was slowing his breathing. Just a touch. Easy on the muscles, he thought. The curtains were drawn back. Outside the light was fading. He could see the cathedral. No other windows. No dark corners. He felt danger. Not from this man. Where then? He didn't know. He said nothing.

'If harm were meant, Mr Sanctuary, then there have been more reasonable opportunities.'

Still nothing. This time the stranger's sigh was genuine.

'Very well, if you insist. I had rather hoped to discuss a matter of mutual interest.'

The hand waved apologetically.

'A trite expression, but so accurate as we both know.'

Sanctuary clenched and unclenched his right hand feeling the weight and bulb of the heavy key tab. Not much, but useful for throwing. His people did not go in for hat-skimming and exploding cigarette-lighters. He waited.

'My visit this evening is, shall we say, not a Departmental matter. But, on the other hand, my people may choose to make it so.'

He caught the interest in Sanctuary's eyes. The smile was easier.

'Oh yes, have no doubt, Mr Sanctuary, you and I are on the same payroll, indirectly, that is.'

Sanctuary's mind was speeding through the possibilities. If the stranger had anything to do with the Department he would have contacted him less dramatically. He would have known how to identify himself. Perhaps he did but for some reason wouldn't. No plastic card. Not unusual. Another Department? Five didn't work like this. Anyway, this one was too top-drawer. He was tapping the tips of the pyramid.

'I have to tell you, Mr Sanctuary, that I have made certain inquiries and it does seem that at this stage your, shall we say, investigation is of a somewhat preliminary nature. The circumstances of friend Fisher's death are thought obscure. It would, Mr Sanctuary, be better if they remained so.'

The man paused. The silence invited Sanctuary to reply. He didn't. His mind was still in top gear. Was Fisher working for someone after all? Another desk in the Department without Sanctuary knowing. Perfectly possible. Happened all the time. The best operations kept to themselves. Then why hadn't the Deputy mentioned it to Dorothea? If another section had used Fisher as a freelance, which was pretty commonplace, then the Deputy would have been told as soon as the murder report had surfaced. Sanctuary would have been called in at once. Not their pigeon, as the Deputy was fond of saying. Let someone else snoop. He wanted to question the stranger. But the only advantage he had was silence. He needed that advantage. His senses kept signalling danger and he still didn't know where the pulses were coming from.

The fingers had stopped tapping. The hands were now neatly folded.

'This is all too unnecessary.'

The sigh was deeper, longer, exaggerated, exasperated.

'Very well.'

That was the second time. Sanctuary was pleased.

'Let me tell you what you are to do. You are to return to London, in your own time, say, after lunch tomorrow, and report that there is no evidence whatsoever of circumstances that would interest your Department. The file will be closed.'

Sanctuary made his clenching around the key tab more obvi-ous. The stranger pretended not to have noticed. He had. He pressed on too quickly to maintain his total authority. His voice, at home in establishment parlours and among whispered meetings overlooked by marbled, sightless statesmen and por-

124

traits of long-dead chamberlains, now took a sharper tone. In a hurry. For him the game of monologue had grown tedious.

'Now, you'll immediately want to know why. Sadly, I cannot tell you. That is a matter of extreme national and, may I say, international importance and I hardly have to explain to you of all people that there are occasions when reasons and decisions are best kept among a few. You, Mr Sanctuary, will not be surprised to learn that you are not among that few.'

The shaggy head was still. The eyes uncooperative but not sullen. Simply, not coming out to play by the stranger's rules.

'One other thing, Mr Sanctuary: arrangements are in hand to provide the police with a satisfactory explanation for our friend's killing. If it's of any consolation it will be very neat and tidy and eminently plausible. No one will accuse you of having fallen down on your job.'

Very carefully, with such natural elegance, the stranger got up. His suit jacket which had remained buttoned slipped into perfectly tailored lines. He nipped at the white cuff of his shirt. A royal gesture before some tassled cord is pulled to reveal yet another public duty performed.

'You will excuse us, won't you?'

As he moved towards Sanctuary, the bathroom door swung back. The second man stepped into the room. Sanctuary clicked his memory file. Six one, six two? Brown hair. Eyes darker than the charcoal of his suit. Not fat but not slim. Short stubby hands at his sides but not relaxed. Jacket open. Just in case. A dull gold ring. The stranger paused by the door close enough for the quiet scent of his soap to reach Sanctuary.

'And, by the by. Don't worry about your new friends. I think you may find they too will lose interest in this most disagreeable affair. Particularly if you forget where your loyalties lie.'

He swung back the door.

'So nice to have met you.'

He was humming 'Ten Green Bottles' to himself as he headed for the stairs.

22

Once the usual crowd had eaten, the yacht club bar slowly emptied of all but the hard core of drinkers. Nothing heavy, Les thought, just what a town pub would call the regulars. He had never drunk much himself, especially when he was behind the bar. He had enough trouble with getting the right change. Sums were not his strong point and no one ever asked Les to chalk the darts score. In fact no one ever asked him anything much other than to pour another round.

The telephone call was unexpected. Not many people called him, certainly not at the bar. Les did not have many friends. In fact he had none. Most of the people he knew were at the club. The Members regarded him as Les the Barman and would wave if they saw him outside, but he had never been invited anywhere. He did not envy them their boats and, some of them, their money. He had never been bothered by the Tenth Commandment and, if he lived in dreams of wealth and possessions, few would have known. The people who talked to him were mostly the late drinkers. Even then they talked at him and never encouraged him to give an opinion, express a sentiment, reveal an emotion. Les's main function, apart from serving one more drink after closing time, was to supply the magic words that made him a good listener.

'Really? Then what happened?'

The perfect barman. So, when the barmaid said there was a call for Les in the hallway box, there was little nudging and winking. He was only important when he was late for work or eager to get home to his houseboat on closing time. And, when he returned to the bar and said he had to nip out for a moment, the barmaid looked questioningly, but no one else did. After all Les was flat-chested.

126

He did not take his bicycle. The boatyard was not far. As he walked by the thin lines of late cars and beyond the dinghy park he felt pretty pleased with himself. He had liked Mr Fisher. He had always had time for a chat. They hadn't been friends, neither of them did that sort of thing. But Les reckoned they had a good understanding. He wondered what this letter was about. The bloke on the 'phone said it was important. Explained a few things about the Commander, he had said. Naturally he didn't want to get mixed up so, if Les met him, then he could have it. No questions. Just pass it on to the right people. Leave him out of it and maybe there'd be a drink in it for Les. He'd liked that. He liked to be appreciated. The barmaid appreciated him, especially when he quietly rescued her from the gawpers and touchers. She had once told her mother that Les was sad. Lonely, she'd said. All by himself in that old houseboat. She would always feel sorry for him, but Les reckoned he was pretty lucky. He did not have responsibilities. He was healthy in spite of what he was attempting to do to his lungs. You've got to die of something was Les's motto. Yes, as he padded across the shingled yard towards the big boathouse, Les thought he really had it made. Fresh air. Nice place to be. No worries. Friendly people he could leave behind at closing time. He could walk to work. He liked the job. What more could a man want? And, what was more, it was his for life.

23

Sanctuary waited for twenty minutes, mulling over the visit. It stank. He was still bothered. If he were being told to back down, then why was it not a direct instruction from the Department? There would be nothing strange about that. It had happened before. He didn't always like it. Priestly said it was because Sanctuary had so little faith in injustice. Priestly spent a great deal of his time looking for opportunities to sound clever. One day someone would laugh. But not this time. This did not ring like the Department's bell. He wondered how much they knew. Was that why Dorothea wanted him? Whoever the stranger was, he would surely know that he would check with the Department. There was no way in which they could threaten him to put in a false report without the Department's agreement. It wasn't as if he had anyone who was close enough to be dragged in. He was looking for the 'phone cards as that thought crossed his mind. There was no one they could threaten. No hostage to be taken. No one here was that close.

He closed his eyes. It was ridiculous. But then it always was. He knew there was no one, but did they know? If they did not, then the target was obvious. He hoped not.

Sanctuary left the building by the side entrance. He was not trying to hide, he needed his car. Anyway, he thought, they would not have waited. If there was a tail he would soon spot it. This part of the world at this time of night had about as much cover as a blood-stain on a white sheet.

He tried the 'phone box beyond the roundabout heading south. Dorothea was out. No answer 'phone. She would not be far. He headed for the back lanes. It was now dark though the moon was good. If there was anyone following they would be easy to spot – or they'd hit a tree. Sanctuary didn't mind which. He grinned as he changed gear; they'd probably be gassed by the time they caught up. The old Alfa's blue smoke trail was quite distinctive.

The black-pitched pottery doors were shut. The house was in darkness. Only the porch lantern welcomed any traveller and warned off intruders. He banged on the front door, the heavy wrought-iron dolphin thudding solemnly. He was about to go when an upstairs light came on. He waited but there was no sound of movement from inside. He knocked again, gently this time, and called out. The hall sprang into light and he heard a click from the lock and then a chain removed.

Isobel had been asleep and looked it. The dark blue kimono was loosely tied and she was busy knotting her hair with a cotton woggle as she led the way into the kitchen.

'Coffee?'

She'd switched on a small light over the Aga range and was filling the aluminium pot, not waiting for an answer, and stretched her eyes in a further effort to wake up.

'So much for an early night.'

She was not yet awake.

'I'm sorry.'

'Good.'

She was wondering why on earth she had let him in.

'I was worried. I've had a visitor. I wanted to make sure you're okay.'

Isobel pulled the kimono closer to her body. The cotton was very thin.

'That was very thoughtful.'

It was a very formal observation. The gurgling expresso was used to being woken at all hours. The coffee was very dark and she sipped, watching him over the brim of her cast-off pottery, while he told her the tale of finding himself the new owner of the *Madrigal* and then about the stranger. He left out the bit about Les and the man the barman had seen talking to Stuart the night before he was killed. He was breaking rules but he didn't much care. He was no longer sure what they were supposed to be. But she was not quite asleep.

'So Pete was right?'

'About?'

'You being something more than interested. Not just a friend.'

'I thought we'd been through that.'

'Maybe.'

She yawned, closed her eyes and stretched again. He wondered if she slept in the kimono. There was nothing else. She opened her eyes and saw his glance, pulled the neckline closer.

He told as much as he needed to and he believed her when she promised, almost irritably, to keep it all to herself.

'Where do I fit in?'

'You could be a target. That's why I'm here.'

'Thanks.'

The irony came with a shrug of the shoulders. The kimono slipped but her eyes did not.

'Funny. You don't look like a paranoid.'

'I'm not kidding. These people, whoever they are, and I promise you I don't know who they are, want me to cover up something that's clearly very important.'

'You don't know that it is.'

'I didn't until this guy turned up with his gorilla.'

'But why would it all involve me?'

'You were a friend of Stuart's, you sailed the *Madrigal* with him. They don't know how much he told you.'

'Nothing.'

'They don't know that. Come to think of it, nor do you. He could have said something that didn't sound important or you may have forgotten.'

She shook her head. The wisps that had escaped the dark cotton band bounced in disagreement. He needed to disturb her.

'Stuart's wife has surfaced.'

It disturbed her.

'I thought she was, well, gone. Where is she? Here?'

He wondered again how well Stuart and Isobel had known each other. It was his turn to shake a no.

'Washington, I think. The police told me.'

130

'Why?'

'She read about it.'

'No. Why did they tell you?'

'Suppose it was not the sort of thing they needed to keep to themselves, or Leonard didn't.'

It sounded thin as explanations went.

'Or they wanted to see how you would react.'

'Or how you would. Perhaps they think you were close. Others may get the same idea.'

'That's a bit far-fetched isn't it? Guesswork.'

'Why? In this business most of it's guesswork. And another thing, there's you and me.'

'The police aren't interested, surely?'

'Damned right they are. But I'm more bothered about the thugs who turned up tonight. They could easily think that we're, well . . .'

Embarrassed. He hadn't said anything but part of him wished he had.

'Well what?'

The mug was down. The eyes directly into his. Not quite indignant. Not far off it.

'Well, what the tabloids call "just close friends".'

'That's nonsense.'

She straightened, her back arched, and hitched the wrap close to the nape of her neck. The kimono had not been designed for serious late-night conversation across a softly lit room, even it were a kitchen. He looked at his coffee mug. There weren't many other places to look.

'They don't know that. There are certain people who would make assumptions and act on them rather than leave anything to chance.'

'What sort of people?'

'The sort of people who think nothing of blowing away two men.'

Isobel looked at the floor. She didn't want to believe him.

'You knew about the guard? Didn't you?'

She nodded.

'Pete called.'

131

'And it doesn't bother you?'

'Of course it does, but it's got nothing to do with me. How many more times do I have to tell you? Are you deliberately trying to frighten me?'

He was. She had known the answer, but it was better coming from this uncombed schoolboy. It seemed he attracted trouble and she wanted to be out of the magnetic field. She firmly intended to stick to clays and glazes.

'Okay, I get your point.'

'Thanks for your offer of help but, frankly, no thank you.'

'Just wait a minute.'

She rode over him.

'If you and I keep our distance and you disappear back to wherever it was you came from, then the whole mess will go away.'

'It's not that easy.'

'Let's try it, shall we?'

She was topping up the mugs.

'What about Stuart?'

'Dead. If you're right and your sinister friends are right, then that seems to have been the business he was in. As hurtful as that may sound, that's the size of it. His business, not ours. Anyway, not mine.'

She looked at him again. Searching to see if he had taken on board what she was trying to say. His face was battered but strangely innocent. Isobel wasn't as calm inside as she tried to make out. She had tried to sound tough. Hard. All she had done was frighten herself, but she knew that she was right. Potters didn't get involved in things like this. Whatever things like this were. She didn't really know. When he replied, he sounded tired.

'You think it'll be as easy as that?'

'As what?'

'As finding a sandpit to bury your head.'

'I don't need one. I'm a potter. Not a very good one, but that's what I am. A potter. I am not in the habit of toting a Derringer in my stocking-top and hiding micro film in my G-string. Okay?'

132

Sanctuary looked at this slim figure now refusing to meet his eye, speaking head lowered as if she were reading from a crib hidden in her lap. He could frighten her even more. That would be easy. But he wanted her to understand that the sort of people he had met that night did not simply go away. The Departmental report might close an official file, but it wouldn't lock away the fact that Stuart Fisher had stumbled on some major secret which had got him killed. It would not lock away the secret and that secret would be protected as jealously as it had been on the day Fisher was about to board the *Madrigal*. Isobel Rolfe would not be able to hide behind her pots, dishes and plates if someone came looking for her. Rusty and Pete would not be able to protect her. Salty folklore and mystical phrases from some cross-legged make-believe guru would not stop a .762 round at fifty metres. He told her all this. She remained quite still. He was being dramatic. Why not? He did not know her well. But he wanted to.

She saw the beam of lights across the yard just before he picked up the sound of the car. The lights and noise disappeared at the same time as the ignition was switched off.

'Pete?'

She shrugged. She didn't know.

The scrape of his chair on the quarry tiles made her jump. She was very awake.

'Stay where you are.'

He looked towards the back door. It was locked. He didn't have to tell her to be quiet. Leaning across the sink and peering through the small-paned windows didn't tell him anything. Whoever had stopped hadn't come into the pottery drive. The quiet clunk of a car door was just audible. In the half-light he put his finger to his lips and listened. One door. Just one of them. Out of the car anyway. He was about to go through to the front of the house when there was a heavy thud of the dolphin's head. He took the girl by the hand and shooed her up the stairs. Another knock. Through the grotesque distortion of the spy-hole, the elliptical features, the gold-rimmed spectacles splashing smiling light back at him from the porch lantern, were blessed relief. He opened the door.

'Well, well, well.'

There were times when Leonard could think of very police-man-like things to say. Sanctuary eyed him for a moment, then looking beyond the Chief Inspector to the lane stepped back to let him in.

'It's the Chief Inspector.'

It was a pretty obvious remark. It was the best he could do. It was one of those evenings.

Isobel appeared at the top of the stairs bending slightly to see who it really was. She came down perhaps too quickly. The soft skirt of her kimono parted before she could gather it together. The deeply tanned legs and the defiant stare she gave the detective drove all thoughts of chivalrous explanation he might have had from his mind. Leonard was far from the cool academic who had confronted them at the police headquarters.

'I see I'm interrupting something. You'll have to forgive me.'

It was not much but it had the right result.

'And what the devil d'you mean by that?'

Sanctuary had a wild look to him but, instead of putting the fear of God into the policeman, he appeared as a slightly ridiculous 1930s British Bulldog figure bristling to defend a lady's reputation. Leonard ignored Sanctuary.

'Good evening, Miss Rolfe.'

He looked at his pocket watch. Snapped it tight.

'I hope I didn't get you up.'

Isobel paused on the bottom step and looked down into his eyes. There was nothing. He could smell her clean scent. His eyes gave nothing. Then a flicker. The red rims might have been sleepless nights. The knowing but not accepting. The loneliness. He looked away. She knew. She moved into the kitchen, no longer trying to catch the swirl of her skirt. Sanctuary was covering well. What was going on that could drag Leonard out at this time of night? Was this a private visit? After all, did policemen normally go about by themselves, especially when calling at a lady's house this late at night? Leonard did not bother to reply. Sanctuary was not the girl's lawyer.

The policeman had seated himself at the kitchen table. He

eyed the two coffee mugs and casually put his hand around the nearest. It was quite warm.

'I suppose I don't have to ask if you both can account for your movements this evening?'

'Why?'

Sanctuary's question was full of defiance rather than curiosity.

'Corroboration's a very tidy explanation.'

Leonard looked at the coffee pot, bubbling and orientally scented. The girl was leaning back against the warmth of the red enamelled range. She watched him without speaking. Waiting for him to answer his own statement. She didn't offer him coffee.

'Can you?'

'What if we can't?'

He wondered if Isobel were mocking him. He couldn't be sure.

'It would be best if you could.'

Leonard looked away again and then at Sanctuary. The policeman was holding to the rim of his temper. Sanctuary sensed there was no point in antagonising Leonard. Whatever had brought him out to the pottery had to be important. Unless? He didn't quite know what, unless he was thinking about . . . but there was always an unless in these affairs. He thought back to the instructor at the Department's induction school. 'Trust no one and assume they mistrust you. You'll get on fine that way.' It had been a cynical observation and hadn't always worked. Sometimes, though, it was about right. There were no rules that always worked. So, help out Leonard and ease him down.

'Well, earlier this evening I was at the yacht club.'

'Anyone see you?'

'The barman. Les. You phoned. You should know that.'

'It was a woman who answered. What time did he see you?'

'Don't really know. Eight? I left shortly after you 'phoned. Eight-fifteen?'

'Go on.'

The voice terse.

'I chatted to your constable on the pontoon. But you must know that too. Then back to the hotel. Reception would know.'

He remembered the colonel and his wife.

'Nothing else.'

'Then?'

'Then nothing.'

There was a pause. Isobel was swishing the coffee dregs in her mug. Leonard's fuse was burning furiously. Isobel dampened it – just a little.

'Then he came banging on my door and woke me up just to tell me that Stuart had left him the *Madrigal* or something.'

'When was that?'

'Just before you arrived.'

'Really?'

She didn't bother to squash the innuendo. She wanted it to end. Wanted them to go and never come back. She wanted to get to bed and hide under the soft cotton sheet and pretend the world had something else to do other than involve her in murder and the smut of assumption from a policeman whose breath smelled of too much coffee, whose eyes were watery when she looked into them and whose nails were softly manicured. She glanced at Sanctuary and inwardly winced. Nor did she need this dollop defending her honour in his most cack-handed manner.

'Now look here, Leonard, what you've heard is true. All this "really" stuff can go to hell in a handbasket as far as I'm concerned. Miss Rolfe was asleep when I arrived. I woke her up and that's it.'

'That's what?'

Leonard wasn't backing down.

'That's all there is to it. And, frankly, I think you've got a bit of explaining to do.'

Leonard was tired. He was confused by events which followed no logic. He was getting pressure from the Old Man who wanted a good clean clear-up to sign off his career file. He was hungry. He was lonely. He was, above all, angry. He didn't look at her when he spoke.

136

'And, if it's not a too indelicate question, where have you been all evening?'

'Here. Why?'

'Can anyone vouch for you – apart from Mr Sanctuary of course?'

'No. Should they have to?'

Sanctuary moved towards the girl. It was an instinct to protect. He sensed he might make matters worse by doing so. He stood alongside. No touching. No arm about her shoulders though her clipped answers were all she could manage. Leonard's mouth was open. Sanctuary cut him off.

'Okay, Chief Inspector. You've had your game. Let's switch channels. What the hell's going on?'

Leonard's arms were on the table. He picked up Sanctuary's tepid coffee and sipped from it. He hated anger, especially his own.

'When did you see the barman?'

'I don't know. Whenever it was you 'phoned. I've told you. Why?'

The hiss and sigh this time reflected revulsion as well as anger.

'Someone . . .' his pause was not for effect, 'someone, some animal, stuck a knife in him tonight.'

'Oh God! Oh no!'

Leonard's blinking was furious.

'Oh God yes, Miss Rolfe. Yes, they did. And when they'd done that, Miss Rolfe, they cut out his heart and left it in his mouth.'

24

Isobel Rolfe was in a state of cold shock. Sanctuary had sent her off to bed and told her whatever her reputation he was bedding down on the sofa for what was left of the night. He had then cursed Leonard for his amateur dramatics. Leonard had said nothing. They both knew what he was doing. She was either a brilliant actress or she knew nothing about Les's killing. They both knew which was true.

Leonard had promised police protection but had come clean on numbers. There were going to be gaps. Putting one constable on one front door tied up five policemen. He suggested that Isobel should get away for a few days. She refused.

Once the girl had gone to bed Leonard and Sanctuary stripped off their mental jackets. This was not simply a triple murder inquiry. It was Leonard who made the observation.

'How many murderers know how to cut out a heart? Even know where it is?'

'Or are ghouls enough to do it?'

Leonard nodded.

'If you know something, Sanctuary, you'd better come clean or I'll have you, I'll have you.'

Sanctuary didn't answer. He was in the larder. If she had any, it would be in here, he thought. She had. He came back with two glasses and an almost-full bottle. He held it up to Leonard.

'Please.'

He poured two very large Glenmorangies, wondered how Isobel could afford it and made a mental note to replace it.

'So what happened?'

The police did not know very much. At about eight o'clock, no one was that certain, there had been a telephone call for

Les. A man's voice, the barmaid had said. She had taken the call in the public box used by members. The Secretary wasn't in the club so Les was in charge and had said he would be back in ten minutes. He wasn't. By eight-thirty, the barmaid was getting angry. The bar was busy and no Les. She had called his houseboat to see if he had popped back. Perhaps he was ill. One of the members had helped out behind the bar and no one had known anything else until the police arrived at ten-thirty.

'Who called you?'

Leonard held out his glass for more.

'The two fellows who found him. Security guards. They've been patrolling in pairs since the youngster was found on the beach. One of the side doors to the boatshed was open. They checked and . . .'

'Found him.'

'Threw up.'

'Still some light.'

'Not in the shed there wasn't. The blade was big. In the back and out the other side. That's very big.'

'And then the amateur surgery.'

Sanctuary took more than a sip at the single malt.

'Not so amateur.'

'Messy.'

'Surgeons wear smocks.'

'Meaning?'

The policeman had undone his waistcoat. The braces were brown with leather tabs and buttonholes.

'Meaning that whoever did this was prepared. An overall would have protected him.'

'Him?'

Sanctuary's question was not simply a reaction.

'Would have had to have been an Amazon. This was a big job. Very wet.

Leonard nodded to the ceiling.

'Too wet for your friend.'

They talked for another two hours and by the time Sanctuary got through to Dorothea she was worried. It was four in the morning. She had hardly slept. The telephone had been

139

chattering since shortly after midnight. The Department wanted to know where he was. Yes, they knew about the barman and the guard. Was there a tie-up? He said he thought there had to be, or at least they had to assume there was until a better hypothesis appeared. He was wanted back for Morning Prayers at nine-thirty. The Deputy had been on himself and Priestly was suggesting that he, Priestly, take charge of any investigation into the Department's involvement. For the moment, the Deputy was keeping the ever-gloating Priestly in his place, but he knew that Priestly would make his feelings known along different corridors.

The Department had received a call through the duty officer. One of the Branch had picked up the barman's death on the midnight line and tied it to the security guard murder. An alert duty officer had noted that one of the Department was in the area. It had been a quiet watch and he had been going through the homeside off-base list on the green screen. Not unlikely for their mainly overseas Department, very few personnel were off-base in the UK. That night, there were three: the usual two on rotation with the Security Co-ordinator in Northern Ireland, and David Sanctuary. The interest was easily established. Any incident, however unconnected, was always logged when a member of the Department was in the area. Sanctuary realised this was bigger league than he had ever played, or even realised existed, which given that he was on the inside was something else, as Dorothea would have said. It was exactly what she did say when he told her how gruesome the killing had been. That she had not known. There was no way in which he could stay out. He had to come in for Prayers.

25

Isobel had been persuaded to close down the pottery for a day or two and by seven in the morning she had moved a sleeping bag and toothbrush on board Pete Hogarth's boat. Perkins had appeared with a couple of two-way radios and a check-in channel. It wasn't much, he had said, but it was better than the isolated house. Before Sanctuary left for London he promised to be back by the evening. Isobel had given him the same look of trust she had shown when the policewoman had led her away for interrogation. He was determined to get back although he already guessed the Department would try to block his return. But he had promised. The early-morning sun was already drying the overnight dew on the splintery pontoon. A slight breeze freshened his stubbled face. In different times he would have recognised a small piece of heaven. But now he felt nothing but gloom as he drove away from the basin with its tall masts standing silently to attention. When he arrived at the Department he knew that he had been right.

He was ten minutes late. Prayers had started. Like Mass, they were said even if no one attended. The Deputy was in his oak carver at the head of the long black refectory table around which they all sat during these morning briefings. Priestly was in full flow as Sanctuary slipped into his seat alongside Dorothea with a brief nod from the Deputy.

'Altogether, Deputy, I would say that this adventure comes under the heading of *reductio ad absurdum*. There is absolutely no way in which the Department should have got itself involved. It is, to say the least, regrettable.'

'That is death's habit.'

The Deputy was never happy when Priestly was in one of his self-righteous moods, which was most mornings. One day,

Priestly would sit in the oak carver. The Deputy thanked his lucky stars that he would be long gone. However, Priestly had a point. He usually did. The Deputy cleared his throat, which was his way of announcing a decision.

'It was right that we should have had a look at Fisher's death. After all, he was known to us. But perhaps we should have handed over to the Branch to hold at least a watching brief for us. You should all know that we are now taking a back seat but I don't want the screen switched off.'

Priestly smiled.

'Perhaps I may . . . ?'

'Perhaps you may not, Charles.'

Something was clearly concerning the Deputy although he had chosen not to pass on whatever it was that had got to him that morning. He looked at Sanctuary.

'Anything?'

Sanctuary ran through most of the events of the past few days. He described the deaths as he knew them of the guard and the barman, and noted with no satisfaction the light forward lean of Priestley's well-barbered head when he got to the removal of Les's heart. He described Leonard in some detail and gave quick portraits of the rest of the cast. He spent more time on Roberts than he had intended and less on Isobel, as he had intended. He mentioned the telephone call from Jane Fisher. He did not mention his hotel visitors.

'Recommendations?'

Sanctuary could see the writing and had heard the text. Somewhere between the two he slipped in with his one plausible thought.

'I have struck up a very favourable relationship with the investigating officer.'

'Leonard?'

The Deputy liked everything clear and precise. No chance of misunderstanding.

'Leonard. I agree that this is not a Departmental investigation. However . . .'

He paused and looked along the table. Eight pairs of eyes were waiting. Only Priestly wasn't looking at him. Priestly was smiling, head slightly bowed, and toying with his slim gold pencil. He was waiting to pounce.

'Considering that there could be a Departmental interest at the end of this affair, my recommendation would be that I keep in touch, on an informal basis of course, with the Chief Inspector.'

Priestly pounced.

'I must say, Deputy . . .'

Priestly did not land. The Deputy closed his leather folder with a snap.

'Thank you, Dorothea. Thank you, gentlemen.'

He stood and moved back to his large mahogany desk with its brass-hooded light and chestnut pipe-rack full of Dunhills, one of which he smoked every evening before returning to the flat he rented behind Harrods. Sanctuary, the last to go, was about to close the door when the Deputy called his name and pointed to the seat by his desk. He scribbled on a memo pad for a moment then swung round in the leather captain's chair.

'Well?'

Sanctuary wondered how much the Deputy knew.

'Who were they?'

The Deputy shook his head. Knew all about the visit to Sanctuary's hotel. Didn't know who they were. Sanctuary told him almost word for word as he remembered it. Descriptions. Timings. Quotes. Style. The lot. He waited. The other man, craggy, bushy-eyebrowed, easier in tweeds than the grey chalk stripe, picked up a long stem briar and rubbed its bowl along the side of his nose.

'I've had C telling us to back off.'

'He say why?'

'Not our pigeon, that's what he said.'

'Whose then?'

The older man was tapping the point of his nose with the empty bowl.

'Not ours.'

'Who got at him? It's too early for it to have gone to the Committee.'

'Permanent Secretary? Yanks? Security People? I suppose

143

we could have stumbled on a cross-over. It wouldn't be the first time we've bumped into one of their jobs.'

'None of these, come to that none of ours, goes in for this style. This is the Bulgarian School, not us.'

'It's happened in Northern Ireland. You know that.'

'That's taking out known terrorists.'

'It's illegal so anything's possible.'

'But that's all been set up from Hereford.'

Sanctuary thought about it. They both did.

'You don't think it's Army do you?'

'Could be. If it is then it's out of order, as your policeman friend would say.'

'He wouldn't. He's not that sort of policeman.'

'Whatever.'

The Deputy eyed the tobacco bowl. Not until after six o'clock, as the lady once said.

'This flashing red would have had to have come from the Co-ordinator in that case. Northern Ireland Rules don't operate on this side of the water.'

'Some say they should.'

The Deputy wondered if Sanctuary did. He thought not. He hoped not. Sanctuary was thinking aloud.

'Perhaps the Rules have changed and we're about to find out.'

'I wonder. There'll be seven different types of carnage if we've decided to play it their way.'

The Deputy got up and walked to the window overlooking Downing Street. The white net curtains made good cover.

'That's exactly what they'll want us to do. The New York dollars would pour into Dundalk like there was no tomorrow.'

The front door at Number Ten was open. There was a casual recess Cabinet. A Committee probably. A couple of Ministers were arriving. He could see the Secretary of State walking across from his office. There was no Press pack gathered out-side. No expectations. No worries. Officially, government was on holiday. On the warm south coast, the local morgue was on time-and-a-half. He turned. Looked at Sanctuary. He liked him. He trusted him. He would have made a good missionary.

144

'Is that what you think, David?'

Sanctuary raised his hands like a sympathetic pawnbroker.

'We'd have known. At least the Department would have been told.'

'On something like this? SAS or whoever operating on the mainland. Taking out known IRA? No trial? Just a gun?'

The consequences were too horrible.

'Lot of public support.'

Sanctuary was right. In the short term. But would the Department know? At the very top. Yes. But it would be a very hot potato. It might go no further.

'We're guessing.'

The Deputy sat down at the long table. They were fencing. They both knew this was a kiloton headache.

'You realise the obvious thing about this business?'

Sanctuary nodded. He knew.

'It could be even bigger than what we're discussing. Fisher talked about the big one. That's nuclear. My visitor mentioned international implications. Anything going on that's unusual?'

The Deputy leaned back and eyed the world map on the opposite wall as if expecting a flashing light to solve their problem.

'Hardly. Usual round of Middle Eastery, a bit in Central America, though nothing much that's our pigeon, and that's about it.'

'Nothing with the *kreml*?'

'Nope. Few bits and pieces in the Ukraine. Arms-flogging, that sort of thing, but nothing on this scale. You're . . . you're certain they were in the trade?'

Sanctuary nodded.

'Or had been. You know what it suggests, especially if you take Fisher's point about a rotten apple?'

'Exactly.'

Sanctuary looked up. A sudden thought.

'What was all that fuss about Ignatiev being out of area? Tie in with the Ukraine?'

The Deputy shook his head.

145

'Ignatiev's an ace shit. Two or three like him. They come up all the time.'

'No chance of Ignatiev being into someone?'

'Here?'

Sanctuary nodded.

The Deputy sucked his teeth. He didn't want to believe any more. He liked hypotheses. Always felt disappointed when they were concluded, which was why he didn't do crosswords. It was a complication of his personality that really liked everything neatly tied up. No formality but, equally, no surprises. This, he thought, was going to be full of them. He was back at the window. The street was empty except for the policeman and a grey-jacketed messenger. He had decided.

'What do you want to do?'

'Just as I said in Prayers. Keep in touch with Leonard. That way we have an inside track without getting involved officially.'

'Okay. Listen. You look tired. That's official. See the MO. Get some deheat tablets. Tell her you can't sleep. Why don't you take five days' leave? Report in twice a day to either myself or Dorothea. Not here. Home. The screen will show you off-base on leave in the UK. Move out of that hotel. It's up to you where you stay.'

'How about the *Madrigal*?'

Sanctuary was grinning. The Deputy was not.

'I don't want to know. Five days. Okay?'

He didn't wait for an answer. His head was back in the bureaucracy of buff and pink folders. When the mortice clicked behind Sanctuary, the Deputy looked up and stared for a long time at the green-baized inner door. He picked up the yellow private telephone beneath the Whitehall briefing television. Tapped a three-digit number and asked two questions. There was little expression beneath the angry eyebrows, little to tell how this disappointed and lonely man felt as he listened to the answers.

26

The *Madrigal* was unlocked when he arrived on board. Isobel was below getting her ship-shape. He had called the yacht club before he left London and dragged Pete away from his lunchtime heart-starter, as he called the first drink of the day. Pete hadn't said much on the telephone. He was non-committal when Sanctuary told him he was moving on board.

'See you then.'

Pete had his over-and-out voice on. Presumably the whole bar was listening. But all was quiet on the southern waterfront, which was all Sanctuary wanted to hear.

Isobel had got things in good order. The ripped cushions were with the police who hadn't given up looking for some telltale evidence of misdemeanour. She had found cotton-covered bunk mattresses and squashed them into position. Apart from the jammed navigation repeater all the instruments were up and running, back on bulkheads or in their racks. Rusty had turned up with a less than new compass and it was as good as it was ever going to be. Pete had fitted a couple of spare batteries and the girl had the small diesel ticking over to charge them.

She looked better. Isobel was one of those people who responded to a lie-in and sunshine. She was back in her old shorts and what appeared to be the only T-shirt she had. Once on board, even the flip-flops had been discarded. She felt at home. When Sanctuary tossed his canvas bag below she had it dropped into the hanging locker before he'd sat down with the mug of coffee she handed him. Isobel squinted into the clear blue sky and then at him.

'She needs sailing.'

He nodded. He was glad she'd suggested it. On the way

down from London he had decided that if he were to carry off his cover of being on leave then he wanted to get the boat to sea. He had another reason: he wanted to attract attention. The best way of doing that was to set sail. But he didn't want to put Isobel in any more danger.

'I'll take her out tomorrow.'

'By yourself?'

Her voice doubted he was capable of single-handed sailing.

'Why not? I'm not planning a transatlantic crossing.'

She laughed. The first time he had seen her face so cheerful.

'The Atlantic's easy. It's sailing in these waters that's the hard part. You've got more tide and traffic than anywhere else for three thousand miles. And you've got forty feet here to squeeze into berths. She's not for single-handed unless it's fair to middling and you know her.'

He nodded. *Madrigal* looked good, but she was a handful.

'Sometime. Okay?'

'What's wrong with now?'

She was already unlacing the mainsail cover.

'She's all ready. Tide's right. There's enough water.'

'Well . . .'

'Scared?'

They came off the berth with Isobel at the helm. The *Madrigal* was long-keeled and had a mind of her own going astern. As they entered the lock and grabbed the hanging lines from the blackened walls there were enough people to see them for the word to spread. Everyone in the basin now knew the *Madrigal*. By the time they were approaching the bar buoy, anyone who was interested knew the *Madrigal* had put to sea.

There was a stiff breeze and the boat bit to windward like the thoroughbred she was. Isobel had given him the helm shortly after they'd left the harbour and he could feel the strength of the *Madrigal* through the long curved and varnished tiller. Two points of the starboard bow, the big island looked clean with a promise of pastel scenery cut and pasted there from some railway travel poster. His eye travelled up the full set of the main and the enveloping tight curve of the big genoa as it wrapped from forestay to well abaft the beam. He braced

148

himself as the sharp bows dipped and cut through the slight chop of seas not yet disturbed by the uncomplicated wind. He felt released. The girl had gone for'd, tidying the foredeck, and he watched the sure-footed way she moved about the narrow deck, easily at home. She caught his look and smiled. Here they were untouchable. For a wistful moment he wished they could simply sail by the great tower that would come up on the starboard side and continue south and then west. Biscay. The Azores. From there anywhere they wished. The *Madrigal* would be faithful. It was Isobel, handing him yet more coffee from the tiny galley stove, who broke the spell. They had hardly spoken. There had been no need. The easy course to windward had been swift. The sun strong and very warm even in the late afternoon breeze.

'We should be heading back. We've got to leave a couple hours for the bar, otherwise we'll be out for the rest of the night.'

'So?'

Her laugh was easy again. Relaxed. There was no suggestive tone to his voice and she didn't want to return to the basin and all that it had come to represent during the past few days. They hadn't talked about the murders. Hadn't talked about Stuart. It wasn't callousness. She was trying to escape. He was trying to clear his mind. She watched him for a while then looked ahead to the southern horizon. A container ship, fat, low and slow to turn and stop, was sailing into the deep-water channel, heading for the waiting cranes of Southampton. A frigate, smudge-grey in the distance, seemed dead in the water but wasn't. A big Dutch ketch, bicycles lashed to the midships hatch, overhauled them, all sails set for the far-off French coast. She would be there by early morning. Isobel did not want to return. Not yet.

'How about the island?'

She nodded towards the coastline, now abaft the *Madrigal*'s beam.

'I don't know the way in. Where?'

'Don't worry about it. The charts are up to date. Remember? I'm in the business. Anyway, I don't need them.'

149

There was no bragging. She had sailed these waters plenty of times to know the island. Everyone did. There was no discussion. No decisions to anguish over. Sanctuary nodded.

'Going about then.'

He pushed the helm away from him, freed the mainsail cleat, and in the same motion played then tightened the sheet while Isobel ran out the headsail. They worked quietly quickly and easily together. Sanctuary brought the *Madrigal*'s head up into the wind, teasing the ropes and then deftly hauling in on the starboard side as the *Madrigal*'s white sails crossed her centre line and she once more dug into the short seas, the wind now on the other side, soon to be broad enough to take them to the island's northern coast.

Isobel kept them clear of the Shrape and headed for the Prince Consort buoy until they entered the fairway and picked up a deep-water private mooring owned by a friend of Stuart's who had taken the southerly passage earlier that month. She was busy on the VHF radio and raised Pete, telling him where they were and not to worry. He was short and cleared at the first opportunity.

'What was all that about?'

She raised her eyebrows.

'Who knows? He's not one of life's chatty people.'

Sanctuary wasn't sure what to think. Nothing was impossible and he was in two minds about mooring. Isobel was scrambling onto the coach roof wrapping and securing the mainsail.

'Give me a hand?'

He found himself reaching across her while she made fast. She smelled of sun and scrubbed thin cotton. He backed off a little. He needed her confidence. Nothing had changed. Five hours' cutting through spray didn't put any distance between him and the Department's objectives. Why? Who? What next?

Later they rowed ashore, paid their respects to the Harbour Office which knew about the arrangement on the mooring and knew too the notoriety of the *Madrigal*. They both got odd looks and the questions were too casual. Before nightfall they had found a pub for dinner. It was nothing special but nervous energy sometimes produces unexpected appetites. They ate

150

long and well, for the most part hardly speaking though Sanctuary got the impression the girl was making all sorts of judgements.

It was when he went up to the bar to order that he felt someone was watching. He looked about as casually as he could. A first-timer glancing at the photographs of famous yachts and nautical bric-a-brac. The expected collection of locals and visitors, all in conversation with someone. No loners. No one out of place, too intent on the bar menu or by themselves watch-glancing as if a friend were overdue. Instinct is misleading, he thought, and, although he wasn't fool enough to dismiss the instinct, the realist in him knew that nobody other than Pete and the Harbour Office knew they were there. Furthermore, no one at all could possibly have known they were going to the pub. They themselves hadn't known until they were outside and spotted the slate menu against the doorframe.

Back at the table, he let his gaze wander though didn't make much of it. He didn't want to frighten Isobel and he didn't want to scare off any watcher. If there was one, and he (or even she) knew he had been spotted, then he would fade – and be replaced. In the bar, everyone was a stranger to Sanctuary. Shadow-spotting was a long shot. Once or twice on the way back to the jetty he had the same sensation of being observed. He suggested a longer stroll than they had intended on the pretext of getting some exercise, but window-gazing and double-crossing a narrow street didn't produce a tail. Yet, he didn't think it had been imagination. Because he was talking to the girl and keeping a look-out at the same time without letting her know, Sanctuary's gentle encouragement had Isobel talking even more about herself and her pottery than she had imagined she might. By the time they were back on board the *Madrigal*, they were as easy as old friends. They relaxed in the snug light of the oil lamp, drinking foul coffee, talking about pieces of their past lives.

Curled up in his spare sweater, three sizes too big for her, Isobel told him about the man she should have married and the foolhardiness that had stepped in their way. He thought he could sail the Atlantic single-handed. Perhaps he could have done. The American coastguard had found some wreckage. Not much. Never him. Sanctuary had said he was sorry. He was, and she believed him. When she met Stuart in Cairo he had meant very little. A casual meeting by the hotel pool. She liked him because he wasn't heavy. It was a four-day stopover for her and the airline crew, and she was keeping one step ahead of the senior pilot who regarded her as a perk of his seniority and her refusal to climb into his bed as simply playing hard to get. They had flown back to Heathrow that evening and when, months later, Stuart turned up they had joked about his Lochinvar role on the edge of the Hilton desert.

'He wanted me to make some plates. He'd collected some leaves from the copse by the harbour and I pressed them into the designs.'

'I can't imagine him collecting leaves. He always seemed, I don't know, very basic. Very sailorish, whatever that means.'

'He was. But he was also quite artistic. Did you never see his water-colours?'

Sanctuary hadn't. They had been in each other's apartments in Moscow, but he didn't remember any paintings. Jane Fisher dabbled in photography. Some of it was erotic. Enormous grainy black-and-white nudes covering two walls. The sort of photography from which it was necessary to stand well back. When you did, lots of slim forms almost touching. Teasing. Very Jane. He had once asked where she had found the models. Jane had laughed and called him nosy. This was Moscow, she had said, one did not ask. But no water-colours.

'What happened to them?'

Isobel didn't know. They were pretty awful but he liked them. She supposed they were in the cottage. That was locked and taped by the police. Perhaps one day they would see them. Isobel shifted somewhere in the giant folds of his sweater. She was tired. Ready for sleep. The *Madrigal* was gently riding at the mooring. The motion and the easy lapping of the water against the hull was soporific. But he wanted to know more.

'What did he paint?'

'Mostly seascapes. There isn't much else once you've done

152

the cathedral and the harbour villages. He didn't do those anyway.'

She uncurled and stood, half-stretching, in the cramped gangway. Almost childlike, ready for her teddy bear and bed. Almost. Too tall. Too blonde. Even snuggled beneath the blue oiled wool, too much movement. Erotic. Jane would have said so and would have stalked her with her Nikons.

'Sleep. You can have the sleeping bag. I'll be fine in this.'

Her yawn was genuine. She tugged at the sweater and brushed by him towards the for'd cabin, her long slim legs even more graceful in the warm yellow light than in the brightness of the day's sun. She paused, leaned forward and, almost without touching, brushed his head with her lips.

''Night.'

It was a whisper.

He heard her snuggling down as he stretched out on the hard cruising berth in the main cabin, his head pillowed on a rolled-up sail bag. When she called good night, her voice was very sleepy. Not teasing. He lay on his back looking out through the hatchway and into the clear sky. He could see the bright loneliness of Arcturus, sentinel long stop to the Plough and its vague pointers to modest Polaris. He wondered how many times Stuart Fisher had stretched out there watching the shifting sky and the dust twinkling light years beyond. No, he hadn't realised Stuart painted. He could hear the girl shifting in the cosy fo'c'sle.

'What sort of seascapes?'

There was silence. But she wasn't asleep. He tried again, his voice low in that vague timbre before sleep comes.

'Anything in particular?'

'Usual thing. Nothing special. Places where he'd sailed, I suppose. Why?'

'Nothing. Just wondered.'

Sanctuary had been given five days. There was no such thing as nothing. And, for the four days left, he couldn't afford to just wonder.

27

By six o'clock the next morning they were making ready for the return sail. The air was fresh and the stiff breeze that had faded by the time they had tied up the evening before had veered and the warmth picked up as it crossed the sweltering continent would soon be with them. Some of the magic of the night had melted. The shared wine, the feeling of playing truant from the horrors ashore and the dawning that they liked each had been good. There were no complications.

Now, as Sanctuary swung the *Madrigal*'s head into the approach to the basin, the tensions of dry land returned. There was no need to search the shoreline for darkening omen. It was not hiding. It had been waiting for an hour since Sanctuary had, as promised, called Pete on the VHF telling him they had just crossed the bar. Pete had listened out for their call and then shut down. But visitors have ears and it was not Pete on the harbour wall.

Sanctuary looked up towards the lock walkway as they slipped through the open mechanical jaws. Leonard nodded his good morning and Sanctuary raised a silent hand in return. The policeman eyed the girl, barefooted and lightly clad, on the foredeck. She looked back at Sanctuary. The smile was uncertain and held its own shrug of inevitability. It had been a few hours of escape. Of such innocence reputations are firmly made.

Leonard met them at the pontoon. He said good morning in an almost just-as-I-suspected tone and watched the girl neatly drop the spring over the first bollard. He held the boat's bow as she quickly made fast the head rope.

'Coffee?'

Sanctuary remembered Dorothea's solution to any tense moment and relaxed a little when Leonard nodded.

'How did you know we were coming in? Pete?'

'Mr Hogarth? Yes. I was at his vessel when you called.'

Isobel was relieved. She trusted Pete. Coincidence was no one's fault. Sanctuary thought it convenient.

'Just happened to be there?'

'No. I was looking for you both. Your boat was gone and I knew where Miss Rolfe was staying the night. Or at least I thought I did.'

'We changed our minds.'

There was a lilt of defiance in her voice. The Islander in her was not used to answering questions.

Sanctuary sipped at the coffee. It tasted better this morning, even from tin mugs. He stretched his legs to the other side of the cockpit and Isobel smiled and budged him over for more room. It was a moment of new friendship which Leonard interpreted as intimacy. It annoyed him. He looked ridiculous in his waistcoated tweeds.

'Well?'

Leonard was startled by Sanctuary's question. He had been about to tell them anyway. Now he would have to return serve. He didn't like aces.

'Well what?'

'Why did you want us? Presumably you were looking for us both.'

Leonard put down the empty mug and stared across the lines of yachts. Twenty metres away, Rusty was sitting cross-legged on the foredeck of the ketch. He was splicing a rope's end. He couldn't possibly hear at that distance but Leonard felt uncomfortable. There was enough of the policeman in him to be suspicious of everything and everybody when he was offstage. Leonard liked people in his office. He hated his office with its washable desk top and nylon-tile carpet. Yet it worked. He wished they were there now. He preferred the grottiness of institutional environment. Taking people out of their environment was a good tactic. Put them in designer grot and they lost most of their confidence. It worked. He wasn't sure why, but it did. This was a moving boat even though it was safely moored. It was a confined space. He didn't know how it worked. These two were relaxed. Perfectly at home on its narrow decks, with its ropes and lines that did things which he knew nothing about. He was out of place. He was fearful of touching anything in case it triggered a reaction that would cause damage or make him look foolish. Leonard believed in Chaos and its causes. His instinct was to hit out at what he saw as their secret and their smugness in the hope that the innocent beat of his wings would cause a catastrophe in their confidence. He did.

'Your friend was into drugs. In a big way.'

'Who was?'

Leonard had been watching Sanctuary. He had not expected the girl to be the one to reply.

'Fisher. Who else? How many friends have you got running cocaine?'

Across the way, in earshot, a large French sloop up from Bordeaux was running its diesel. She had passed them shortly before they came through the heads and had berthed not long before the *Madrigal*. It had been a long, battery-draining, single-handed haul. The skipper, a middle-aged blonde, was leaning over the stern checking the engine cooling water as it gurgled and threw up into the harbour. She stood and hitched her narrow denim bikini top into place and smiled across at Sanctuary. He was thinking of his visitor and the promise of explanation. He smiled back, not seeing her.

'You're out of your blasted mind.'

Sanctuary's response was not venomous. Emphatic. The smile was fixed, no humour, only taut anger. Isobel was staring hard into the policeman's eyes, searching for the cruel joke which she wanted to believe was hiding behind the harsh statement.

'Am I?'

'You know damn well you are. Stuart Fisher never touched the stuff and most certainly never got into the running business. We both know that.'

156

'Perhaps you didn't know him as well as you think. After all, you told me yourself you hadn't seen him for some time.'

'I can't believe you.'

Her voice was quiet, anticipating more to come, knowing that her disbelief would be seen as naivety.

'Can't or won't?'

It was a predictable response but she wanted to go on.

'Both. He simply wasn't that sort of person.'

'Ah, so, Miss Rolfe, among your many experiences are those which allow you to confidently identify drug-smugglers? Fascinating.'

A customs officer had arrived at the French boat, drawn to the yellow flag flying from the mast where it boldly requested free pratique. He had come in search of forms and manifests. The woman, in search of clearance, put out a hand and another smile of welcome. They went below, he with his attaché case, she with another hitch of her bikini.

Isobel flopped back. She felt defeated. Cheated. No confidence. She looked at Sanctuary. His hands were back in his trouser pockets, furiously scrubbing at his thighs.

'Okay, Chief Inspector. Out with it.'

His voice sounded as if he was weary of the whole affair. He was not. Leonard looked at them both and removed his spectacles and began cleaning them with a gingham handkerchief. He took his time, wetting his bottom lip with his tongue as he did so, then looped the wire arms behind his ears and blinked into vision.

'The barman had a locker in the club. We didn't know about it until last night. Roberts mentioned it.'

'Why?'

'He wanted to know if it would be all right for him to empty it for whoever they got to replace him. He didn't have a key and busting it open would look suspicious. Or so he thought.'

He paused, waiting for a sneer that didn't come. He had underestimated the impact of his accusation. A locker was something Perkins should have thought of immediately. He had not. Instead they had searched the houseboat. That had been

157

as clean as a deckhand's cubby hole, everything in miniature and in its place.

'Don't tell me. A signed declaration from Les and Stuart that they'd been partners in Golden Triangle Inc.'

Sanctuary's voice was full of contempt for what he guessed would follow.

'As good as.'

Leonard waited for some response. The girl was looking down into the cabin, not wanting to hear any more. Sanctuary's eyes never shifted. He was defying Leonard to carry on with his melodrama. He did.

'Whatever loyalties you want to hang on to I'm sorry to tell you that it was all there. If it's any consolation, your friend seems to have been killed because his conscience had finally pricked him.'

The girl turned her gaze on the policeman.

'Impossible. Stuart wasn't like that.'

Leonard could see the tears coming. He felt no sympathy. Emptiness. It didn't bother him. That night in her house, this woman had looked deep into the uncertainty and pain. Now she was pleading. Let her.

'I tell you he wasn't. I know. I knew him.'

'Really?'

She was too upset for the dart to get through. Sanctuary was not. He had calmed down. Now he wanted to know what the police had found and who had put it there. Leonard didn't need his notebook. He had opened the locker himself. There hadn't been much but it had been damning.

'Your friends Les had four post-dated cheques and a letter signed by Fisher.'

'What's so remarkable about that?'

'Five grand each? In my book, that's remarkable for a barman. It was the letter. It said it all. Here. See for yourself.'

Leonard took a folded sheet from his inside pocket.

'Go on. Read it. Then tell me I'm wrong.'

Sanctuary unfolded the white paper. It was a photocopy. It didn't take long to see why Leonard was so smug.

158

Les,

I'm getting out. We've had a good run but the more I
think what this stuff's doing to people – especially kids
– the more I think we've got to pull out. Hash was one
thing, cocaine and crack are different ball-games. Strictly
off-limits from now on. Here is your money. Whatever
you do, do not bank it all at once. And you need not
worry about me, the money's there. Remember, it will
look bad if you suddenly flood your overdraft with 20K.
Take my advice and open four different building society
accounts. Then be careful how you spend. I'm pushing
off to France for a few weeks. These people aren't going
to be too chuffed when they realise we're not picking
up. They're nasty bastards so take some more advice and
split. See you some time. Stuart.

The letter was typed and signed in what looked like Fisher's
small neat handwriting. The girl had been reading over his
shoulder. She looked away again. She did not want to believe.
She did not believe. Nor did Sanctuary.

'Is that it?'

'It's enough, isn't it?'

'You know damned well it isn't.'

Leonard was not put off.

'For good measure, in fact for extremely good measure, we
found two plastic bags in the locker full of the finest example
of the Colombian National Product.'

'Now I know you're trying it on.'

Leonard was not trying it on. The letter was genuine. They
had opened up Fisher's cottage and compared the paper and
the typeface with the stationery and portable Imperial in his
sitting-room. The signature was made with Fisher's fountain
pen. The distinctive green ink was unmistakable. The matching
was perfect. The signature, the dead man's. As he recited the
list of evidence both actual and circumstantial, Leonard began,
for the first time since he had finally got to bed at three that
morning, to feel uneasy. And it was not simply Sanctuary's
confidence that was throwing him. Something, he was not sure

159

what, was warning him that he had jumped to too many conclusions.

'Listen, Leonard, this stinks. Think about it.'

Leonard had thought about it. He was uneasy because he never believed evidence even when it was admitted. That had more to do with his nature than a sense of policework, which he detested anyway.

'There's nothing to think about. Your friend was a runner. He gets Les involved; by the size of the pay-off I would say on a pretty big scale. He decides he's had enough, or has made enough, and decides to quit while he's ahead. He was an amateur. It's common. Bangkok Hilton is full of backpackers who'd planned to do just one trip.'

'I tell you, he wasn't.'

Sanctuary put a gentle hand on her bare arm. She was cold. He put his arm about her slender shoulders and she instinctively moved closer. He ignored the policeman's expression. He would think what he would think anyway, especially after last night. Leonard's voice was now almost a whisper though no one else was in hearing distance. Rusty had disappeared from his splicing perch. The Bordeaux sloop's engine had been cut and the Anglo-French Customs and Excise discussions were apparently in progress still. The pontoon was quiet and empty.

'But, once you're in with these people, there's no such door as out, not on your terms anyway. And, if your friend was shelling out mega cheques to the hired help, this was a very big business indeed.'

'So your theory is that they found out he was quitting and killed him?'

Leonard nodded.

'And the barman?'

'Very gruesome. Very gruesome. I can't imagine there will be many more defectors in the foreseeable future, do you?'

'You're wrong on this one, you know. Quite wrong.'

'So you keep telling me. But it ties in with a couple of points. Les had a record. Nothing big-time. Receiving. In the old days he would have been into cigarettes, booze, watches. Nothing

160

big but enough for the rummagers to watch to see who his friends were.'

'But there hadn't been any suspicions. Or had there?'

'That's true.'

Isobel waved her hands. It was a pathetic gesture.

'Well then, how can you just sit there and accept all this?'

'Squeaky clean doesn't mean innocence, Miss Rolfe – in anyone.'

The bitchiness was unnecessary. He regretted it. But he was tired. He knew also that whatever he'd retrieved from the locker might get a rough ride in court. Except, of course, there was no one to take to court and, the way things were looking, he did not believe there ever would be.

'Very neat, isn't it?'

Sanctuary's voice was reasonable. He was thinking aloud but wanted to lodge his thoughts in the other man's mind.

'Tidy. Yes. But it doesn't have to be convoluted and messy before it's true.'

Leonard stood. He stretched his arms in a praise-be yawn to the clearest of English summer blue skies. He was not unintelligent. He had had doubts. A couple would always loiter in the shadow of his reasoning. But there was one single reference that tidied the investigation. Perhaps two.

'I know, you think this was planted.'

Sanctuary's stare said that he did. Leonard smiled. He quite liked what Perkins called 'the big fella from London'.

'Think about this: there was no way in which we would have got round to the locker. We didn't even know it existed. We weren't meant to find it. Secondly, Fisher left a letter with his solicitor. It explained everything.'

Sanctuary was interested. Mentally, he sat up.

'What sort of letter. Who to?'

'To his solicitor. He spelled it out. He'd been running, what he called contraband – now there's a sweet old-fashioned phrase for you. He wanted Tupman to know this, in the event of his death, as Tupman put it.'

'Why?'

'Oh, don't worry, he was quite explicit. If he got himself

161

killed he wanted someone to pay. The only problem with that is that he did.'

'Did what?'

The voice was very quiet. Not wanting answers but wanting explanations.

'He did pay, Miss Rolfe. Very dearly. You see, your friend, whom you knew so well and who wouldn't hurt a fly, fingered his partner. It was the amiable old soul Les who was the go-between between the organisation and your honest and true friend. Perfect. Les the barman, everyone's friend. Always there polishing glasses and listening to hard-luck stories and, it seems, fixing couriers in their smart little ships.'

Sanctuary's arm was outstretched, returning the unwanted, unbelievable letter. Leonard showed him the flat of his hand.

'Please, be my guest. It's only a copy. I have plenty more.'

'A fake.'

'No, Mr Sanctuary, not a fake. It's the real thing, unlike, I'm afraid, your friend. I'll be in touch.'

He stepped ashore. The triumphal exit. Without turning, he raised a senatorial short arm in farewell and retreated along the sun-bleached pontoon to where he had left his bicycle.

Sanctuary did not need to tell Isobel that it wasn't true. But he did. It was a good way of cooling down. He started to boil more coffee and then gave up. Neither of them wanted it. This was real, not soap opera. He was below, searching in his bag for his note from Stuart, when a clear and elaborate 'Ahoy, *Madrigal*' rang out.

'Well then, missy? Where's our hero?'

Sanctuary half-emerged from the main cabin, his head and shoulders poking into the open cockpit. Pete, an old blue cap covering his baldness, was grinning down at him and the boat dipped to starboard as he clambered aboard. A mellow baritone from somewhere above Sanctuary's head was full of welcome warmth.

'We thought it prudent, Mr David, to stand off until the curious policeman had taken his leave.'

Pete was laughing, both his arms about Isobel.

'This little runt had all his vents on the wind but he couldn't

162

hear a dickeybird. Why I feed him I don't know. So what did Super Sleuth have to say? Don't tell me he nicked you for cradle-snatching and taking and sailing away Queen's evidence?'

From anyone else in the circumstances, the jargoned banter would have been intolerable. From Pete, it was exactly the easy-going mood they both needed. Isobel found a strength in her voice hidden from her when Leonard had been there. She told Rusty and Pete about the note, the cocaine, the cheques, the typewriter, the green ink and the letter to Tupman. They listened in silence, Pete filling his yellowed pipe and then poking the dead match alongside the others in the thin band around his short peaked cap.

'Well? What you think, pig?'

Rusty's eyes were bigger, rounder and browner than ever. The large head propped on the stubby fist gently bounced and settled like a balloon on a breezeless pond.

'Circumstance had little respect from inquisitive lawyers. But that is of no consequence if this policeman wishes simply to close his mind to the truth and substitute a motive which, after all, however suspect it may be to us, does give him a reason for the killings. Up until now he has been without reasons.'

Isobel was shaking her head. A slow-burning anger that was yet frustration.

'You think he doesn't know that?'

'Course he does, missy. He's not stupid. He only looks it. No, I'll bet you a quid to a bent bit that he knows exactly the size of the problem. What you think, master?'

Sanctuary knew exactly what he thought. But his reason sounded just as unlikely as Leonard's evidence appeared.

'Simple at first. All this evidence turns up. Leonard can't ignore it. There's pressure on him to solve the crime, which isn't the same as making an arrest.'

He paused, regrouping his argument. Pete wore an expression which suggested that he knew what was coming, almost urging him on as a proud parent might prompt a nursery-rhyming five-year-old.

'He's a good enough policeman to know that it's very neat.

163

At the same time, it's often the case that victims are so damned arrogant, or careful or even innocent, that they don't have time to hide or destroy evidence.'

'But what about the letter to the solicitor?'

'Tupman? I don't know.'

Isobel thought she did.

'That sounded as if Stuart did have time. And what about you? He suspected something was happening or could happen, otherwise he wouldn't have got in touch with you in the first place.'

Sanctuary knew she had a point about Tupman. He had not liked the man but he was trained well enough not to let this dislike colour his judgement. The letter to the lawyer bothered him. Maybe it explained Tupman's attitude when the two had met. Pete had a simple explanation.

'If this whole thing's a set-up, then a grand confession to Tupman would be simple to fix.'

'But if Stuart had written a letter like that he wouldn't simply have stuck it in the postbox, he would have delivered it.'

'What's that supposed to mean, missy?'

Pete had got her point but he wanted Isobel to expand. He wanted to bring her into the hunting of the conundrum.

'That man Tupman would have seen Stuart and told the police that this was really the letter that Stuart gave him. That makes the idea of another forgery less likely.'

In the centre cockpit of the French sloop, the customs officer and the denimed skipper were saying goodbye. There was much smiling. They could hear them chatting farewell. On board the *Madrigal*'s coach roof, Rusty raised a point they'd all been thinking though had not mentioned.

'The cursed lawyer could indeed be solicitor to some conspiracy.'

Pete spat a shred of tobacco into the harbour.

'What the little runt means is that this Tupman matey could be in it up to his neck.'

'But the letter could be genuine.'

Sanctuary hadn't wanted to say so, but someone had to.

'We've got to accept that, whatever we may feel, none of us

164

really knew that much about Stuart. The two letters were pretty damning.'

He leant across Isobel and reached into the cabin rack where he had left the copy of the letter to the barman together with Stuart's original note to him. He showed them to Pete.

'Anything strike you as odd?'

Pete's eyes skipped back and fore like an accelerating tennis umpire. He shook his head and handed them up to Rusty. The strong white teeth enlarged his knowing smile when he spoke.

'Yes. One is typed. The one to you is handwritten. Why might this be so?'

Sanctuary nodded.

'That's what I was wondering.'

He was back on the bench and looked sideways to Isobel. Her eyes were closed, her head back, avoiding the consequences though not the conversation.

'Well?'

She opened her eyes and looked at him and shrugged.

'You heard what the police said. They found the typewriter in the cottage. It all matched, even the ink and the handwriting.'

'The trappings of the pen and machine are set easily to deceive perhaps. Our eyes guide our senses of reason and we are convinced of inevitability and, too readily perhaps, ignore possibility. Is that what you are saying, Mr David?'

Sanctuary grinned. Whitehall memoranda were easy compared to Rusty's mock rhetorical prose.

'Why should he write to me in ink and to Les and presumably Tupman on a typewriter? That's all.'

The girl spotted his mistake almost as quickly as he had.

'Because, when he wrote to you, he was in the bar and not at home.'

'Well done, missy. Bull's-eye.'

Her eyes were closed again. This time screwed up. They opened. Suddenly. Like a surprised ghost-hunter.

'Wait a minute, wait a minute. What typewriter?'

Sanctuary put his hand on her bare arm. Urging her to remember.

'Go on.'

She was wide-eyed and awake. Excited. She had discovered the seven-letter word in Stuart Fisher's confusing Scrabble.

'He didn't have one. I know, I know. Of course he didn't. I remember him showing me the word processor when he got it. He'd gone into town to buy a typewriter and they'd sold him a word processor for nearly the same money.'

'You're sure, missy? Real sure?'

'Course I am.'

She punched Pete on the knee in her excitement.

'I remember now. He was tickled pink with it. That's where I got all my letterheads and invoices. He did them on his word processor. He didn't have a typewriter.'

The question, when it came, was deeply toned and rounded of vowel.

'So, good people. Who did, we wonder?'

There was no answer.

'Okay, master. As we thought, we've got ourselves a war. Do we pull out or do we join battle?'

Sanctuary looked at the others in turn. Rusty's domed forehead was wrinkled and his eyes were wise. Trustworthy. But to what use? Isobel was no longer frightened. Her slim body was no longer tense. One brown leg rested easily against his without any need to shelter or seek protection. Uncomplicated company in a cramped cockpit. Pete, who was sitting on the chromium pushpit rail, sipping from his angled beer can, had posed the question and was now looking into the distance but tuned for an answer. When it came, it was what Pete had expected.

'What happened to Les wasn't minor league.'

'You think it's not ours, master?'

'It's not yours.'

'But you're the pro, is that it?'

Sanctuary nodded, though it was not the whole answer. When it came, it was from Isobel.

'We go for it. Whatever it is.'

'This is so unwise, and fortune will favour only the wise as three unfortunates have shown us.'

166

Isobel reached up one hand and touched Rusty's bare foot. It was a thank-you gesture.

'If we back off and let the police wrap this up as they want to, then Stuart will be remembered as nothing more than a cheap drug-runner. At least we should be trying to prove he wasn't.'

Sanctuary's hands were behind his head and he was thinking aloud again.

'Right, but let's be practical. We've no way of proving Stuart was innocent without setting ourselves up as a poor man's Pinkerton agency. If we do that, we go into the burglary business, act against the police, and risk getting thrown into jail. And we have the security guard, Stuart and Les as reminders that we may get ourselves and perhaps other people killed.'

Pete sucked at the last of his beer. Raised an eyebrow at Sanctuary.

'So when do we start? Come on, you're the one with job experience, not us.'

'How about looking inside the cottage?'

'Breaking and entering, master? That's against the law.'

'Even with a key?'

Her voice was quiet with a hint of mischief.

'You have, missy?'

She nodded.

'He gave it to me to deliver his plates. It's still hanging on the rack in my kitchen.'

28

Sanctuary's check call to Dorothea produced an unexpected bonus. She had traced the contact for Jane Fisher. The woman was living in Washington DC where she was running the European end of an import-export agency with a former American diplomat. He recognised the name. So they had stayed together. The Department's man in the embassy said they were occasional visitors to diplomatic parties, especially trade and cultural receptions. Anything on the partner? Dorothea was guarded. It was an open line.

'You might have met him during your Sad Sam days. He was a Company man.'

'Still?'

'Not officially. He left his former employers when he and Mrs Fisher went into, eh, partnership. On the other hand . . .'

'He keeps in touch.'

'And he could be very backroom.'

'Where is she now?'

'Washington, as far as we know. Why?'

'I'm not sure. She is, from memory, an unpredictable woman.'

'Not quite the stereotype embassy wife it says here.'

He remembered the next morning and the taunting invitation to dinner when Stuart got back from Warsaw.

Dorothea's edgy voice brought him back. The Deputy had asked after his health. She had been bothered by his contact call from the island. There was also a general Z-Note on the investigation.

'That makes it official, Davy. Hands off. This one's not for us. No one will mind if you come in.'

'I would.'

He was calling from a harbourside doorless telephone. The overalled man waiting to use the box was pacing a few feet away. Discreet just, but making it clear that he disapproved of reverse-charge calls. Feeding small coins encouraged brevity. Dorothea was reading from her briefing notes.

'We hear it was drugs.'

'Wrong.'

'How wrong?'

'Very.'

The man had lit another cigarette and made sure David could see him looking at his wrist-watch. Dorothea was trying to cool Sanctuary's frustration.

'The plods are happy.'

'We're about to change that.'

'Who we?'

He could hear the anxiety.

'Must go, someone here.'

'Davy, be very careful. There's something else you ought to know.'

'Quickly then.'

'Ignatiev's definitely out.'

'Where?'

'Last heard, via Cairo.'

'Why there?'

'We're not sure, but he is.'

'Look, I must go. See if you can find out what he was doing, will you?'

'I'm on to it now, but there's little to go on. And there's something else.'

'I'll call you later. Just one thing, see if there's anything on Fisher in Cairo during the past few months.'

'Was he?'

'How the hell do I know? That's why I'm asking. Bye.'

Even as he replaced the receiver and apologised to the workman for hogging the only box on that side of the basin he was quietly cursing himself. He had been rude, which was not in his nature. He had been rude to the one person he could trust. He nodded to the workman, got into his car and headed for town. As he drove, Sanctuary worried about the news of Ignatiev. The GRU had trained him, sent him to the special forces, the Spetsnaz, where he had been trained to kill. Ignatiev had enjoyed the training. His file said so. Sanctuary knew it off by heart. He had written it. Dorothea should have known more. He wondered who did and why they weren't telling her.

When he caught up with Leonard, Sanctuary told him about the word processor. Leonard listened politely. Upstairs, the Old Man had been happy with the situation report. They both accepted that, for the moment, there was little chance of an arrest. The Old Man wasn't even too sure that he wanted one. The evidence would go down in court even if it were genuine. They both knew that. Sanctuary's story about the word processor was worth a look but it was just as circumstantial.

'Just because Miss Rolfe didn't see a typewriter doesn't mean that it didn't exist. And we have it. If he had thought of buying one it could have been because he wanted to replace one. I have to tell you, we are satisfied. The typewriter is real. We are in the processing of double-checking and matching the type and keys. Besides, I don't imagine even Miss Rolfe saw everything he had.'

He skipped on, ignoring Sanctuary's look of disgust at the cheap jibe.

'Perhaps he used it for things he didn't want to keep on disk.'

'He could have wiped anything he didn't want to save.'

'A typewriter is very convenient even in this day of megabyte efficiency. Put in the paper and off you go.'

Leonard tapped his fingers on the desk, demonstrating his point if not his touch-typing.

'No switching on. No loading. No messing about with printers.'

He folded his arms. His point was made. It was, as the Old Man had remarked, very tidy. That bothered him. He didn't tell Sanctuary that.

'You don't want to believe it, do you? You're happy with *prima facie* evidence and that's it as far as you're concerned.'

'If that's meant to be provocative it won't work. What's your version then?'

170

'Stuart Fisher discovered something which he thought was of national importance. Someone killed him because he was getting too close to whatever was the truth of the matter. To give you and whoever else might be officially interested a motive for his death, they rigged the drug-running. QED.'

Leonard smiled the smile of the don hearing out the sincere but harmless hypothesis of his research student.

'What about the barman?'

'It enforced the drugs story. It was also possible that he knew something. Don't forget, barmen see and hear things when others believe them out of sight and earshot. As a bonus it was a very explicit warning sign.'

'Which you intend to ignore?'

'Don't you?'

'I'm a policeman, Mr Sanctuary. You, as I understand it, are a tourist. Officially on leave. No official, nor semi-official, standing.'

'Right.'

'But you're here.'

'Right.'

'Again.'

'How do you rate Tupman?'

'Surely he's not part of your conspiracy theory.'

'Why not?'

'Tupman is one of the great bores of the northern hemisphere. He was born here, educated privately just twenty miles away. Boarded from the age of eight. Took a first at Oxford. Returned here to become a junior partner in a law practice started by his great-grandfather. He is not simply a pillar of society, he *is* society, under which all pillars uphold everything he stands for.'

Sanctuary, head on one side, contemplated Leonard's face. The curly hair, the freckles he had not before noticed, the blinking eyes, the gold-rimmed spectacles. Still the intelligent veneer? Or the real thing?

'Fisher left me a letter saying he was on to something.'

'Of course.'

'Why of course?'

'Otherwise you wouldn't be so certain of your ground. I believe you when you say he was not an exceptional friend, so why else would you be determined to set aside our evidence?'

The real thing.

'You would like to see it?'

'Of course.'

'May I see Stuart's letter to Tupman?'

It was in yet another buff folder. Again, a copy. The original was in a plastic envelope locked in a grey locker along the corridor. The contents were more or less as recited by Leonard on the boat. Typed and unremarkable. Two points bothered David. He said so.

'The typing's perfect.'

'Reasonably. Under a glass it's uneven. The Qwerty row is inconsistent, differing pressures, which suggests that it wasn't a trained typist, more likely an amateur – self-taught. Fisher was self-taught. We've seen his Navy record. No courses.'

'I didn't mean that. There are no mistakes. No crossings-out. No whiting-out. That's not bad for two pages of confession presumably under some stress.'

Leonard picked up the copy and traced it line by line. Without looking up he nodded agreement.

'You said two points.'

'Instead of Yours sincerely, he signs off Yours aye.'

'Very Royal Navy. Even more reason to believe it genuine.'

'Yes, very Navy, but not in this context. It's normally used informally and therefore usually to friends. I hardly imagine Tupman was a friend. A confession's pretty formal.'

'A slip of the pen.'

Sanctuary did not contradict the policeman. The fact that he was offering an explanation suggested Leonard was having doubts.

'Is the typewriter here or in his cottage?'

'Here, why?'

'Just wondered. Would you have any objections if I had a look in the cottage?'

'You know better than that.'

Sanctuary's shoulders signalled it was an idle request.

172

On his way back to the basin, Sanctuary made a detour. He had intended waiting until nightfall. That was at least six hours away. The Deputy's nervousness meant he could not afford six hours. Isobel's instructions hadn't been hard to follow. There were a few flint houses, but this was the only one by itself, thatched and on a bend. As he slowed to get a better look, a green car was trying to get out into the lane. It was a dangerous bend. Perkins recognised the Alfa Romeo. It was no use trying to hide. He stopped and went over.

'I know I'm not allowed in, but would you mind if I looked at the outside?'

Perkins wasn't sure. There'd be no instructions on looking. Looking at what? Sanctuary simply wanted to glance around to see where his dead friend had lived. Perkins didn't mind as long as he touched nothing. He stayed in the car for a couple of minutes, but when Sanctuary had not reappeared from the back garden he heaved himself out of the protesting Vauxhall and waddled along the side path to find him.

Sanctuary had already looked into the back porch. The half-glass door was mortice-locked and bolted from the inside. The small French window to the dining-room was bolted. No lock. The top windows were wooden and sashed. There was a burglar-alarm box above the reeded bathroom window. Sanctuary could see it was a dummy. He fingered the door key in his pocket. It would have to stay there. The front of the house was hardly hidden from passers-by and certainly not from stout policemen.

Perkins turned the corner on cue to find Sanctuary sitting on the garden bench enjoying the sunny view across flat grassland. He had been waiting for the policeman to seek him out. He wanted Perkins to talk to him.

'I got to be getting back. You know, things.'

'You want me to go then?'

'Be better.'

'I'm not going to break in if that's what you're thinking.'

Perkins looked at one shoe.

'Not really.'

He looked up. He didn't like dealing with this Sanctuary. He was official somewhere and that made Perkins uneasy.

'I saw the Chief Inspector earlier. He seems to think it's all cut and dried. Drugs. What do you think?'

Their meeting would get back. Better to keep it above board. Apparently. Sanctuary was smiling. Seemed relaxed enough. Nice enough bloke really. Not many people ever asked Perkins what he thought.

'Looks like it. It's usually something like that. There's always a reason.'

The high voice had more to come.

'People are not always what they seem. Sorry about that.'

Sanctuary waved a hand.

'Thanks. I'm not sure the Chief Inspector's right. But he could be. After all, you've more experience of this sort of thing than I have.'

'Surprising how things turn out. Look at this place for example, he's got it all there. Makes you wonder then, don't it?'

'Got all what there?'

Perkins thought it was obvious. To him it was.

'Well, I mean. Nice little place like this. All done up. Must be worth a tidy sum. What's he want to get into exotics for? Nice pension coming in from the Navy people. Then there was the business. He wasn't short of a bob or two. Was he?'

'I didn't realise he had a business. Exactly what I was talking about. You people are the pros. Something that doesn't make sense to me does to you.'

Perkins smiled and sat on the bench beside Sanctuary. He was right of course. Policework was putting together all the small things. Some people didn't appreciate that. Some times even the guvnor thought it was a waste of time. He, Perkins, didn't. It was all right being flash and having degrees and things but, when it came down to getting a good nick, well, it was being a good copper, wasn't it? No good getting someone in the hurry-up wagon if some smart-arse brief gets it blown out of court. Was there?

174

Sanctuary nodded in admiration. Perkins liked that. This one was okay. Bit toffee, but okay.

'So when someone goes bent you have to look outside as well as in. Could be a woman. Could be he needs money.'

His laugh nudged Sanctuary in the ribs.

'Course, could be both.'

Sanctuary added his knowing chuckle to the chorus. Spear-carrying to Perkins wasn't difficult.

'Why would he need money? You said he was comfortable. A business?'

Perkins had found the remains of a half-eaten chocolate bar. He was carefully picking pieces of pocket fluff from its naked end. He offered it to Sanctuary who shook his head and waited. Perkins took a bite.

'Take the business. Import-export. Well, it all looks good on that computer of his. Fancy places. Big-time addresses. Freight numbers a mile long. But the truth is, well,' he munched at the last dark segment, 'it didn't add up to a row of beans, did it?'

'No?'

'Course not. Wasn't a brass farthing coming in. All wind and piss. Nothing in the kitty. I know, it was me who had to check his bank account.'

Perkins gave him one of his smiles, difficult to spot beneath the beard. It was time to go. Perkins had other things to say, but nothing of importance. The six hours were now important. There were things to be done.

Instead of turning for the coast road, Sanctuary drove back to the town. He was wondering how he could unofficially get sight of Fisher's bank statements. The Department could do it in a couple of hours. The Department wanted to stay out of this. He found a pay 'phone and called Dorothea again.

'I'm sorry.'

Her laugh was warm.

'Don't be silly. Just take great care.'

'Don't worry.'

'At least allow me to do that, Davy.'

Sanctuary pictured her. Remembered again the warmth of the park.

175

'Okay, nanny. Listen, there's something else. Can you get sight of Fisher's bank statements?'

She promised to do what she could without raising blood pressures. Priestly was in the room. Sanctuary could hear his smile in Dorothea's voice. She told him also what he had failed to hear when last they spoke. Fisher had been involved in a minor scandal when he was in Cairo. Drugs were used at a party of junior diplomats and businessmen. The evidence suggested Fisher had been the supplier.

'Why didn't we know about this before? When he was on the books?'

'Apparently the whole thing was hushed up. No one wanted a fuss because it involved a couple of dips.'

'Who?'

'We don't know.'

'Someone must.'

'Does it matter?'

He thought about it for a moment, tapping his fingers on the glass door.

'I suppose not. Where was the report, though? That matters.'

'It's only just appeared. It was kept in Black in case it was needed.'

'In our Black?'

'Right. It wasn't so much against him, but there was always the chance that one of the businessmen or the foreign dips might be useful one day and a little reminder might sway them along our aisle. Usual thing.'

'We're sure?'

'Yes. Sorry.'

Dorothea was telling him that his hypotheses and refusal to believe the obvious were losing him credibility with the Deputy – his only ally. He knew that.

'I take it there's nothing more on Ignatiev. Was he there at the same time?'

'Nothing. Don't know. Not yet. We've got pretty limited access on this one. Slavonic's being unhelpful and Cairo as usual spends most of its rain-forest budget on watching other

176

Arabs. I'm still trying. But frankly I'm drawing blanks all round.'

'Blocking or nothing there anyway?'

'Bit of both.'

'That means we're on to something. Keep going at Ignatiev. Try the GRU watchers. They must have something.'

'Davy, we have no official interest. It's like trying to get a sirloin from a starving lion.'

'What about this man, Pete Hogarth? What about Interpol? That's all open source.'

'Nothing. Not unless you can give me any more. Okay?'

He said yes and was about to put down the telephone when another thought struck him; it was an obvious one which was perhaps why he'd missed it.

'Just one more favour for the computer. See if there's anything under the *Madrigal*.'

Sanctuary was feeling gloomy as he walked back past the cathedral to where he'd left his car. Where was Ignatiev? He was too big to disappear and clever enough to do just that. There was something else bothering him. Tupman and the blasted letter. He was certain the lawyer was hiding something.

He called into the office but Tupman was out. The receptionist was memorably frosty. He was walking through a crooked back street, deep in thought, when he caught an uncertain, but cheerful hello and looked up to see the brighter side of Tupman & Frobisher half-smiling, but going by. He called out and Mrs Dent stopped. The smile was there still.

'I thought you were ignoring me now you're a ship-owner.'

They exchanged pleasantries and banter about no Greek tycoon having to live afloat and it was a simple and casual meeting until Sanctuary asked about the missing letter. Mrs Dent's professional mask did not quite hide her easy-going nature, but she clearly had no wish to get mixed up with something she thought was a matter for the partners. He pressed her in the most general manner and she said that she had never heard of anything other than the document she had witnessed.

'Mind you, if Tupman received it directly from Commander Fisher, there may have been an instruction to keep its very

177

existence secret. People have very odd requests. Ask Mr Tupman, he would know.'

'I did. It seems to have slipped his mind.'

'Not a figment of yours?'

'Stuart Fisher was not the sort of man to make mistakes.'

There was an edge to his voice that lowered the legal portcullis. She was tall. Her glasses were large, oval-framed. He could see from the curve of the lens they were not worn for cosmetic reasons. Mrs Dent had a very serious gaze when she wished. The tortoiseshell spectacles gave her an almost academic air which he found quite trusting and rode easily with her cheerful features. Now her look was considered and her words carefully chosen.

'Without being callous, Mr Sanctuary, and without any experience in these matters, I imagine that people like your friend who are in a position of considerable danger are prone to making mistakes which they would otherwise avoid.'

'Is that what your boss told you to say, Mrs Dent?'

'Good afternoon, Mr Sanctuary.'

She was gone, her wicker shopping-basket firmly in the crook of one arm, before he could apologise for what the Deputy would have called a particularly unhelpful and tactically weak remark.

He found Pete and Isobel where Rusty said they would be – in the yacht club bar. Roberts was talking to them and Sanctuary's arrival pleased him. The Secretary was now part of the circle.

'I was just giving our friends here a sitrep. We've had all the Press down here all day. I've given more interviews than Elvis's mother. They took their time catching on but, now they have, well, they needed a bit of talking to. Give them something to write up and they'll go away happy instead of pestering.'

Sanctuary was glad he had not been around. The Deputy didn't really need one of his people splashed over the tabloids.

'Tell David the rest. It's too amazing.'

Isobel's voice was dull. Disappointed. Weary once more.

Roberts smirked. He could handle it. No problem.

'Oh, them? We've had another visit from the local sheriff. Very interesting so to speak, as the Chinese say.'

Pete looked about him as if he were searching for a cuspidor.

'The guy's full of shit. He reckons that Les was not only into running, he probably had something to do with Stuart's murder.'

Roberts was not letting another moment of glory pass him by. He knew how to pull an audience. He bent his head and lowered his voice to not much above a whisper. It worked. The three of them instinctively leaned towards his platform.

'The latest constabulary theory is that Les had something on Stuart, probably about the drugs, told whoever Mr Big was and Mr B waits across the creek, pulls the trigger and then wastes poor old Les because he knows too much. Not bad, eh?'

Sanctuary was furious.

'What in hell's name made him say something like that?'

Roberts's head was as steady as a glazed toby jug. He held their attention if not their admiration.

'Oh no. Not Leonard. The other one, the fat slob. He was in my office most of lunchtime. Sniffing around for info. Course I never told him a thing he couldn't have found out if he used his eyes and ears. But that one's used to exercising his gnashers not his brain.'

The eyes flicked from face to face searching for reaction.

'Why tell them anything? It all seems so horrid. Now everyone believes Stuart was into drugs. I even had him,' with her eyes, Isobel pointed to the red stripe in his usual spot at the end of the bar, 'suggesting that I must have known about it.'

Roberts was about to launch into another round of his conversation with Perkins when Pete slid from his stool and touched Isobel on the arm. He had heard and had enough.

'Come on, missy.' He nodded to Sanctuary. 'We'll see you back on board, master.'

His snub to Roberts and half-wave to Sanctuary were on the hoof before Roberts could register his surprise and adjust his authority. Pete was off with Isobel at his side. The Secretary's recovery was tinged with enough bitterness to obscure any dignity he had hoped to salvage. Roberts, more than most, felt

179

real or imagined insults and had never doubted the satisfaction of revenge.

'If he thinks he can jump in where Stuart left off, he's another thought coming, I can tell you.'

He nodded furiously.

'Perhaps he simply thought it was better to spare her any more details. She's pretty upset still.'

Roberts looked at Sanctuary with the nearest he ever showed to surprise.

'Don't tell me our little Miss Stuck-up's got you on a string as well?'

'Not at all. I'm just making the point. He's been a good friend and that's what she needs at the moment. It can't be very nice for a woman to be living an easy-going life and within a couple of weeks be worried stiff that someone might stick a knife into her.'

'Well, I'll tell you something on the old net. Between you and me, Okay?'

He paused, looking for Sanctuary's nod of consent. He continued without it.

'He's the last little bastard I'd trust my daughter with, or anyone else for that matter. Mr-yo-ho-ho-Hogarth knows all about sticking knives in people. Receiving me?'

Roberts looked at his watch. It was a large, important-looking chronometer, not the sort that comes with a five-litre can of engine oil. He was in his time-is-money mode. Red stripe was hunch-backed, sipping coffee from a polystyrene cup and doing what he did most of the time he wasn't sailing – eavesdropping. Very few took him seriously. Most knew that he made up what he didn't overhear. That was the difference between red stripe and the Secretary. Roberts would reach conclusions, but never jump to them. Years in the Navy had taught him to keep everything he knew close to his chest and let it out a piece at a time and then at a price. Which was what he was doing now. Sanctuary made an opening bid.

'I must say it's good to have someone with your background on tap. There's something to be said for being able to patch into the old net.'

180

Roberts had spent a lot of his life not being appreciated, which was one of the reasons he kept very much to himself. Keeping mum meant not having to remember the aitches. He liked metaphors did Roberts. He liked Sanctuary's sentiment. This fellow was right of course. Being on the old net was invaluable. Not many were. He accepted Sanctuary's generous offer. After all he didn't know too much and unlike red stripe he was not about to add fiction to fact. Fiction got found out and that meant being embarrassed. Roberts nodded to the door through which Pete had disappeared with Isobel.

'He's got a bit of form. That's all.'

Sanctuary worked on what he hoped was a admiring smile.

'Trust you to know.'

Roberts picked up the bonus and leant against the bar. To a stranger, he could have been a member. Only to a stranger.

'Something to do with laundering money from something big. Bullion, they say.'

'Who says?'

Roberts tapped the side of his nose. Now that would be telling, said his finger. Sanctuary needed a little more.

'How much? Where?'

'The word is it was in the big Ks. One guess was low millions. The money went the Costa del Blag route.'

'Spain?'

'That's right. Hilltop haciendas or whatever they have. Time-share apartments. He fixed it and took twenty per cent.'

'When?'

'Five years back.'

'This is good stuff?'

'I only deal in quality, Mr Sanctuary, only quality.'

The water-colour eyes told Sanctuary nothing more. He wondered why Dorothea's computer had not identified Peter Hogarth especially as it was connected to the Security network throughout Western Europe.

'What's that got to do with knives? Money-broking is something of a grey legal argument.'

'Oh, his kind are all above board when it comes to the business side. No, Mr Sanctuary. I suspect there was never a

181

balance sheet out of place. But, as you know, it's not only thieves who fall out.'

'He had a partner?'

'Two of them. One of them did more than fall out. He fell overboard. They say it was in Biscay. Bit of a green one blowing at the time. Our Mr Hogarth's partner took an unscheduled make-and-mend over the side. Most unfortunate. For him.'

'No suggestion of foul play though?'

Roberts's laugh was carefully rehearsed. Cynical and worldly wise.

'Oh, plenty of suggestion but no proof and then there was the other one. The other partner. Got pissed one night in Marbella and ended up with a knife between the ribs.'

'Where was Pete at the time?'

'In bed with his alibi.'

'But nobody ever proved anything.'

'Shouldn't imagine the old spics tried very hard. Just crossed the two of them off the unwanted list.'

Sanctuary tried to imagine how much was true and how much hearsay. He came to the conclusion that for the moment it did not matter. He would speak again to Dorothea. But there was one loose end dangling that Roberts might tuck in.

'And Rusty? Where does he come into all this?'

The Secretary did not know any more. He looked at his wrist-watch and then at the bar clock. With a promise to see Sanctuary later, Roberts slipped away under cover of time and a pressing engagement.

When Sanctuary got to Pete's boat, it was getting dark. His thoughts about Roberts's information were not clear. Roberts could be repeating rumours and attempting to give them some authority in order to advance his own reputation. Even if it were true, so what? Did that make Pete any less of an ally? Could he be mixed up with Stuart's death? For the moment Sanctuary's main concern was the cottage. He had not really expected to see it that afternoon, but under cover of darkness it would be pretty simple to get in, find the water-colours and, if Perkins had not confiscated them, the disks showing Stuart

182

Fisher's business affairs – or, if the fat policeman were to be believed, lack of them. Pete immediately agreed that there was no need for them all to go. Rusty intoned ideas of what he called 'diversionary tactics'.

Isobel insisted. If he was going so was she. She pulled on denims and an old blue sweatshirt without waiting for any argument. She knew the inside of the cottage and where the water-colours were. Pete and Rusty stayed on board. A little music and activity might be amusing if they were being watched. It meant also that any watchers' resources would be stretched if they split up. Sanctuary did not mind too much. If there were dangers, they would be in the harbour where everyone knew he and Isobel were, not at the cottage. He wanted also to talk to Isobel about Pete.

Sitting alongside her, one foot propped on the dashboard ledge as she drove her bumping, noisy truck at breakneck speed, he told Isobel Roberts's story. The girl was less than impressed although more and more she was learning to trust nobody.

'That man's a nasty bit of work. Why believe him?'

'He didn't make a big deal of it.'

He didn't tell her of Roberts's suggestion that Pete had designs on her.

'There's always malicious gossip. Most of them in the club haven't anything else to do.'

'This isn't most of them. It's only Roberts.'

'He's no proof.'

As she said it, Isobel remembered the past few hours and the way she had learned that proof could be arranged to suit the occasion.

They drove past the cottage and along the road for a mile and then turned down the lane leading to the pottery. There was half-moonlight. Enough to see by. They parked the red truck close to the pottery and she led the way across the back garden and over a stile into a darkened pasture. She knew the way and within twenty minutes they had crossed the field without disturbing a dairy herd, skirted a copse and fetched up

183

on the nettle and orchard patch behind Stuart Fisher's empty cottage.

Sanctuary tried the wall and a couple of loose flints fell. He cursed softly. He saw nothing.

For ten minutes they rested easily by the low wall, watching for any sign that they had been seen. There was enough light for a sentry to have noticed their approach through the platoons of apples and pears. The occasional car's headlights caught the side of the building or the hedge, but none slowed for more than the bend. No driver's head turned to where they might have been seen. Without speaking, he led the way to the side path and they crouched again. Three more minutes. But nothing moved. He nodded and within thirty seconds they were in the front porch and then into the still house. The front door opened onto the living-room and they waited again for their eyes to clear through the gloom. Sanctuary, with a finger to his lips, watched from the edge of the front window. Apart from a few more cars, there were no signs of prying eyes. Isobel went through to the tiny kitchen to watch from the back of the house. She returned and smiled the all-clear. He put his hand over hers as she instinctively reached for the light switch and shaded his torch beam, keeping the diffused light low to the red carpet and away from the window. In the corner, on a leather-topped partner's desk, was what Sanctuary was looking for. The grey computer and keyboard were standard units. They were plugged in. He angled the screen towards the wall and pulled Isobel towards the desk.

'Stand there. Try and block as much light when I turn it on.'

'Why not draw the curtains?'

'Because the plods would know they weren't drawn when they left.'

'But there's no one there.'

'We don't know that. Stop arguing.'

'Why are we whispering?'

He grinned and switched on.

'Because it's romantic. Now, keep your eye on the road.'

Within a few seconds Sanctuary had the menu on the screen and was scanning the processed envelopes of titles. He had clicked into four lots of accounts before he found what he was looking for and then only because the title jarred. Kukla. It was not in Cyrillic. It did not have to be. The transliteration was simple enough. Kukla, the Russian word for doll. Sanctuary called up the file just as Perkins had. It was all there. Or, rather, very little was. The Kukla International Transaction Agency showed a series of import and export dates, cheques in, cheques out, an address in Arlington, Virginia, a second in Geneva and a third in Cairo. The accounts were simple. Perkins had been spot-on. Freight details were in commercial codes and numbers. There was no description of what was being imported and exported. Costs appeared to balance income. The bottom line of the Kukla International Transaction Agency was a long zero, nor was there any indication of directors. Sanctuary wondered who was pulling the Kukla strings. When had Stuart Fisher joined them and what had he joined? On a stand by the desk was a laser printer. Sanctuary wondered. This was a pretty sophisticated package. Hardly a bargain substitute for a type-writer. He clicked the mouse and cursed the warm hum of the printer. While he was waiting he flipped through a box of disks. The rest were straightforward. Household accounts, navigation programmes, boatyard and sailing expenses and back-up disks. He was tempted to slip them into his pocket, but reckoned the police would have a detailed note of everything in the house including the software. The last page came through the printer and he tucked the accounts into his shirt and switched off.

'Right, where are the pictures?'

'In front of you.'

There were six water-colours hanging in a square in clip frames. In the dim light they meant little to Sanctuary. He could see they were coastlines painted from seaward. They appeared to be different views of the same place although neither of them could identify the stretch of land. He stared at them for five minutes, trying to memorise the main features. Perhaps Pete would know. He must have seen most of the local coasts, assuming that's what they were. The paintings were in blues and greens for the sea and browns and whites for the land, with distinctive black flicks for buildings and landmarks.

They had one thing in common: they were poorly painted. Stuart Fisher was clearly no artist. Yet he had thought them worth framing and hanging. Why?

Isobel was running her torch back and forth across the desk top. She then opened each drawer.

'Notice anything odd?'

There was a wisp of triumph in her question.

'What?'

'No spare ribbons. No Tipp-Ex. No carbon paper. For someone who is supposed to have had a typewriter that's odd, don't you think?'

A car sped past, breaking sharply for the bend and throwing a beam of headlight into the room. Instinctively, Isobel swung and half-toppled. He caught her by the shoulders. Neither moved. And then the light was gone. Sanctuary did not let go. For a moment, the magic of conspirators was recaptured and she leant easily against him, her head close into his chest. The moment went by just as did another car.

'What's upstairs?'

'How should I know?'

Isobel's answer was sharp enough for Sanctuary to regret having asked. He reached for her hand and tugged in the direction of the narrow dark stairway.

'Do we have to? We've got what we came for.'

He could hear the nervousness in her voice.

'You never know. There may be something.'

'What?'

'Haven't a clue. May as well take a look. You wait here. Don't move.'

'Don't worry. I won't.'

The mock nervousness, even whispered, was convincing. He kissed her forehead, smiled though she could not see it, and turned to the steep stairs.

He allowed a full beam of his torch. At the top he could see three open doorways. As he approached, the one ahead reflected his light from the tile and chrome. The bathroom. He switched off and felt his way to the small landing. He turned to what must have been the back bedroom and looked back to

186

see Isobel halfway up the narrow stairs, holding on to both bannisters as if ghosts were about to spring from the very walls. Sanctuary grinned.

'I said wait there. I'll just check.'

Even in the half-light he could make out the brass bedstead and heavy Victorian mirrored wardrobe sticking out into the small room like an elaborately carved blockhouse. There was another seascape on the alcoved wall above a bow-fronted chest of drawers. He stepped around the bed to get a closer look. As he did so, he caught a shadow movement at the bevelled edge of the looking glass. Instinct threw his arm into the air and he started to cry out a warning. His feeble arm was swept away. His voice was never heard. A massive pain burst through the side of his head, then another at the front, and he felt himself going down with a roaring in his ears and a shower of red light across his closed eyes. Somewhere through a dark, spinning, disappearing tunnel a shrill frightened scream tried to get through.

29

Priestly had dined well. Yet again. Now he was smiling the smile of those with a talent to damn. He had walked across St James's Park and, although it was gone eleven o'clock, had returned to the Department as a matter of tactical course. Dropping in late in the evening meant that he was seen to be interested rather than keen, and it required no effort. Nor did his visits inconvenience his home life. He had none. Priestly's rooms, like his mind, were well organised and uncluttered by close friendships. There was no one to go home to and a chance meeting with, say, the Deputy was always of value, or most certainly could be if played correctly. Priestly played every public opportunity correctly.

This evening, there had been no Deputy, only Dorothea. She too had dined, but with friends, and her loose summer frock – Priestly imagined Dorothea in frocks, never dresses – almost roused Priestly's long-buried desires for young company. Priestly preferred the company of older women. They tended to like him and often had influential husbands. He had picked up Sanctuary's file from Dorothea's desk and for the first time had seen the extent of the mystery surrounding Stuart Fisher's death.

He had every right to read the file, except that there was an unwritten rule which said that unless a member of the Department needed to read a file, then it was better that she or he did not. Priestly rarely observed unwritten rules unless he had created them.

'Our David's beach seems full of exciting games. I do hope he will not let us down.'

'You surprise me.'

Dorothea watched him flipping over the green-covered file.

188

'No, I don't. You're being deliciously sarcastic. Why is Sanctuary involved still? I thought we were warned off?'

'He's on leave.'

'Come now, my dear. That contrived moment is long past. Why, I repeat, is our little boy playing in the sand?'

Dorothea got up and looked at the overnight tray. There was nothing of importance there. A couple of Grade IIs from Washington. The usual assessment of the parlous state of the Russian leadership. A backgrounder on the next day's meeting of the US Secretary of State and his Israeli counterpart. Six lines on unofficial weapons sales by the Ukrainians and a summary of the latest satellite intelligence – or so the Americans said. They were five hours behind London and their close-of-play reports always had an urgency that never quite made it across the Atlantic. Nevertheless, Dorothea studied them with the sort of attention she normally reserved for an interesting lunch menu. Priestly was amused.

'You do realise that three murders is no place for any of our team. Nasty gutter Press gather on these occasions and we wouldn't want dear David to be the subject of speculation, would we?'

'He knows how to look after himself.'

'You do not sound at all convincing, my sweet. Not at all. Nor did you on the telephone today.'

'It's difficult enough without anyone trying to put the boot in from this end.'

She was reading still and wished she had not said it. There was no need to antagonise Priestly. But his reaction was not what she expected.

'Are you two, ah, just close friends?'

'Sorry?'

She looked up. But Priestly had stabbed and was now back in his file. When he spoke, the exchange had never taken place. The point never raised.

'What do we know about this little boy? Ah,' he peered at the file, 'ah, Benjamin Lomax.'

She was back at her desk, wondering if there would be a late check-call from Davy and how she would handle it in front of Priestly.

'Nothing. Should we? He's just a local kid who may or not have seen something. The police have nothing on him.'

'And his parents?'

'Not that I know. Should we have?'

'I suppose not. As you so correctly remind me, dear Dorothea, this is a police matter and we have no interest apart from it being something of a pastime for David.'

'What sort of thing should we have?'

Charles Priestly was far from being Dorothea's favourite person in the Department, but she knew him to be one of the brightest. When he said something that concerned a project or programme, she took note. She had to. Others were always interested.

'Well, my dear, there's nothing here about the evidence he has thus far given. Nothing on his parents, especially his father. I knew some Sussex Lomaxes once, though I hardly imagine from this address that they were the same family. And there is no police assessment. How odd. Don't you think?'

'Nothing to say?'

'Now that I would call odd. And nothing on protection.'

'Mind you, there's no suggestion that he's in any danger. You see that David went to talk to the mother.'

'But got no further than not today thank you.'

'Perhaps there's no reason to get further than that.'

'And perhaps, perhaps, dear Dorothea, other visitors to Lomax Towers might not be so personably polite as David.'

He was right. She said she would mention it to Sanctuary next time he came up. Priestly liked that. It was nice to see Dorothea acknowledging his authority. Yes, he liked it. But he was not yet finished.

'And should we not be asking about this, ah, Miss Rolfe? After all, his initial report was interesting. Then nothing. It would seem that the young lady has found a way of persuading our little boy that she's above suspicion. How clever of her, don't you think?'

30

Sanctuary moved but did not moan. It was dark. He was lying face-down on a carpet. The carpet was wet. Sticky. So was the side of his head. It was blood-sticky. His blood. There was quite a lot of it. Some of it was weeping through a slowly congealing gash across the eyebrow, beneath which the eye was swollen to the size of an avocado stone and closed. The other eye was pressed into the bloodied carpet. It made seeing difficult. His head felt as if an axe had only just failed to cleave it in two and he lay, still wondering where he was. He could hear breathing. It was his but it took him a few seconds to realise that. The sound in his head was clogged, then lunging and buzzing to the front of his brain and reverberating around what were supposed to be the hollow places. Instead they were stuffed with coloured pains. He tried to listen for outside sounds. He did not know if he could hear any. It began to dawn on him that he knew exactly where he was. The musty material by his open eye was the heavy drape of a candlewick bedspread. It was Stuart Fisher's bed. He was, presumably, where he had fallen. He rolled as best he could. The bedroom door was open, a small cane chair on its side stopped it from closing. He wondered if it were there deliberately.

When he moved again, he thought his back was broken. It wasn't but he was quite willing to believe it was. Something, someone, had worked him over. He had never hurt like this. He was pretty sure that he was alone in the room. If there anyone around he could hardly take them by surprise. In his state, he wouldn't have lasted one round with a teddy bear. And then, as his head started to spin in a different direction, he remembered Isobel. Where was she? Remembered her clutching the bannister rail. Apprehensive. Afraid. Of what?

191

Had she known? Of course not. Of course? He managed to get to his feet and then stumbled. He wanted to throw up. Heroes were supposed to be made of better stuff than this. Heroes were lucky. They were scheduled to appear in the next reel. He wasn't sure he was still in the script. By the time he made it downstairs his eyes had become playful binoculars sliding in and out of vision. But he could see as much as he needed to. The main room was empty. He lurched into the kitchen. Bare.

Isobel had gone.

His head protested and his stomach came up in sympathy. He collapsed over the kitchen sink. The cold water cleared his head until he stood upright. He unbolted the back door and stood for a couple of minutes dragging in cool night air.

It took time, but eventually he could stand. In the living-room, a small, leather-topped wine table was on its side. He didn't know if he had knocked it over or whether it was a sign of a struggle. There was none other. The front door was shut and he could hear the unconcerned ticking of the mantelpiece clock.

He was tempted to switch on the lights. But didn't. His torch was probably somewhere upstairs. A car went by, its headlights sweeping the living-room wall for a brief moment. The paintings were there still and the computer. He felt in his shirt. The spreadsheet of Kukla's business efforts was gone. So was the box of disks he had left by the keyboard. How long had he been unconscious? He peered at his wrist-watch. His vision couldn't cope and in the half-light his watch was dull and time-less.

Steadying himself against the mantel he focused on the clock. The green luminous hands were at one minute to seven. Sanctuary shook his head, slowly. He could not have been out all night. Anyway, by seven o'clock it would be broad daylight. He stared at the clock. It had to be right because it was wired up to the mains. His mind was yelling instructions. Trying to get through the fuzzy pain. But it was clockwork. A cocky, tin-cased, twin-belled, wind-up-and-get-you-up alarm clock. And it had not been there when they broke in. Now the yell became a scream. It was coming up to the hour. Suddenly his head was as clear as the bells that were about to ring. The big hand was reaching for the twelve as he ran for the back door, sprinted across the small garden and hurled himself with a great roar of anger and pain over the low wall into the nettles and clumped grass of the scruffy orchard.

He hit the ground as the bomb exploded.

It is surprising how much energy is left and how much pain is overcome when the mind is frightened. Sanctuary dragged himself in agonies of mind and body away from the wall and across the orchard. Keeping to the thick hawthorn hedging, he made his way back the way the girl had led him from the pottery. A couple of times he paused to catch his breath, throw up, take bearings and listen for wailing police and fire alarms. When they came they seemed distant and remote from the loneliness he felt. His first priority had been to get away. Now he paused by the stile to check his injuries. The right eye had gone fifteen rounds with a contender and would remember every jab and cross for days to come. He could only feel the side of his head but, with his index and middle finger like blunt scissors, he found the deep ridge beneath the drying blood. He ripped his sleeve from his shirt to make a rough bandage that could cover the whole of the top of his head. He explored his spine and rib-cage. He was sure something had cracked and his lung hurt. He spat onto the wooden foot-bar of the stile. No blood. One kind of mercy, he thought.

For perhaps twenty minutes he watched the outline of the pottery and Isobel's house. He could see the cab of the truck even though it was in a shadow of the converted barn but there was no sign of life. He kept watching. There had been no sign of life at Stuart Fisher's cottage.

Sanctuary approached the house from the back. The windows were uncovered and, as he moved from back to side to front, he found the frames secured, the doors locked and, as far as he could see by shading his good eye to the windows, the rooms undisturbed. There was no sign of Isobel. He had not expected any. The truck's bonnet was cool. He had not imagined it had been anywhere. But for the moment he was resorting to basic mental checklists and, for that same moment, all the ticks were there. Until he switched on the headlights. Someone had been into the pottery. The padlock hung crookedly in the wrought-iron staple.

Sanctuary's instinct was to take a look. His common sense told him to drive away and be back at the yacht basin as soon as he could. He got down from the truck, the headlights full on, and limped across. The unbolted door squeaked as Sanctuary eased it back. The door was open enough for him to squeeze through. Then a sharp kick from the inside hurled the door wide. The second kick took him full in the stomach and he collapsed onto his knees, his forehead and nose propping the rest of his torso before he rolled on one side.

'If you move, Mr Sanctuary, you will be shot through the back of the head.'

The voice was clipped. Military. Fortyish. Very believable. Sanctuary stayed where he was though it was unlikely he could have got up anyway.

'Oh, shit!'

'You are quite fortunate, Mr Sanctuary. Quite fortunate.'

'You have a strange way of proving it.'

'You are alive. That, for the moment, is quite fortunate.'

Sanctuary should have felt dreadful. He did. But his mind was still fitter than his body. From everything he had seen and had not, from the cold military efficiency spitting from this stranger, Sanctuary was figuring that, if they had intended to kill him, they would not have bothered to warn him. He would have been dead before he hit the floor.

'Why didn't you kill me in the cottage?'

'Why should we? We do not deal in indiscriminate and unnecessary punishment.'

Sanctuary closed his eyes. A reaction to his agony. His protests came in gasps.

'Trying to bomb shit out of me was pretty unnecessary.'

'Frankly, Mr Sanctuary, we expected you to have left Commander Fisher's house before you did. The explosion was a simple warning.'

'Simple! Same as Les?'

'The barman? Not important.'

194

There was a shifting of a foot behind Sanctuary. Whoever it was was getting bored. Sanctuary hoped it wasn't due to nervousness although he somehow felt these people didn't trade in such sensitivities. He wanted to keep them talking, but he did not give himself much chance. He tried.

'He wasn't really mixed up in drugs. You know that.'

'That, Mr Sanctuary, was your last warning. Go back to the Department. Please your Deputy. We're not in the business of taking out you people. But, if you keep breaking the rules, then out you go. Okay?'

'Where's Isobel?'

There was a slight pause. Not a sigh, but an impatient intake.

'She is your insurance premium, Mr Sanctuary. Do as you're told and you get her back.'

'Otherwise?'

'There is no otherwise.'

The brogues turned and walked towards the door. Sanctuary raised his head to see their owner. Which was when he learned the hard way that three times is unlucky.

It took a long time for him to regain consciousness. They had left him where they hit him. He had vomited at some point and maybe the stench brought him round. It was getting light. One of the blue-overalled messengers in the Department was forever telling Sanctuary that there was always someone worse off than yourself. As he sat, back to the pottery wall, legs stretched awkwardly before him, he could not imagine who that someone might be. Sanctuary was a big man. Well built. Tough. Someone who had enjoyed the brutal energy of eighty minutes' Rugby football and who had always been in the fore-front of any hard, bashing, bruising rush for the line. But not this. He felt he had been put through a bottling plant, clipped, nudged, clamped, juddered, stamped, filled with a vile liquid, and crowned with an air-tight, steel, serrated cap.

As dawn filtered through the dusty panes and half-open door, Sanctuary could see that the devastation had not been confined to his body. The visitors had methodically smashed every piece of pottery in the barn. Blue glazed plates, autumn fawn pots and jugs, chocolate and cream dishes and bowls lay broken and grinning like neatly displayed relics of a holocaust.

Sanctuary was weary of it all. Physically hurt and tired. His head drooped, his mind hardly strong enough to cope with the uncompromising, bestial thoroughness of the past few days. These were men so ruthless and so indifferent to suffering that they could unconcernedly leave him to live. Now they had Isobel. Sanctuary knew they had long crossed whatever Rubicon had separated them from violence in pursuit of their goal. To them, Isobel was a lever to force his retreat to the anonymity of the Department and the official indifference of official investigation. He knew too that brown brogue's reference to the Department meant they had an inside knowledge that made him shudder. How did they know? How high did their leadership extend? Was this what Fisher had meant when he said that he had run out of people to trust? Sanctuary's focus had improved. His mind was whistling through the options as his eyes were scanning the shattered clays and glazes. He did not hear Leonard approaching. Didn't know he was there until the policeman spoke.

'Well, well, well. You have been having fun, haven't you?'

For once Sanctuary was pleased to see them, even the Fat One, who was clumsily tugging his spiral-bound reporter's notebook from his pocket. Leonard moved further into the pottery and stared about him. Perkins's counter-tenor did not conceal his surprise when he saw the carnage and then got his first good look at Sanctuary's face.

'Jesus!'

Sanctuary ignored Perkins. Perkins did not notice. He was gazing about the pottery like a junior constable who has discovered his first fantastic and highly illustrated porn library in a priest's bedroom.

'Who did this then?'

Leonard would have asked the same question in a less direct manner, but Perkins got the same answer.

'I don't know.'

'Really?'

Sanctuary looked up at Leonard. The blinking was furious.

196

The gold-rimmed spectacles were once more being scrubbed on his tie.

'I said, really?'

'I heard you. It's true. The nearest we got to formal introductions was being beaten up in the dark and then a ground-level view of a pair of brown shoes. I'm what you would call an unreliable witness. How did you know?'

'Know what?'

'To come here?'

'Somebody blew a hole in your friend's house. I tried the boat. This was second on the list. Anyway, let's have a look at you.'

By the time Leonard had driven Sanctuary to the casualty ward, he had got most of the story. By the time the sister and houseman had finished cleaning, stitching and patching, and had accepted that Sanctuary would let them X-ray his skull but wouldn't stay, Leonard had got the rest. He had made his own decisions. He told Sanctuary to stay put until he got back.

Within seconds of getting into police headquarters, Leonard had rung new alarms. The murdering, the bombing and now the kidnapping were beyond him. The Old Man said he was taking charge, blaming Leonard for everything.

'What the fuck's sake is happening, James? We've lost control of this one.'

'We were never in control, sir.'

A display of anger had to be exhibited with dignity. The Old Man had read that in a biography of a king. That's how he felt at that moment. Great title he might have, but his only power was in the hands of subordinates. Now the one courtier he had trusted was telling him no one had been at the wheel and his ship of state was out of control.

'Great! Now you tell me. And what about this Sanctuary chappie? I'm being asked, James. Asked, I tell you. And I have no answers. I'll get the Chief Constable to lodge an official complaint. Home Office hates that.'

The Old Man was feeling slightly better. Only slightly. Leonard found himself defending Sanctuary.

197

'He's taken a bad beating.'

'Good.'

'Maybe.'

'No. Good. There's some luck in this. The damn thing has got so big that no one would expect us to be able to handle it. The people who matter know we're not in this sort of business. Nevertheless, I might say that, if resources are drafted in, they will be as an aid to us, not to elbow us out of the bloody way and take all the herograms when it's wrapped up.'

'And if it's never wrapped up?'

'Don't worry. It will be. I'm assured from the very top.'

'Oh good.'

It was softly spoken. It was Leonard at his most sarcastic. The Old Man knew and took another sip of tea.

'What more do we have about the girl?'

'Nothing. She's gone. Your instructions are being carried out to the letter.'

'What does that mean?'

'Your instructions are being carried out to the letter.'

Few other than the Old Man would have got beyond the innocence of Leonard. The boardroom pose, the searching of the Constable for inspiration, the swinging of the high-backed executive chair, right ankle resting on left neatly tailored knee, gave them both time.

'Right, James. What do you want?'

'Wherever they have the girl is wherever they are.'

The Old Man worried the copper bracelet on his wrist, staring past Leonard as he thought through the implications of his protégé's simple observation.

'And if we concentrate our efforts on the kidnap rather than the murders?'

'Then we will put them under pressure.'

'How will they react under pressure? Do we know?'

'How can we? We can guess. They might crack and run.'

'Unlikely.'

Leonard nodded his agreement. The spectacles were off again, the gingham furiously at work.

198

'At the same time, they'll be reluctant to expose themselves by any further outings.'

'Why do you think they're still around? Tell me that, James.'

'I don't know that they are. What I do know is that they could have gone after killing Fisher. They didn't.'

'Or, if they did, they came back.'

Leonard did not need to nod. But he did. It wasn't agreement. It was encouragement. Because the next point of his logic had to come from the Old Man. It did.

'Which means there remains something, or someone, on this patch they want but don't know where it is.'

The Old Man was warming. He wanted this one tidied before he finished. He still had an eye for the starched collar at the Palace. But he was also excited. It had been a good career. There had never been one of these. There was pressure from the top and even above that. He smiled at Leonard. It was the smile of a much younger man.

'I'll ask you again. What do you want?'

'Whatever reinforcements we get, either from here or elsewhere, will do the leg-work and pile on the pressure. This is the perfect opportunity for someone to have access to all the information that comes from that operation but to work more or less on his own.'

'The boy who climbs through the fence while the rest stand at the vicar's gate.'

He thought the Old Man would have forgotten.

The eight-year-old. The others, slightly frightened, asking politely if they could get their football from the vicarage garden. The frosty, irritated, even angry parson telling them no and demanding their names. The lad, slipping away from the rear of the group and squeezing through the high, secluding laurels onto the neat lawn. Picking up the prized ball. The summerhouse door not quite closed. The other face, the beautiful youth, sneering to hide his nakedness. The lad, flustered and uncomprehending, back to the freedom of the lane, running to where the others would come once their roll had been answered, 'truthfully mind you'. The Old Man remembered, and he knew.

'Something like that.'

'We pile on the pressure, you work alone. That it?'

'Yes.'

Leonard picked up Sanctuary at the hospital in the girl's truck. Perkins and his green-armoured chocolate bar had been left behind. Perkins would keep in touch. Perkins figured that meant Leonard would get in touch when he wanted him and not before. He was about right.

The two men exchanged few words. Leonard said sorry a couple of times when the clutch juddered. Sanctuary, his head in seven different shades of agony, told him not to worry.

Sanctuary was thinking. Or trying hard. He had managed to get through to Dorothea from the hospital. A hallway 'phone had not been the place Sanctuary would have chosen to report through, but it had had to do. Dorothea had been agitated. Unlike her. She had wanted him to come in. The Deputy was washing his hands. Sanctuary hadn't known how much time he had before Leonard's return and he had brushed aside the warnings.

'Look, ask your green friend about Kukla International Transaction Agency. Got it?'

'Kukla as in china doll?'

'Or puppet.'

'Maybe. What else?'

'Bank statements. Update on his wife. Names of people at Cairo party.'

He had paused, long enough for Dorothea to have heard.

'Go on.'

'Have a second look at Isobel Rolfe.'

Dorothea heard.

'Problem?'

'She's gone.'

'A runner?'

'Lifted.'

'When?'

He had told her as much as he could in a not very accurate Department shorthand, missing out the gruesome details of the

200

attempts to remodel his face. But she had guessed from his voice, distorted by bruised muscles and swollen lips, that something was wrong. Even seventy miles away, Dorothea realised Sanctuary was holding back. She had told him as much and he told her in the most affectionate manner he could muster to go to hell. Dorothea thought Sanctuary was probably all right.

'Anything for me?'

'Not much. We've drawn a blank on the *Madrigal*. All the maritimes read out tonnage and registrations. It's not an exclusive name by any means. We think it spent a lot of time in the Mediterranean recently. Maybe Alexandria. That make sense? Nothing odd, though. I'll send a hard copy care of the post office. But I've put it through again on World Net. Other agencies may show up with something.'

'What about Hogarth?'

A trolley rattled through the swing doors from the ambulance ramp. Dorothea was talking and he missed some of what she had been saying.

'. . . his money as a copyright lawyer in the pop business. Advised a few bands on investments. Then specialised in overseas property. Investment for others, taking a percentage. Any good?'

'Mostly Spain?'

'All over, it seems. There was a spot of bother in Spain but nothing proven.'

Leonard appeared and Sanctuary made quick goodbyes. As they headed for the doors, the receptionist called the policeman. Handed him a note. It had been left for Sanctuary. Now he sat in the jogging truck rereading it. Trying to make sense, knowing that sense had different rules and he was now beyond them.

Be sensible Mr Sanctuary.
Go home.
For your friend's sake.

Inside the envelope had been a small lock of Isobel's hair. Melodramatic. Effective. He had shown it to Leonard. They had asked the inquiries office who had delivered. No one knew.

It was a busy time. Leonard glanced over from the wheel and smiled glumly.

'You got to hand it to them. They knew you would be there.'

'How the hell did they?'

'Does it matter? They did. It wouldn't have been too difficult. The hospital was an obvious place to go and the truck's . . . distinctive?'

'But why?'

'Presumably to prove they could find you whenever they wish. Anyway, at least we know they haven't pulled out. It's a reasonable guess that Miss Rolfe is not far away.'

'If she's alive.'

Leonard sighed. He had already thought that a distinct possibility.

'You want to pull out?'

'You really think that would make any difference?'

They both knew that the kidnappers would never let Isobel go. Sanctuary and Leonard would have to find her. If they stood any chance they had to keep moving. Keep everyone guessing, including their own people. From this moment, Sanctuary and Leonard would have to dump suspicions of each other. It would be a strange team. They needed to work quickly. Leonard never worked with anyone. Perkins was right. Leonard was not a good copper, but he was a good Chief Inspector. He dropped a gear as they approached a roundabout and then swung through onto the main highway.

'Tell me more about those paintings.'

Sanctuary had been thinking about them without coming up with answers.

'Why should he paint something which isn't local without putting a name to them? And why paint so badly and then put the stuff on the wall so everyone sees he's a lousy artist?'

'Arrogance?'

'No.'

Sanctuary was staring out of the side window at the flat-lands stretching towards the sea and thinking how different from the coastline in Fisher's water-colours. The truck was batting on at eighty miles an hour and past a signpost for Southampton and

202

The West. They were heading well away from the yacht basin and the *Madrigal*. Leonard caught Sanctuary's question before it slipped out.

'Portsmouth. Queen's Harbour Master.'

The traffic was heavy. Buses, trucks and long high dark-blue naval lorries with military numberplates lumbered for position on the approach roads to the Naval Dockyard. It was twenty-five minutes before they drove through the Unicorn Gateway, picked up a pass from the constable and were parking in the Visitors Only bay beneath Semaphore Tower.

They rode up in the tiny lift and found the Queen's Harbour Master in his wide office with its panoramic view over the waterway. He was middle-aged, elegant in his well laundered white shirt and gold shoulder-tabs. His faintly raffish air matched Leonard's tit-bit that QHM, as he was known in the naval wardroom, not only had his own smart harbour barge, he also had a very famous actor brother. There was a trace of the family thespian when he spied Sanctuary's plaster and bandaged head and obvious limp.

'Well, I'd hate to see what the other fellow looks like.'

There was a moment of silence, broken when the sailor threw back his head with a roar of laughter and called for three coffees. They were admiring what he called the best view on the south coast when a young Wren arrived with two cups and saucers and her boss's Sail Navy mug of what he called 'NATO Standard. Milk with two sugars.' More head-back laughter and they got down to business.

'Mr Sanctuary has seen some pictures, Ralph. We want you to identify them.'

31

The Deputy was furious. He had been instructed. The Department had Instructions which, unlike laws, were never open to interpretation. Instructions were issued by the three Deputies, or, *in extremis*, by Controller. An hour ago, at his too smart and new office on the south bank of the Thames, Controller had instructed the Deputy. Instruction meant tacit criticism. The only time anyone at his level was criticised in that way was when the Department was being threatened by gale-force politics. To Controller, there had to be something approaching a hurricane, more reasonably called Accountability, before waves broke over his particular stretch of the embankment of the capital's river. Under no circumstances could the Department operate with the freedom it needed if it were to be made accountable other than in the most informal manner. Consequently, the Department rarely, if ever, operated in concert with other agencies. Joint Operations meant someone or, worse still, some body assuming responsibility. That depth of formal undertaking could only mean Accountability. Furthermore, members of the Department kept out of trouble. There was no such thing as explanation.

'You will,' said Controller, 'understand what to do. Immediately. I am puzzled, old man, why you allowed it to get this far. Mm? You know the rules: at the first sight of blood we off-fuck. Mm? My White buzzed this morning. The only time He buzzes on my White is to ask me and Stella for dwinkie-poos. This morning, no invitation. He spoke succinctly on this matter for perhaps fifty seconds. I was not expected to answer. Am I clear, old man? Mm?'

The Deputy had nodded. The others preferred to stare at their blank note-pads. No one ever took notes.

'Good. Then I'll let you get on, old man.'

The less than subtle dismissal was grumbling through his vanity when the Deputy returned to his room overlooking Downing Street. He waved Dorothea, not to the conference table but to the deep armchair by his desk.

'Okay. Bring him in. Today. That's an Instruction.'

Dorothea took a deep breath and what Priestly insisted were her bosoms rose and fell beneath the damp cotton of her summer dress. She, along with hundreds of other summer walkers, had been caught out by the gloom and opening of the heavens.

Dorothea, like the rest of them, had been lulled into thinking that summer could go on for ever. She had sheltered, but few ever escape a sudden storm.

'You're wet.'

The Deputy was stretching for a too-early briar. It was an incongruous observation, considering his mood and sense of urgency, but it covered some of his embarrassment.

'Cloudburst.'

'Bloody right there is.'

He scratched too harshly at a matchbox and the flaring head fell to the green blotter.

'Where is he?'

'Out of contact. We've had one check-call. You know the girl's been lifted? By them.'

'According to C, it's a re-run of the first day of the Somme and flaming David Sanctuary is responsible for the lot.'

'That's ridiculous.'

This time the match made it to the overfilled bowl and through clouds of smoke the Deputy puffed and gave a staccato recital of the morning's meeting. Controller had not been asked if another agency were involved. The Deputy had raised the matter. Controller ignored the question. No one present pushed him. The Department's interests had been noticed by Five and the Metropolitan Police Special Branch. The Commissioner had mentioned it over their monthly breakfast. The CIA Station Chief wanted to know if his people at Langley need be interested. Controller's view was that this was not a matter for the Department, nor should it have been. The warnings had come down. Controller did not say from where. The Deputy had pointed out that a matter of national security could be involved. Controller had said it was being handled with great finesse until Sanctuary showed up.

'And another thing. Who's been poking into Kukla International?'

Dorothea showed her surprise.

'I have. Why?'

'Bloody CIA raised it this morning. Their compu-guard or whatever they call it showed someone was tapping into information. What's this about?'

'What's their interest?'

'It's one of theirs, that's what.'

'Langley's?'

'Yes, flaming Langley's. Everything's flaming CIA over there. Whoever's running the Covert Desk seems to believe his first job is to set up an undercover company. Anyway, lay off. Why were you snooping?'

'David asked me to. For what it's worth, I've drawn a blank.'

'No you haven't, you've got up Langley's nose, they've got up C's, he's got up mine. He's right, Sanctuary's causing more trouble than a flea at bedtime. No one's allowed to sleep. Where's Charles?'

'Carlton Gardens. Do you want him to go down there?'

Another match and the Deputy's eyebrows curled tightly in satisfaction.

'To bring him back? You're joking. I'd rather send Kosov.'

Dorothea allowed herself a smile. The smug KGB Resident at the Soviet Embassy was loathed by the Deputy who considered the new détente as the most dangerous state of East-West relations since Cuba.

'I know which one Davy would rather have alongside him. Charles does wear his ambition rather publicly sometimes.'

'Too right. Someone has been nobbling C from on high. I knew that days ago. But someone has been feeding Departmental info from below. Ambition I can get along with. Being screwed by my bloody milk-monitor is something else.'

206

'Shall I go?'

He tamped the smouldering cherry rough-cut with the back of the matchbox and looked into the air. Instructions were one-dimensional. No compromise. He had never seen the job of Intelligence as a game for consenting governments. In his experience, being sidetracked meant being bogged down and this was no different. David Sanctuary had to come in or be brought in. There were aspects of this affair the Deputy disliked, but he recognised there were probably things he did not know, would not know. He looked at Dorothea for some time. She was fond of David Sanctuary. She called him Davy when she wasn't looking. So did he. But the Instruction was clear and so were the consequences.

'No. No one does.'

'What happens if he doesn't check in today?'

Dorothea met his gaze. The Deputy looked away. There was a sudden spitting, then an urgent tapping at the window ledge.

'Then we cut the rope.'

It was raining again. Hard.

32

The skies over the Solent were clear. Sanctuary and Leonard were on their second coffees. The Queen's Harbour Master was on his fourth. He never drank tea. For two hours they had gone through Sanctuary's attempts to recreate the sketches and then to match them to the naval officer's knowledge of the coastline. As he pointed out, it was remarkably difficult to find the rocks and marks, if Sanctuary did not really have a photographic memory and, even if he did, the badly painted pictures, seen by dim torchlight, were less than easy references.

'Any chance of getting a look at the paintings?'

According to the policeman, there had not been much left of the inside of Fisher's cottage. The bomb appeared to have been taped to the chimney-breast.

'Not really, Ralph. Not really at all.'

The QHM looked from one to the other and nodded. He did not ask why.

'Fair enough.'

He was sitting back on a tall stool, sipping from the seemingly ever-full mug.

'You know, what I find curious, is why the paintings should have been so bad. I paint a bit myself and I'm not very good. But, when I was worse, my paintings were better. That sound Irish?'

Leonard was interested. His glasses were being cleaned.

'You mean when you began it was painting-by-numbers stuff.'

'Right. It was only when I gained a bit of confidence that I stopped trying to paint perfect reproductions of whatever it was I could see. Or thought I could.'

Sanctuary shook his head. Winced and wished that he had not. He had forgotten how bruises bumped together.

'Perhaps he was simply a dreadful artist. Had no talent whatsoever.'

Ralph smiled. His natural politeness forbade him to make his point too forcefully. But he made it anyway.

'People with no talent whatsoever don't take up painting. Were there any other paintings about?'

Leonard had been over the cottage with a policeman's fine tooth-comb.

'Nothing much. A few daubs of his boat. Weren't bad actually. And quite a good one of the view from the lock. But nothing as smudged and blobby as the ones on the wall.'

Sanctuary was tired and he hurt. He was getting impatient. He got up from the chart-table high-stool and stretched out his hand to the Queen's Harbour Master. Somewhere, perhaps not far away, was Isobel. The more he thought about her, the more he wanted to get her to safety. It had been a nice try but they had wasted enough time.

'Perhaps he was simply trying to tell everyone that he may have been a good yachtsman but he couldn't paint for toffee.'

Leonard, embarrassed by Sanctuary's impatience, smiled at Ralph.

'Think about it, will you? Let me know?'

'I take it it's important?'

Leonard nodded.

'You could say that.'

The two men drove out of the old naval city each deep in his own thoughts. Sanctuary's disappointment was obvious. It showed in the tight lines at his eyes. Leonard had accepted that the pictures might give some clue to the mystery behind Fisher's death. Neither was naive enough to believe that an 'X marks the spot' sign would have been painted into one of the watercolours. Yet both were open-minded enough to understand that, given the pressures under which Fisher had lived during his last few days, perhaps even weeks, he might have resorted to some sense of theatre. Leonard had not been at all scathing about this last possibility.

'It's reasonably well documented. People in his position can easily develop what appears like a persecution complex. Part of it suggests that no one is to be trusted. So, rather like old widows, they start leaving clues to their reasoning behind the persecution. What we must never do is dismiss those signs. Among them is to be found a solution. Often it is never found because the logic has escaped the ploy itself, but,' he waved his hands in a shrug of reassurance, 'well, let's say we would be silly to ignore the less conventional forms of investigation.'

It was the sort of explanation that continually baffled Perkins. Unpolicemanlike, was the Fat One's expression.

It had started to rain. Instead of heading towards police headquarters as planned, Leonard pulled into a side-road running parallel with the main highway.

'The lad?'

Leonard shook his head.

'His mother. She's the one he would have talked to. Or, rather, she's the one who would have heard anything he said.'

There was no sign of WPC Rose. Leonard had left instructions. Maybe whoever was guarding had gone inside for a cup of tea. It happened.

Leonard left Sanctuary in the cab and banged on the door. The windows were shut tight and the front curtains drawn. Maybe the sun. Stopped any fading. But it was raining. Leonard banged again. Nothing. He looked through the letter-box. The hall was neat, brushed and wiped down. It was empty.

The black Ford that had been parked along the road when they pulled up drove off without any apparent urgency, waited politely at the joining lane of the highway, and then slipped into the traffic flow and was gone. Sanctuary, watching Leonard trying to make himself heard, hardly noticed the car and, when he thought about it, it was too late to get the number. He felt there was a passenger, but could not be sure. Modern headrests made people-spotting difficult. He mentioned it to Leonard. There was little they could do. The Lomax home seemed empty, as if the family had gone away. The two men banged on front doors either side and then worked along until Sanctuary got an answer from Number 42. He said he was supposed

210

to be delivering to the Lomaxes. Had she seen them? The grandmother shook her head. She had not. But that was not surprising. Kept themselves to themselves, those Lomaxes did. What with him being a gypo and all that, they was bound to, wasn't they? Sanctuary said thank you and returned to the truck. Leonard had similar luck. Mrs Lomax had gone out shortly after breakfast, but no one had seen her come back. Bennie? She had been alone. Mr Lomax? No one knew. Maybe painting up Midhurst way, they thought. Council, wasn't he? Leonard was worried and drove back to the police station, stopping only to drop off Sanctuary at Tupmans.

Before he got down from the truck, Sanctuary wanted the answer to a question he'd floated at Leonard some hours ago. Perhaps now the policeman would answer.

'When you talked about Tupman, you didn't mention Mrs Tupman. Know her?'

Leonard was leaning his forearms on the steering wheel. He nodded.

'Sad woman. Married the boss.'

'Lived happily ever after?'

Leonard shook his head.

'No way. Car crash on their honeymoon. She's been in a chair ever since.'

'Who was driving?'

The policeman's eyebrows answered.

'Don't know for sure, but I would have thought he was. Never struck me as the type to allow a woman to do a man's job. Has he you?'

Sanctuary had one more.

'What about his PA, the blonde?'

'Not sure. She's only been here for six months or so.'

'Where was she before? Local?'

'Not that I know. Perkins said something about London. The Secretariat of the Law Society, I think.'

He tried one of his smiles.

'Ask her.'

The ash blonde was in the reception area when Sanctuary went in. He did not ask her. Instead he apologised for the way

211

he had spoken when they had met in the street. She smiled. It was warm enough. She looked concerned. His face was very purple and yellow. The games-playing had stopped. She had read the newspapers, heard the local news and the office and city gossip. Tupman was with a client. There was a chance that he would be free for about ten minutes in about fifteen.

'Any good?'

'Very good.'

'Can I tell Mr Tupman what it's about?'

'I'm not entirely sure.'

'I'm afraid Mr Tupman is terribly busy. Of that I'm entirely sure.'

'Well . . .'

'I'm afraid well is not quite enough. However, I shall see what I can do.'

There was something of the schoolmarm about Mrs Dent. He had been ticked off. He looked at her closely. He could imagine the willowy Mrs Dent quietly oiling the machinery of an old-established and influential institution. The vaults and rooms of Chancery Lane and the carefully preserved Oxbridge air of the Inns of Court would be a natural habitat for this breed of woman. He wondered why she had migrated to the south coast. The fair hair flicked and the slim, clean cotton shoulders heaved with Mrs Dent's undisguised exasperation.

'If you're still looking for a letter, Mr Sanctuary, then I'm afraid you're going to be out of luck. And, if you would accept a little advice, should you raise it with Mr Tupman I suspect it will turn out to be a very short interview indeed.'

Tupman was as sour as on Sanctuary's last visit. Sanctuary was not bothered. Not impressed. Sanctuary had been beaten, bombed, his friend had been killed, someone had kidnapped Isobel, they would probably kill her – if they had not done so already. As he stepped into the smug, over-stuffed trappings of Tupman's room, Sanctuary snapped. There was no public display. Something inside barked 'enough'. By the time Sanctuary dropped into the visitor's chair he had decided that Tupman was to be his first target. Tupman was openly shocked when he saw Sanctuary's battered face.

212

'I must say, Mr Sanctuary, that events have got somewhat beyond our understanding, would you not agree?'

Sanctuary was lounging. He sat to ease the breaks and bruises, but not his mind. Ten years earlier, he had worked through a Resistance to Interrogation Exercise with Special Forces. Pounding the snow hills. Freezing. Hiding. An ambushed rendezvous. Thrown into a stinking wet hut. A smug, lean, bald skull, sneering and ruthlessly slitting edges of his mind and his intellectual stamina. The other one. Dark. Short. Welsh. Sympathetic. Friendly. Far more dangerous. Sanctuary had survived. Had not broken. He had been well briefed. Told what to do. Knew that in forty-eight hours he would be back on the train to London. Later, the Department sent him on the cleaner version, Debriefing Course No 24. Sheraton. Carpets. Embossed wallpaper and accents. Much harder to handle. Sanctuary had done the course. He was about to take on Tupman. It would have to be quick.

'That's a bit of an understatement.'

His yawn was open, only half-smothered.

'Sorry. Haven't been to sleep for a couple of days. Excuse me.'

He rubbed his eyes and cheeks as if searching for circulation and fresh energy. Tupman had, from Mrs Dent's preamble, expected a more belligerent tone from this large young man. Tupman was surprised, but not yet off-guard.

'Most tiring. Most tiring and equally disagreeable. Now, ah, Mr Sanctuary, as you know, I have made it clear on a previous occasion that no other correspondence has been placed in my safe-keeping for your attention, so I doubt if there is any way in which I may help, or even advise.'

Mr Tupman was now sitting back. He had no need to hide in files and ribbon-bound documents. Or had he? The throb of the long vein snaking to his pate pumped uncertainty into his complacent countenance. He waited for an answer.

'What do you think Fisher might have done with his letter if he did not give it to you, Mr Tupman?'

Sanctuary's eyes on the lawyer were as lazy as he could make them appear.

213

'I have no idea.'

'Then you accept there was a letter?'

'No, Mr Sanctuary, I do not. I said I have no idea.'

But he did not tell Sanctuary to leave.

'Mr Tupman. I need your help. Actually, to be precise, I need your guidance.'

Sanctuary got up and began a slow pacing of the stained floorboards. Tupman was at first surprised by the movement and then recovered, sitting slightly to one side in his large chair, a gold and ebony paper-knife in one hand. Sanctuary gave the impression of coming to a decision and Tupman found himself tapping his clean blotter to the four-four time of the other man's tread.

'I have said, Mr Sanctuary, I would help you, but it is beyond me how I may.'

'Just hear me out for a moment. Okay?'

Tupman shrugged. He had still not asked Sanctuary to leave.

'Stuart Fisher wrote two letters to me. One told me that he was worried. The second explained why. The first one reached me. In it, he said that he left a letter with you.'

'Mr Sanctuary. Mr Sanctuary. Mr Sanctuary. This really is too tiresome. We have been through this once. I told you then that I found your attitude objectionable. There's nothing more to say.'

Still he didn't tell him to go. Sanctuary was thinking quickly. Why was Tupman containing his anger? Why was his contempt below the surface, albeit only just? Try again. Keep it reasonable. The soft, reasonable approach. Remember the embossed wallpaper. He leant against the street wall, by the window, allowing Tupman to look beyond the net curtains for refuge.

'I know how frustrating this must be for you, sir, but as you have pointed out the tempo has changed and more people are asking questions. I'm only one of them.'

'I must say that is not my impression. It appears that you, and you alone, Mr Sanctuary, choose to assume a tenacity quite beyond the interests of a friend of the deceased.'

'The police are.'

214

'But you are not the police. It is their job to ask questions. Not yours. Why not leave it to them? Unless of course – '

'Unless of course what?'

Tupman let the paper-knife fall. It made little noise.

'Unless, Mr Sanctuary, you masquerade. And, should your mask slip, then we see you as something more than a friend of Commander Fisher's.'

'We?'

Tupman ignored the question.

'And unless, of course, there are specific matters which have come to your notice. Possibly, just possibly, if I knew of those matters and could judge their substance, then it is conceivable although remotely so, that I could be of more help. Though I hasten to say that I doubt it.'

Tupman attempted a smile. He was not much rehearsed in similar expressions. It showed. As the lawyer's loom of friendliness faded, Sanctuary's eyes opened. Tupman was under orders. Why else would he be so communicative? Someone must be behind Tupman. They wanted to know how much Sanctuary knew. Tupman had been instructed to find out. Right. The rest was going to be easy. Tupman didn't know that. Gently does it.

'That's very considerate of you, Mr Tupman.'

Tupman's expression thought so too.

'Ah, you mentioned, Mr Sanctuary, a letter that you had received. Do you remember what was in it?'

'Word for word.'

Good. For the first time, Tupman was having to ask questions.

'Do you happen to have it with you?'

Sanctuary shook his head.

'But you could get it?'

'I suppose so. Would it be useful?'

'Until we see it, who may tell?'

'When you say "we", do you mean other people?'

'An expression alone, Mr Sanctuary. Just an expression.'

'A Royal one.'

'Something similar. Now, I suppose we could start by hearing what you remember of the letter's contents.'

'I'm not sure that would be in order.'

'Why ever not?'

'It's very difficult, Mr Tupman. I'm not sure if you have any right to see the letter.'

'Come now.'

'I'm afraid not. I wonder, if you could just give me a couple of simple answers, perhaps I could arrange for you to have a copy.'

Tupman's face gave little, but enough for Sanctuary to sense that the lawyer was under tight instructions. Tupman had not replied. He was fiddling with the paper-knife. It looked oriental, long-bladed and surprisingly sharp along one edge. Sanctuary made his first move.

'You see, Mr Tupman, you have interested us for some time. In fact before Stuart Fisher's death, your name appeared on our file.'

It was Tupman's turn.

'You, ah, said "our"?'

The hesitation was enough to scuff his preferred display of confidence.

'Not Royal. Our.'

Sanctuary's voice remained friendly. The edge was there for Tupman to hear when he was ready.

'But how could I be of any interest? And I singularly fail to see what this has to do with the present situation.'

'As you have learned, Mr Tupman, tentacles stretch from the most unexpected crevices, especially in our business.'

Sanctuary was flying by the seat of his pants. He had no idea of Tupman's connections. He didn't even know for certain that he was on the right track. He certainly didn't know where he was heading. But then, as the Course Number 24 instructor had reminded his class, help came from the subject. Tupman simply helped Sanctuary over the next bridge of information.

'You should know, Mr Sanctuary, that my influence goes beyond this city. Yes, indeed, I may say that influence is considerable and that you would understand its significance if I

216

were in a position to elaborate. Which of course I am not. It is sufficient to say that I would be grateful to know the contents of the letter and any other thoughts that you may have surrounding the, ah, unfortunate death of, ah, our friend, the Commander.'

Sanctuary plunged.

'What happened to Fisher's letter to me?'

'I have told you before there was no letter.'

'Wrong. There was. Both you and I know that. Mr Tupman, I should remind you that a number of people have been killed. Another is about to be.'

'Who?'

It was a quick and natural reaction from the lawyer. It was one word ringing with urgency. Fear. Sanctuary continued the corporate approach, but now at the run.

'We know. You will find out. What happened to the letter? You gave it to someone. Who?'

'I tell you – '

'Forget what you've told me. Just think about it. You were not the only one to see the envelope.'

Tupman's sense of tragical history was finely tuned. He lost a layer of his reluctant tan.

'Preposterous. Absurd. Preposterous. No one would have seen the letter.'

He recovered quickly.

'There was no letter.'

'It is, I suppose, a question of loyalties, Mr Tupman.'

'My staff are perfectly loyal. This is going too far.'

'Really? Loyalty is a strange affair, Mr Tupman. In a place like this, one doesn't have to dig too deeply to find all sorts of stresses. Even beneath the most respectable blankets.'

'I beg your pardon?'

Just a little more pressure.

'You're very well respected in the city.'

Tupman raised his brows. Of course he was respected. The family had been in the city almost as long as the Church.

'Stress is not always caused by disloyalty, Mr Tupman. Sometimes the perception is sufficient. If, for example, someone believes another is disloyal, the anguish is sufficient to produce the stress, even if the suspicion is unfounded.'

Tupman's face was a mask. The tufts of dark hair over the ears were even more grotesque when viewed from a standing position. It was as if they had been glued on the wrong sides. Tupman's skin stretched tautly across his cheek-bones, the lips tight as if the mask were about to explode in cruel rage. It was not. Tupman had not reached that point. Nor would he. He resorted to rage and sneering too often to have any left for emergencies. Instead, the mask was firm, the tight black eyes moving behind the façade as if from some eighteenth-century sinister pageant. It was for Sanctuary to go on.

'For example, some would expect absolute loyalty. If there were the slightest suggestion that loyalty had waned, then the penalty would be severe.'

'Your moral philosophy is an unsound as it is inappropriate.'

The letter knife was spinning in Tupman's fingers, boring the beginnings of a hole in the precious desk. Sanctuary pressed on.

'The connections you mention.'

'Yes?'

'We both understand their definitions of loyalty. You stick to their rules or else.'

Tupman's eyes were fixed on the spinning steel. Sanctuary slipped in his own blade.

'If we let it be known that you had cooperated with us, frankly, Mr Tupman, I would not give much for your chances of making next month's Rotary lunch.'

'That is a nonsensical suggestion. I cannot imagine your argument.'

'Mr Tupman, this is not a playgroup. Let me spell it out. I represent a determined organisation. As you can see, I've been the subject of some pretty rough attention during the past twenty-four hours. The same people have killed three men. I don't have much time, Mr Tupman. If you don't come clean, then I have no problem with making out you have cooperated. I believe you'd be a dead man if I did.'

'Nonsense.'

218

There was little conviction in Tupman's voice. There was even less in his once-haughty expression when Sanctuary fired his next salvo.

'I don't care a shit, Mr Tupman. Whether it's nonsense or not, whether or not I'm right, does not matter. If I drop the word, then you are fingered. Okay.'

There should have been a grandfather clock to count the seconds of tension. Instead, the rumblings of distant town traffic reminded that, elsewhere, life went on. Elsewhere, ordinariness was safer, comfortable, reassuring, rarely frightening. Tupman, whose whole life had been geared to ordinariness, safety in convention and by his own ways fear in others, was frightened.

'You don't understand.'

The voice was distracted. A betrayed lover. Sanctuary was not yet ready with the balm. His thoughts about Isobel and what might have happened to her stepped up the uncompromising cruelty his instincts had dragged from his personality. He had no other weapon, therefore he would use it.

'Frankly, why should I? Fisher didn't. The others didn't. I came in here. You treated me like shit. You sat there and played the big man. You are not a big man, Mr Tupman. One word from me and you would be dead. You wouldn't get further than tonight. You would be dead. Do you know what they did to the barman? Of course you do. They cut out his fucking heart, Mr Tupman. That's what they did. Took a knife and cut it out. Someone put in his hand and pulled out that heart while it was hot and bloody and still trying to beat. They yanked that heart, Mr Tupman, out of his chest and stuffed it into his fucking mouth. Mr Tupman, I tell you, one word from me, one word that you have cooperated, whether or not it's true, means that someone tonight, maybe even tomorrow, who fucking cares, will cut out your heart and stick it in your mouth. You're nothing, Mr Tupman. Nothing. Fancy that? Look at you. Your hands are shaking, Mr Tupman. You are fucking shaking. Next you'll be pissing yourself because that's what happens, Mr Tupman. That's what happens when someone starts to fall apart. As far as I'm concerned, they can fucking have you

219

because I want someone to pay for Les, and for Stuart, and frankly, Mr Tupman, it may as well be you.'

Tupman clenched his hands. They would not stop shaking. He had never experienced such an onslaught. But he knew the truth in Sanctuary's gutter hardness. He had no excuse, but he made one.

'There is no choice. There never has been.'

Sanctuary wished Leonard were with him to play the nice guy. It would be quicker. Taking the hard man off the boil was tricky. He needed to keep up the pressure but at the same time let Tupman in to talk.

'Stop fucking me about, Tupman. You either go with me or I make a call. Which one? It's up to you.'

The eyes moved slowly to focus on Sanctuary who was once more seated, almost confidentially, in the client's chair.

'Yes.'

'Yes what?'

Sanctuary remembered once as a child hearing his father explaining to a patient why life is sometimes best if it comes to an end. The old man had always thought he would be the first to go. Through the open window. Sanctuary had heard. When the old man reached home and the empty bed, he would weep. But, for the moment, he took comfort in the doctor's words and his right by learning and standing to recite them. Now, Sanctuary, who had learned to play every trick in the Department's own book, hoped to God he was right.

'She has been ill. Few would blame you.'

'Mr Sanctuary, this is . . .'

He was going to say outrageous and maybe a few other things, but did not. Pressure comes in harsh waves when senses of decency, decorum and reputation are offended, when respectability is dressed by a sneer for others' misdoings and the fear of being found out can be tolerated no longer.

'You were discreet.'

Tupman sighed. Not discreet enough. Sanctuary wanted to know who had found out. What they had found out, although he could guess. How they had. How they contacted Tupman. Where he contacted them, although he suspected the lawyer

220

was never allowed to do that. Who and how and where were the answers he needed to find out why Fisher had been killed and where Isobel was being held – if indeed she were alive still. And he had even less time than when he started.

'Did Mrs Tupman know?'

The pain in Tupman's cold eyes was answer enough.

'They said they would tell her. It would have killed her. That may, Mr Sanctuary, sound trite to you, but I assure you it is not meant to be.'

'Go on.'

Now Tupman wanted to tell. To tell someone. Discovering a key unlocks a jumbled cupboard of secrets in the guilty. The jumble is greater in the ashamed. Now Tupman's relief spilled across the desk to where the kind son of a fly-fishing GP sat waiting, no scorn in his expression.

'I am very human. Same desires as normal men. I am surrounded with ludicrous temptation. Ludicrous, Mr Sanctuary, because I am talking about cocktail parties, dinner parties, Friends of this theatre and that festival, sprinkled about me with beautiful, desirable women. But, Mr Sanctuary, I must not touch. Instead I am a respectable practitioner of the law held in esteem and considered to be a model of how a gentleman should be, considerate, kind and understanding to a wife who, Mr Sanctuary, is a cabbage in a wheel-chair. I am admired for my kindness and my celibacy. I will tell you, Mr Sanctuary, celibacy is nothing to be admired. And so I found comfort elsewhere.'

Tupman was now slumped in his grand chair. His chin was on his chest. He was spent.

'And they found out.'

Tupman's nod was almost imperceptible.

'Yes. Pure, pure, pure chance.'

He looked up. The smile on his face was Tupman's own physical reflection of irony.

'When?'

The wave of the open palm and the raised nostrils said it did not matter when.

'When? How?'

'Oh, a couple of years ago. Miles away from here where it could never have mattered.'

The sigh reminded Tupman how wrong he had been.

'When did they contact you?'

'I thought you knew.'

'Who?'

Tupman's sneer was not for Sanctuary but for the bad luck he felt he'd been dealt.

'You don't, do you? You don't, Mr Sanctuary, understand the length of those tentacles.'

Sanctuary waited. Tupman was drawing mental breath. He would tell.

'One indiscretion. One moment of stupidity. I was on a holiday.'

He laughed as if the very idea of Tupman enjoying himself was impossible to imagine.

'An educational tour, Mr Sanctuary, well it certainly turned out to be just that.'

'What happened?'

'It matters?'

'Course it does.'

'I suppose so. We had come back to the hotel after a hot, dusty, worthy day. I came down for dinner, got talking to a nice young man from the British Embassy, the Cultural Attaché, I believe. We dined and then went to a party in a villa.'

'And?'

'And that was that, Mr Sanctuary. Very much so.'

'There were girls and you were, eh, compromised. Photographs. The lot.'

'Oh, there were girls all right. Yes. The lot, as you so delicately put it.'

'And?'

'You still don't understand, do you? Frankly, if I had been caught in an embarrassing moment with one of them, well, I suppose one could have pleaded the stress of an unnatural marriage.'

Sanctuary then understood. He looked away.

'Yes, Mr Sanctuary, the British Diplomatic Corps has much

222

for which it should answer. An indiscreet moment with a pretty girl in a far-off land? Yes, I suppose that would have been embarrassing. I would never have forgiven myself. But I would have survived.'

'It was worse than that?'

'What is worse? Finding out about oneself? That is worse? Realising that the protest that one is red-blooded and hungry for the opposite sex is a self-inflicted illusion? That is worse? Finding comfort in a moment of beauty? Knowing that afterwards he was mocking me in my self-disgust? That was worse?'

Tupman had stopped shaking. Now there was no fear. Exhaustion.

'A couple of years ago, you said?'

'I did, didn't I.'

Tupman had spilled. His confidence, but not his bullying, had returned. Sanctuary guessed the answer, but asked his question.

'Where was this?'

The tutor's head was back. The eyes on the ceiling as the dim undergraduate was allowed into the last secret of his learning. The head came forward, almost with a snap. The eyes sharp in some curious triumph.

'Cairo, Mr Sanctuary. Cairo. That's where I met Commander Fisher. It was his party.'

'Then what?'

'Then nothing.'

'Really?'

'Really. Not immediately anyway.'

'Fisher set you up?'

'Is that what it was? No. Not set up. An opportunity maybe. But not set up.'

'For what?'

'I suppose for the future. For coincidence to prosper.'

The chance for Sanctuary to return to his harsh inquisitor's role was gone. He had now to tease as a bedside doctor might diagnose cause and seek effect.

'Was Miss Rolfe at the party?'

'Who?'

223

The curiosity was genuine.

'What did Fisher do?'

'Nothing. I told you, it was an opportunity, not a grand scheme.'

Tupman was back staring at the paper-knife as if it might at any moment open an escape to another memory which would clear his mind and life that had once been so comfortably mundane.

'He must have done something.'

Tupman looked up.

'Why?'

'Because the coincidence is too great, Mr Tupman. Too great.'

'But isn't that what coincidence is? A great impossibility that comes true?'

'Who then. Someone else at the party?'

Tupman nodded, preferring not to speak. Sanctuary could not afford the momentum to slacken once again.

'Tell me, Mr Tupman.'

'Why should I?'

'Because that way you get to live.'

'You think that's important?'

'There aren't any second chances if you change your mind.'

The lawyer's sigh was not one of contemplation, nor frustration. Weariness perhaps. He would tell.

'About six months ago I had a visitor. Someone I had known at Oxford.'

'Here?'

Tupman nodded. Continued.

'Yes. We had not seen each other in years. In fact we had hardly known each then. He'd been on my staircase, but we'd not had much in common.'

'What did he want?'

'He told me that he worked for the Government and that I could be of some service.'

'The British Government?'

'Mm. Mm.'

'What sort of service?'

224

'He didn't say. Not immediately.'

'But you agreed.'

'Not immediately.'

It was Sanctuary's turn to sigh.

'Don't piss me about. I'm just as serious.'

Tupman's look was full of contempt. Tupman was on a different plane. A man suspended in a moment beyond death.

'You have done your job, Mr Sanctuary. Time is now mine. Not yours.'

Sanctuary leaned across the desk and picked up the telephone, dialled nine, waited for a line and then tapped out a ten-figure number. Dorothea's voice was welcome. He was glad Priestly felt himself too grand to answer.

'Can't answer questions. Re-check Tupman and put it about that he's willing to cooperate.'

Dorothea was saying that she assumed he knew what he was saying because she did not. Tupman's calmness was running for cover.

'Wait one moment, Mr Sanctuary, one moment. Please, one moment.'

'Just a minute.'

Dorothea did not reply. But she was there. Sanctuary didn't bother to cover the mouthpiece.

'Well?'

Tupman's fingers were linked in Anglican prayer.

'They used our cottage. We've got a cottage. They used it for meetings and to set up what they called, ah, an event.'

Tupman seemed to think that was enough. He looked up from the corner of one eye. It was not.

'Go on.'

'They've been staying there. It's in the trees on the north bank of the harbour. It is very, ah, private.'

'Who they? Your old friend?'

'Yes.'

'Who else?'

'A couple of others and, ah . . .'

'Yes? Who?'

'A foreign person. He came in by sea. We have a landing stage.'

'D'you know who he was?'

'By chance, I do. He made a telephone call. I heard his name.'

'Which was?'

'Ignatiev. At least that's what he said.'

At the other end, Dorothea quietly replaced the telephone handset.

33

When he left Tupman and Frobisher, Sanctuary said nothing more than goodbye to Mrs Dent. She said something about having been in for longer than she had expected and that she hoped the meeting had been useful. He did not reply. He was walking into police headquarters when he met Leonard coming out. The policeman looked haggard. The Fat One was trying to keep up with his boss without puffing. He kept up but as they crossed the yard he was puffing. Leonard stopped in front of Sanctuary. Looked hard. Said nothing. Cocked his head and Sanctuary followed his direction to the green saloon. They were swinging into the traffic before anyone spoke.

'Where are we going?'

Leonard looked fixedly at the dashboard. The Fat One, both hands on the wheel, did not dare speak. Sanctuary, cramped in the back, figured he would find out soon enough.

It was not a long drive. The ambulance was outside, its twin back doors open, the blue light flashing still. More yellow tape cordoned the street. The nearest neighbour was ten houses away. She could not see much.

Bennie was upstairs on his bed. A dragon kite hanging from the ceiling corner kept away evil spirits, and old trainers were tied to the cheap whitewood cupboard door, saved and treasured for who knew what reason? On the floor, an exercise book lay open, the felt-tip lines carefully written, striving for a C-grade one day, because he knew he could and so did his mum whatever they said down the school about him not trying and always fidgeting in class.

In death, Bennie was quite still.

In the kitchen, Mrs Lomax sat at the oil-clothed table. WPC Rose, for once looking helpless, still had her hat on. She was

227

making tea. Leonard pulled out the plastic-covered stool and sat across from the silent woman. He took both her hands in his. She looked up. Didn't try to draw away. Maybe didn't see him. Didn't ask why?

'What did Bennie tell you?'

She said nothing. She looked at the teacup set beside her without knowing what it was. Shook her head.

'Heard something, didn't he?'

Sanctuary leaned against the kitchen cupboard. There was no room but he wanted to hear. He nudged shut the door to smother the falsetto of the Fat One. Leonard tried again.

'He told you something. Didn't he, luv?'

'What?'

'Something. He told you, didn't he? Something. What he saw at the harbour?'

She shook her head. Neatly scraped-back hair, grey and lifeless, making no fuss as it was rocked side to side.

'He didn't see nothing.'

'Heard something then?'

'No.'

She peered into his face. Searching for something he knew could never be there. Bennie was dead.

'When then?'

'After.'

'When?'

'Dunno.'

'When was that?'

'Maybe yesterday. I had to go out. Up the shops. He wouldn't come. I told him to wait for me here. Not to go out like.'

'Did he?'

She nodded.

''Spect.'

Leonard's eyes were full of pain. She saw some of it and felt sad for him.

'He told you?'

She nodded. Eyes on his. Hands moving. One thumb rubbing her sore knuckles under his palms.

'He went down there. Told him not to. He did.'

'He saw a man?'

'Said he did. Same one as before.'

'Before when?'

'Same as before.'

'On the day?'

'Think so.'

'What he tell you, luv? Something?'

'Said he heard him in the 'phone box. One without the door. You know?'

He said he did.

'What did the man say?'

'Gave somebody a number. Said they'd call when it was done.'

'What was done? D'you know?'

She shook her head.

'You know what number?'

'Same as his dad's. 876. His car number. 876. Only twice.'

Leonard looked at Sanctuary. When Sanctuary spoke it was softly and from a great distance.

'You mean 876876?'

Mrs Lomax did not hear Sanctuary's voice. She nodded at Leonard.

'That's right. It's Lomax's car number. Only twice. That's how, that's how Bennie got it in his head. He told me.'

'You're sure, luv? You're sure?'

The woman pulled her hands away. Looked at them as if they were never hers and then at the kindly policeman with his funny glasses and mucked-up hair.

'Course I'm sure. Course I am. Bennie wouldn't lie. He's a good boy you know. Wouldn't lie.'

The door opened. Leonard looked around, anger in his soft eyes. It was Perkins, a fat hand holding the edge of the door like a vaudeville act about to make an entrance.

'Sorry, guv. Need a word.'

He sensed his poor timing.

'Important. Real important, guv.'

229

Sanctuary closed the kitchen door behind them and they stood crammed in the tiny scullery.

'Well?'

Leonard's voice was tired.

Perkins looked from one to the other.

'Just come through, it has.'

His head flicked in the direction of the front door and beyond it the flashing squad car, its radio chattering to unseen ears.

'Come on then.'

'Tupman. Seems he's blown himself away.'

34

Sanctuary had almost forgotten about Pete and Rusty. The afternoon had been long, rough and bewildering. It was now evening and he parked the Alfa near the ramp down to the *Madrigal*'s pontoon. Leonard had promised to meet up in an hour. It would be twilight. Sanctuary told the policeman that he intended to check out Tupman's cottage. It was the best lead they had. It was the only one.

When he told Leonard as much of Tupman's story as he believed the policeman needed to know, Perkins had proved his local knowledge, but not his intelligence.

The cottage was along a track leading from a lane that meandered about two miles from the natural harbour's tree-lined north shore. Perkins had been there a couple of times, once for a break-in, another time to pick up some old deck chairs Tupman had promised for the church jumble sale. You couldn't miss it according to Perkins. The track was straight up to the cottage for a hundred and fifty yards. The trees either side had been cleared back after the 1976 drought as a fire break, Sanctuary and Leonard looked at each other, their expressions glum. If Isobel were being held there, there was little chance of approaching undetected in the numbers needed to have any chance of a rescue. Perkins was all for calling in a couple of helicopters and the headquarters' hostage squad – maybe the army. Even as he offered the idea, Perkins saw the flaw. Getting into the hideaway was one thing, getting the girl out alive was another.

It was Leonard and not Sanctuary who suggested using the *Madrigal*. Perkins added another thought about the cottage which convinced Sanctuary that the chances of getting close were slightly less than evens – which was about the best he could hope for. The Fat One remembered that the front of the small house commanded a splendid view down the waterway towards the headland. Long ago, a thick copse of conifers had been planted to form a horseshoe windbreak as well as to provide privacy. The break in the shoe was the window on the harbour and faced south-west. The yacht basin was to the east. Sanctuary's plan was full of high risks, but no one had anything better. Now, as he explained his idea to Pete and Rusty, he could see their doubts and something verging on disbelief in their faces.

The three of them were below in the *Madrigal*, crouched over the local chart. It was just dim enough for a lamp to be needed to show them the depth marks, buoys, shorelines and channels. It all looked easy on the Admiralty cartridge paper. Pete was sceptical.

'I have to say, master, you've got to be out of your tree if you think this'll work. Pig?'

Rusty, kneeling on the side-berth, ran a thumb along the channel from the lock gates to the first bend in the basin approach.

'Imperfect is an understatement. But Mr David has, this one must presume, certain experience in these matters.'

Sanctuary dredged a grin.

'The most dangerous thing I've ever done in this business is fill in an expenses claim.'

Pete sucked on his empty and yellowed clay. It was a hiss and whistle of disbelief.

The three men did not hear the car door. But they heard Leonard's quick, neat footsteps. There was hardly room as he ducked below. The policeman looked at all three.

'The number. It came up inside fifteen minutes.'

'And?'

'It's the cottage.'

Pete rubbed his chin with the back of his hand. He wasn't happy.

'Let's get this one straight. You stay below and we sail her out of the basin. Right?'

Sanctuary nodded.

232

'We take her down-harbour towards the trots. Yes?'

He pointed to the line of moorings a quarter of the way between the basin and the headland.

'Keeping as far over to the north shore as you can. Can do?'

More pipe-sucking. Rusty's head was on one side as he looked at the bulkhead chronometer.

'That means going within this hour, Mr David.'

'Sure?'

'Oh yes. Oh yes. There'll not be enough water to get in unless we do.'

Pete ran the parallel ruler from the point where the cottage was hidden by the conifers to the pencil mark he had made in the channel.

'And then,' he paused like a surgeon outlining an incision mark on an anaesthetised patient's belly, 'you slip over the side just here.'

'Hopefully the tide will carry me downstream and I can get ashore this side of the trees. You carry on and anchor or pick up a mooring at the head of the trots.'

'Where they'll see us, master. Or we hope they do.'

'They'd better. We have to assume they see us leaving, or at least you two. The way the tide sets here,' he dabbed at the chart where the trees hid the yacht basin from the cottage, 'I reckon I'll have two minutes before she comes into their view again.'

'It's not long, matey. Not long at all.'

'Which is why we can't go in the dinghy. In this light they'd spot it a mile off and, anyway, I'd have to make too much noise keeping her on course across the tide.'

Leonard was shaking his head.

'If you took the boat, I could come with you.'

'And do what? No. I'm better on my own. You watch from the mooring. If it starts to go wrong then you can call in Perkins and his 7th Cavalry. You're the only one who can do that. You can't if you're lying in a ditch with a hole in your head,'

Leonard wasn't finished.

'Won't they think it odd that we've anchored?'

'Maybe. Hope so. If they see the *Madrigal*, which they must,

233

even in this light, then they'll be spending their time watching you. Hopefully.'

'If indeed, it must be understood, they remain still in the Tupmanry.'

Sanctuary sat back, resting against the bunk cushions. He hoped they were. Whoever they were. If they were not in the cottage, then Isobel would be gone. They were already running out of time. He squeezed by Pete into the fore-cabin and pulled out Fisher's wet suit from the hanging locker.

'Let's go then.'

As they went through the lock, Leonard and Sanctuary, hunched in the tiny fo'c'sle, were well hidden from curious eyes. If the lock-keeper thought it strange that Pete and Rusty were taking out the *Madrigal*, then he did not say so. Instead, in the few seconds that it took them to pass through the lock, he wanted to know if they expected to be back that night; his inquiry sang out clearly above the *Madrigal*'s diesel and he accepted Pete's shrug with a wave and added a warning that the lock would be closed at ten. It hardly mattered. There would be too little water in the channel for their long keel until the early hours of the morning. Once out, they were gone for the night.

In his tiny office, Roberts was scratching and scrawling at a revised catering budget sheet. Through the half-open window he heard the knock of the *Madrigal*'s engine as she entered the lock channel and for a moment he watched through binoculars as the vessel's thoroughbred lines set up a small white bow wave in the failing light. Pete and Rusty were no more than a few feet away as Roberts panned the tripod along the boat's course. The Secretary nodded as if he understood, which he did not. But he nodded again, pulled a slip of paper from beneath his blotter, mouthed silently the number written in black ink, picked up the telephone and dialled a London number. As usual, a machine answered. The husky, distorted voice could have been anyone's.

Pete stood easily in the cockpit's centre, the busy throbbing of the engine-shaft reverberating through the deck to the soles of his canvas shoes. He gently pushed the tiller away from him,

234

easing the boat's head a little to starboard. Rusty had gone for'd to hand in the bowfender and was now unlashing the painted anchor in case they could not pick up a midstream mooring. That done, he glanced aloft to the white light at the masthead which glowed feebly against the darkening sky and then over his shoulder to the far shore, wondering if tide and dusk would aid their expedition. Pete nodded towards the mainsail tied neatly in bunches on its boom. The two men, after years of sailing together, needed little more than unspoken signs, and Rusty scrambled onto the coach roof and began loosening the nylon lashings.

Holding the tiller between his legs, Pete puffed life into his old meerschaum, flicked the dead match over the leeward side and looked back to the slight wake and the receding basin with its spills of masts stacked beyond the harbour's wall. An evening sail as casual as a stroll for a man with a dog and a pint in mind. With an easy sweep, *Madrigal*'s bow came to port, then steadied as Pete brought the tiller to midships, heading the slim blue vessel towards the line of downriver yachts moored in the far distance. The evening was still except for a slight breeze over the boat's port quarter. Pete set the engine in neutral, let the boat drift on its own momentum and ebbing tide; then, with a hand signal for'd, eased the block-and-tackled boom line as Rusty quickly handhauled the mainsail, ignoring the ratchety and noisy mast winch. Slacking away more of the line, Pete saw the white sail fill until the *Madrigal* picked up an extra knot from the stern breeze. He bent, switched off the engine and touched the boat gently once more to the north shoreline, keeping one eye on the blinking digital repeater on the bulkhead before him. According to the echo sounder, they had three metres of water beneath them, but, as Rusty dropped quietly into the cockpit, they both knew that if Pete edged too far from the main channel on the falling tide the *Madrigal* would find herself shelved by the mud humps of the natural harbour and stuck fast until high tide, there for all to see.

35

The Deputy's telephone was silent now. Dorothea felt numb.
The Deputy's request for an immediate conference with Controller had been refused. There was no matter on which they
might confer had been the reply. All that had been decided
had been done on the understanding that there could be no
further discussion. The Department was now Dark. Its role
had been withdrawn. Controller had given an assurance to the
highest level that the Department was no longer interested,
had no residual interest, had no reason to revive an interest,
and had no one off-base who would be in any way interested
in what was taking place along the south coast. Asked to elaborate, Controller said he knew no more. Asked then who did
know, Controller had said nothing. He said again, the Department was officially Dark. The Department's safety curtain had
been lowered, its audience ushered away, its cast disbanded,
its set struck.

'Why? Why? Why?'

He supposed Dorothea's cry a plea not a question.

'We backed him. We lost. That's why, isn't it?'

The Deputy's voice was miserably tired. Now he had the task
of explaining to himself why he had been right to let Sanctuary
have so much rope. The days of expendable staff were, he had
thought, over. The Third Worlders talked about dumping and
'letting go'. Some Americans still muttered about 'wet jobs'
but, to the Deputy, it was all cowboy stuff, played by cowboys.
Mentally, he shrugged. What could we expect from Washington
when one department would actually murder officers in other
departments, and innocent bystanders too, rather than jeopard-
ise operations. In London, matters had never been like that.
Only story books had a fund of stiff upper lips to test the

236

credulity on the points of Intelligence fangs. The days when there were stiff upper lips had been figments of wartime imaginations. The days when he thought he had control had never been. He knew all that. He had always known it, but conveniently it had slipped his mind. Now, David Sanctuary was being sacrificed to protect an operation about which he knew nothing. Someone did. That someone was outside. There was a tap, almost a scratch, at the door and it opened before he could bid.

Priestly was tight-faced. His skin was stretched. The smile was missing. The Deputy swung in his chair and nodded towards the high-backed leather hall seat on which Priestly occasionally pleased himself with moments of papal imaginations. The Deputy was waiting.

'Well? What do you hear?'

'I took afternoon tea with a friend. We enjoyed buns.'

Priestly's preamble was his way of saying that he, Priestly, knew of their contempt for his own private links and comforting intelligencers, but here was the watermark that distinguished his carefully cultivated network of insiders and their obvious hopelessness. The Deputy knew the game, but was not willing to play, not while he held the cup. He rolled the dice again.

'Yes, yes, yes. We know that. And?'

'Has David mentioned Ignatiev during the past few days?'

Dorothea nodded. She did not mention the reference to Fisher, nor the Cairo connection, although she guessed it had surfaced on Priestly's tea tray.

'In a nutshell then. I'm afraid our dear David has stumbled into something and consequently it would seem, as the eulogist remarks, we shall never see his like again.'

The Deputy thrust his palm up towards Priestly, who was still not quite smirking.

'Come on, Charles. Don't piss about. What's being said?'

Priestly ran his fingers across his smooth hair and crossed his ankles.

'Ignatiev has been on the Watch List ever since he went back to Moscow. Right?'

Again Dorothea nodded. She had initiated the Watch Tasking

237

and had grumbled when Overseas Three had produced little in the way of monitoring, nor had Photographic. When she spoke, her voice was impatient, she did not want Priestly to upstage them. Even in a crisis, there was a temptation to score. Perhaps because it was a crisis.

'He went back four years ago. He's been out a few times. He surfaced again after the August Coup. Spent time in London, we know he bought an apartment in Geneva, presumably with GRU money. We think he backed another in Paris, maybe one in Düsseldorf and he's been out three times in Cairo.'

The Deputy had lit his pipe. Between puffs he rasped the obvious question.

'Where does he fit in?'

Priestly recrossed his ankles and glanced down to make certain his patent leather shoes were not scuffed.

'It doth seem, my dears, that the *Glavnoye Razvedyvatelnoye Upravlenie* has been extremely busy during the past few months and that Ignatiev has been its busiest body.'

The Deputy had spent years fighting the KGB, he knew little of its military counterpart, the GRU. Priestly was telling him that they had been watching the wrong bear. He needed to be convinced.

'The GRU is finished, isn't it?'

'Certainly not. I'm reliably told that for the past two years the GRU has been regrouping. We've been studying the KGB reforms and they've let us. The Army had its face lifted and its hair-dos are legend. Military Intelligence has pressed on. But I have to tell you that according to my information the Ignatiev Gamble has got everyone on the run, largely I suspect because it's been the best-kept secret. As we all know, they are the only secrets that really matter because they're the ones which get us into war – or so we learn fifty years on.'

Dorothea was wearing a thin sweater about her shoulders and now she tugged it in as a scarf. She was not cold, but her senses were chilly.

'Charles, please. Can we get to the point?'

The Deputy nodded.

238

'What in the devil's name is the Ignatiev Gamble?'

Priestly was centre-stage once more.

'Right. The word is that the GRU regrouped after the shuffle at the top. It's the old story of Soviet middle management swaying from side to side and avoiding decrees and missives. They saw what was happening outside and they, or at least a somewhat influential group of them, knew that the whole structure of security was disappearing. We've known this for some time, have we not?'

Dorothea satisfied him with a yes. The Deputy did not bother. Priestly took another breath.

'Well now, when they saw what happened to Gorbachev, the Commonwealth, the army and even to Yeltsin whom, apparently, they detested, they decided that there had to be a plan, a scheme, a ploy, to throw the whole reform off-balance.'

The Deputy still had not received his answer.

'Ignatiev? What about Ignatiev?'

'Ah yes, dear Viktor Alexandrovitch. The intellectual of the GRU, or so some imagined, including, if I may point out, our own people. About three years ago, Ignatiev became the senior Viking for the GRU insiders. As you know, in the old Soviet Intelligence cells, the Viking controlled his own runners and hit men, the Borzois. Well, the new set-up was so controlled, so secret, that Ignatiev actually had other Vikings working as Borzois.'

'How do we know this? If it was so secret I doubt if we could have penetrated.'

The Deputy's point was a logical observation. Even though contact with the GRU would not have had anything to do with the Department, there was likely to have been an eyes-only memorandum. There had not been. Priestly's answer was a surprise.

'Forty eight hours ago, a photocopy of a file with all this background was sent to the private address of my teatime friend. There was a note with it which suggested that the original had never gone into the Green Basic. But, everything on Ignatiev was in that file.'

The Deputy looked from one to the other.

239

'In other words someone is covering up. Someone in our own Department. Shouldn't that have come to you?'

Dorothea nodded.

'Reasonably.'

'And?'

'It didn't.'

The clock struck a waltz to accompany an answer. None came. Priestly was about to continue when the Deputy interrupted.

'Author?'

'Of the original report?'

'Mm. Do we know?'

'Oh, indeed we do. It was Fisher. Hand-written to Controller. Although there is no evidence that it ever reached him. And, before you ask, we don't know who sent the copy. But it has to be internal to know the address. Yes?'

More silence. Then Dorothea opened wide the thoughts of the others.

'Why didn't Fisher send it to us? We'd handled him in the past.'

'I don't know. We don't know that he didn't. But it would seem that, if he did, then it never reached us.'

Dorothea was remembering the text of Fisher's note. Trust was hard to come by. Priestly was off again.

'Ignatiev's vision was simple, its execution complex and uncompromising. Ignatiev believed, and does still, that his grand plan would kill three birds. It would, in the somewhat irregular jargon of my informant, "screw the peace process, re-establish the state's reliance on the military, thereby stopping the rot and, for good measure, fuck the Ukrainians".'

On Priestly's lips, the expletive was quite inoffensive. The Deputy was sitting upright. The pipe was out.

'Explain.'

'But of course. Three years ago, Kravchuk in the Ukraine had the most unseemly to-do with Moscow. Yes?'

More nods. This time from both of them.

'At the heart of the contrariety was Kravchuk's refusal to let Moscow dominate Ukraine, particularly as this might well have

240

resulted in Kravchuk being set aside by his own people. The main area of contention was who ran the Army. Yes?'

Dorothea had worked on the study paper.

'More importantly, who had control of the Navy and nuclear systems.'

Priestly allowed a condescending nod of agreement.

'And there was the inner bull at which Ignatiev directed his shaft. The GRU in Ukraine stayed loyal to the ideals of the old Chief Directorate of the General Staff. In other words, to Ignatiev's merry folk.'

'What's this to do with Cairo? With Fisher?'

The Deputy didn't need Priestly the contemporary historian. He wanted Priestly the informant. The Deputy had a man in the field hanging on a thread. He wanted action, not a political science lecture.

'And Davy?'

Dorothea hugged her arms and wondered if Priestly's apparent indifference was real.

'Mm. Yes indeed. Cairo. The Fisherman and, of course, your dear, ah, Davy. Mm, I must say, I've never seen him as Davy.'

The hand came down, the pipe-rack jumped.

'Tell.'

'Well, it appears that Ignatiev's team in Ukraine which, incidentally, included those darling Russian SAS-lookalikes, the Spetsnaz, had the whole thing under control within a couple of weeks. The scheme was quite simple. They decided that two nuclear warheads should be detached from the Ukrainian arsenal and exploded in the UK and the United States. Friendly, eh?'

Dorothea listened to the evening chimes interrupting the ticking mantel clock, the Deputy listened to his own warning bells.

'The Ukranians are not that stupid.'

'I would offer the thought that they are in no way at all stupid. This was simply a GRU operation.'

'Was?'

'Excuse me. Is.'

241

Dorothea's voice was distant as if she had seen a sign riding a far cloud.

'It is not credible. Not at all credible. Anyway it doesn't explain whatever Davy's into.'

'It is credible, my dear, and it does explain. In our rather superior way, we think it incredible because we enjoy our society and we do rather well by it. Also, we have relaxed, if you call looking about us for jobs to do relaxing. But, if you are an idealogue like Ignatiev and his friends, if you feel threatened, if you believe that the Gorbachev-Yeltsin legacy has no organisation and even less authority to institute controlled reform rather than idealism that leaves your society threadbare, if you believe all this, my dear Dorothea, then you may well have a totally different perspective of what is and what is not credible.'

The Deputy was nodding once more. Could be.

'Cairo? Fisher?'

'Having a warhead is one thing. Doing something with it is quite another.'

'You said two.'

'I did, my dear Dorothea, but, alas for poor Ignatiev, even his people could handle only one of the very special kind they wanted. You see they wanted what I'm told used to be called an NDB, a nuclear depth bomb. A rather nasty depth charge. The idea was to manipulate some of the trigger mechanism and place it in a British harbour and, well, blow it up. But the problem was how to get it here. In those beautifully frosty days of the Cold War, they would have sent it round in a cargo ship or a trawler, or even a container truck; after all, that's how they used to put in their Spetsnaz exercise teams.'

The Deputy was tapping out his pipe on the heel of his hand.

'A yacht.'

'A yacht.'

Dorothea looked at one, then at the other.

'The *Madrigal*? How?'

'As far as we know, Fisher was working for the Americans. We think he teamed up with them in Moscow, not officially you understand.'

'But he was still in the Navy and, anyway, didn't his wife go off with someone in the CIA?'

'Certainly it appeared so and, to the bystander, why should she not? She was someone in the CIA anyway. Still is. The split was managed. He left the Royal Navy and joined up with a group that had been operating from Cyprus.'

'Corde?'

Priestly nodded.

'Precisely. Corde was put in by the CIA as a freelance group while the hostages were still in Beirut. They ran their own narcotics business and a little arms dealing. Their rather disreputable cover was supposed to give them the inside information on the skulduggery of the Middle East. But after the Lockerbie inquiry, the inside one, not the public one, then they were quietly pulled out. There were too many accusations that the whole Libyans-did-it story was wrong and that Corde would be revealed. But, by that time, they'd taken an interest in the really big arms deals that were being set up in the Central Asian Republics.'

'Wait a minute. Wait a minute. This is getting too dense for me.'

The newly packed pipe had gone out again. Matches were being struck in pyrotechnic fury.

'You mean, Corde kept going?'

'I do mean that.'

'But they'd been shut down by Washington. Isn't that right, Dorothea?'

'Right. Mind you, after the Oliver North business, nothing is surprising.'

Priestly beamed. His point made for him.

'Precisely. They were beyond anyone's control and, suddenly, they struck gold. They infiltrated the ring that was trying to buy tactical nuclear warheads from the Ukrainians.'

'From Kravchuk himself?'

'Not at all. From the Army. Fisher got involved in Corde. They needed a disaffected figure. Hence the business deals for him in Cairo. Although most of the dealing was done elsewhere, Cairo was the general crossroads.'

243

'Not Damascus? Not Tripoli?'

Priestly allowed himself a modest shake of the head.

'Not at all. After the Gulf disagreement, the Syrians were keeping too much of an eye on anyone in Damascus in case the tendrils of the egregious Saddam curled about dear Mr Assad's foothold.'

'Tripoli?'

'Everyone was watching Tripoli. However, it seems that Corde caught on to Ignatiev's scheme which was portrayed, initially, as a business arrangement for an unspecified weapon.'

Priestly eyed Dorothea's expression of doubt.

'And before we cry "unlikely", my dear, let me whisper Supergun? Everyone thought that nonsense until it happened. Yes? After the event, all seems clear. On the day, there is little but the fog of scheming, especially if one is expecting nothing to emerge from whatever international mist one is monitoring.'

She wanted to hear more.

'Go on.'

'Enter Mr Fisher. Or rather, neatly slotted in by Corde, appear Mr Fisher. Ignatiev knew him. Ignatiev knew, or thought he knew, that Fisher's wife had gone off with anything but a gentleman from Langley, Virginia. Ignatiev knew, or thought he knew, Fisher as an old friend, or at least acquaintance, with very little gruntle for his society and a typical two-gins-before-eleven-a.m. ex-colonial servant. More importantly, one with a fancy for very photogenic and exotic parties plus a boat riding at a mooring in the harbour of Alexandria.'

'Was it?'

'Most certainly. Fisher had bought the boat in, of all places, Minorca, although why I should say "of all places" I really don't know, considering it used to be one of ours in the days when Nelson had one eye.'

The Deputy walked over to the bureau and poured water from a cut-glass decanter. He sipped as he stared across the way to the other side of Downing Street. He nodded in the direction of the black door.

'Do they know all this?'

Priestly did not know. He said as much. For the moment it was not important to the Deputy.

'Tell me, Charles. Let's assume all this is true.'

'Yes.'

'Then three questions.'

'I have one.'

The Deputy shrugged aside her intervention.

'Just a moment, Dorothea. Charles, question one: are you suggesting that Fisher's boat was used to transport this warhead?'

'We think most certainly it was.'

'Did he know what the cargo was?'

'We can't know that. It seems unlikely. According to Fisher's report, they tried him out with other cargoes. He sailed to Gibraltar, the Azores and once to Ceuta. Nothing special, but his business as courier to Ignatiev was being established.'

The Deputy was shaking his head. Part bewilderment. Part disbelief.

'He was Ignatiev's personal Borzoi and this was being okayed by Corde, presumably Washington and, as far as Fisher knew, someone in London. Bizarre.'

Priestly tended to believe the whole operation confirmed his long-held view that the Intelligence gatherers spent too much time watching the doors and not the windows and therefore missed the really juicy titbits. The Deputy was under pressure and it was starting to show and he was finding it difficult to take Priestly's story at face value. The *Madrigal*'s part in the tale seemed incongruous. He said so.

'I really can't see why they would use a yacht. After all, they would have little control unless they put on board one of their own men and, anyway, why not use one of their own ships?'

Again, Priestly did not really know the answers but what he did know gave him more guesses than the other two.

'Any other vessel was being watched, especially any with Ukrainian connections which would have had to come through the Bosphorus.'

'Including submarines?'

'Nothing like that moved out of the Black Sea for months.

245

Don't forget the Navy was tied alongside except for the big carrier. No. We think it came out in a small cargo vessel, perhaps a coaster, and a rendezvous was made with the *Madrigal* at sea. We think off Hammamet, but we can't be sure. Anyway, the cargo ship returned and no suspicions. Mm? Question two?'

'Okay. Try this. Why do it?'

'Still simple. Explode the nuclear weapon. Not too much damage. Blame the Ukrainians. Moscow feels threatened, improves the authority and the emergency rating of the Army, Washington and London go on alert and even when they come off the hawks say this shows we can't believe in peace dividends, defence budgets are raised, deterrence is big business once more, Moscow has no option but to complete the restoration of the armed forces, return to general tension, crack down in Russia and the rest of the Republics go hang, the First Chief Directorate is back on the throne and the ghosts of Suslov and Ogarkov roam happily.'

The Deputy finished his glass of water and saw the assurance in Priestly's expression. Even the smile was back.

'And back to the days when the Soviet military believed the only stability came from fear and that freedom meant instability and the eventual destruction of the state, of whatever persuasion.'

It was Priestly's turn to nod.

'And don't forget, they have Balkan proof that freedom produces misery. You said there were three questions.'

The Deputy was back at the window, looking into the street.

'Why didn't we know about this? And why kill Fisher if he played Ignatiev's game?'

Priestly's sigh was genuine.

'I don't know the answers. But with whom I took tea had a disturbing hypothesis. If it is all true, and I hasten to bid that it is more likely than not to be so, then to reveal it would run the risk of it getting, let us say, beyond an acceptable tight circle. If it remains in that tight circle and if, or rather when, the matter is resolved, then life between London and Moscow can continue normally as if nothing has happened, because

246

nothing has. As to Fisher, well, I'm afraid the belief is that he was killed because he had played his part and therefore had to be destroyed, especially as it seems he was beginning to wonder why nothing was being done. Don't forget, he had written a report. If someone read that report and that someone was already in the circle, then Fisher would have to be relieved of any further duties. Mm?'

The Deputy flipped open the folder and read the copy of Fisher's letter to Sanctuary. He had run out of people he could trust. He pushed it across to Priestly, who instinctively took out his gold propelling pencil.

'What did he mean?'

Priestly answered without raising his head from the photostat.

'One doesn't truly know. But,' he looked up, paused, 'perhaps just that. My tea companion's fear is that certain of our community, perhaps those in the most holiest sanctum, do know, and wish success to the Ignatiev Gamble. It would, after all, restore the status quo ante, when indeed stability reigned and uncertainty had its advantages.'

'You mean, senior people, maybe over the road, are willing to risk the effects of a nuclear explosion? Nonsense.'

'Nonsensical perhaps, Deputy, but in such a state of mind not nonsense.'

The Deputy flopped back in his chair. He was rubbing the still-warm stem of his briar against his nose.

'And Sanctuary's stumbled into it and was about to up-fuck the whole operation. And therefore he has to go the way of Fisher.'

There was no reply. He looked at Dorothea.

'Sorry. You had a question?'

She had. It started as a whisper and arrived firmly.

'Two. You're pretty certain that the warhead was delivered in the *Madrigal*?'

Priestly's slight bow was that of a priest receiving a chalice.

'As certain as we can be. Certainly the vessel is, or so I'm told, quite capable of retaining its stability. I'm told that, in matters of ship construction, the *Madrigal* is reinforced, long

247

in the keel and also very deep. The weapon itself is relatively small and the technical assistance, although not necessarily the detonating procedure, also from Spetsnaz, would have travelled by other means – probably as mates in long-distance refrigeration lorries. I, we, understand this to be a regular method of inserting their agents.'

The Deputy had listened to Priestly, but had kept his eyes on Dorothea. He had anticipated Dorothea's second question but wanted to hear it from her.

'And?'

'And, well, the most obvious question. If this is true, where is this warhead and when is it set to explode? And . . .'

She paused. Help came from the unlikeliest source. Priestly.

'And do we really leave our David to burn?'

36

Sanctuary had been in the water for ten minutes. It was cold, colder than he had imagined. There was no sun to warm his forehead, not his eyes which were already feeling the sting of salt and whatever else had silted into the farm-banked channel. But, so far so good. Still hidden from the shore by line of sight and the envelope of the *Madrigal*'s genoa and mainsail, he had slipped over the port side without a splash and had trodden water as Pete sailed the boat on towards the lower reach moorings.

Now, he allowed the tide to carry him downstream and used his flippered feet to kick him at an angle across the set of the current towards the shore. In the increasing gloom of the evening he had good cover, but he knew also that summer strollers might spot his bobbing head and raise the coastguard.

Sanctuary was banking on the dusk, the slight chop of the water and the darkening shoreline to rescue him from those who meant well and to protect him from those on the far wooded side who did not. It was not hard work. The tide was setting him in line with his target, a point on the almost flat shore among mud boulders and weed where the crooked thorn trees stood as a ragged stockade between the water and the clearing that led up to the cottage.

By now, the breeze was running with the tide and the lapping water was coming from behind. But still Sanctuary found himself gagging on great mouthfuls of foul water. Ahead of him, the upturned-bucket shape of a port hand buoy told him that the main channel would soon be shelving and, as he reached the steel marker, he steadied himself, holding onto its chain while he tried to get bearings.

A brown gull, in its first season of freedom and oblivious to this blobbed creature below, perched atop the buoy, and together they surveyed the shore. The gull's interest soon called it elsewhere, but Sanctuary had to take his time. It was difficult to see from water level, but he was beginning to have doubts about the approach. The plan relied on the screen set up by the trees and shrubs on the north-eastern bank. But, if he recognised the blind spot, surely those in the cottage would have spotted the weakness long ago. From now on he had to assume that somewhere, just inside the tree line, someone would be standing sentry. He was about to let go and continue his drift, when he picked out the urgency of a small boat's engine.

At first he could not make out the direction, but then he spotted the squat hull shape and open day-cabin of the small converted fishing boat. It was heading downstream from one of the side-channels and towards him. For a moment he wondered if he had completely miscalculated. None of them had thought about water-borne sentries. The boat was getting nearer and he shifted round to the other side of the buoy.

Then he realised that the vessel was indeed heading right in his direction, but not for him but the buoy. Sanctuary made a quick assessment. The marker told the helmsman that he had to pass not between the buoy and the shore, but on the other side. As the boat neared, Sanctuary gently tugged himself around the rusting can, keeping it between him and the approaching boat. He knew that sailors instinctively look at marks as they pass or go round them and, just when he judged the boat to be abeam, he pulled himself beneath the surface and crawled hand over hand down the anchor chain. He counted to forty while he listened to the bubbling echo and turbulence of the propeller and when his lungs were about to burst he forced himself to rise rather than lunge to the surface; as he did so, the wash from the hull bounced him into the can and he wished for a curse to cover the pain as his bruised and wounded head thumped against the buoy. The boat was far gone.

The night seemed older and he had difficulty in picking up the shoreline and the humps of black clay boulders. When he did, he found that he had drifted further downstream than he had intended and was already dangerously close to the end of the tree line and the clearing that allowed the team in the cottage a panorama of the innocent harbour. He managed to swim against the current for a little way, but it was running too quickly for him. He guessed the tide might be ebbing at about two knots and, good swimmer as he was, Sanctuary found it too strong to stem. He was worrying about where he would end up when the problem was solved for him. First the webs of his flippers, then his knees, touched and scraped the bottom and he rolled over in weed and black slime before coming to rest against the wreck of a long-abandoned clinkered workboat.

Sanctuary estimated that the trees were no more than twenty loping paces away and for five minutes or so he crouched and waited and watched. Nothing. The breeze stirred the leaves and some sea reeds, but there was no sign of patrolling eyes. Nothing to suggest he had been seen. Perhaps they were waiting for him to move. He felt safe against the frames and strakes of the old wooden hull, and behind him the black waters and hidden far shore did nothing to give him away. He looked about and knew that he was doing nothing but putting off the moment when he would have to make his move.

He checked his only weapon, the long jungle blade treacherously serrated on one side and now safe in its scabbard strapped to his right thigh. It was Pete's. Sanctuary had not asked him why he had it. Now, he felt like an ageing gunfighter and was certain that in another era he would have taken a slug of rye before moving on. Instead, Sanctuary cupped both hands beneath the shallows and scooped up a mound of the stinking black slime. Carefully, he rubbed the muck into his face and head. He had no idea if it would stick as camouflage, but he had long decided that, as he was about to embark on a hiding-to-nothing, he needed every trick to stay in with a chance of success. Infection in the head gash seemed a minor risk.

Far across to his right and downstream, a large motor cruiser was churning the conservancy board speed rules into nonsense as its skipper drove it hard to the lock channel to beat the falling tide and spice the long hard day at the vessel's duty free cross-channel bar. The boat was lit inboard like some 1930s transatlantic liner and two spotlights erratically swept the course ahead. The vessel's passengers and crew were already unwinding and the rock tapes blared across the tatty but genteel waterway.

Sanctuary blessed the roughnecks and their crude disregard for the sailorman's code. It was the diversion he needed. More importantly, it was about the only one he was likely to get and, as the noise blasted to new heights, Sanctuary pulled off his flippers and ran in a double crouch for the trees. At every pace he expected to feel the vicious punch as a high-velocity bullet thudded into his gut. None came and he collapsed into the undergrowth with a feeling of surprise, relief and for a moment, nervousness bordering on exhaustion.

Across the water, the cruiser was completing its ultimate act of oafish buffoonery. With one huge engine running ahead and the other astern, the vessel was turning about on its own axis. From where he lay in the ferns, Sanctuary could hear more plainly the raucous music and see what appeared to be ten or twelve figures huddled in some curious dance on the flying bridge. The lock-keeper's lights were on but there was no sign that he was opening the front gates. Perhaps the thought of the partying crew attempting to dock alongside expensive glassfibre hulls was too much for the cautious keeper. Drunk in charge of a gin palace was a state best kept in the outer harbour rather than in the confines off the multi-million pound inner basin.

There were three or four whooshes and the sky was lit with flares from the cruiser. Sanctuary hoped that whatever was going on would not be resolved quickly and that it would divert the complete attention of the watchers in and around the cottage. He pushed his flippers even further into the ferns and set off through the trees towards the laurels and where he knew, from the map, the cottage squatted by the water's edge.

It was the whiff of cigarette smoke that alerted him. The dark figure was about three trees ahead by the line of shrubs, his back to Sanctuary. He was leaning slightly forward, totally absorbed in the manoeuvres of the cruiser. Sanctuary stopped. Waited. The figure ahead shifted his feet and took another drag on the cigarette. The action did not suggest someone expecting

252

visitors. Sanctuary wondered what to do. He had thought it through during the swim. Then was now. He wondered no more. Very slowly he pulled the long blade from its holder and moved forward, at each slow pace searching the ground ahead for moss patches to deaden his step. The cruiser crew had found another supply of flares. The man leant back, perhaps surprised. At that instant, Sanctuary swung his arm with all his mustered strength and sliced the half-metre of scalloped steel into the side of the man's neck. The jet of blood spurted into Sanctuary's face and chest as the man crumpled at his feet. Sanctuary staggered into the laurels. From the shadows of the cottage a man's voice called. Not an inquiry. Light-hearted. About the boat. The voice was Russian. Sanctuary searched his vocabulary.

'Glupy. Ochen glupy.'

He made his comment on the sailors' stupidity as short, as guttural and as non-commital as possible. From the shadows, another laugh.

'Da. Glupy.'

It had been enough. Sanctuary was trying to rub away some of the blood. His face, he thought, he could live with. Or die with. His hands were different. They had to be dry. He wiped them on the dead man's trousers. As he rubbed the webs of his fingers over the sharp leg-bones, Sanctuary was surprised at the slimness of the man's form. He had expected a more muscled torso. A standard Spetsnaz. Maybe they were not.

Sanctuary did not care. He now had a second target. The other man had called him. No one else. This suggested there had been only two men on guard outside. The cottage was curtained and behind the red drapes lights burned clearly in the downstairs rooms and one, faintly, in an upstairs window.

The cruiser was turning and looked as if it had given up hope of getting alongside that night and was heading downstream, perhaps to anchor off the head until the morning. He could not rely on another diversion and he wondered what they were doing on board the *Madrigal*. He wondered too who these men were. He had no light and, anyway, he did not believe he would find any identification on the body. He wanted some.

253

The Russian had thrown him. Who was he up against? The men who had come to his room at the hotel were English, at least one of them was. Or a good clone? As he pulled the body further over, the almost-severed head fell against his knee. For a second he stared. Then felt nothing. He was beyond that.

He reached inside to search the jacket and found the shoulder holster. Under the right armpit. Left-handed. It didn't matter now. The gun was a Heckler and Koch. He wasn't good at guns, but he recognised the weapon. Big. Powerful. A two-handed affair. It would stop a big man at fifty paces, if you were good enough to hit him. You had to have big hands as well as a good eye for such a gun. He wondered why the slim man at his knees had chosen it. He must have been very good indeed. Then so were the others. But he knew that already. The task now was to get whoever was inside the house outside.

Sanctuary had heroic ideas about kicking open the door and steaming in with all guns blazing. But the only advantage he had was that he knew he was there and they did not. Against him were numbers and, most importantly, if Isobel were in the cottage, he did not know where she was being held and how. Tied up? Walking freely? Upstairs? Downstairs? In the old boatshed by the jetty? The boatshed. That was it.

He was about to move through the laurels towards the water's edge when he saw the other man emerge from the house's shadow towards him. There was nothing he could do except move. If he stayed where he was he would be seen. If he made no noise, then the other man would become suspicious, because he would expect his colleague to be prowling.

'Vlad?'

Sanctuary grunted a reply. The other's response was suspicious.

'Vlad?'

He had paused. He was no more than twenty feet away.

Sanctuary sank further into the shadows, unsheathed his knife, unzipped his wet suit and started to pee noisily into the laurels, leaving his hands free about the metal handle. The other man laughed at the sound.

The man sensed rather than saw something was wrong when

254

he was at the edge of the bushes. It was not soon enough. His cry was not firm enough to raise an alarm, his hand not quick enough as he went for his gun. Sanctuary turned and lunged. The long knife went into the man's gut between his crotch and waistband. The two-handed upward wrench tore his stomach, his entrails and jammed hard against the breast bone. His open agony and disbelief were frozen in his dying eyes just inches from Sanctuary's blood-greased face as he lowered him like a carcass on an abattoir hook to the damp ground.

Sanctuary vomited uncontrollably over the open-mouthed, sightless face at his feet. For an age of seconds, turned away from the mess beneath him, Sanctuary stooped, hands on knees, gasping in gulps of air, his mind spinning in his own disbelief. He wanted to stop now. To stop. The programme that had managed his mind's survival kit so far kicked him into the next window. He had to go on.

He reached down to pull out the knife. It would not come. He turned away and started for the boathouse. Stopped. Went back. Put his foot on the man's chest, slipped, tried again and jerked out the knife. This time he did not attempt to wipe it. Instead it slipped into its lair more easily than before. He went into the trees and searched the first man's trouser pockets and found what he was looking for.

The boathouse was empty. Had been for years. It was open to the water and the landing stage and he heard the scurry of rats in the furthest corner. In the half-light he could see dirty boat-covers hanging from the tarred walls. From the other corner, where the rats had set up home, Sanctuary gathered old paint tins and half a can of fuel top-up. He splashed the cover and the summer-dried walls and took the dead man's cigarette lighter and turned up the flame. At first, the dust sheet smouldered, then it caught. The explosion of the fuel filled the shed as he ran back past the cottage to the safety of the shadows.

It took four or five minutes, but then he could see the flames and sparks across the roof of the cottage. Another minute and the cottage door swung open. Two men ran out, calling, and headed for the boathouse. Sanctuary, the Heckler and Koch in

255

both hands, was up to the main window as they rounded the corner away from him. The room was empty. He went through the doorway with the fury and determination of a wronged quarterback and took the stairs three at a time.

The room in front of him was half-lit by the window lamp. Isobel was lying spreadeagled across the iron bedstead, her ankles and wrists tied to the corner posts. She was naked. A dark-haired man, flattened nostrils, Mongolian cheek-bones, erect, soiled underpants around one ankle was struggling into his trousers. He got them as far as his calves, stumbled in his panic and fell to one side. Sanctuary shot him twice. Once in the nostrils. The second time where his nostrils had been. A memory of Vietnam flashed through his mind. A soldier ejaculating as he killed. He now knew why. He was no longer afraid, Isobel was screaming. Sanctuary called her name. She did not hear. Kept screaming.

'Isobel. It's me. Me!'

His wild, bloodied, muddied, figure bent over her. He slapped her face. She screamed. Then stopped. He took out the knife and slashed wildly at her bindings, grabbed her arm and headed for the stairs. It had all taken seconds.

They reached the bushes as the first of the men returned. He was running. Still calling. The other man was behind. Now they stood either side of the open door. One was clearly visible in the door light. Sanctuary was tempted to shoot. He might easily have missed and, anyway, he did not want to give away their position. The boathouse was like a beacon lighting the cottage in silhouette, dancing shadows where they crouched.

Sanctuary, still with a strong grip on the girl's arm, led her to the shore on the other side of the house and under cover of the tree line pulled her quietly into the water. They had not spoken.

The water was fast-running and Sanctuary floated as a life-saver might, on his back with the girl held lightly under the armpits. If her minders searched, then they did not do so in the waterway. He doubted they could be seen within seconds of drifting into the main channel. Behind them, small craft were speeding across from the boatyard and marina.

256

It took no more than twenty minutes and they found themselves at the edge of the trots and the visitors' moorings. In the dark he could see hull lines, but had little idea where the *Madrigal* might be lying. He tried a quiet call, but the effort of keeping the silent girl afloat and turning his head to get his bearings left him with a mouth full of dirty water and nothing else. He turned and tried again.

The current was now taking them across the line of boats which had swung on their moorings stem onto the ebbing tide. Three times he called and was about to give up when he heard Pete's distinctive voice from a hull just a cable's length away. He splashed, tried a wave and within seconds heard once again the same voice.

'Okay. Got you.'

The horseshoe lifebelt slapped the water in front of them as they drifted through the first line of buoys and, inside thirty seconds, he had Isobel hooked on, and the two of them were being pulled across the current to the low freeboard of the *Madrigal*.

37

Once Pete and Leonard managed to haul them on board, Rusty cast off from the mooring and, under a running jibsail, they sailed downstream. Pete said no to the engine and to the main channel. Instead he threaded through the moonless inner corridor of moored yachts and, it was not until they reached the lower channel and the broad stretch of water before the headland, that Pete put on as much canvas as he could raise from the big genoa and the full mainsail.

They were now heading to sea and, with some luck, would be well beyond the reach of whoever searched for them far away on the north shore. Through the head and now running to the bar buoy and on, the *Madrigal* cut through increasingly choppy seas, sometimes lifting on a peak and rarely thumping into a trough. Pete would keep her heading until they had put comfortable distance between them and land. Until they knew where they went from here.

By the time they were clear of the bar, Sanctuary had given his version of what had happened. He made it sound easier than it had been and gave no mention of the uncompromising way in which he had executed, pig-sticked and blasted his three victims. The swim down-channel had got rid of much of the gore. But he was still a bloodstained mess as he crouched below in the slippery warmth of a cowled sleeping bag.

In the forward cabin, Isobel, by now cleaned and dressed in an old white boiler-suit, lay curtained off, curled in her own womb of horror as she listened without hearing. The hesitancy in Leonard's voice said he did not want to know the full story but he wanted to know everything.

'You're sure they were Russian?'

In the half-light, Sanctuary shook his head.

'No. They spoke Russian. That's all. And not enough for me to tell. But it sounded right.'

'And nothing to suggest who they were?'

'We didn't wait.'

'What about . . . ?'

Leonard nodded towards the fo'c'sle. Sanctuary shrugged.

'Shock. Won't say anything. You've heard. Nothing.'

Leonard was saying that they had to get her to speak. Sanctuary was not listening. He could see only the agony in her face. Lashed to the polished brass corners. Naked. Bruised. The cynically white bed-sheet and lace pillows. He could remember only the rage. The need to destroy. To seek awful revenge that was not his to seek. He had not told them. He would not. He turned back to Leonard. The policeman had finished speaking. The question he had posed loitered in his eyes. He saw Sanctuary's eyes. Cold. Nothingness. Leonard felt frightened.

Sanctuary shrugged off his quilted shawl and stretched into the cotton trousers Leonard handed over as he went on deck. Sanctuary looked at his hands. They felt sticky. He rubbed them together. They were dry. They felt sticky.

He ducked inside the for'd curtain, and sat on the edge of her bunk. It was dark, but he could see her face. The eyes open. Sightless. Her breathing was beyond her as if the body, having drifted to some other plane, motionless, needed no effort, little support. At some point, she had pulled an old towel about her shoulders. He reached back into the main cabin and tucked her into the warmth of the sleeping bag. Isobel stirred, but did not look. He whispered her name. Nothing. He tried again, simple questions. The eyes flicked, her brain registering under the soft, subliminal interrogation. Somewhere, whys and whens and whos were being washed onto patient cells, awaiting the gentlest of sympathetic keys before responding.

The boat lurched into a steeper wave. The wind had backed and was now fresh, maybe force four to five. They were out of the shelter of the land and the *Madrigal* was slicing her way to the south. He could hear Rusty on the upper deck and the ratchety grind of the main winch. The further they sailed, the

259

further they were away from the problem. He needed to know the size of that problem before they went too far. They could not beat for ever.

Sanctuary put his hands to her temple, gently brushed away tired strands of fine blonde hair and stroked softly just as his father had done because his mother had not. Isobel's eyes closed and, once more, he whispered her name. Then again, the same questions. Slowly. But how much time? Perhaps all in the world. Perhaps none.

Once more, the *Madrigal* lifted, dumped down, and he heard the rattle of the disturbed anchor cable in the locker ahead of him. He heard the shift of the mugs and tins in the main cabin and the slide of a ruler, slipped from its notch in the chart table. He felt the strain of the hull as it stiffened, then flexed and ploughed on.

A soft hand, nails torn like the palms into which they had dug so deeply to complete the agony and hush the screams, came from beneath the quilt, searching first for his hand, then for his arm. He whispered her name, willing her back to the moment. He had to know what she had heard. What she now knew. Her hand was pulling him without any strength, stroking him.

He leant forward in the cramped cabin, beneath the down cover, and she nuzzled her face into his bare chest, her hands exploring in a dream of her own where touch was tender, gentle, not harsh, not brutal. Beneath her cocoon she snuggled to his hard flesh and he cupped her warmth in his hands and murmured in her ear. When she spoke, he hardly heard but did not interrupt and when they had done she did not remember and he covered her and left her and she slept.

38

In the main cabin, Sanctuary switched channels and called up the shore station. It didn't take long. Ship-to-shore priority was something of an adventure for the routine monitor. Dorothea was there. She had not been crying. But now she might. He told her. She told him. It was insecure. Dangerous. He needed to know. When they broke off, Dorothea, picked up her leather overnight-bag from the hall, left a note for Mr Dorothea, closed the front door behind her, ignored the lift, took the stairs to the basement and went through the laundry entrance. In the blue Ford saloon on the main street, the driver dozed while the other man kept an eye to the third-floor window in which Dorothea had left a lamp burning.

She walked through the service alley and waited near the entrance. There were no signs of watchers in the side street, but she waited for two minutes in the shadow until she heard what she had hoped for – a group chatting noisily on the way home from the nearby pub. As the drinkers approached the alley entrance, Dorothea stepped out, picked up their pace and walked just in front of them, hidden from any eyes watching the junction with the main road. She turned the corner into the now-closed shopping thoroughfare and searched the oncoming traffic for a taxi. Dorothea was looking too far ahead to notice the Jaguar slowing down beside her until it was alongside. She tried not to show surprise. Priestly was at the wheel. He did not smile. The back door was opened and a gruff voice from the far corner told her to get in. Dorothea hadn't much option.

39

On deck, the wind was whipping through the rigging and the *Madrigal* was shipping seas across the foredeck. The icy water ran the length of the top deck, most spilling through the gunnels, some washing its way aft and over the quarter. Peter had changed tack and they were now making five knots to south-south-east. Miles off, Sanctuary could see the running lights of large vessels. Container ships, bulk carriers, ferries. All sailing innocent passage. Over his shoulder, he could see the loom of a flashing light. He thought perhaps the Nab. He didn't know. It might be important later. Not now. For the moment they were standing off the main routes, away by themselves. When he'd opened the cabin door to the cockpit, three pairs of eyes had pierced his. Three anxious relatives searching for news of a daughter.

Sanctuary had to raise his voice, almost shout at the three leaning high on the starboard bench.

'If she's half right, we're in the shit. If she's completely right, everyone's in the shit.'

The cabin hatch slammed in a toss of a wave and Rusty dodged below to secure and to brew chocolate. Sanctuary squeezed in between Leonard and Pete, who was now oil-skinned and firmly wedged in the cockpit's corner, a strong bare hand on the varnished tiller. He spat to leeward. Leonard repeated his question.

'What does she know?'

'They've dropped something in Portland Bay, the harbour, by the naval base. On the sea bed.'

'What?'

Sanctuary did not look at Leonard when he replied.

'She doesn't know. Something. That's all. She's not the

world's best witness at the moment. She said there's a chart on the wall in the cottage. It was marked.'

Leonard bent his head in the increasing wind to Sanctuary's face.

'How did she know? What it meant.'

'Don't know. But she reads charts. Don't forget she corrected Fisher's charts of Portland.'

Pete was scratching his stubbled beard with the back of a wet fist.

'Drugs? You think that's the business, master?'

Sanctuary remembered the night visit to his room. The pressure from London. The viciousness of death visited upon Les, Bennie, the guard. He knew. Dorothea had told him. For the moment there was no need to say. He shook his head.

'Wrong league. The only thing we know is that tomorrow morning's D-Day for whatever they dumped. She says they talked downstairs.'

Leonard was blinking.

'Wait a minute. How did she know? You said they were Russians.'

Sanctuary shook his head.

'I said they spoke Russian. She said they had visitors. Then they used English. Always talking about the day after tomorrow. Everything centred on that forenoon. Thursday.'

'Pig!'

One of the cabin doors swung ajar. The brown deep eyes called a question. Pete had shifted the two men further for'd in the cockpit and was shouting instructions through the open door.

'Make sure all's secure below. It's going to blow a bit. Half a hooley by the look of her. Rig the lee-cloth for the missy. Don't want her falling arse-over-tit. And keep your shitty little paws off her. Okay? Then get up here.'

He spat again. He grinned his sharp-pegged leer. Pete was in his element.

'You want to go about, master? Portland from here'll be a piece of piss.'

Leonard was peering ahead. He'd given up on his glasses.

Rusty had tied them with a spare piece of halyard line. They were salty but clinging still to his sharp nose. He needed to get back in charge, although of what he wasn't sure.

'Wait a moment. Let's get a couple of things straight. Okay?'

Pete, eager to bring the *Madrigal*'s head into the wind and then on to the other tack, glanced at Sanctuary. Pete had no doubts about who was in charge. He'd pulled Sanctuary out of the water. Sensed the strength. Felt the whiff of controlled brutality. Pete Hogarth had run some strange people. Rum buggers, he called them. This one was something else and this was not the man who had slipped into the water before the dusk had set to darkness. If Leonard did not know, he would find out. Best let the new boss give the orders. Best to take them.

For now, Sanctuary nodded quietly to hear out Leonard. Pete knew hearing in some was not the same as listening. Leonard hesitated. Perhaps he too was on the point of commitment. Had to be, anyway. Just needed to admit it. To himself. The single door opened and Rusty handed through mugs, then disappeared below. Leonard sipped and talked.

'All we know is that a girl, who is in a highly drained state, tells one of us that something, we don't know what, has been dumped in Portland Bay. Right?'

There was no reply. But no dissent. He continued.

'We know that, if this is the link we've been looking for, well, then it's got to be important. People, normal people, even villains, don't go about blowing away bystanders unless it's very big indeed. Right?'

Sanctuary nodded.

'I'm a policeman. I see things differently. I'm telling you that this isn't something that we simply toddle off to Portland for and see if we are right. Hell, we don't even know what we're looking for. This league is way ahead of anything any of us has played. Another thing, I don't know what went on back there, but I'm not a fool. It wasn't simply Lochinvar rescuing the maiden from the keep. Look at the state of you both when we got you on board. They were very nasty dragons, Sanctuary, and not one of them was chasing us. Why?'

264

Sanctuary drained his mug. The wind had long cooled the black chocolate. But that was all. In an office, he would have got to his feet, signalling the interview was at an end. In the cramped cockpit, with the policeman wild-eyed in his uncertainty, more had to be said. Leonard, too intelligent for the Fat One to understand, could not understand what was now happening; he needed someone to make his conscience understand. Sanctuary's eyes were hard. No turning back.

'You forgot something else. Why didn't they kill her?'

He nodded towards the cabin where Isobel slept. He didn't wait for answers.

'They hadn't gone soft. But she gave me a name. She heard them. They were waiting for the man with that name to call. He had not. They wouldn't have done anything, gone beyond any of their instructions without his say-so. I know them now. They're Borzois. They were waiting for their Viking.'

Pete paid off the *Madrigal*'s head as he sensed a gust and the sloop slid through a trough and steadied herself on the shelf of the wind. He'd half an eye on Sanctuary.

'Dogs, master?'

'The old Soviet military intelligence had a hardcase wing. Intelligence-gathering. Everything from great secrets to running agents to stealing and buying information. Some of them were trained like our SAS.'

'Spetsnaz?'

Leonard had read about them. Everyone had.

'Right. Fanatical sometimes. But the leg-work was done by juniors. Men who were earning their spurs. If they got caught, so what? They called them Borzois. The tsars were Vikings. Vikings gave orders. Borzois barked. The Viking running this operation has gone to ground. That's why she's alive. I reckon he's in Portland.'

'Who is this Viking? If you're right.'

It was Leonard's final challenge.

'I am. His name's Ignatiev. That's why we're going to Portland.'

'Ready about?'

Sanctuary eyed Leonard. The policeman nodded.

265

'Ready about.'

Pete pushed the tiller away from him. The ropes ran through the stainless-steel blocks. For a second or so the headsail flapped as the bow came up into the wind. The starboard winch clicked furiously and the boat dipped into the lengthening sea and spray.

Below, Rusty watched the compass repeater swinging on to the course, checked the Decca position, cursed the fall-back repeater still jammed on some nonsense latitude and longitude and, on the chart, laid off a new course to take them south of Portland Bill.

40

Before midnight, the wind had once more backed and the seas had raced at them from the port quarter. But the wind and current had been good. They'd been lucky. When they'd come about for Portland, the current had been on the turn and for more than four hours had boosted their westerly passage, sometimes by two knots. And now, with the morning sun a couple of hours off its meridian, the *Madrigal* stood well out to sea and below the horizon of the coastline and the perilous Race that swirled about the headland.

The council of war had been brief and one-sided. Leonard had been violently sea-sick and was tucked down in a quarter berth where the close air hardly cleared his head, which for the moment was exactly where and how Sanctuary wanted him. Before he went to his bunk, Leonard had tried to put through a call to his friend, the coffee-swilling Queen's Harbour Master. He'd drawn a blank, said it was urgent, had given the *Madrigal*'s call sign and promised to listen out on the message transfer times. As he hit the quarter berth and called down for the end of the world, or at least his part in it, Leonard had heard Pete telling Rusty to monitor the shore station reports. Then, for Leonard, welcome oblivion as the *Madrigal* hit yet another long swell.

Sanctuary did not want the *Madrigal* sailing into full view of Ignatiev. He was banking on the violent weather change of the past twelve hours and the yacht's anonymity in the long waves and increasingly frequent showers and squalls to hide them until the time was right to sail close in to the harbour. His plan was to stay below the horizon until dusk and then, unlit, come close enough to Portland for him to get ashore using the inflatable. It was Pete's knowledge of the waters that helped Sanctuary make up his mind.

'This weather's here to stay for a couple of days, master. That rubber duck's got nothing more than a couple of knots in good conditions. You'll either capsize or end up in the Atlantic. Anyway, once you get close the outboard'll be like a search-light. We've got more chance bringing her in under canvas – that's if you happen to know where we're going?'

Pete knew who was in charge. He knew also almost every-thing was being left to chance. Sanctuary did not reply. He was never going to tell them all he knew. Nor would he pass on what he'd heard from Dorothea. He had no right bringing them this far. He needed the *Madrigal*. She was his safest way into whatever would happen at Portland. If he were to get out, which at that stage he doubted, then the boat would be the only way. He therefore needed Pete Hogarth's seamanship and his local knowledge. As part of the package came Rusty. The girl was on board because she was in no state to move. Leonard he might need later although he was useless for the moment. The *Madrigal* was overcrowded. Fortunately two were hooked into their bunks, out of the way.

Rusty was making even more soup.

'It is wise, Mr David. The warmth is good for us. For all of us.'

On cue, Isobel emerged from the main cabin. Gone was the warm tan, the skimpy summer T-shirt, the swing of her body. The carefree expression was haggard now, the eyes dulled, the rims worn red from tears. She was bagged up in a one-piece, salted sailing overall, a thick-collared blue sweater poking above the stick-down flap. The clothes had been Stuart Fisher's. She did not look little-girl lost and wistful, only tired, listless and in need of air. The wind was sharp and the spray persistent. She crouched in the lee of the cockpit hood. Still cornered, her arms wrapped about her bunched body like a vagrant waiting for the soup kitchen. She shook her head when Rusty offered a mug of soup and then took it and sipped, not seeing the pain and concern in his eyes.

In silence they battled back and forth along the coast with

268

Rusty at the chart table, logging, calculating, calling course changes, pinching from the tide to give to the wind. It was uncomfortable. It was tiring. Pete had rigged a crude helm check while Rusty completed his second job, fixing the automatic tiller control. By the afternoon, they started taking a lot of water. It was getting wet below and Rusty and now Isobel took turns pumping the bilges. Water had come through the for'd hatch and now, it seemed, through the stern tube. The *Madrigal* was seaworthy but, as Pete put it, 'as damp as a bride after two gins'. It was an unfortunate expression, but by that time no one was taking offence. All minds were on the uncertainties of the hours to come, even Leonard who surfaced in time to pick up the call from the Queen's Harbour Master.

Leonard could almost hear the panto slap of the thigh when he told Ralph they were bound for Portland.

'That's it! The paintings. Portland, but not the usual view. It's in the bay looking towards the breakwater. Anything for me? Over.'

The policeman told him what they knew, told him also that he had to trust what they said, ask no questions, take whatever action he thought necessary with his own people. Ralph seemed remarkably unflapped.

'No probs. There's a routine. What we can't handle we'll chuck at the Booties. Over.'

Leonard was feeling ill again and not much ready for cryptic clues.

'The who? Over.'

'Booties. Grunts. Royal Marines. SBS. SAS with flippers. Right? Don't fret, dear boy. We'll hack it. Just one point that'd be helpful. If there's trouble, when d'you think it'll show? Over.'

'The bets are on tomorrow. Over.'

'Oh dear. Oh dear. Thursday War day. Oh dear. Over.'

'Say again. Over.'

'Thursday War. It's an exercise we run from Portland. It's about to be shut down but until it is it's as near to the real thing we can get. Aircraft, whirlies, subs, damage control, the lot. Puts the ships' companies through their paces. There's an awful lot of traffic about. If someone's planning something, they couldn't have picked a better day. If it's Thursday it must be war. Okay? Over.'

'We may need help. Over.'

'My dear boy, we'll be there. See you under the clock. Or in heaven. Over.'

41

They tried to sleep but could not. Isobel had returned to the fold in a distracted way. She had no smile to show her thanks when Rusty fussed about her. He did not mind. To give her something to do, Pete let Isobel take a trick at the tiller on the long tacks out to sea. The runs and beats made life a little easier than the uncontrolled lurchings of holding the boat head-to-wind. Leonard had found, from somewhere, sea-legs of sorts and, as long as he kept on deck in the cold sprayed air, he could think clearly of the night to come. It was Leonard who pointed out that heading into Portland was unnecessarily brave.

'That's where we need to be, but why not make it into Weymouth? If your man's in Portland at least we'll be less obvious. There can't be many boats sailing in at last night. He'd spot us a mile off.'

Sanctuary was below, braced against the *Madrigal*'s pitch and yaw as he bent over the detailed chart, trying to second-guess where Ignatiev's team would have dropped its cargo. He looked about the cabin, now restored after its many rippings and searchings. He knew he could not be right, but deep inside there remained a belief that the secret was somewhere on board the *Madrigal*. He returned to the chart. Leonard had a point. It was too open for snooping and presumably anything suspicious would be reported to the Navy. At this stage he didn't want that to happen. Pete was waiting for Sanctuary's instructions.

'What you say, master?'

Sanctuary waved a delaying hand and read their position off the Decca. He tapped the second repeater to double check, but once more the neat rows of meaningless digits were unresponsive. He cursed technology and his own short temper and drew a pencil line from the first Decca fix to a beacon inside the harbour channel.

'Okay. Take us in on due west. We'll tickle the rest of the way when we get closer. You're looking for a quick flashing on the port bow and then a double green on the starboard. Then we'll pick up a double red somewhere between. That's your heading. I'll give you exact course when we see the lights.'

Rusty was on the coach roof and Sanctuary heard the first hiss of a canister as he finished inflating the dinghy. He was right. They might need it. Sanctuary was tempted to call up the Pier Master's office for a berth. It would have been routine for any innocent yacht. He resisted the thought and checked the chart once more. The Cove moorings were shallow, but he would send Pete out once they were ashore. It was while Sanctuary was checking the Pilot Book that he noticed some dull photographs of the coastline now on the starboard beam. He remembered the bad water-colours, perhaps sketched from sea level where all the world looked strange. The Queen's Harbour Master had said Portland from beyond the breakwaters. It could have been anywhere. It wasn't. He handed the open book to Leonard.

'We're on target.'

It was dark again. The wind had dropped, though the breeze was defiant enough as the *Madrigal*, her headsail furled and mainsail dropped, motored between the furthest points of the channel, alongside the deeper berths. There was no signal from the Pier Master's office and the Customs light gave no flicker of having seen them. Pete did not want to hang about if they were not needed. As he put it, there was no point in Sanctuary's only back-up scraping the bottom just when he needed to get out in a hurry. They arranged to contact each other at regular intervals. Leonard was certain he could get alongside a radio once his NATO-standard friend arrived. There was little talking now; they'd done that and Pete dropped the engine into reverse for a few seconds and hove to with just time for Sanctuary and Leonard to slip over the side into the dinghy. On the evening-lit quay, onlookers gave them interested glances but no more than might have been expected from bystanders. Sanctuary was in the dinghy, holding her easily alongside the boat's port quarter, when Isobel, the sailing suit and sweater discarded, started to climb down. His look said no.

'I'm coming.'

He pushed away from the dark blue hull.

'No.'

'You may know Ignatiev. I'm the only one who's seen his friends. You need me.'

By the time they were ashore, the *Madrigal* was passing the Harbour Master's office heading for the open sea and Rusty was unlashing the mainsail ready for hoisting.

From the shore, a dark-haired man, unremarkable in black tracksuit and trainers, watched the *Madrigal*'s departure through sturdy infra-red binoculars.

Leonard headed for the privacy and telephone of the central police station. Sanctuary and Isobel pounded both sides of the harbour, keeping away from lamped patches, watching and listening for any signs of Ignatiev. By the time Leonard rejoined them, it was clear they were time-wasting. Neither Sanctuary nor the girl really knew where they should look and only Leonard had any leads.

The Queen's Harbour Master had driven over from Portsmouth. There was a small problem. The Navy was at its most obdurate in these situations, reluctant to do anything which would cause trouble. Ralph was trying to solve it on the old boy net and his reputation. He had contacted London. Security had been informed. If it is possible to get blank looks on telephones, Ralph was getting them. Another man might have gone to the pub, or called the duty officer and left it at that. Ralph knew Leonard. He knew something was going on. His instinct said stay out of it. He hoped he had nothing to lose. His thespian brother would have thought him splendid.

Ralph's old Alvis was maroon, large and obvious. Sanctuary and Isobel sat in the deep leather rear seats and listened to Ralph's report.

'My oppo here is an old friend. I've also had a word with SOO.'

'Sue?'

Ralph apologised to her.

'SOO. Staff Officer Operations. We were at Dartmouth together. He's briefed FOST, sorry, what we used to call Flag Officer Sea Training, that's the admiral when he's at home. He's apparently quite excited and MOD's now into the act. There's only one problem. Nobody in Whitehall seems to know anything about this.'

The sailor looked over his shoulder. Gave Sanctuary a please-be-honest-with-me look. Sanctuary looked from the side window.

'You gave Ralph the number I gave you?'

Leonard nodded. Ralph shook his head.

'Oh yes, old man. Done that. Itsy-bitsy problem. Some duty wallah said ta very much, squire, but don't know what you're talking about.'

Sanctuary, hands in pockets, was scratching. Now the scratch became almost a tearing motion.

'Man or woman?'

'If you'll forgive my saying so, old man, bit of both. Sorry. Bit cheap that. But it's true. Oh, and when I mentioned your name, he, she or it, ah, said never heard of you.'

He appealed to Leonard, sitting beside him in the front seat.

'It would be *très* useful if someone would let me in here.'

It was Sanctuary's decision. They needed a little more if they were going to be of maximum use. He remembered Dorothea's words. Had missed the warmth. Had disregarded the fear. He wondered if she had got out in time. Where was she? She would have been useful. Wouldn't have needed the telling.

'Okay. Can we drive on? Portland?'

Ralph nodded.

'It's very close, but I can give you the scenic tour if you like, along the strand until you're ready.'

Sanctuary nodded to the rear-view mirror through which Ralph was watching, just his humorous eyes visible under bushy brows. The sailor switched on and pressed the starter. The Alvis gave a deep, throaty, gurgling chuckle and stole away from the kerb in search of Regency arcades and late holiday-makers walking off suppers until it would be decent to return

274

to their boarding houses. As he talked, Sanctuary watched the streets and, most of all, the people.

'All I can tell you is straightforward. There's no proof I can give you. Okay?'

'Fine, dear boy. Transmit.'

Sanctuary's voice was cold. It came from a vending machine. It would give the exact weight, no change, nothing more. Have a bad day.

'A man called Ignatiev is GRU. Russian military. Okay?'

Ralph nodded. Isobel was looking out of the other window. Leonard had turned. The attentive policeman still. Almost the accomplice. Almost.

'Ignatiev has organised at least one small nuclear device to be shipped in here. It's somewhere on the sea bed.'

The humour had disappeared from the mirrored eyes. Leonard was blinking, rubbing at his spectacles with a yellow duster he'd found in the leather door-pocket. Isobel was deeper in the seat beside him, her head flopped back, her eyes closed. She was the first to speak.

'Why?'

'Doesn't matter. It's about power. Nothing to do with us. Okay?'

It was Ralph's turn. He changed gear in time to his question. Accelerator off. Clutch down. Gear stick shifted. Clutch up.

'You're more than certain?'

'Yes.'

'Fuck.'

Leonard was shaking his head. Not disbelief.

'If this is true, why's no one doing anything? Why are they saying they don't know you?'

Sanctuary's eyes, in the half-light, showed no emotion.

'There's been a black on it. Fisher believed someone at the very top was involved. We don't know. We simply have to . . .'

Sanctuary was interrupted by Isobel. He wondered why he hadn't thought of it.

'We simply have to show ourselves instead of hiding.'

She was looking at him, ignoring Leonard and the driver. It could only be the two of them.

'They know us. They want us. If we want them, we have to give them some bait. That's us. You and me.'

42

He looked slimmer. Maybe thinner. Perhaps it was the black tracksuit. But then he saw her. He moved quickly. It was the walk. On the balls of his feet. Short paces. An over-sharp footballer. She had seen that walk, seen him, from her upstairs cell window. He ducked into the first opening, an alleyway by one of the tall waterside houses. Sanctuary had followed her pointing finger although the man had gone. They did not run but Isobel was almost trotting to keep up with Sanctuary's stride as they reached the opening. Tracksuit had disappeared.

In the alley, a small boy, too young to be out so late, was squatting on his haunches by an open front door. He was reading a comic. He did not look up as they went by. The alleyway led through to a narrow lane. The yacht basin must have been close by. It was quiet. No traffic. Sanctuary thought he could hear the frapping of rigging and shrouds. Nothing to the left. Nothing to the right. He had gone. Isobel looked back. The boy was still in the doorway. He was looking at them. She walked back, smiling as easily as she could.

'Hello.'

The boy didn't answer. Stared at her.

'We seem to be lost.'

He was eight or nine. The comic was almost done. He looked down at the game where you had to join up numbers to make a picture. He was tracing the numbers with his fingernail.

'We were, eh, trying to catch up with our friend. Did you see him? Black tracksuit?'

The boy looked up. She had baggy blue trousers and a sweatshirt. She'd got big thingies. Bigger than his sister's. He'd watched them bouncing when she went up before. He tried not to look at them. She'd got a nice voice. Wasn't local. He'd have known. He nodded.

'Good.'

She was crouched with him. He could smell something funny. Didn't smell good. He looked at her teeth. Maybe she didn't clean them.

'Did you see which way he went?'

He shook his head. Isobel stood. Sanctuary was watching from the corner. Impatient. Waiting. She started to go.

'Prob'ly he went home.'

The boy was concentrating on his comic.

'Really?'

He nodded.

'You know where he lives, then?'

'One of the holiday flats. By the shop.'

She smiled again.

'That's right. Now I remember. Eh, which shop? That's the bit I can't remember.'

She was looking back to see if Sanctuary was waiting. He was. The sweatshirt was stretched. The boy was looking at her breasts. She caught his eye.

'Round the corner. You know. Where they sell the sailing stuff.'

They were bigger than his sister's. He could feel himself blushing. He scrambled up and went in, slamming the door behind him.

The boat chandler's was unlit. Sanctuary peered through the window. There was a special offer on anti-foul paint. He could see brightly coloured waterproof jackets on a circular hanger. There did not seem to be a back office. All was dark. At the side of a white door there were four oblong buttons. Flat 1, Flat 2, Flat 3, Flat 4. Sanctuary stepped back. There was light in the top window. He wondered which way the flats were numbered. In real life, Sanctuary would have had an American Express card to slide into the crack between door-jamb and catch. It would have swung open, probably quietly. In his real life, Sanctuary had not found much call for a credit card at the cottage, on the boat and now in the back streets of the ferry

278

port. He didn't need it. It was Isobel who tried the obvious way in. She turned the handle. The street door was not locked. Sanctuary put his hand on her arm, gently closed the door, and led her back to the corner of the street.

'If they're there, then fine. But there's no point in us rushing them like the reverse balaclava-and-stun-grenade loonies. We'd be useless with one-inch holes between our eyes. Go and pick up Leonard. Tell him where I am.'

Isobel started to argue. Didn't get far. She wanted to kiss his cheek but didn't do that either. Instead, keeping close to the wall, she headed in the direction of the town and where Leonard and the sailor had promised to meet by the clock tower. Isobel had her own thoughts; they were no longer the wishy-washy ideas of someone caught in a melodrama. She had no concept of danger. She had been there. She was back. She was part of what was unfolding. If she thought of revenge it was not retribution. Her right hand clenched and unclenched an imaginary blade. She wanted to be holding something so sharp that to see the curve of steel would frighten. She wanted to cut and slice those who had savaged. She wanted the bare belly of a man who was no more. A cut, a slice, a folded skin. She wanted to see his head rock from side to agonising side as hers had. She wanted to hear his shrieks just as she had heard the futile screaming inside her head as she had at first twisted and wrenched and then succumbed, seeing nothing but a fire behind her eyes. She wanted to get rid of her pain. She did not see about her. She did not see the Jaguar parked behind an old van.

Sanctuary no longer believed in luck. He did not believe open doors were doors someone had forgotten to shut. And so from the corner shadow he watched the top window and listened for the rattle of the discarded Coke can he had placed by the white door.

It took nearly an hour. The light burned on. Once an old lady shuffled along the street, men's carpet slippers easing her corns, a stiff clip-top handbag hanging regally from the crook of her bent arm. If she noticed Sanctuary in the alley shadow she gave no sign. Sanctuary watched her coming and kept an eye on her going. He didn't trust anybody until he was dead.

He heard the clatter of the real thing but not the door. The light burned on. Tracksuit looked both ways, hugged the wall as he short-stepped towards the brighter street. Six one, six two? Brown hair. Not fat but not slim. A dull gold ring. He had started to peer into the alley's gloom when Sanctuary's arm came about his neck. He was slammed against the hard stone wall, a pulverising knee crunched into his tracksuited testicles and, as he slumped on his side, both hands instinctively holding his wounded groin, a size eleven shoe belted into his face, crunching into his nose and splitting his cheek-bone. Sanctuary grasped him by surprisingly long hair and trouser seat and thrust him onto his belly with his head bent back and bloodied face pressed against the wall.

'Where's Ignatiev?'

Silence.

Sanctuary stood. Kicked him hard between the widened buttocks, knelt, tore at his collar, snatching back his head until the throat was stretched and arched that it might tear.

'Where?'

The man could not speak. He was choking on his own blood. Sanctuary banged his face against the wall.

'Where is it? Where's the warhead?'

The man was gasping. Dawning unconsciousness. Close. He tried to slump. Sanctuary yanked his head. The shattered cheek and pulped nose sounded like beef slapped to a butcher's bench before chopping. Sanctuary's mouth was by the man's ear. He could smell the gagged vomit.

'Where? Where is it?'

This time he did not batter the wall. He didn't want him unconscious. Not yet. Instead, holding neck and hair, Sanctuary grated the man's face against the stone. He tried to scream. Could not. No room in his throat to scream.

'Where?'

The voice was hard to hear. The accent thickened by race and gore.

'Fort.'

280

'What?'

He pressed and shredded as the man went silent.

'Where?'

The breath was hardly there. The voice just.

'Fort.'

'Fort? What fucking fort?'

'Fort.'

He pressed the bared and splintered bone into the pointing, and twisted as he would a freshly cut lemon for cocktails.

'What fucking fort?'

'Fort Head.'

'What?'

There was an air-gassed phut. Another. The man's body jerked the first time. Not the second.

Sanctuary rolled and came into a crouch in the darkest hollow of the alley. A man was standing by the entrance. Tall, slim, slightly stooped. Too arrogant to hide. The long barrel of his semi-automatic made even longer by the silencer.

'Hello, Sanctuary. So you still play this game.'

Ignatiev's accent was as Sanctuary remembered it. Cultured. Tight. Spare. There was none of the throat-clearing sounds of peasant centuries experimenting in a new tongue. Ignatiev was a Russian because that's what it said on his diplomatic passport. Sanctuary said nothing. Cursed inwardly his short breath.

'As you, Sanctuary, would say, a sprat. So, now you know, or think you do. And it does not matter, because it is your turn, my dear friend.'

The corner light was on Ignatiev's face as he turned. He was smiling. Perfectly cleaned and maintained teeth. The horrendously expensive Australian in James Street was to be congratulated. Sanctuary remembered the sad-faced instructor in Wiltshire.

'If there's nothing much left, gentlemen, you can always stick a question between you and the trigger. Make it ludicrous. Officially, it's supposed to come under Dislocation of Expectancies. Unofficially, it's called throwing the bugger off guard. Chancy, but could be more effective than prayer.'

Sanctuary took a chance.

'Why did you lift the girl when she was working for you anyway?'

He shifted a couple of feet. The shot didn't come. The smile had gone.

'Don't be so fancifully English. Dear Miss Rolfe simply got in our way. The fools should have done with her.'

'They were told not to.'

'Of course not. They were told nothing. That's why they did nothing.'

'By your people in the Department. They wanted no more killing, especially one of our own.'

'Come now.'

'She's worked for us since Cairo. Your people recruited her. Fisher did.'

No answer. Sanctuary pounced.

'Now they've pulled the plug. Chickened. You're on your own.'

The arm was moving. Sanctuary's voice had given direction. Range.

'No, Sanctuary. You are. It is too late for anyone to pull out. Especially you.'

Sanctuary felt the splinter of brick a micro-second before he heard the shot. He rolled. There was another ricochet. No gassed and smothered shot. A sharp toytown crack. But from the other end of the alley. Ignatiev was running. Away. Up the lane. Away. Sanctuary could hear feet. Many feet. He had no way out. But Ignatiev was gone. The feet were slowing. Three figures at the alley's head. One with a gun.

'Do come out, David. This is becoming all rather silly.'

Priestly was being pompous.

43

The Deputy had no liking for what was going on. He disapproved. Dorothea was concerned for David and trying not to show it. Priestly had put away his handgun and was walking back to the Jaguar. Priestly's instinct was that he would be followed. He would forever rely on his instinct to be followed rather than directly instruct. It had advantages, including the fact that the Deputy was following him. Following, denying the still form.

'Get in.'

Sanctuary eyed the Deputy. He trusted no one. Perhaps Dorothea. Fisher could not have been wrong.

'Why you here?'

'Get in.'

Sanctuary shook his head.

'Why?'

Seething. The Deputy clapped his arms against his sides.

'Get in for God's sake. The place'll be crawling with plods.'

'Why?'

Priestly was in the car. Tapping a soft-gloved finger on the driving wheel. The Deputy had opened the door. He nodded in the direction Ignatiev had taken.

'You're in trouble, David. This is another game. Not our stuff. You're on fire. We came to get you out.'

Priestly's glance up from the driving seat was his most patronising.

'We're not asking for gratitude. But you are rather alive, dear boy. You were about to be positively dead. One suspects the Sanctuary family tree would not have stretched to a reasonable turn-out at the crem had we not appeared. So yours, if I may suggest, is not to reason why.'

Sanctuary ignored him.

'How did you know?'

The Deputy's voice was at its gruffest. Old school of the Department. The last of them.

'You'd told us the town. You were in a boat. We saw you land. We lost you. After that? Frankly luck.'

'Why didn't you make contact immediately?'

Priestly allowed a hint, a cultivated hint, of impatience.

'You didn't need us. Not then. That, though God knows why, that is why we're here, David. Now, coming?'

Sanctuary shook his head. Looked at Dorothea. She was pleading. The voice was soft, almost lost in the late summer air.

'Time to come in, Davy.'

He turned to go. The Deputy had opened the rear door.

'Where the hell are you going? In.'

Sanctuary turned to face him. The head was across the roof from where Sanctuary was standing by the rear bumper. Priestly was watching him in the wing mirror. Sanctuary nodded.

'Ask him.'

Priestly looked away. The Deputy's gruff was now growl.

'Ask him what? What the blazes are you talking about?'

Sanctuary's eyes had not left the mirror. Priestly was back, staring.

'He's the best shot in the Department. He couldn't have been more than twenty feet away.'

He turned again. This time he went. The long strides were more a run as he made off in the direction Ignatiev had taken.

Behind him he heard the ignition. He didn't look back. From the chandler's doorway, a rumpled figure, unseen from the Jaguar, fell in beside him.

'Who were they?'

He said nothing. Took Isobel's hand.

'You must tell me. It's important.'

They were beyond the lane, the alley, the street far behind them. He stopped. He seemed even taller in the half-light.

'Why?'

'One of them came to the cottage.'

284

Sanctuary grabbed her by both arms, his bent head now inches from hers.

'You're sure?'

She nodded. A child's head nodding to be believed. Memory triumphant. Fear sweeping aside boldness, calculation, determination. Sanctuary looked back. The street was clear.

'Right. Which one?'

'I don't know.'

'You must.'

'I don't. I couldn't see them. I was in the doorway.'

'How d'you know then?'

'The voice. I heard it. But it was one of them. I know . . .'

'What did he look like?'

'I don't know that.'

Sanctuary relaxed his grip. His sigh was long and infuriated.

'I don't. I never saw him. He was downstairs. But I heard him.'

The shot shattered the window by Sanctuary's shoulder. He threw Isobel to the ground and ducked into the middle of the road. Wherever he was, Ignatiev wanted him, not her. The second shot was wide of the target and he ran forward, crouching and yelling.

'Run. Run back. Keep running.'

He heard her go. Lights were on. Windows were opening. The gunfire. The shouting. The breaking glass. He reached the corner. The busy street was innocent as charged. Gunfire? No silencer. Silencer blunts range. Maybe. Why not closer? He heard the voices. Ignored the questions, the did-you-see-thems?, the what's-happenings?, as he ran back to the corner and the chandler's. The Jaguar was gone. He wondered where. Wondered why. Which one? Now it did not matter. It would. Now there was no time. She was waiting. Frightened. The hands shaking. No longer clenching and unclenching vengeance. He grabbed her wrist and headed for the centre. Somewhere he could hear the police siren. They would find the alley. Wrong body. But never mind. It would do. Why no silencer? Too many questions. What was Fort Head?

285

44

The sailor told him. Of course he would know. Now they were heading along the short journey to the base. He watched for the Jaguar. Saw others. Never that one.

'It's on the Outer Breakwater in the naval base, old bean. Why?'

'That's where the warhead is.'

Leonard was once again leaning over the back of the leather passenger seat.

'Certain?'

He didn't reply.

'How d'you know?'

Sanctuary looked at the girl. She was still. He put out a hand. Touched her. He could feel the forearm muscles stiffen. Then relax.

'All right?'

She nodded. The hair escaped from her top-tie. She wasn't.

'I just do. What chance of getting your people to check it out?'

Ralph shrugged his shoulders, gripping and ungripping the huge-spoked steering wheel of the aged Alvis.

'We haven't a mine-hunter on stand-by. I'm told it would be the morning.'

Leonard snorted.

'That's potty. This is an emergency, isn't it. Not a training exercise.'

'Look, old bean, I can't whistle up a ship that isn't anywhere in sight. Normally, there is. Today, there isn't. By the time one's flashed up from Pompey and here, well, of course it could take hours.'

286

'Divers. You must have them on stand-by. What about the Royal Marines or whatever you called them?'

'SBS? I'll give it a go.'

They were approaching the barrier and Ralph slowed the engine to a stop. The young security guard peered in the car and then at the identity card offered by the Queen's Harbour Master. Ralph looked apologetic.

'I'm sorry. We'll have to sign in. Everyone out.'

It took ages. Sanctuary and Isobel had no means of identification. The guards, no longer the sound sailors who would have more easily accepted the say-so of the Commander, were reluctant to let them in. It took telephone calls and valuable minutes before lines in books which wanted to know names, rank, status, service numbers, contact numbers, registration numbers, seemingly a *Who's Who* entry, were satisfied. Tabbed with plastic identity cards which could have applied to anyone, they drove on. Sanctuary had said nothing through the rigmarole at the security box. He was thinking what had to be done. Where Ignatiev was. How much time they had, or did not have.

'Can we get hold of some diving gear? Flippers, mask, gas?'

'Can you use it?'

The girl answered before Sanctuary.

'I can. I've been diving since I was a kid.'

Sanctuary looked at her. She was telling the truth. She'd gone beyond bravado.

'Yes.'

'I'll try.'

Ralph did not sound confident. He had pulled up by an embankment leading to a row of wartime single-storey huts. He guided them down narrow stone steps and switched on the corridor light. Small rooms which he called cabins were to the right and left. There was a strong smell of soap and steam central heating. Ralph opened the first door. There was a bed, a chair and chest of drawers.

'The heads are halfway along. If anyone asks, you're Sea Rider Evaluation, SRE, and I'm your escorting officer. It doesn't mean anything but it'll do. Wait here, I'll see what I can do. Can't promise. But I'll try.'

The outer door slammed on its spring and he was gone. Isobel looked in the mirror. She seemed surprised as if she didn't recognise herself. She had changed. Leonard would never know how much, and said nothing as she went off in search of a shower. He eyed Sanctuary. It was the first time they had been alone since they had left the yacht basin. He was fishing for the yellow duster which had found its way into his jacket pocket. Sanctuary was lying on the bunk, legs bent at the knees, hands behind his head. Eyes closed. He must not sleep. Must not. He felt drained. Leonard, polishing almost done once more, was leaning against the chipboard chest of drawers. The mirror reflection exaggerated the nodding of his curly head. Without his glasses, Leonard was another one on the edge. A referee would have made him take the full count. Sanctuary thought he would probably frighten small children. Now he was mouthing something as if trying to find the right form of words. He did.

'I've spoken to my people. They said the cottage was like an abattoir.'

Sanctuary turned on his side. Face to the wall. His voice was muffled.

'Pity.'

'Is that all you can say? Pity!'

Sanctuary said no more. Leonard did.

'I'm supposed to be taking you in. It's a nightmare. It makes Beirut look like Bournemouth.'

He might have gone on but Ralph arrived back with a great deal of clattering and banging. He had raided the Clearance Diving Office. The flippers were one-sized. There was one wet suit. There were only two gas bottles, but he had found three underwater lights. Isobel came back and Sanctuary handed her the wet suit. It wouldn't fit him anyway. He needed her, or someone, below in case something went wrong. It had to be Isobel. There was no one else. Ralph had lost his seadog veneer.

'Best I can do, I'm afraid. I've raised the general alarm. SOO's put a block on tomorrow's exercise, for the moment. I've told him this is all hush-hush, which I suppose it is. He called in a mine-hunter and we should have a Clearance Diver in a couple of hours. We can wait or go. What's it to be?'

'We go.'

'I've jacked up the inflatable. But, until the team gets here, we're on our own.'

Sanctuary nodded his thanks. Another time and he would have shaken hands. There were no longer other times.

Isobel was stripping off. Leonard turned away. Ralph looked embarrassed as the girl stood for a moment, naked, damp from the shower that could not wash away the past few days or the physical bruises. She stretched, then bent to struggle into the rubber suit.

They left Leonard ashore. If there were to be back-up, he knew where they were heading. He did not mind. His nerve had not left him. Now he was drained.

Ralph piloted the rubber boat along the inner side of the breakwater, passing the three blinking lights that warned of the danger beyond. They reached the end of the mole, rounded beneath the quicker-flashing red lamp, and immediately felt the rougher chop of the open sea. Ralph held the dinghy into the breeze while they tested the compressed air bottles, strapped them to their backs and took the long thin line the sailor had secured to the bow-ring.

Sanctuary and Isobel had not spoken. He could see she had been telling the truth by the way she handled the diving gear. It was Isobel who helped him check the balance on his air, showed him the O-ring and, when he had the mouthpiece in, touched his fingers on to the demand valve button. Ralph's brief eyes-upward and smile had been reassuring. She knew what she was doing. Sanctuary was going to need her down there. Ralph was shouting above the engine. They were getting close to the middle of the entrance.

'You'll not see a thing down there, old bean. Get a good grip of those flashlamps, otherwise you'll take a wrong turning and end up in Baltimore.'

Sanctuary didn't really hear. Isobel must have. In spite of her tenseness she managed a smile as she washed her mask, slipped it over her head and nodded ready.

289

He went first, sitting on the boat's edge and dropping without fuss and backwards into the surprisingly warm sea.

Immediately they needed the lights as they pushed through the undercurrent. It was deep, deep enough to take the vulnerable hull of a frigate. It took time, but they searched in a zig-zag exactly where he now believed Fisher would have dropped the nuclear mine; in the centre of the channel where given the right moment, the right codes, maybe even the delayed effects of engine noise or magnetism, a passing hull would trigger the horror encased in the weapon.

In the dense water, they must have swum over the cylinder two or three times. He found it by touch, his body at forty-five degrees to the sea bed, his flippers scraping, but not sensing. Isobel tugged at the line they were both holding. She was shining the powerful beam below. It reflected and refracted about them, but he could see something. He arched, then bent, and pushed downwards, helped by the girl. He did not want to touch. His face was two feet away from the casing before he made out the Cyrillic markings. They meant nothing to him, no more than did the mystery of packaging marks in his own language. But these were not in his own language. That was enough. The canister registered neatly in the description Ralph had given him as they made from the shore.

'Not sure what you could be looking for. Never seen one meself. They picked up some tech from the Yanks, MK 57 and Mk 101, or so they tell me. Stuffed it into a modification of something called Silex. Seemed unlikely at the time. We only got confirmation when the Yeltsin bean took over. Even then we didn't know for sure.'

'Know what it looks like?'

Ralph had shrugged in the darkness. The doubt was in his voice.

'Not really. Mind you, there aren't too many combinations. Rounded, but not a ball, you know. More cigar tube. About as long as us.'

He'd tapped the size of the four-man rubber boat.

'Anyway, if your pal was on the level, it couldn't have been that big, could it? Not deck cargo for a yachtie all the way up from the Med? Read me?'

Here it was. Nothing to see. A sleeping canister, rounded at one end, too fat to get his arms around, but only just, and a little longer than his height. Isobel was on the other side, she had let go of the line and with a light touch and gentle flip was steady. He moved his arm slowly as her mask came up and he pointed with slow-motion signs to the surface. It was time to go.

From behind Isobel, the murky water glowed as three lights approached. He was relieved. The cavalry had taken its time, but the naval divers would know what to do. As Ralph would say, this was their part of ship.

Animal instincts are fine-tuned to danger. There was something too swift, too predatory about the way the three figures converged. He tried to warn. He pointed. She did not see. Then started to turn. Sanctuary was helpless. This was not his environment. He could not swim as he had supposed.

Sanctuary found himself falling away instead of going forward. He dropped his light, which probably saved his life. He felt a hand at his leg, then his ankle. He kicked as he had as a child, terrified of nothing more than seaweed. The hand was gone. The kick took him away. Falling still. Now one foot was bare, but Sanctuary was hidden, away from the glow. He could still see forms but nothing he knew. He got closer. He could hear noises but could make out only fear. Then he saw her, the lamps moving in a nightmare's arc. He saw one of the forms behind the girl, then another, they were struggling, writhing cumbersome water-snakes. He saw an arm, then in the glow he saw the mask, the mouthpiece, ripped from her face. They were holding her. Even in the dull light, bubbles streaming from a silent throat. There was no strength in his pleading. Nothing in his willing. No lines that could switch on hope. Then nothing as he fell further away.

He had touched the bottom but had no idea where he was. No bearings except up. He swam forward, then on, then to the left, to the right, he did not know where. He found himself rising. Hopeless.

291

Sanctuary surfaced to awaken the world. The waters about him were rising and falling. For a moment he was in a trough. Then a peak. He tried to look about, but could see nothing in his mask. He pulled it from his face and unbuckled his tank, letting it fall away, then floated on his back, half expecting the worst. He no longer cared. He guessed from what he could remember of the tides that he would be carried towards the shore. A wave lapped his head and he swallowed even more foul salt. It made him turn, which was when he saw the rubber dinghy. Calling was no good. The sea was winning. He was swallowing too much. His energy was draining. He turned again and made the final effort of long, windmilling backstrokes until his flapping arm struck the boat's slippery side. Sanctuary grabbed at the looped life-lines, was dunked beneath another wave top as he did so, gulped for air and choked more water, tried again, got a hand on the stiff cord and pulled himself about.

Ralph was hanging over the side staring at him. His throat had been ripped open.

45

It was Leonard who pulled Sanctuary from the water. Sanctuary had tried to get into the drifting boat. Could not. Instead he began the painful swim, towing the rubber catafalque to the distant shore. Dorothea was standing above them, a powerful pencil torch dancing across his near-spent body, the beam snapped off when it crossed the lifeless sailor.

Leonard dragged him as best he could. He wanted to swear. Did not.

'Where's Isobel?'

Sanctuary did not answer. He lay face down, spewing quietly into the cold earth.

'What's happened? Where is she?'

Sanctuary's eyes were closed. He refused to remember. The blurred face. The darkness. Nothing. His voice when it came was a low chant.

'They must have found Ralph. Followed the line down. Dead.'

Leonard wanted to look away. He could not. Ralph's body had slipped into the stern of the boat. Twisted as he would never have allowed himself to be in life. Did not matter now. Sanctuary felt a hand on his shoulder. Through his bile knew even then a soft scent. A park somewhere, ice creams melting light years away.

'Davy?'

The tenderness was too faithful, too caring. He heard his name, not her agony. He wanted to know. Which voice?

'Where are they?'

She told him. She had left the Deputy and Priestly in the main town. They were on the hill overlooking the bay, the Deputy talking to London on his scrambled car telephone.

Dorothea had weighed the options, made a priority telephone call of her own and within five minutes of arriving at the base barrier had been handed on to Ralph's Dartmouth friend and, once he had seen her identity card, redirected to the shoreline and Leonard. An SBS team was due any time and the Staff Officer had withdrawn to complete his briefing orders. She was worried, but she too needed to know.

'Is it there? You found it?'

Sanctuary, slumped on his forearms, looked up, white spittle at the edge of his mouth. He eyed her as a bar drunk might an intruder into his oblivion. He nodded.

'It's there.'

Leonard did not know where 'there' was.

'Where? What is it?'

Sanctuary was spewing again. He finished. There was not much sea water to come out. He wiped his mouth with the back of his hand. Did not look up.

'In the middle of the channel. Between the breakwaters. There were three of them.'

'Shit. Three?'

'Not warheads or whatever they're called. No. Three divers. Frogmen. Came from nowhere.'

Dorothea's hand was again on his shoulder. He didn't feel it. Only a weight he could never shift.

'I couldn't get across. They pulled off her mask. Maybe a knife. I don't know. I couldn't get across the bloody thing.'

Dorothea's hand rubbed his back.

'Could you see any dials? Meters? Control and detonator figures?'

He was shaking his head.

'He said it would possibly be pressure. Could even be timed to go off after the tenth, eleventh, even the fiftieth, hull had gone across.'

Dorothea and Leonard instinctively knew who 'he' had been. Dorothea looked at the beached dinghy as she spoke.

'Possibly? Or probably?'

Sanctuary dug into a corner of his mind, trying to remember exactly what the easy-going sailor had said.

'Could be.'

'Anything else?'

There was. Sanctuary couldn't think of the exact wording. He pulled himself up. He was running down. He could not. Not yet.

'He said it could be a frequency detonation or something. Make sense?'

This time Dorothea said nothing.

Leonard was feeling left out. He was standing, half-expecting the marines to arrive on the remote foreshore. Above and away from them, headlights and sparse traffic suggested little urgency in the night air. He needed someone to do something. He did not know what.

'What does this mean? Frequencies? What do we do about it?'

Dorothea was looking at her folded hands as if they held the key to some tactical catechism.

'Presumably, somewhere, someone has a list of numbers. They have to be fed into a control system in strict order and within a strict time. That system is the detonation box.'

Leonard was surprised. How would she know? But, now, nothing was ordinary, everything reeked of suspicion, chaos and misery.

Sanctuary was back. Dorothea obviously knew far more. Maybe she knew why. Why the mayhem of the past days? Why the warhead had not been exploded long ago and its terrorists long gone? Why the end game had to be played out until the last moment?

'Int. finally came up with it?'

'Mm. Mm. In fact I think someone has known all along.'

'And?'

'The picture looks something like this. The warhead, or warheads, are brought here. The codes for the frequencies travel separately. That would be standard. The technician comes in another way. We think Fisher was killed because he had no further use as a courier and because his relationship with the cousins was blown.'

Leonard was getting lost again.

'Cousins?'

'Okay, jargon for American Intelligence, usually CIA.'

'Fisher worked for them?'

She nodded.

'Yes, sireee, as they say. Not a Company man. Contract. Had done since Moscow. So did his wife. But that's a diversion.'

'What about these numbers?'

Sanctuary's voice was quiet. He would not lose sight now. The explanation would come later, if it ever mattered again.

'We think they're missing. The NSA bird has been eavesdropping.'

She sensed Leonard's confusion. She knew enough. Could tell very little. Had to show the way.

'Satellite. Listens in. Something called a KH–11. Not that good as people say, but good enough. Once we could identify a source for it, it picked up trigger words. The problem was getting the read-out. That came a few hours ago.'

Leonard was up with the game.

'Someone's got the figures. Whoever gets them can detonate the warhead?'

Sanctuary was walking about, bending his knees. Trying to get circulation and muscles talking to one another once more.

'Unless we get to them. What do they look like?'

Dorothea didn't understand.

'Numbers. Digits.'

He stopped his pacing. Digits. Digital. Numbers. Digits. Digital. Dead numbers. Static numbers. Frozen digits. Dead numbers. A dead navigation repeater. He grabbed Dorothea by the shoulders. His face close to hers. His breath stank. She winced.

'How many numbers? Groups of three? Four maybe?'

She was nodding her head up and down in time to his grip.

'I'm not sure. Yes, I think so.'

Leonard was looking between the two. He could hear the urgency. Felt the cold strength in the big man.

'What have you come up with, David?'

David. For the first time. Sanctuary looked at Leonard. What a stupid time to realise he didn't know the policeman's first

296

name, and wanted to. He dropped his hands from Dorothea's shoulders. Turned to the boat. Talked as he went.

'Give me a hand.'

Sanctuary was tugging the corpse from the boat. Dorothea had caught up and was steadying the bow.

'What are you doing?'

'The *Madrigal*. I've known it all along. That's where the numbers are. She's had them all the time. Fisher knew. You're wrong. They didn't travel separately. He had them, but no one knew where.'

'Where then? Where're you going?'

She needed to know. He was pulling the boat's stern around into the water. He snatched Dorothea's torch and waded in until the outboard was clear of the bottom and then heaved himself into the midships. Leonard and Dorothea stood helpless. Stranded. Leonard had to shout over the outboard's first roar.

'Where the fuck are you going, Sanctuary?'

'The *Madrigal*. Call them up. Tell them to meet me on the same course as we came in. Pete'll remember.'

Leonard was shouting another question. He half-ran, a playground sidestepping as if he could catch the boat. Stumbled. Tripped over Ralph's body. He stopped shouting, his mouth working silently, yet another unasked question left on the foreshore. It did not matter. Sanctuary hadn't heard. Hadn't waited. The outboard was on full throttle, the dinghy's bows lifting over the calm of the inner harbour, heading to the gap in the breakwater, to the open sea and beyond the leading lights to his rendezvous with the *Madrigal*.

46

It took half an hour to find the sloop. Sanctuary had curved his course to keep as far out as possible, punching the slight current that swirled about the bay. He did not have a compass, but he went well beyond the channel's end and picked up the lights he wanted. It was hard enough in the *Madrigal*. Even harder in the bouncing sea-level dinghy. He did not need to be accurate, just lucky. He wondered about the frogmen. Wondered if they would spring at any moment from a faster, bigger craft than his own. But he seemed to be alone apart from a couple of bay fishermen well beyond hailing distance. He wondered too about Isobel. But not for long. That would come later.

He sighted the *Madrigal* when she tacked. She was running without lights. It was cloudy. Very dark. He had the outboard running at about the slowest speed it could take and still give him way when she was a couple of cables off his starboard bow. He watched, without increasing his speed, to make sure, as the *Madrigal* short-tacked this, then that, way. A vessel biding its time, keeping its station head-to-wind until the current demanded it should sail on. There was no doubting the low sleek lines, the sharp bow and counter stern, and by the time he was certain he was close enough for Rusty and Pete to have seen his torchlight.

Rusty took his bow-line, within seconds he had scrambled aboard, the dinghy was streaming astern, Pete had the *Madrigal* on a broad reach and they were heading out to sea.

They wanted to ask questions. Asked only one.

'Dead. We were diving. We found it. They found us.'

They did not ask him what had happened. They did not ask him why he had not saved her. They did not ask him why her

298

and not him. If Rusty wanted to ask, he did not. Instead he went below, handed up Sanctuary's old clothes and then disappeared into the fo'c'sle with his misery.

'So, master, it turned shitty. Where to now? Home?'

The idea that the peaceful, organised, manicured yacht basin of sunshine and soothing frappings might be home seemed obscene. He shook his head. They were perhaps three miles offshore and making four, four-and-a-half, knots.

'I want you to show me something. Tell me something. Here.'

He dodged into the main cabin. Pete did not need instructions. He brought the *Madrigal* on to a easier course and put the tiller on autohelm. For a moment the boat skitted her way, then settled. The weather wasn't that difficult for the helm.

Sanctuary was tapping one of the repeater displays on the starboard bulkhead away from the chart table.

'Okay, tell me. What does it do?'

'Piss all, master.'

Pete tried a grin, but the strain of waiting and the iciness in Sanctuary's look didn't give it much chance.

'What's it supposed to do?'

The small black sailing cap was on the back of his head and Pete was scratching at the sparsely covered dome beneath.

'Well, Fisher, he fitted this navset, see?'

He pointed to a similar display box about the size and thickness of a TV-dinner tray.

'Supposed to be programmed so that you can pick up a fix. It works off shore-side beacons. Mind you, me, I don't trust this gizmology.'

Sanctuary's voice was not impatient, although he was.

'Go on.'

'Well, that's about it. As long as you programme it properly, as long as it knows where it is when you switch on, well, it'll give you a pretty good fix of where you are. And it'll tell you a dozen way-points or so. You know, positions and where you're supposed to be going next. Got me?'

Sanctuary looked at the other display.

'What are those numbers, then?'

'Buggered if I know, master. I know what they're supposed to be. Same as the master panel. But they ain't, are they?'

'Why not?'

'Because it's buggered. That's why. What you got in mind then?'

The *Madrigal* was pitching again, but for the moment the helm would hold. The raucous wind and unruly seas were doing their best to make life uncomfortable. Both men however were deep in thought.

'Tell me, those numbers aren't way-points or anything? Not course and speed? Not simply locked in and can't get out?'

'No, master. I reckon that lot's a good old-fashioned bunch of buggers that showed up when the thing went on the blink.'

The wind was getting impatient, the autohelm less sure of itself. Sanctuary was having to cling to the wooden grab rails in the deckhead. Pete was wedged by the galley stove.

'Anyone who wasn't a sailor might think they were navigation figures.'

Pete shrugged. There were few stupidities he wouldn't put beyond shore-side people.

'Spose so.'

Sanctuary had one last question before he was sure.

'If it's broken, why is it still showing numbers? Especially as the batteries were disconnected when she was searched?'

Now Pete was really interested. He didn't know. But he was going to find out.

'There's only one answer, master. It must be on a self-power circuit. First I'd heard of one if it is.'

He reached across as the *Madrigal* lurched again, concern on his face. He didn't like the weather, not this close to shore. He turned back to the display panel and twirled the two black thumbscrews holding it in the swing bracket and slid off the back panel. His surprise was obvious.

'Well, stuff my old boots. Look at this. Someone's put in their own circuit. Very neat and dandy too. Bloody hearing-aid batteries or something. No wonder it's still on.'

'But no connection to the master?'

'Right. Bloody right. Then what are all these figures?'

300

Sanctuary now knew. He never got a chance to explain. The *Madrigal* gave an even more violent lurch. Then a crash, another bump. But this wasn't the wind and sea finally losing patience. Through the leeward glass, Sanctuary could see a white wall, the side of a cruiser. It was rubbing alongside. There was another thud, a crash and both men lost their balance, banging against the galley and chart table.

A dark figure leapt from the cruiser's after-deck and, before either man could do anything, Ignatiev was framed, crouched in the coachhouse doorway. This was not the urbane Ignatiev who had time to spin banter and rehearse his black humour on victims. His look was that of the wildman. The carefully selected, trained, reassessed, retrained, tested GRU agent in the field. This was a Viking above all Vikings. This was the one with sufficient madness to preclude second thought. The *Madrigal* was heaving, the foresail flapping wildly, the boom swinging from side to side. Ignatiev's wildness was now an asset. He was unflustered. His deliberately jammed frame moved with the *Madrigal*'s yaw. The gun as steady as a compass needle always sure on its magnetic master, just as it was now centring on Sanctuary's heart.

'Give me.'

The command came through the velocity of a rifle bullet. The right hand was stretched far enough for the repeater unit. Sanctuary tried for time. He had little hope.

'Why wait until now?'

Ignatiev could not resist his last triumph going without applause.

'We did not know until you told us.'

Sanctuary did not understand. Pete was frightened. Ignatiev took a curtain call.

'We knew it could be here somewhere. On our last visit to your sweet craft, we took the precaution of leaving what your service would call . . . a device?'

Sanctuary felt sick. They had spent so much time looking to see what had been taken and had ignored the fact that something might have been added. Ignatiev was now smiling. So he had a weakness after all.

'As you know, my dear Sanctuary, we have only the best. After all, if we can listen from a satellite, a mile away presents few problems, particularly, my dear fellow, when we choose the frequencies.'

He drew a great breath. He really was mad, thought Sanctuary, but what comfort that might have been escaped him. The hand was out again. The gun still steady. There was no need to cock it. The hand came up until the barrel was ranged on a point between Sanctuary's eyes. Ignatiev's smile had gone. His tongue, pink even in the semi-darkness, flicked the full bottom lip.

'Very well. Your way then.'

Sanctuary sensed the tensing of Ignatiev's trigger finger. Waited. Stared at the other man's eyes. Each man's as cold as the other's. One had won. The other had lost. Neither played a game though both knew the rules. There was a slight movement from behind him. He felt the thinnest whistle of air. Saw the knife strike deep into Ignatiev's neck, its point slicing through the jugular.

Sanctuary caught the gun as it fell to the side-bunk and, with a threequarter's old-fashioned handoff, sent what had been Ignatiev bundling into the cockpit. For a moment, Sanctuary looked back. Brown eyes. In mourning. Sanctuary remembered a report. A death in Spain. A knife. A partner dead. He nodded something that might have been thanks. Brown eyes. Sad. Then gone. Returned to the dark depth of the for'd cabin.

Pete, cursing foully and gathering his strength in doing so, was out into the cockpit after Sanctuary. He watched without emotion, having no time to give judgement, as Sanctuary, steadying himself on the stainless-steel rail of the *Madrigal*'s stern, gripped the automatic with extended arms. The *Madrigal* lunged as if wanting no part in what was to follow. Sanctuary steadied himself just as the man holding the cruiser alongside looked up; he did so in time to see Sanctuary squeeze the trigger. The bullet smashed into his right eye.

The second man was at the wheel on the open-canopied bridge. Perhaps because he was fighting wind and waves to hold the almost flat-bottomed cruiser steady, he seemed not to realise what was going on. He had only half-turned when Sanctuary shot him three times in the back and once in the head. The first man was twisted through the wire side-lines. He was quite dead. Sanctuary, swaying with more than the motion of the tiny hull, aimed once more and shot him through his gaping mouth.

'Borzois.'

As if in mad response, the cruiser veered uncontrollably away, the wind tossing the vessel to one side. The bullets had hurled the helmsman across the engine controls. The starboard engine had gone into full ahead and the spotless, stainless-steel stanchioned boat now began a headless, crazy circling in the turbulence of the white-crested seas.

They turned away.

With Sanctuary gathering the headsail sheets and bringing in the big sail, Pete took the helm, tightened in the mainsail and had the *Madrigal* heading away from the coast and out to the safe deeper troughs of the increasing storm. With the boat's port gunwales dipping low to the waves, the sea once more spraying and running the length of the scuppers. the *Madrigal* was steady.

Sanctuary spent a few minutes going through Ignatiev's clothing. There was nothing. Not even a label on his shirt. He unbuckled the expensive watch and, without thought of ceremony, dumped the body over the port side. He didn't look back.

He went below and picked up the repeater and scanned the numbers. First across. Then backwards. Then from the bottom up. Then downwards. Now they were committed to his memory. He glanced at the master display, scribbled two sets of degrees and minutes in reverse order on the bulkhead, went on deck and tossed the repeater into the water.

Pete had said nothing. He would have liked his pipe. He opened a side-locker and handed Sanctuary a harness.

'She's getting herself worked up to a hooley, master. Wouldn't be right to find yourself over the wall after all this, would it?'

The grin was real enough. So was the emptiness in the face across the cockpit.

'Take us home, Pete.'

'Bloody right.'

'You need a course?'

'Do I buggery? Don't you worry, we'll pick up a mark or two later.'

It didn't take much to alter course. When they had done so, Sanctuary clipped on to the life line and went for'd. The long foredeck was slippery, the water coming across the bow icy. He gripped the mast and cooled beneath the spray.

Going home? No. The club secretary? Home? The ghosts of Les, Bennie? His mum who twisted her fingers in her apron, never understanding. Always at the edge. The guard he had never met? The despicable Tupman for whom only his crippled wife would mourn? The cool, the winsome Mrs Dent? Home? These were unreal people. They did not exist. Isobel had existed. She too had been touched by him. She too. He pulled closer about his throat the dirty towel she had used to wipe away her outrage. Sea water was trickling down his neck, inside the waterproofs he'd found. Fisher's? That, too, no longer mattered.

Isobel had warned them. He remembered one moment when she had whispered. He remembered her voice. Remembered what she had said. Remembered what she had heard. In the street. In the dark. Running. She had heard them talking by the Jaguar. She had heard the voice. He had never asked the obvious questions. What did it sound like? Old? Young? Said with a thin blue strip running at an angle through it? Or the croakiness of too much dark tobacco? Could it have been, at a distance, downstairs even, the deep huskiness a woman sometimes wears when authority becomes her? And, yes, Ignatiev had listened, but how did he know Sanctuary was going out to meet the *Madrigal*? Did someone tell him? That same someone? The Deputy? Priestly? Dorothea? Even Leonard? The voice, no. But he had never been with them until the beach. No one was trusted. Or was there someone else? Was there someone as yet unseen? Had Fisher been so right? Someone much higher up? Someone who would have fitted so devastatingly the wildest dream in the Sad Sam theory? Now still there? Someone who had people who could lie in wait on a damp marsh-reeded bank. Someone who could wait patiently for his prey, assured that he needed but one chance.

The *Madrigal* lurched once more. Dipped. He looked back. Pete was eyeing him. Tending. Not understanding. But there. He turned about and faced the eastern horizon, letting the cold spray crash over him, without moving. It had started to rain. It could not wash away the one moment of warmth, the long moment of agony. It could not wash away the torment. The piercing scream.

Somewhere, there was someone who knew.

Somewhere there was someone who would pay and so slowly that they too would scream and scream and scream and plead for mercy. And they would get none.

Epilogue

In Whitehall, the wind that had drifted the night snow against the Treasury steps had lost interest, had gone to play in the Home Counties. A small flurry of flakes blew from the mounded roof of an abandoned car. High above Parliament, the great clock claimed the three-quarter hour and, in a doorway, a bus inspector checked his watch, stamped thick-soled boots and waited. He glanced at the figure which rose from the Underground. The man was taller than average, unruly hair bared and already flecked, hands deep in his long straight macintosh, shoulders hunched against a sudden gust across the empty square. Without looking up, the man crossed the wide thoroughfare, his unpolished brogues crumping the carpet of snow. The inspector tugged down his peaked cap, re-checked his watch and waited. Far away, towards Trafalgar Square, a dark saloon slithered within feet of where the kerb might have been beneath the piled snow. It was the only vehicle in sight, though the man did not notice. Instead he kept to the road and then into the side street, swept at first light in case some great crisis should call the official Jaguar from Carlton Terrace, even on the sabbath. He turned right through the arch and held out his pass without pausing, without recognising the security man's greeting. The cobbled quadrangle had not been swept, but the wide steps to the double half-glass doors had, and his shoes grated on the dirty pink salt and then scratched at the tiled floor as he passed the guard and headed for the staircase.

Priestly's old desk was as immaculate as ever although Priestly was not there. Instead, from his gilt and slightly chipped frame, Lawrence of Lucknow smiled down on a youth sifting through that morning's tray of cables. He looked up, too quickly, as if expecting the door to have been tapped before

306

opening. Startled, ill at ease. The lord lieutenant's grand-daughter, whose bed the youth had reluctantly left two hours earlier, might have been surprised; the self-assurance she rather admired had deserted him. He started to rise, as a new chaplain might to his bishop, and then hovered in a half-sitting position as the other man eyed him.

'Deputy in?'

The voice was tight.

'Ah yes. We were expecting you. You must be David Sanctu-ary. We've not met. I'm . . .'

Lamely, he did not finish his introduction. His outstretched hand remained empty. Sanctuary ignored him, headed for the inner door, and went in without knocking.

The cherry and briar pipes had gone. So had the creaking leather chair. The brass and green-shaded desk lamp was still there. Now, in the winter gloomy room, it cast its light across the immaculate blotter. That was different. So was the smell. The shaggy-browed man who each day had waited for the chime of six and the first scratching flame of the evening had, as planned, gone. Now there was a new smell, the schoolroom perfume of hyacinths.

The new Deputy did not look up from the closely typed report. Sanctuary let the green-backed door close and slumped into the large armchair now in front of the desk instead of to the side where it had, for as long as he could remember, always been. There had been a lot of changes. None of the important things, except one. The report finished, the Deputy looked up, smiled.

'Hello, Davy. How are you?'

'Okay. You?'

Dorothea nodded. Slowly. With pleasure.

'Mm. Fine. I'm glad you're back.'

'Am I?'

'Of course. Why d'you ask?'

He didn't answer. Instead he looked around the room as if trying to find a missing ornament, a portrait out of place, a clock with an irregular tick. Dorothea tapped the report.

307

'They say you've made a complete recovery. I'm pleased. It's taken time.'

'Six months.'

They both knew that. They'd both been there. Not at the end. Only Sanctuary had seen that. The Department's sanatorium had not been there. He knew she was lying. They had not said that.

The Department's trauma specialist had written of his concern about Sanctuary's long periods of silence, of his refusal to communicate any emotions, and of the apparently restful nights. The specialist said that during waking hours post-combat traumatics could sometimes bottle up emotions even when deliberately provoked. He was disturbed that Sanctuary seemed to have similar control during the night when it would be expected that his anxieties would surface. They did not. After six months, the sanatorium had released him with a recommendation that he 'be returned to light duties' and his case reviewed after three months. Sanctuary knew all this. He had made it his business to see the report. These things were no longer difficult. Sanctuary had re-read the specialist's conclusion and nodded his satisfaction. The man was covering his back. He couldn't figure why his patient wasn't displaying the usual symptoms. He did not, as he told his PA when she typed the report, 'know where this guy Sanctuary's coming from'. Sanctuary had closed the folder, replaced it in the confidential file tray, locked it, and had returned to his room via the hall bathroom where he had flushed the lavatory and banged the cubicle door for the benefit of the duty officer in the sound-monitoring room. He had never intended they should know 'where he was coming from'.

Dorothea was talking about him coming back to the Department in his own time. He interrupted her.

'Where's Priestly?'

She did not look away. The eyes were as warm as they always had been.

'On attachment. GCHQ.'

'How long?'

'Two years.'

308

'Then?'

'Who knows. Why?'

'You jumped him?'

Dorothea managed a small swivel of the high-backed chair. She did not like his eyes. In the gloom they were menacing. She wondered about the silences. The self-control. This time she smiled. No triumph. Simply a Departmental smile.

'I wouldn't have put it that way.'

'He was next in line.'

'Who knows? I was offered it, I didn't turn it down. I must admit, I didn't ask, "why me?". Charles was very nice about it. Hurt, but very nice. He sent me flowers.' She paused, then added, 'From Cheltenham.'

'Delayed reaction or . . . ?'

'Definitely an Or. He was sent to GCHQ the day before I was appointed. Have you . . . have you heard from him?'

'You know the answer to that. All my mail's been logged. You would have seen it.'

'Public telephone boxes.'

Dorothea stared at him for some moments before she spoke again, her voice husky.

'What is it?'

He looked behind her eyes. Saw nothing. For six months he had wondered. There had been Priestly. But now he knew. A mental check-and-balance list had told him nothing. The more he thought he knew, the less confident he had become. For hours on end he had lain on his strictly laundered bed, hands behind his head, staring at the evidence his brain had inscribed on the ceiling. Eventually he knew what something inside had known all along. The answer would only be there when he could see, touch and hear. Now he could.

'Tell me why?'

Her new smile was convincing – for a moment.

'Tell you why what, Davy?'

'You knew what I was doing at almost every moment. You would have seen Fisher's report. You would have green-screened it. Or binned it. You would have seen all the JIC minutes. You would have run the Ignatiev movement file. You

309

were the one who said he was out but not active. You knew I was going to the harbour.'

Dorothea ran a hand along the arm of the executive chair, watching the changing shade of the nap. She sighed a sigh of a wronged adulterer.

'And I was the one who protected you, Davy. I was the one who made sure you had the extra days when the Department wanted you in. I was the one who pushed Priestly's arm away when the knives were out. I was the one who watched your back. I was the one who checked Fisher's file and found it had gone from the index.'

He, too, sighed. Wearily, disappointedly confident.

'Because you wanted to make sure. Because you needed to go through the routine. Because you knew that others could log in and find the same information. You took only one gamble. Ignatiev's movements. It didn't matter then. I was miles away. I couldn't check the file.'

'So?'

'Priestly could. Vicious, spiteful, back-stabbing Priestly. Priestly does not forgive. You were right. The telephone box. All the information he got from his friend including Ignatiev's movements was on your Eyes Only file.'

'Nonsense.'

He took a hand from his raincoat and tossed a back-up disk onto the clean blotter.

'It's all there. Cairo. UK. Moscow. Ukraine. Fisher. Tupman. The lot. Priestly's friends are thorough. You knew. But I needed to see you before I knew.'

She hardly glanced at the disk. Realised it would be a copy. For a moment, Dorothea wanted to go to him, put an arm on his, tell him that none of this was now important. He was safe. It was done. That was the Department. Done. File Logged. File Endorsed. File Closed. But this was not the David Sanctuary who had sat with her in the sun, in deck chairs, dripping with ice cream. Awkward. A little in love. That was then. Not now. Her voice was still warm. Always would be.

'What d'you want? Nemesis?'

'How far? Who else?'

310

Dorothea shook her head.

'We're nothing people, Davy. Pawns. We don't matter. Ignatiev didn't matter. There'll be other Ignatievs. There are different ways of doing things now. I'm nobody. What do you want to do? Kill me? You could. You've done it now. It's easy, isn't it? The more violently you do it the easier it is. Right? Is that what you want to do? And then what? While they hunt you, the next one? Then the next? Then the one after that? Until you're satisfied there are no more? And how will you know? You won't. And what happens when they lay down their markers? The warnings. The hit and run and the 'phone call from your mother to come quickly. What then? Who are you going to blame? Me? Someone higher? Or yourself? Leave it alone, Davy. Chase this tiger and it won't eat you, it'll eat your friends. Don't you see?'

For thirty seconds, maybe more, he stared behind those deep, warm eyes. Still deep. Still warm. He got up, hesitated for a moment while the sad eyes held his, turned and left the room, not slamming, not closing, the door. By the time the youth adjusted his smile, the moment had gone. When he crossed the quadrangle the snow was falling as the man had promised. The guard waved half a salute and returned to the sports pages, and in Whitehall the dark saloon had been abandoned against the Cenotaph.

Sanctuary, hands deeper into his pockets, head bowed into the snow, saw nothing. Remembered only a scream.